For your enjoyment, we've added in
this volume *Bachelor Untamed,*
a favorite book by Brenda Jackson!

Praise for
New York Times and *USA TODAY*
bestselling author Brenda Jackson

"Brenda Jackson writes romance that sizzles
and characters you fall in love with."
—*New York Times* and *USA TODAY* bestselling author
Lori Foster

"Jackson's trademark ability to weave
multiple characters and side stories together
makes shocking truths all the more exciting."
—*Publishers Weekly*

"There is no getting away from the sex appeal and
charm of Jackson's Westmoreland family."
—*RT Book Reviews* on *Feeling the Heat*

"Jackson's characters are wonderful, strong,
colorful and hot enough to burn the pages."
—*RT Book Reviews* on *Westmoreland's Way*

"The kind of sizzling, heart-tugging story
Brenda Jackson is famous for."
—*RT Book Reviews* on *Spencer's Forbidden Passion*

"This is entertainment at its best."
—*RT Book Reviews* on *Star of His Heart*

Selected books by Brenda Jackson

Harlequin Desire

*A Wife for a Westmoreland #2077
*The Proposal #2089
*Feeling the Heat #2149
*Texas Wild #2185
*One Winter's Night #2197
*Zane #2239
*Canyon #2245
*Stern #2251

Silhouette Desire

*Delaney's Desert Sheikh #1473
*A Little Dare #1533
*Thorn's Challenge #1552
*Stone Cold Surrender #1601
*Riding the Storm #1625
*Jared's Counterfeit Fiancée #1654
*The Chase Is On #1690
*The Durango Affair #1727
*Ian's Ultimate Gamble #1745
*Seduction, Westmoreland Style #1778
*Spencer's Forbidden Passion #1838
*Taming Clint Westmoreland #1850
*Cole's Red-Hot Pursuit #1874
*Quade's Babies #1911
*Tall, Dark...Westmoreland! #1928
*Westmoreland's Way #1975
*Hot Westmoreland Nights #2000
*What a Westmoreland Wants #2035

Harlequin Kimani Arabesque

ΔWhispered Promises
ΔEternally Yours
ΔOne Special Moment
ΔFire and Desire
ΔSecret Love
Δ True Love
ΔSurrender
ΔSensual Confessions
ΔInseparable
ΔCourting Justice

Harlequin Kimani Romance

ΩSolid Soul #1
ΩNight Heat #9
ΩBeyond Temptation #25
ΩRisky Pleasures #37
ΩIrresistible Forces #89
ΩIntimate Seduction #145
ΩHidden Pleasures #189
ΩA Steele for Christmas #253
ΩPrivate Arrangements #269

*The Westmorelands
ΔMadaris Family Saga
ΩSteele Family titles

Other titles by this author available in ebook format.

BRENDA JACKSON

is a die "heart" romantic who married her childhood sweetheart and still proudly wears the "going steady" ring he gave her when she was fifteen. Because she believes in the power of love, Brenda's stories always have happy endings. In her real-life love story, Brenda and her husband of more than forty years live in Jacksonville, Florida, and have two sons.

A *New York Times* bestselling author of more than seventy-five romance titles, Brenda is a recent retiree who now divides her time between family, writing and traveling with Gerald. You may write Brenda at P.O. Box 28267, Jacksonville, Florida 32226, email her at WriterBJackson@aol.com or visit her website at www.brendajackson.net.

BRENDA JACKSON

STERN
& BACHELOR UNTAMED

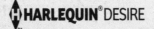

If you purchased this book without a cover you should be aware that this book is stolen property. It was reported as "unsold and destroyed" to the publisher, and neither the author nor the publisher has received any payment for this "stripped book."

ISBN-13: 978-0-373-83792-2

STERN & BACHELOR UNTAMED

Copyright © 2013 by Harlequin Books S.A.

The publisher acknowledges the copyright holder of the individual works as follows:

STERN
Copyright © 2013 by Brenda Streater Jackson

BACHELOR UNTAMED
Copyright © 2009 by Brenda Streater Jackson

Recycling programs for this product may not exist in your area.

All rights reserved. Except for use in any review, the reproduction or utilization of this work in whole or in part in any form by any electronic, mechanical or other means, now known or hereafter invented, including xerography, photocopying and recording, or in any information storage or retrieval system, is forbidden without the written permission of the publisher, Harlequin Enterprises Limited, 225 Duncan Mill Road, Don Mills, Ontario M3B 3K9, Canada.

This is a work of fiction. Names, characters, places and incidents are either the product of the author's imagination or are used fictitiously, and any resemblance to actual persons, living or dead, business establishments, events or locales is entirely coincidental.

This edition published by arrangement with Harlequin Books S.A.

For questions and comments about the quality of this book, please contact us at CustomerService@Harlequin.com.

® and TM are trademarks of Harlequin Enterprises Limited or its corporate affiliates. Trademarks indicated with ® are registered in the United States Patent and Trademark Office, the Canadian Trade Marks Office and in other countries.

Printed in U.S.A.

CONTENTS

STERN   7

BACHELOR UNTAMED   189

Dear Reader,

I love writing about the Westmorelands because they exemplify what a strong family is all about—mainly the sharing of love and support. For that reason, when I was given the chance to present them in a trilogy, I was excited and ready to dive into the lives of Zane, Canyon and Stern Westmoreland.

It is hard to believe that *Stern* is my twenty-sixth Westmoreland novel. It seems as if it was only yesterday when I introduced you to Delaney and her five brothers. I knew by the time I wrote Thorn's story that I just had to tell you about their cousins who were spread out over Montana, Texas, California and Colorado.

It has been an adventure and I've enjoyed sharing it with you. I've gotten your emails and snail mails letting me know how much you adore those Westmoreland men, and I appreciate hearing from you. Each Westmoreland—male or female—is unique, and the way love conquers their hearts is heartwarming, breathtaking and totally satisfying.

I love writing stories where best friends fall in love. In this story, Stern and JoJo are best friends who understand each other and want the best for each other. I enjoyed how they finally realize their relationship is based on more than a close friendship—it is grounded in true love.

I hope you enjoy this story about Stern and JoJo.

Happy reading!

Brenda Jackson

STERN

* * *

To my husband, the love of my life
and my best friend, Gerald Jackson, Sr.

Happy Birthday to all the members of the
1971 Class of William Raines High School in
Jacksonville, Florida. You know what milestone
we hit this year and we are still the greatest. Ichiban!

To my good friend Linda Reagor.
Thanks for the hunting lesson. I appreciate you!

Greater love hath no man than this,
that a man lay down his life for his friends.
—*John* 15:13

THE DENVER WESTMORELAND FAMILY TREE

Raphael and Gemma Westmoreland

Stern Westmoreland (Paula Bailey)

Thomas (Susan)

Adam (Clarisse)

Dillon (Pamela) ①

Micah (Kalina) ⑥

Jason (Bella) ⑤

Ramsey (Chloe) ②

Zane (Channing) ⑨

Derringer (Lucia) ④

Riley (Alpha) ⑧

Canyon (Keisha) ⑩

Stern (JoJo) ⑪

Brisbane

Megan (Rico) ⑦

Gemma (Callum) ③

Adrian

Aidan

Bailey

⑪ Stern

① Westmoreland's Way
② Hot Westmoreland Nights
③ What a Westmoreland Wants
④ A Wife for a Westmoreland
⑤ The Proposal

⑥ Feeling the Heat
⑦ Texas Wild
⑧ One Winter's Night
⑨ Zane
⑩ Canyon

One

"Stern, what can a woman do to make a man want her?"

Stern Westmoreland, who had been looking through the scope of his hunting rifle, jerked his head around at the unexpected question, nearly knocking the cap off his head.

He glared at the woman beside him who was staring through the scope of her own rifle. When a shot rang out, expletives flowed from his lips. "Dammit, JoJo, you did that on purpose. You asked me that just to ruin my concentration."

She lowered her rifle and frowned at him. "I did not. I asked you because I really want to know. And if it makes you feel better, I missed my target just now."

Stern rolled his eyes. So what if she had missed her shot *now?* Nothing had stopped her from taking down that huge elk yesterday when he had yet to hit anything, not even a coyote. On days like this he wondered why he always invited his best friend on these hunting trips. She showed him up each and every time.

Lifting his rifle and looking through the scope again,

he drew in a deep breath. He knew why he always invited JoJo. He liked having her around. When he was with her he could be himself and not a man trying to impress anyone. Their comfortable relationship was why she'd been his best friend for years.

"Well?"

He lowered the scope from his eye to look at her. "Well what?"

"You didn't answer me. What can a woman do to make a man want her? Other than jump into bed. I'm not into casual sex."

He couldn't help but chuckle. "I'm glad to hear that."

"What do you find funny, Stern? It's okay for *you* to be into casual sex but not *me?*"

Stern stared at her in astonishment. "What in the heck is wrong with you today? You've never been into drama."

JoJo's expression filled with anger and frustration. "You don't understand, and you used to understand me even when nobody else did." Without saying anything else she turned and walked off.

He watched her leave. *What the hell?* JoJo was being temperamental, and in all the years he'd known her she'd *never* been temperamental. What in the world was going on with her?

Deciding he wasn't in the mood to hunt anymore today, he followed JoJo down the path that led back to his hunting lodge.

After a quick shower, Jovonnie Jones grabbed a beer out of the refrigerator, pulled the tab and took a refreshing sip. She needed that, she thought as she left the kitchen to sit outside on the wooden deck and enjoy the picturesque view of the Rocky Mountains.

A few years ago Stern had stumbled on this lodge,

an old, dilapidated place that sat on more than a hundred acres of the best hunting land anywhere. In only two years, with the help of his brothers and cousins, the building had been transformed into one of beauty. It was a perfect hunting getaway. It offered black bears, deer, fox and other wildlife, but this was mainly elk country.

The lodge had been a good investment for Stern. When he wasn't using it, he leased it. It was a huge two-story structure with eight bedrooms, four full bathrooms and wooden decks that wrapped all the way around the house on both the first and the second floors. The common area included a huge kitchen and dining area and a sitting room with a massive brick fireplace. Plenty of floor-to-ceiling windows provided breathtaking views of the Rockies from every room.

She eased down in one of the outdoor cedar rocking chairs. Even after her hot shower and cold beer, she was still feeling frustrated and angry. Why couldn't Stern take her seriously and answer her question? It should work in her favor that she was best friends with a man most women believed to be the hottest thing on legs. Stern got any woman he wanted. If anybody ought to know about a woman's appeal, it should be him.

JoJo chuckled, remembering. In high school, girls would deliberately pretend to befriend her for no other reason than to get close to Stern. It never worked for long because once Stern learned the truth he would drop them like hot potatoes. He refused to let anyone use her. To him, friendship meant more than that. If those girls didn't want to be her friend because of who she was, then he wanted no part of them.

In truth, most of the girls she'd known in high school, and even some of the women she knew now, preferred not to hang around with someone who wasn't very girly.

JoJo preferred jeans to dresses. She liked to hunt, practiced karate, could shoot a bow and arrow and knew more about what was under the hood of a car than most guys. Of course, that last skill set had come from her father, who had been a professional mechanic. And not just any mechanic—he had been the best.

A deep lump clogged her throat. It was hard to believe he had passed away two years ago. He'd suffered a massive heart attack while doing something he loved—working on a car. Her mother had died when JoJo was eleven, so her father's death had left her parentless. She'd inherited the auto mechanic shop, which had given her the opportunity to come out of the classroom and get under the hood of a car.

After she had gotten the teaching degree her father had wanted her to get, she'd obtained a graduate degree in technical engineering. She had enjoyed being a professor at one of the local community colleges, but owning and operating the Golden Wrench was what she truly loved.

"So are we still on speaking terms?"

Stern placed a tray of tortilla chips and salsa on the table beside her. He then slid into the other rocker.

"Not sure if we are or not," she said, reaching over and grabbing a chip to dip into the salsa and then sliding the whole thing in her mouth. "I asked you a question and you didn't answer me because you assumed I wasn't serious."

Stern took a sip of beer and glanced over the can at her. "Were you serious?"

"Yes."

"Then I apologize. I honestly thought you were trying to mess with my concentration."

A smile touched her lips. "Would I do that?"

"In a heartbeat."

"Well, yes," she admitted, trying to hide her amusement. "But I didn't today. I need information."

"On how a woman could make a man want her?"

"Yes."

Stern leaned forward in his chair and pierced her with a dark, penetrating gaze. "Why?"

She lifted a brow. "Why?"

"Yes, why would you want to know something like that?"

She didn't answer right away. Instead she took a sip of her beer and looked out at the mountains. It was a beautiful September day. A red fox flashed through a cluster of pine trees before darting between a patch of woods to disappear.

After she'd gathered her thoughts, she turned back to Stern. "There's this guy who brings his car to the shop. He's sexy. Oh…is he sexy."

Stern rolled his eyes. "I'll take your word for it. Go on."

She shrugged. "That's it."

Stern frowned. "That's it?"

"Yes. I've decided I want him. The question is, how can I get him to want me, too?"

As far as Stern was concerned, the real question was, had JoJo lost her ever-loving mind? But he didn't say that. Instead, he took another sip of his beer.

He knew JoJo better than he knew anyone, and if she was determined to do something then that was it. He could help her, or she'd find help somewhere else.

"What's his name?" he asked.

She slid another chip into her mouth. "You don't need to know that. Do you tell me the name of every woman you want?"

"This is different."

"Really? In what way?"

He wasn't sure, but he just knew that it was. Using the pad of his thumb, he rubbed the tension building at his temple. "First of all, when it comes to men, you're green. And second, for you to even ask me that question means you're not ready for the kind of relationship you're going after."

She threw her head back and laughed. "Pleeze, Stern. I'll be thirty next year. Most women my age are married by now, some with children. And I don't even have a boyfriend."

He wasn't moved by that argument. "I'll be thirty-one next year and I don't have a girlfriend." When she looked over at him, he amended that statement. "Not a steady one. I like being single."

"But you do date. A lot. I'm beginning to think that most of the men in town wonder if I'm really a girl."

He studied her. There had never been any doubt in his mind that she was a girl. She had long lashes and eyes so dark they were the color of midnight. Those eyes were staring straight ahead now, looking out over the thick woods. She had her bare legs lifted in the rocker with her arms wrapped around them. Her pose emphasized the muscles in her limbs. He knew she did a lot of physical work at the shop, but the two of them also had memberships at a gym in town.

She had changed out of her hunting clothes and was wearing cut-off jeans and a short top. She had gorgeous legs, long and endless. But he knew he was one of the few men who'd ever seen them. She opened the shop at eight and closed after five. It wasn't unusual for her to work late if she had a car an owner needed. And during that whole time, she wore an auto-mechanic's uniform splattered with grease. A number of men would be surprised how she looked wearing something other than that uniform.

"You hide stuff," he finally said.

She glanced over at him, frowning. "I hide what?"

"What a nice body you have. Most of the time men see you in your work clothes."

Her frown deepened. "Well, forgive me for not wearing stilettos and a slinky dress while I change a carburetor."

A vision of that flashed through his mind and he smiled as he took a sip of beer. "Stilettos and a slinky dress? You don't have to go that far, but…"

He glanced over at her and saw she was pouting. He kind of liked it when she pouted. She looked cute.

"But what?"

"You would probably gain more men's interest if you were seen around town after hours in something other than jeans and sweats. You're a female, JoJo. Men like women who look soft and sexy once in a while."

She studied the contents of her beer bottle. "You think that might do it?"

"Probably." He suddenly sat up straight in the rocker. "I have an idea. What you need is a makeover."

"A makeover?"

"Yes, and then you need to go where your guy hangs out. In a dress that shows your legs, a new hairdo—"

"What's wrong with my hair?"

Honestly, he didn't think there was anything wrong with her hair. It was long, thick and healthy. He should know. He'd helped her wash it numerous times over the years. He loved it when she wore it down past her shoulders, but these days she rarely did.

"You have beautiful hair. You just need to show it off more. Even now you're hiding it under a cap."

He reached over and took the hat off her head. Lustrous dark brown hair tumbled to her shoulders. He smiled. "See, I like it already."

And he did. He was tempted to run his hands through it to feel the silky texture.

He leaned back and took another sip of his beer, wondering where such a tempting thought came from. This was JoJo, for heaven's sake. His best friend. He should not be thinking about how silky her hair was.

"So, you think a makeover will work?"

"Yes, but like I said, after the makeover you need to go where you think the guy's going to be—with a date. Whenever you pull it all together, I'm available."

She met his gaze. "Not sure that will work. If I'm with someone, he might not check me out."

"Most people around here know we're best friends and nothing more."

"He's new to town and probably won't know that."

Stern thought for a moment. "You're probably right. I wouldn't come on to a woman if I saw her with another man. But you want him to accept you as you are. The woman who works as a mechanic during the day and the same woman who can get all dolled up at night, right?"

"Right."

Stern smiled. "Then I suggest you let him see you with another man. Makes it obvious that you can be sexy when you want to be and that other men appreciate you. I bet once he's seen you, even if you're with me, he'll contact you for a date. And then when he does see you in your work clothes, he'll look beyond the uniform and imagine what's underneath."

Stern's smile faded. For some reason the thought of

men checking out JoJo that way, of men calling her for a date, bothered him. Suddenly, he was thinking that maybe a makeover wasn't such a great idea after all.

"That's a wonderful idea, Stern! As soon as I get back to Denver I'm going to get started on the makeover. First, I need to find out where this guy hangs out. Then I'll find the name of someone who can make me look pretty."

"You're already pretty, JoJo."

She patted his hand. "Ah, that's sweet of you to say, but you're my best friend so your opinion of my looks doesn't count. I'll get in touch with your cousin Megan for the name of her hairstylist, and it shouldn't be hard to find a makeup artist. Then, I'll go shopping. I'll get some of your other cousins and sisters-in-law to go with me because they all like to shop. I'm excited."

He took another sip of his beer. "I can tell."

Why did her interest in a man bother him? The only reason he could come up with was that she was his best friend and he didn't want to lose their special bond. He didn't want to lose *her*. What if this guy found it strange that a man and woman were best friends? What if he pushed her to end the friendship they'd shared for years?

His gut twisted. His brothers and cousins had always said they wouldn't want any girlfriend of theirs to have the sort of close relationship with another man that he and JoJo shared. What if this guy thought the same way?

Stern did not like problems, and he always preferred dealing with them head-on.

Stern frowned. "What's his name, JoJo?"

She chuckled. "You don't need his name, Stern. Besides, you'll find out soon enough when I set my plans into motion."

Stern took a sip of his beer. He couldn't wait.

* * *

Later that night, JoJo lay in bed staring up at the ceiling. Things were going better than she'd planned. When she realized back in the spring that she was developing feelings for Stern, she had been horrified. How could a woman fall in love with her best friend?

Rather suddenly, it seemed. On their last trip here to the lodge in April, she had come downstairs one morning, ready for another great day of hunting, only to find Stern still in his pajamas. Or, partly in them. He had on the bottoms but not the top. And in that instant, on that day, she'd seen him not as her best friend but as a sexy man who had the ability to stir any woman's blood. He had certainly stirred hers. She hadn't been able to stop staring at his massive shoulders, his impressively broad chest and perfect abs. And once she'd started thinking of him as a sexy man, she couldn't seem to stop. By the end of the day she'd been a basket case.

But it was more than just sexual chemistry messing with her mind. By the end of the trip she'd realized she had fallen in love with him. Maybe she'd always loved him, but until that day she had accepted their relationship as nothing more than a very close friendship. Now, her heart wanted her to admit what she'd been denying for years.

She'd known she had to come up with a plan or risk losing her best friend forever. She might have fallen in love with Stern, but she knew he didn't love her. He was one of the most eligible bachelors in Denver and his weekends were filled with dates.

So one day two months ago, when she read a romance novel a customer had left behind in the break room, an idea popped into her head. She would find another man to fall in love with, someone who could take Stern's place in her heart.

She'd been inspired by the heroine in the book, who was also in love with a man she couldn't have. To shift her focus off of the forbidden man, the heroine began dating her next-door neighbor. Eventually she fell in love with her neighbor. At the end of the book the couple married and lived happily ever after.

Okay, so it was pure fiction—but it was still an idea that had merit. On that day, JoJo had decided to become the owner of her destiny, the creator of her own happiness.

She'd just been waiting to run into someone interesting. For the next two months, she'd waited. And just when she thought she would never meet a man who could pique her interest…in drove Walter Carmichael needing a new set of spark plugs for his Porsche.

Something about him drew her attention, and he didn't have a ring on his finger. She quickly dismissed the notion that his good looks, impeccable style and suave manner reminded her of Stern.

When she did a routine customer-service follow-up call, she found that Walter had a nice phone voice, too. He had everything going for him. Now she had to make sure she had everything going for her. And the best person to help her was her best friend, the man she was trying not to love.

Two

Stern looked up when he heard a knock on his office door. "Come in."

It was Dillon, his oldest brother and CEO of Blue Ridge Land Management, a firm that had been in their family for more than forty years. Dillon was the one in charge, their brother Riley was next in command and Stern and his older brother Canyon were corporate attorneys. His cousin Adrian would be starting in a couple of months as one of the company's engineers.

Dillon entered Stern's office then closed the door behind him and leaned against it. Stern had seen that look on Dillon's face before. It usually meant he was in a world of trouble.

"Any reason for your bad mood today?" Dillon asked, staring him down. "Your first day back from vacation and I'd have thought you'd be in a good mood, not the opposite. I heard hunting went better for JoJo than for you, but please tell me that's not what has you upset. You're not a sore loser. Besides, thanks to her father, she not only knows everything there is to know about cars, she's also an expert marksman, a karate champ and a skilled archer. She's been showing you up for years."

Stern tossed a paper clip onto his desk and stared at it for a long moment before glancing up and meeting his brother's gaze. "I'm well aware of all JoJo's skills, and that's not what's bothering me. She informed me while we were on our trip that she's set her sights on another target—and it's not an elk. It's a man."

Dillon raised a brow. "Excuse me?" He moved from the door to take the chair in front of Stern's desk.

"Just what I said. So maybe I am a sore loser, Dillon. JoJo has been my best friend forever and I don't want to lose her."

Dillon stretched his long legs out in front of him. "I think you better start from the beginning."

So Stern did. Dillon said nothing while he listened attentively. When Stern was finished he said, "I think you're getting carried away and not giving JoJo credit for being the true friend that she is. I don't think there's a man alive who can come between you two or mess up your friendship. I think it says a lot that of all the people she could have gone to for advice, she came to you. She trusts your judgment."

Dillon stood. "If I were you, I wouldn't let her down. And as far as your bad mood, you know the rules, Stern. No one can bring personal garbage into the office. Canyon just got back from his honeymoon and is in a great mood, understandably so. Yet you were going at him about every idea he tossed out, just for the hell of it. You owe everyone at the meeting, especially Canyon, an apology and I expect you to give it."

Dillon then walked to the door and opened it.

"Dil?"

Dillon stopped and turned around. "Yes?"

"Thanks for keeping me in check. I'm sorry I behaved inappropriately."

Dillon nodded. "I accept your apology, Stern. Just make sure it doesn't happen again." He then walked out and closed the door behind him.

Stern rubbed his hand down his face. He could handle anybody's disappointment but Dillon's. When their parents, and uncle and aunt, died in a plane crash nearly twenty years ago, they'd left Dillon and his cousin Ramsey in charge. It hadn't been easy, especially since several Westmorelands had been younger than the age of sixteen. Together, Dillon and Ramsey worked hard and made sacrifices to keep the family together. Dillon had even gone against the State of Colorado when they tried forcing him to put the youngest four kids in foster homes. Those were just a few of the reasons why Dillon deserved his utmost admiration and respect. Even now, he helped keep the family together.

Presently, there were fifteen Denver Westmorelands. Stern's parents had had seven sons—Dillon, Micah, Jason, Riley, Canyon, Stern and Brisbane. Uncle Adam and Aunt Clarisse had had eight children: five boys—Ramsey, Zane, Derringer and the twins Aiden and Adrian—and three girls—Megan, Gemma and Bailey.

Over the past few years, everyone had gotten married except for him, the twins, Bailey and Bane. In June Megan had married Rico, a private investigator; Canyon had up and married Keisha Ashford, the mother of his two-year-old son, last month; and Riley and his fiancée, Alpha, would be getting married at the end of this month. It was still a shock to everyone that his cousin Zane, who had once sworn he would stay a bachelor for life, would marry his fiancée, Channing, over the Christmas holidays.

Stern tossed another paper clip onto the desk before picking up the phone and punching in Canyon's extension.

"This is Canyon."

"Can, I apologize for acting like a jerk in the meeting today."

There was a slight pause. Then Canyon said, "It wasn't your usual style, Stern. We haven't argued in years. What's going on with you? I leave to go on my honeymoon and come back and you're not yourself. What happened on that hunting trip with JoJo?"

Instead of answering Canyon's question, Stern said, "Let's meet for lunch and I'll call and ask Riley to join us. My treat."

"What about Dillon?"

A wry smile curved Stern's lips. "No need. He just left my office after chewing me out, so he's straight."

Canyon released a low whistle. "Glad it was you and not me."

"Hey, JoJo, we need a new set of tires for a '75 BMW and I don't think we have the model number in stock."

JoJo glanced up from her computer screen and smiled at the older man who'd stuck his head in her door. Willie Beeker had worked for the Golden Wrench for more than forty years, first with her father and now with her. He'd been set to retire the year after her father's death and she knew he'd only hung around the past couple of years to give her the help and support she needed. Although he'd trained a number of good men, any of whom could step into his shoes, no one could take his place.

She'd known Beeker all of her life. He and her father had become best friends while working together as mechanics in the army. Her father had gotten out of the military, returned home to Denver and married. Years later, the two friends hooked back up when Beeker had divorced and moved to Denver. While growing up, she'd seen Beeker as more than one of her father's outstanding employees. She'd considered him an honorary uncle.

"No problem, Beeker. I'll start checking around immediately."

Beeker entered her office. "Things were crazy off the bat this morning, and I didn't get the chance to welcome you back and ask how things went last week."

JoJo leaned back in her chair and smiled. "I brought down an elk on the third day."

"That's great, girl! You didn't make my boy too mad, did you?"

Her smile widened. "Um, maybe just a little. But Stern will be fine."

She couldn't help remembering their final days at the lodge. They'd put up their hunting rifles and pulled out the playing cards and checkerboard. He had whipped her hands down in all the games except one, and she had a feeling he'd felt sorry for her and had given her that one.

JoJo always appreciated unwinding at the lodge with Stern and this past trip had been no exception. After their first conversation about her makeover, he hadn't wanted to discuss her request again, which made her think he wasn't crazy about the idea. But he had promised his help and she couldn't ask for more than that.

"Did the 2010 Porsche come in while I was away?"

Beeker raised a brow. "No. Why?"

"Just curious. It's a nice car."

"You sure that's all you admire?"

She held Beeker's questioning gaze. "Yes." Since her father's death he'd stepped in as a surrogate father to her, but she didn't want to worry him needlessly.

Beeker nodded. "So you think he'll ever settle down and marry?"

Now it was JoJo who raised a brow. "Who?"

"Stern."

JoJo frowned. How had they moved from the driver of the Porsche to Stern? "I don't know. Why do you ask?"

Beeker shrugged. "There have been a lot of weddings in his family lately. His cousin Megan in June, Canyon last month, Riley later this month and Zane before the end of the year. The single Westmorelands seem to be falling like flies."

"Stern dates a lot, but he doesn't have an exclusive girl."

Beeker chuckled. "If anyone would know, you would." He checked his watch. "Let me know when you locate those tires so I can send Maceo to pick them up."

Maceo Armstrong was her newest employee, fresh out of mechanic school. "I will."

It took JoJo less than thirty minutes to make a few calls, find the tires and dispatch Maceo to make a run across town. It was only then that she allowed herself to consider Beeker's question about Stern. Like she'd told Beeker, Stern didn't have a serious girl right now. But she knew that didn't mean he wouldn't meet someone eventually. After all, as Beeker had said, there had been a lot of Westmoreland weddings and engagements lately. Because of her long friendship with Stern she also was close to his family.

She'd known that Canyon had been quite taken with Keisha Ashford three years ago, so his decision to marry wasn't a surprise. But she had been surprised at Megan's marriage, only because of the swiftness of the romance between her and Rico Claiborne. And Riley's and Zane's decisions to marry were definitely shockers. Could such a thing happen to Stern? What if Stern began seeing a woman seriously and the woman convinced him to end his close friendship with JoJo out of jealousy? So far it hadn't happened, probably because none of the women he dated saw her as a threat.

Stern would be a good catch for any woman. Besides being handsome and wealthy, he was a nice person—insightful, kind and considerate. And she didn't just think that because he was her best friend. He dated a lot, but he never treated any woman shabbily. He let them know up front where he stood in regards to relationships and he'd said more than once that he had no intention of settling down or thinking about marriage until after his thirty-fifth birthday. That meant he only had five years to go. And he'd only have that much time if some woman didn't come along to sweep him off his feet. JoJo had never worried about that before, but the family trend seemed to be that the Westmoreland men were vulnerable to love.

JoJo shook her head. *Vulnerable?* She couldn't imagine that word connected to Riley or Zane. And because she knew them so well, she figured that if they were making a long-term commitment, it was because they deeply loved the woman they were marrying.

And because Stern never did anything half-step, there was no doubt in her mind that one day he would meet a woman and fall in love just as deeply. And when that happened, where would it leave her? She knew the answer without having to think hard about it.

Alone.

That meant she had to move forward with her plan. It would be imperative to have someone special of her own before Stern met someone and married. Pushing away from the desk, she stretched her body before grabbing a clipboard off the wall. As she left her office she knew pursuing Walter Carmichael was more important than ever. In a few days she would know where he liked to hang out and then go from there. Wanda, her fiftysome-thing-year-old know-it-all receptionist was on it and if anyone could find out the information it would be her.

Like Beeker, Wanda was another trusted employee who'd worked for the Golden Wrench for years—ever since JoJo was in high school. It had been Wanda who had explained to JoJo why it meant so much to her father that she take those etiquette classes and dance lessons, although she'd hated every minute of them. She much preferred being under the hood of a car instead of acting like a simpering idiot the way most teen girls behaved. She and her father had compromised. He would let her go hunting with him and Beeker and take the karate and archery classes she loved, if she learned what she needed to know to be a lady every once in a while.

She'd never been interested in boys the way other girls had been, mainly because the boys sought her out and not the other way around—it hadn't been for her looks, but for her wheels. Thanks to her dad, she'd always driven a smooth-looking muscle car, a guy's dream. And just as Stern had known the girls' motives for faking friend-ship with her, she'd been very much aware of the guys' motives. That was yet another reason her friendship with Stern meant so much to her.

Whether it happened in a few months or in the next year, one day he would be forced to end their friendship. And the last thing she wanted him to do was feel guilty about having to cut her loose.

Then there was that other problem she'd found herself contending with during their weekend away: her new-found attraction to him. More than once while they'd been playing cards, when his attention was squarely on

the hand he held, her attention had been squarely on
him. When had that little mole on his upper lip started
to look so sexy? And when had long eyelashes on a man
become a turn-on?

If those thoughts weren't bad enough, when he had
dropped her off at home and given her the usual peck on
the cheek and hug, she had felt her heart pounding deep
in her chest. Yes, she was into Stern bad, and the only
way out of it was to turn her attention to another man.

Still, the memory of Stern singing in the shower, whis-
tling through the lodge while he cooked breakfast or
humming late at night while they sat together on the deck
playing checkers was embedded in her brain.

She was so lost in remembering that she didn't slow
her pace when she rounded the corner until her body hit
the solid wall of a man's chest.

"Whoa. Going to a fire, Jo?" Stern asked, reaching
out to steady her.

She seemed to blush, and he couldn't help wondering
what she had been thinking about. He had a feeling her
thoughts hadn't been on work.

"Stern, what are you doing here?" she asked, sounding somewhat breathless.

He lifted a brow. "Any reason I shouldn't be here?"
he asked, releasing her and then turning to fall in step
beside her.

"No, but it's Monday and we just got back yesterday."

"I know but I met Riley and Canyon for lunch at McK-
ays, and thought I'd check to see how things are going
since I was in the neighborhood."

"Oh."

Was that disappointment he heard in her voice? Did
she wish it had been that other guy—the one whose name

she refused to give him—to show up unexpectedly and not him? That thought didn't sit well with him. "You don't sound too happy to see me."

She glanced over at him. "Don't be silly. I'm always happy to see you."

He didn't say anything for a moment. Was he being silly? Was the whole issue silly—the very issue that had nagged at him and kept him up last night to the point where he had snapped at his brothers this morning? Had he gotten chewed out by his oldest brother for nothing?

Pushing those questions to the back of his mind, he asked her, "What are your plans for later?"

"Um, nothing. I haven't unpacked yet and will probably do that and laundry. Why?"

"No reason."

They entered one of the bays where Beeker and another one of her employees had a car up on the lift changing out the struts. Stern greeted the men as he and JoJo passed through.

"How many cars do you have to work on today?" he asked as he continued following her to the bay she normally used. He watched as she glanced down at her clipboard. "So far there are only five scheduled. But you know how that might end up on a Monday."

Yes, he knew. Back in high school, when her father was alive, he and JoJo had been hired out to do odds and ends in the shop. He had enjoyed learning from her father and Beeker and all the other guys. And Wanda had been a hoot. JoJo's father's death had hit him as much as it had hit her. Joseph Jones had been a man Stern had looked up to, a man he had respected, a man who'd spent a lot of time with him.

Stern had spent as many days and nights with JoJo and her father as he had at home. He'd gone on hunting trips with them. Mr. Jones had taught him the proper way to handle a gun and Beeker had taught him and JoJo how to shoot.

"You want to take in a movie tomorrow night?"

She glanced up at him and he wondered why, in all the years he'd known her, he had just realized how mesmerizing her eyes were.

"A movie?"

"Yes." They'd gone to movies together a number of times, too many to count, and never had they considered them dates or anything more than two friends hanging out. Why did he suddenly feel that this invitation was different?

"What's playing?" she asked, eyeing him suspiciously. "The past couple of times we went to a movie we saw ones that none of your girlfriends wanted to see. So you took me. Must be one of those blood and guts flicks."

He couldn't help but chuckle because she knew him so well. "There is this new action movie that came out this weekend. Riley claims it's good."

"And the reason you can't find a date for tomorrow?"

"Not trying to find one. We still need to talk."

"About what?" she asked, checking her watch.

"About that request you asked of me at the lodge."

She stopped walking and hung the clipboard at its designated place on the wall. "If I remember correctly, you didn't want to talk about it."

She was right. The more he thought about the makeover, the more he thought it wasn't a good idea. If a man only cared about outside appearances, then he might not get to know the JoJo that Stern knew from the inside out. She had a heart of gold, and she was cheating herself if she pursued a man who would only zero in on her looks.

But he knew JoJo and she had made up her mind

about this guy whose name she refused to give him. The thought of this unnamed man made him mad, and then madder each and every time he thought about him. So Stern decided that the best thing to do was to keep an eye on her and make sure she didn't get into trouble or into any situation she couldn't handle.

"Well, I do want to talk about it now, and I'm thinking a makeover might not work after all."

She frowned. "Why?"

He shoved his hands in his pockets. "Your mystery man won't get to know the real you."

She rolled her eyes. "He can get to know the real me later. First, I need to get him to notice me. So I think the makeover will work, and you did say you would help me. Don't try wiggling out of it now."

"I'm not." He paused. "I just don't want you to get hurt."

"Hurt?" She glanced around as if to make sure none of her employees were within hearing range. "Are you saying you don't think that a makeover will help me? That I'm so much of a reject that even a makeover wouldn't do me any good?"

"No, that's not what—"

"Well I've got news for you, Stern. I've seen even the ugliest of women and men become beautiful and handsome. So there's no reason to believe a makeover can't do wonders for me, too."

"That's not what I was insinuating, JoJo."

"Doesn't matter. I'll show you," she said, then walked off toward the first car she would be working on.

He rubbed his hand down his face in frustration. What was going on here? He and JoJo never fought or argued about anything, and now they seemed to be bickering back and forth about every damn thing.

All he'd said was that he didn't want to see her hurt. Why would she think he'd meant that a makeover wouldn't help her? In truth, he knew it would help her and that's what he was worried about. Men would be coming on to her for all the wrong reasons.

He glanced over at her as she leaned over the car to look under the hood. He couldn't help noticing how her work pants stretched tightly over her backside. Her perfectly shaped backside. Damn, why was he checking out JoJo?

He drew in a frustrated breath. "I'll call you later."

"Whatever," she mumbled without even bothering to look up.

Stern left, feeling as if he'd made the situation between them worse instead of better.

Three

"Here's the information you wanted on that Carmichael dude."

JoJo looked up into the face of a petite blonde who didn't look her age. A copy of Wanda's birth certificate in her employment file indicated she was nearing sixty, but if you asked Wanda she would swear she wasn't even fifty yet. And since she had the face and figure to back it up, no one had dared to call her on it.

JoJo picked up the card Wanda had tossed on her desk. "He lives in Cherry Hills Village." The Village was one of the most affluent suburbs in Denver.

"You're surprised? Look how he dresses. Look at the car he drives. Not to mention what he does for a living."

JoJo nodded. "He's thirty-one, the same age as Stern. And according to what you've found out, he's not in an exclusive relationship."

"Also like Stern."

JoJo shifted her gaze from the card to Wanda, who was pretending to peruse JoJo's bulletin board. She'd known Wanda long enough to recognize the smile the older woman was trying to hide. "Well, yes," JoJo admitted. "Like Stern."

Wanda tilted her head and met JoJo's gaze. "Come to think of it, there's a lot about this Carmichael man that would remind a person of Stern. Is there a reason for that?"

JoJo decided she didn't want to hold Wanda's gaze any longer. The woman was sharp. "What do you think?"

JoJo couldn't resist watching Wanda out of the corner of her eyes. She saw Wanda look thoughtful for a moment before she said, "Do you really want me to tell you what I think, Jovonnie?"

JoJo tried to ignore the tension building at her temples. Whenever Wanda called her by her full name JoJo knew Wanda would go into "it's time I tell it the way I see it" mode.

"Don't you have a switchboard to cover? You are on payroll," she reminded her.

"Don't try pulling rank on me, young lady. This is my lunch break, and need I remind you I am entitled to one?"

"No you don't have to remind me, but I'm working through mine, so if you don't mind, I—"

"I do mind," Wanda interrupted, resting her hip on the edge of JoJo's desk. "And the reason I mind is because I think you're making a big mistake."

Seeing that she wouldn't be getting any work done until Wanda had her say, JoJo tossed her pen on her desk and leaned back in her chair. "Evidently, you want to get something off your chest."

"I do."

JoJo nodded. "All right, you have the floor." She placed the card down on her desk.

Taking JoJo at her word, Wanda stood and paced in front of JoJo's desk. Wanda was a beautiful woman who had gone through two marriages. The first had ended in death and the other in divorce. Wanda would tell anyone that the second marriage had been a mistake because she'd tried to find a man who could replace a husband who was irreplaceable.

Wanda had fallen in love with a cop at the age of twenty-one, and he'd left her a widow with a newborn baby at twenty-eight. She had remarried at thirty-four and divorced at thirty-seven. She and her ex were both still single and remained friends. It wasn't unusual for him to drop by the shop every so often to take Wanda to lunch or dinner.

Tension now throbbed at JoJo's temples. She had a ton of paperwork to do, and like she'd told Stern, she needed to go home to unpack and do laundry. She'd become impatient with the pacing when Wanda finally stopped, snagged her gaze and said, "You've fallen in love with Stern."

JoJo was glad her backside was firmly planted in the chair or she would have fallen out of it. She was totally positive she hadn't given her feelings away so how had Wanda figured things out? JoJo didn't want to believe what her father had always jokingly said about Wanda: that she had a sixth sense about stuff that wasn't any of her business.

When JoJo didn't say anything, but just sat there and stared, Wanda said, "Admit it."

JoJo quickly snapped out of her moment of stunned silence. She reached across her desk and picked up the pen she'd tossed aside earlier and pretended to jot something down on one of the documents she picked up. "I won't admit anything. Don't be silly."

"Not silly, just observant. And you should know by now that I don't miss a thing."

JoJo replaced her pen on the desk and tilted her head. "And just what do you think you haven't been missing?"

Wanda smiled. "The way you've started looking at Stern when you think he won't notice. The way you smile whenever you see him. How excited you were to go on that hunting trip with him. You acted like it was your first time when you do it two or three times a year."

JoJo waved off her words. "All circumstantial evidence."

"Yes, but then you decide to check out a guy who could be Stern's clone. To me that's an obvious sign."

JoJo nibbled on her bottom lip before allowing a frown to settle on her face. "You make me sound pathetic."

Wanda shook her head. "Not pathetic. Just confused."

Now it was JoJo who needed to stand. Instead of pacing, she moved to the window. It was a beautiful September day, but all she had to do was look up at the high mountains to know Denver would get an early winter. And a pretty cold one, too.

She turned around and, not surprisingly, she found Wanda leaning her hips on JoJo's desk. "Let's just say your theory is true. Mind you, I'm not saying that it is," JoJo said. "But let's say, for the sake of argument, that it is. What's wrong with me moving toward a sure thing instead of getting hung up on a lost cause?"

"Why would you think Stern is a lost cause?"

JoJo thought long and hard about Wanda's question before answering. "He's only a lost cause when it pertains to me. I know him. He's my best friend, and he knows that's all he'll ever be to me. There's no need for me to waste my time wanting more. Knowing that, I'd go to a plan that might work."

"Walter Carmichael?"

"Yes. He's just what I need to move ahead in another direction." *Away from Stern.*

"And what if that doesn't work?"

JoJo smiled. "It will. I intend to learn from the best."

Wanda stared at her for a minute. "Please tell me you're not doing what I think you're doing."

JoJo shrugged as she went back to her desk and sat down. "Okay I won't tell you."

Wanda shook her head. "It's not going to work, JoJo. When one man has your heart you can't replace him with another. I learned that the hard way."

JoJo watched as Wanda squared her shoulders and walked out of the office. One day, JoJo decided, she would have a long talk with Wanda and get the facts about what had happened with her second marriage. Why had it been so difficult to move on and fall in love again with a good man?

JoJo was certain it wouldn't be that hard for her to shift her affections from Stern to Walter. She'd never been married to Stern, after all. Falling for another man shouldn't be difficult.

In a way, she was looking forward to showing up at the Punch Bowl on Saturday night. From the information Wanda had just provided her with, it seemed that's where Walter hung out on the weekends. She'd heard it had live entertainment and was a nice place to dance, a place where women went to meet men.

She drew in a deep breath knowing this weekend she would be in that number.

"This must be serious." Zane Westmoreland opened the door to his cousin.

Stern walked past him and into the living room. "What makes you think that?"

Zane shrugged as he followed. "You're here. I can't recall the last time you came visiting."

"You've had a house guest and I didn't want to intrude. I heard she's gone for now." Stern was talking about the woman Zane would be marrying over the holidays. Stern was still somewhat in shock about that. If anyone had told him that his cousin Zane, the one man who not only knew women like the back of his hand but who also enjoyed them tremendously, would settle down and marry, Stern would not have believed them.

"Channing had to go back to Atlanta for work. She'll be moving here from Atlanta permanently next month."

"Think you can last until then?"

Zane smiled. "Not sure. She'll be back in a few weeks for Riley's wedding. We'll spend Thanksgiving with her folks and then we marry on Christmas Day."

"Sounds like you have it all planned out," Stern said, sitting on the couch and stretching his long legs in front of him.

"I do." There was a pause. "So what brings you by on a Monday night, Stern?"

Stern would think the reason he'd stopped by was obvious. Zane, who was six years older, had a reputation for knowing women. Not just a little about them but practically everything. Before he'd become engaged to Channing, Zane had been the family expert on the subject, and Stern figured the kind of knowledge Zane possessed didn't dissipate with an engagement.

"It's JoJo."

Zane's brow lifted. "What about JoJo?"

Stern released a slow breath. JoJo had been his best friend for years so everyone in the family knew her. "She asked me for a favor."

"What kind of favor?"

"She wanted me to tell her how to make a man want her. There's this guy she's been checking out. Only thing is, he doesn't seem to reciprocate the interest, so she wants me to tell her what she needs to do to stimulate that interest."

Zane nodded. "Oh, I see."

Stern frowned. "Well, I sure as hell don't."

"You wouldn't."

Stern's frown deepened. "What is that supposed to mean?"

A slight smile touched Zane's lips. "It means that since JoJo's your best friend, you're too close to the situation. If you were another woman it wouldn't be a big deal, but because you're a man, to you it is a big deal."

"Of course it's a big deal. Why should she worry about making a man want her? If the guy doesn't have the sense to want her on his own, why should she worry about it?"

"Because she evidently wants him and wants him to want her in return. There's nothing wrong with that."

Stern figured there was a lot wrong with it.

"So what did you tell her?" Zane asked.

Stern leaned back against the sofa cushions. "When I didn't take her seriously at first, she copped an attitude. That's the last thing I needed so I offered a few pointers. I told her that she probably should wear more dresses. JoJo has great legs, and she should flaunt them more. I also suggested she stop hiding her hair under a cap. Her hair is one of her strong points. I particularly like it when she wears it down."

Zane nodded again. "Anything else?"

"I told her that after her makeover, she should find out where this guy hangs out and go there, impress him as the new and improved JoJo. I told her if she decided to make such a move then I would go with her."

"Why?"

Stern's brow bunched in confusion. "Why?"

"Yes, why? Why do you feel the need to go with her?"

"Because I don't know the guy," he said defensively. "She won't give me his name or tell me anything about him, other than that he brings his car in to get it serviced from time to time."

"That's all you need to know. If you ask me, that's more than you should know. JoJo is a grown woman who can take care of herself."

"You don't know that."

Zane chuckled. "We're talking about JoJo, Stern. The same woman who can hit a target with a gun *or* a bow and arrow with one eye closed. The same woman who has a black belt. You and I both know she can take care of herself, so that means there's something else bothering you. What is it?"

Stern frowned as he stared at the floor and mumbled, "Nothing."

Zane didn't say anything for a minute. "There is something, Stern. You didn't come here because you wanted to see my pug face. There's something bothering you, so come clean. I can only help if you do that."

Stern paused. "I'm afraid, Zane."

Zane lifted a brow. "Afraid? What are you afraid of?"

"That I'm going to lose my best friend. What if she gets serious with this guy and he has a problem with our relationship? You've said enough times that you wouldn't want any woman of yours to share the kind of relationship with a man that JoJo shares with me."

"You won't lose her," Zane said, trying to reassure him.

"You can't be certain of that, and I can't take that chance."

Zane shook his head. "You're going to have to trust her judgment."

"I trust hers. I just don't trust his."

Zane rolled his eyes. "But you don't know him."

"Exactly," Stern said, standing. "That's why I need to find out who he is and check him out."

"I think you're going at it all wrong."

"I don't," he said, heading for the door. "Bye, Zane. You've given me a lot to think about."

"No, I didn't. I suggest you examine your own feelings for JoJo," Zane replied. But Stern was already out the door and didn't hear what his cousin had said.

The next night JoJo stepped onto her porch and inhaled deeply to fill her lungs with crisp mountain air. She had put her hair in a ponytail before placing her favorite Denver Broncos cap on her head, but instead of her usual jeans and T-shirt, she was wearing a blue blouse and a pair of black corduroy slacks. She'd also grabbed a jacket because the evenings were turning cool.

She heard a sound, turned and then smiled at the man coming up the steps. Her heart raced. Stern's well-toned physique was displayed in a pair of jeans, a blue Western shirt and a Stetson. He looked way too handsome for his own good.

She checked her watch. "You're on time."

"Aren't I always?" Stern said, glancing around. "I hope you don't stand out here on the porch waiting for all your dates."

JoJo adjusted her cap. "You aren't a date. Come on," she said, grabbing his arm and heading down the steps. "I've already locked up and turned on the alarm. The movie starts in twenty minutes."

"Whoa, what's the rush? There's not much traffic out so we'll make it."

She knew he was right, but she was looking forward to tonight. Any time she got to spend with Stern made her all giggly inside. She was certain those feelings would pass once she knew more about Walter. And speaking of Walter...

"I'm going to get that makeover this weekend," she said as she got into the car and buckled her seat belt.

Stern glanced over at her after buckling his own. "Why?"

She felt the huge smile that spread across her face. "I found out where my guy hangs out on the weekend and I plan to show up."

Stern held her gaze for a moment and then asked, "Where?"

"I'll tell you only if you promise not to show up."

"Not making that promise, JoJo."

She rolled her eyes. "Then I won't tell you. Why are you being difficult about this, Stern? Do I show up at places where I know you'll be taking your dates?"

"No. But I'm not the one asking for advice on how to reel someone in. Besides, I want to make sure he doesn't get disrespectful with you," Stern said, pulling out of her driveway.

She frowned. "Dammit, Stern, I can take care of myself. If I can catch his attention, we'll talk, listen to music and dance. It shouldn't be hard to tell if he's interested."

He turned to her when the car came to a traffic light. "But he'll be interested for the wrong reason."

"I can handle it."

He grunted. "So you're really going to go through with this?"

"Yes. Of course. I thought we cleared up the issue of

how serious I was last week." He was acting too much like a big brother to suit her.

A couple of hours later, to her way of thinking, Stern was not in the best of moods. The movie was good and she had enjoyed it, but each time she stole a glance at him, he was frowning.

"That sour look will get stuck in place if you don't get rid of it, Stern," she teased as they walked out of the theater.

He looked over at her. "Funny."

"You don't see me laughing. The movie was your idea, but I don't think you enjoyed being here," she said, sliding into the car when he opened the door for her.

"I enjoyed the movie, and I enjoyed your company."

JoJo wasn't convinced. She glanced at her watch. "It's early. You want to drop by McKays for coffee?"

"That sounds good."

At least he wasn't in a rush to get her home, she thought. "I talked to Megan about the guy that does her hair, and she suggested I talk to Pam, so I'm doing that tomorrow. I hope she'll be able to recommend someone who can do my makeover. She always looks good. In fact, all the women your cousins and brothers married look great."

Pam was married to his oldest brother, Dillon. A former movie star who'd been a regular on one of JoJo's favorite soaps years ago, Pam had given it all up to return to her home in Wyoming to raise her three younger sisters when her father died. That was when she'd met Dillon.

"What if I told you I like the way you look?" Stern said, intruding on her thoughts.

She rolled her eyes. "You would since you're my best friend. Besides, I'm not trying to impress you, remember? However, I appreciate the fact that you gave me some advice at the lodge. It's advice that I'm putting to good use since I consider you an expert on what men like. I'm going shopping on Friday, and after talking to Pam I'll be contacting someone who can perform miracles on my hair and help with my makeup."

He didn't say anything. He just redirected his focus on the road. But she would swear she could hear his teeth gnashing. Why was he upset about her setting her sights on a guy? When minutes passed and she could feel the tension radiating between them, she couldn't stand it any longer. When he pulled into McKays' parking lot and brought the car to a stop, she turned to him as she unbuckled her seat belt. "What's wrong with you, Stern? I thought you understood. Why do you have a problem with me going after a guy I want when you do the same with any woman you want?"

Stern didn't say anything for a long moment. "Is it wrong for me to want to protect you, JoJo?"

She drew in a deep breath. Little did he know, she was trying to protect him...mainly from herself. If Stern had any idea that she'd fallen in love with him, he would probably race toward the nearest mountain, away from her.

"It's wrong if I don't want to be protected. You're acting worse than Dad ever did. Even he had the good sense to loosen the binds when I got older. In fact, he would tell me all the time that I needed to get out more, date, get dressed up and meet boys. He didn't worry about me because he knew I could take care of myself. Why don't you?"

"That's not it."

She lifted a brow. "Then what is it?"

Stern frowned, not knowing if he could explain how he felt without sounding selfish. Was he willing to deny her a chance to be happy just because he didn't want to lose her? "Nothing. I'm just in a bad mood. Sorry."

He started to open the car door to get out when she reached out and touched his arm. "Why are you in a bad mood?"

He shrugged. "Craziness at the office. My first day back yesterday didn't go well." No need to tell her how he'd been a jerk in front of his brothers and how Dillon had read him the riot act. "Work was piled high on my desk. I have a lot of cases to prepare for this week. A ton of stuff to do with little time."

He saw the sympathetic look in her eyes and felt like a heel for stretching the truth. The number of files on his desk was manageable and had nothing to do with his mood.

She patted his hand. "Don't worry about it, Stern. You can do it. You always do. You're bright. Intelligent. A hard worker. And you have a good head on your shoulders."

He couldn't respond. What she'd said was the JoJo way. She'd always had the ability to make him believe in himself even when the odds were stacked against him. Like when he'd wanted to play basketball in high school but his grades hadn't been the best. She had tutored him and when he'd wanted to give up, she wouldn't let him. She'd encouraged him by saying some of the same things to him then that she had said just now. And, dammit, she always had him believing it. "Thanks, JoJo."

How in the world had he been blessed with a best friend like her? A lot of people considered them odd because of their unique friendship. And there were some, like his cousins Bailey and the twins—Aiden and Adrian—who thought they would eventually become more than friends. He had told them time and time again that he didn't see JoJo that way. She was his best friend and nothing more. He refused to think anything had changed.

"Ready to go inside?" he asked her.

"Yes, I can use the coffee. I need to finish inventory. We're running out of supplies too soon. Something isn't adding up."

"Then I'm sure you'll find out what the problem is," he said, getting out of the car. "You're always on top of stuff."

He came around the car to open the door for her. "Thanks for the vote of confidence," she said.

"No problem."

Pushing the car door shut behind her, he took her hand and together they moved toward the entrance of McKays, a popular restaurant in town. It was only when they were inside and greeted by the hostess that he released JoJo's hand.

And only then did it occur to him how good it had felt holding it.

"Thanks for the movie and coffee tonight, Stern."

"Don't mention it," he said, following her inside her home. Whenever he took her out, he would come in with her and check things out.

After their little discussion in which he had explained why he was in such a bad mood, his attitude had vastly improved. Over coffee, he'd joked about Aiden and Adrian and their plans now that they had finished college. Aiden, who had gone into the medical field, was doing his residency at a hospital in Maine. Adrian, who'd gotten a master's degree in engineering, would start working for Blue Ridge as a project engineer in a couple of months.

Adrian had decided to travel abroad before returning to Denver to settle down and start work.

She and Stern also talked about all the excitement swirling around the Westmoreland households, with all the recent marriages and engagements. The one thing she noted was that Stern thought it was really funny that some of his cousins and brothers figured he would be next—even though he didn't have a steady girlfriend.

"Everything checks out," Stern said, coming out of her kitchen.

"Only because you scared away the bogeyman." She chuckled and took off her cap, tossing it on a table before removing the band from her hair to let the waves flow around her shoulders. She wondered if the person who would do her hair for the weekend would suggest cutting it. She'd never gotten her hair cut, but if it meant getting Walter to notice her, then she would definitely consider it.

JoJo almost jumped at the feel of Stern's hand in her hair. She hadn't heard him cross the room.

"I love your hair," he said softly, running his fingers through the strands.

His fingers felt good. "I know," she said. He had always complimented her on her hair and she knew from their conversation at the lodge that he thought she shouldn't hide it under a cap.

"Tell me you won't cut it. Ever."

"Umm, can't do that. The hairstylist might suggest I cut it as part of the makeover."

When she heard his teeth gnashing she glanced up at him. They were standing closer than she'd realized. "You're supporting me with all this right?" she asked, trying to sound in control of herself, of her emotions. Why did he have to smell so good?

He didn't say anything as he continued to run his fingers through her hair. Why was heat beginning to flow through her? It's not like he'd never played with her hair before. When they were younger he would pull her pig-tails all the time, and then when she got older, her pig-tails became ponytails and he would pull those, too. And more than a few times he'd helped her wash her hair when they'd vacationed at the lodge. But that was before she'd discovered she had feelings for him, before she'd begun lusting after him. Some of her dreams about him were totally X-rated.

She cleared her throat. "Well, if you still plan to go into the office early, you better go home and get a good night's sleep. And I still have those inventory reports to go over before I can call it a night."

"Yes, you're right," he said, pulling his fingers from her hair and checking his watch. "It's getting late."

"Yes, it is." Was it her imagination or did his voice sound a little throatier than usual? He was still stand-ing there, and he had reached back up to run his fingers through her hair again. Why was her body shifting closer to him? Why was her face tilting toward his?

More heat streaked up her spine and she was swathed in feelings she had never felt before.

And then Stern's fingers tightened on several strands of her hair and he lowered his mouth to hers.

She leaned up to meet his lips, feeling weak in the knees as their lips touched. Sensing she was about to lose her balance, Stern wrapped his arms around her and deepened the kiss. At least she had the presence of mind to grip his shoulders. Voices echoed through her brain: *this is wrong. This is Stern. He's my best friend and we shouldn't be engaging in this sort of thing.* But she ig-nored the voices as sensations overtook her.

And then he did something that made her gasp in

shock. He deepened the kiss even more, literally sucking her tongue into his mouth and devouring it. Never had she been kissed this way. To be honest, she'd never really been kissed at all. That sloppy, wet kiss Mitch Smith had planted on her lips right before Stern had clobbered him, when they'd been in the tenth grade, was nothing compared to this. In fact, it was crap compared to this.

This was the kind of kiss that romance novel authors wrote about—the kind that rendered you senseless and boneless at the same time. She couldn't help wondering if this was a test. Stern knew about her inexperience when it came to men, yet she had boldly set her sights on a man. Was he kissing her merely to show her what to expect? To see how good—or awful—she was?

That wasn't a bad idea, she thought. Then he could give her pointers so she wouldn't mess things up with Walter. Yes, that had to be it. That had to be the reason he was kissing her like this. He was kissing her to give her suggestions afterward. In that case…

She tightened her hands on his shoulders and leaned into him as he sucked on her tongue. She hadn't known a kiss could be so intense until now, and she liked it. It made her pulse throb and heat circle continuously in her belly.

To say she'd lived a sheltered life would be an understatement, but it had been her own choosing. Instead of going away to school, she had remained in Denver to attend college and had even stayed at home, preferring that to living on campus. Her father had tried talking her into going away to school, saying she needed to see the world. But she had convinced him that she was perfectly fine living with him.

She'd never experimented with men. Having her first

experiment be with Stern made more streaks of heat rush up her spine as his tongue continued to tangle with hers.

Why were her hips instinctively moving against his? Why was such a reaction causing shivers to overtake her?

The need to take a deep breath caused her to pull her mouth away.

"Wow," she heard him say and watched him lick his lips.

Drawing in much needed air, she met his gaze. "Well, how did I do?"

He raised a brow. "Excuse me?"

"How did I do? You were testing me, right?"

He shook his head as if to clear it. "Testing you?"

"Yes. You of all people know how green I am when it comes to kissing. I figured you didn't want me to embarrass myself when I let Walter kiss me. So how did I do?"

"Walter?"

Too late, JoJo realized she'd let the man's name slip. But all Stern had was a first name and there were plenty of Walters out there. "Just tell me how I did."

He stared at her for a long moment and then said, "A little more practice wouldn't hurt."

"Oh," she said, feeling disappointed.

"But you surprised me. You're better than I thought."

Her face then split into a wide smile. "I am?"

"Yes."

She nodded, moving from feeling disappointed to feeling elated. "Thanks. I was worried there for a minute."

"Don't be. With a little more practice you'd be off the charts. Now about this Walter…"

If he thought she would tell him anything else he had another think coming. "Don't ask me anything about him, Stern," she said. "Let's get back to talking about the kiss."

He crossed his arms over his chest. "What about it? I said you're good."

"You also said with practice I'd be better. And I want to be better. That means I'll need you to teach me how to be a better kisser."

"For this Walter?"

There was no need to lie about it so she said, "Yes, for Walter."

"In other words," he said as if he needed to make sure they were on the same page, "you want to learn to kiss to impress this Walter guy."

She nodded. Isn't that what she'd said? "Yes."

He just stood there and stared at her for a full minute and she had to force herself not to tremble under his laser-sharp gaze. When he didn't say anything and only continued to look at her, she began nibbling on her bottom lip.

"Well? Will you help me improve?"

"I'll think about it. Now come on and let me out. I'm leaving."

JoJo followed him to the door. "When will you let me know, Stern? I don't have much time."

When he reached the door he turned to her. "Soon." He leaned in to place the customary peck on her cheek. "Don't stay up too late."

Then he opened the door and she watched him leave.

Four

"Any reason you're banging on my door at this hour? It's after midnight, Stern," Zane said, moving aside to let his cousin enter.

Stern went straight into the living room and began pacing. Zane stared at him before plopping down on the sofa. He rubbed his hand down his face. "You want a cup of coffee?"

Stern stopped pacing and stared at him. "No, what I want is advice. I had a date with JoJo tonight."

Zane leaned back against the sofa cushion. "You have dates with JoJo all the time. What made tonight different?"

"I kissed her."

Zane stared at him for a moment, shook his head and then said, "I think we better drink coffee after all. If you don't need a cup, I do." He stood and walked toward the kitchen with Stern following in his wake. Once he set the coffeemaker on and it began brewing, he turned to Stern and leaned against the counter. "So, now do you want to tell me why you kissed JoJo?"

Stern shoved his hands into his pockets. "I don't know why I kissed her. I was playing with her hair one minute and then the next thing I knew, I was practically shoving my tongue down her throat."

"No graphics, please," Zane said, pouring a cup of coffee and then moving toward the table to sit down.

"Well, that's what happened."

"I'm surprised JoJo didn't karate chop you."

Stern decided he needed a cup of coffee after all and went over to the counter to pour a cup. "She didn't because she thought I was testing her."

"Testing her?"

"Yes. She's doing a makeover for that guy I was telling you about. His name is Walter, by the way. She let it slip out. But I don't know his last name."

Zane shook his head. "You're digressing. Please go back to why JoJo thinks she was being tested?"

Stern joined Zane at the table. "Because I know she's never really been kissed, she figured I was testing her to make sure she knew what to do when this Walter guy kisses her. Then, I made the mistake of telling her that she needs to improve on her kisses."

"Does she?"

"Hell, no, I lied. She was good. Too damn good. To be honest with you, the kiss was off the charts. And now the lie has caught up with me because she wants me to help her become a better kisser."

Zane stared at him for a long moment. "Let me get this straight. You and JoJo have a platonic relationship to the degree that she thinks the two of you can practice kissing without anything happening?"

"Nothing will happen," Stern argued.

Zane snorted. "If you believed that you wouldn't be

here, sitting at my table after midnight on a weeknight needing advice."

Stern knew that to be true. "To answer your question, yes she thinks our relationship is platonic to that degree because she sees me as nothing more than a friend. Her best friend."

"Well, can you handle teaching her to improve her kissing?"

Stern stared down into his cup of coffee and then he said, "That's the weird thing, Zane. Tonight, when I was kissing JoJo, one part of my brain kept saying...*Hey, this is JoJo you're locking lips with.* But then another part was tasting a very sensuous woman. A woman who has her sights on another man. While I was kissing her I forgot she was my best friend."

"Sounds like you've gotten yourself in a mess."

"Don't I know it? If I refuse to do it, she's going to think I'm being selfish and don't want her with Walter because I'm being overprotective. But if I do what she's asking, I might lose control and want to take it to another level. A level that can't exist between best friends. So what do you suggest?"

Zane rubbed his chin in deep thought. Then he said, "Do what she wants."

Stern frowned. "You want me to teach her how to kiss for some other man? That Walter guy?"

Zane took a sip of his coffee. "No. If you were smart, you would teach her how to kiss for yourself."

"This isn't funny, Zane."

"And you don't see me laughing, Stern."

Stern stared long and hard at him. "Are you suggesting that after all these years I consider moving from best friends to lovers with JoJo?"

Zane smiled. "Yes, I guess I am."

Anger raced through Stern. "You're off your rocker to suggest such a thing. There's no way I can do that. That's pure crazy."

Zane chuckled. "You kissed her tonight, and I gather you rather enjoyed it. I'm sure this time yesterday the thought of doing such a thing would have been pure crazy."

Stern frowned as he stood up. "I'm leaving. I came here for advice—not for you to get ridiculous on me."

"And you think I'm being ridiculous?" Zane asked.

"Yes. How long have JoJo and I been best friends, Zane?"

"A long time. Since middle school, if I recall."

"You're recalling right. And in all those years, at any time, did you suspect there was ever more between us?" Stern asked, certain what Zane's response would be.

"Sure. All of us have."

Stern frowned. That's not the response he'd expected. "And who exactly is *all of us?*"

Zane shrugged massive shoulders. "Mostly everybody."

Stern stared at Zane for several long seconds while Zane sipped his coffee as if it didn't bother him that he was being stared at. "Well, I hope *mostly everybody* knows they are wrong. JoJo and I have never been anything but the best of friends. I will protect her with my life and vice versa. I have never, ever thought of her as anything other than my best friend."

"So what was the kiss about tonight? You said she thought she was being tested, but I'm curious to know what you thought you were doing. Locking lips with a woman who is nothing more than your best friend? Shoving your tongue down her throat…and those were your words, not mine."

Tension began to build at Stern's temples. He pushed his cup of coffee aside and stood up. "I'm leaving."

"You didn't answer my question," Zane pointed out. "What was the kiss about tonight? Why did you kiss her in the first place?"

"I told you what happened. I was playing with her hair one minute and then the next thing I knew, I was kissing her."

"Playing with her hair? Interesting. Do you do that often?"

"Yes. No. Stop it, Zane! You're confusing me."

"And you're confusing me, Stern. It's after midnight and I'm too tired to debate you, but I'm not too tired to tell you what makes sense and what doesn't. I suggest you go home and think about what happened tonight and decide."

Stern lifted a brow. "Decide what?"

"Whether or not you want it to happen again. You have to make a decision as to whether you're going to teach JoJo how to become an expert kisser or leave it to someone else."

Stern felt a deep lump in his throat. "Someone else?"

"Yes. You know how women are. They only ask you to do something once, and if you're slow to act they'll get someone else to do it. I haven't been to the Golden Wrench in a while, but I bet JoJo has a number of men working there who would love to teach her how to kiss. And it might not stop there."

The picture Zane had painted in Stern's mind suddenly had his blood boiling. "I'm leaving."

Zane remained seated. "Good night."

"And I won't ever ask you for advice again."

Zane chuckled when he heard his front door slam behind his cousin moments later. He took a sip of his coffee and said, "Yes, you will, Stern. Yes, you will."

"Why are you all smiles today, JoJo?"

JoJo's smile faded as Wanda approached. "You're imagining things. I wasn't smiling." She twisted the wrench to remove the battery from the car she was working on.

"Yes, you were, and I noticed you've been smiling all morning. Something happen last night on your date with Stern?"

JoJo lifted a brow. "It wasn't a date. We merely went to a movie. And who told you about it?"

"You did. Don't you remember?"

In all honesty, she didn't. But there was a possibility that she had absentmindedly mentioned it because it wasn't unusual for her and Stern to go out. "No, I don't remember, but it doesn't matter. This is Wednesday, our busiest day of the week, and I intend for it to be a good day."

"So if it's not Stern putting a smile on your face, it must be because you know that Walter Carmichael is here today."

"Is he?" she asked, wondering why her body wasn't reacting. No increase in her pulse. No deep pounding of her heart. No unsteady breathing.

"Yes, he's in Beeker's bay. He looks good as usual."

"Why is he here? He doesn't have a tune-up for another three thousand miles."

"Something about a tear in the leather seat on the passenger side. I heard him tell Beeker it was caused by the buckle from some woman's boot. He wasn't too happy about it. I guess you should go out and say hello to your soon-to-be Boo."

JoJo wiped the grease from her hands before grabbing her clipboard off her desk. She then smiled over at Wanda. "I think I will."

Moments later, JoJo entered the bay where Beeker stood talking to Walter Carmichael. From Walter's profile she saw similarities between him and Stern. Both were tall, well-dressed and handsome. But that's where the similarities ended. Although Stern wore serious expressions a lot of the time, he had a smile that snuck up on you. Stern's smile would curve the corners of his lips and practically take your breath away. She'd seen Walter Carmichael smile only once and that's when she had complimented him on how well he took care of his car.

Both men glanced up when they saw her and she smiled in greeting. "Hello, Mr. Carmichael. Glad to see you again."

"I wouldn't be here if it wasn't for the tear in my seat," he said, sounding annoyed. "I'm just glad you have a good upholstery team. Beeker assures me the seat can be repaired as good as new."

"Then I'm sure it can be." JoJo knew she wasn't looking her best. She was wearing her work uniform, work shoes and a cap, but still…the man wasn't giving her a sideways glance. She decided not to let it bother her. On Saturday night he would see that she could clean up really nice.

"Well, if you need anything else, let me know. We appreciate our customers."

She really hadn't expected him to say anything in return, but it would have been nice to hear something like… thank you. Instead, he turned back to Beeker and began discussing another car-related issue, dismissing her.

She broke into the conversation, saying, "Well, I've got work to do. Have a good day, Mr. Carmichael."

Instead of responding, he merely nodded, dismissing her again as he continued his conversation with Beeker. Seeing he had no interest in her whatsoever, she left Beeker's bay to return to her own. She'd seen the work log; it would be a long and busy day. She didn't have time to be annoyed with a man who wasn't interested. But she hoped she would get his attention when he saw her Saturday night.

Eight hours later, feeling totally exhausted, she entered her home through the garage. As soon as she reached her bedroom she snatched the cap off her head, stripped off her clothes and headed for the bathroom to take a shower. After that, she would rest up a minute and then throw on something casual before heading out to meet with Pam.

Instead of driving the distance to Westmoreland Country, which was on the outskirts of town, she was meeting Pam in downtown Denver. Pam was going to be in town checking out an empty building she was thinking about purchasing for the acting school she wanted to open. She already had one such school in Wyoming, where she used to live, and she wanted to start another one here in Colorado. She and Pam would have dinner together at Larry's, a café around the corner from the potential school building and a short drive from where JoJo lived.

JoJo had worked on a total of eleven cars today, doing various things, from changing the oil to installing a couple of alternators, and she was bone tired. She could barely keep her eyes open when she stepped into the shower. However, once the water hit her face she felt more alive. All day she had been too busy to think about that kiss she'd shared with Stern last night, but on the drive home, and now, she couldn't get it out of her mind. Warm sensations flowed through her just thinking about it.

Of course she'd known she lacked knowledge in cer-

tain sexual areas, like kissing, but even without a wealth
of experience she didn't think it got any better than it had
been with Stern. The man's kiss made her body quiver
inside. There was no doubt he was an expert. She didn't
want to think of the number of women he'd kissed to
reach that status. The idea of the many women Stern
messed around with had never bothered her before, so
why was it bothering her now?

She knew the answer, which was why she'd created
this plan in the first place. She needed a diversion, even
if that meant going after someone like Walter. She hoped
he'd just been having a bad day and that his attitude today
wasn't the norm.

After drying herself off, she quickly went to her closet
to pick out something to wear and suddenly noted that
her wardrobe contained mostly blouses, T-shirts and
jeans. She owned a few pairs of slacks and a couple of
pantsuits—black, brown and navy. But no dresses. Whenever she had to attend a formal event, like a wedding or
a funeral, she wore a pantsuit.

At the hunting lodge, one of Stern's suggestions had
been for her to show off her legs. That meant a shopping
trip. She would bring that up with Pam when they met.

A part of her was getting excited about all of her plans
and the upcoming weekend. In the end, she hoped all of
these changes worked out in her favor.

Dillon stuck his head in the door. "You're still here?"

"Come in," Stern called out as he leaned back in his
chair. "Yes, I thought I would work late to catch up on
a few things. I see that we'll be closing the Harvey deal
next week."

"Let's keep our fingers crossed that it really happens
this time. Karl Harvey has postponed signing this thing

too often to suit me. It will be great if we finally get that tract of land in Minnesota. According to Riley, we already have a potential investor who wants to build a medical complex there."

Stern nodded. "I know why I'm still here at this hour, but what's your excuse? It's almost six o'clock."

Dillon smiled. "I'm meeting Pam later. She came into town to meet with the owners of that warehouse."

"The one she wants to turn into an acting school?"

"Yes, and then later she's meeting with JoJo at Larry's."

Stern raised a brow. "JoJo?"

"Yes," Dillon said, coming into the office, closing the door behind him and taking the chair in front of Stern's desk. "Something about beauty tips or a makeover or something."

Stern tensed at the thought of JoJo moving ahead with her plans. "Dil, can I ask you something?"

"Sure."

"If your best friend asked a favor of you, would you do it?"

Dillon was thoughtful for a minute before he said, "Depends on what the favor is. I won't break the law for anyone."

"It doesn't involve breaking the law."

"Then I'd make sure it wouldn't be immoral, unethical or harmful to anyone. If all that works out then yes, I would do the favor."

Now it was Stern's turn to be thoughtful as he built a steeple with his fingers. "But what if this favor could change the dynamics of your relationship with your best friend?"

Dillon didn't say anything for a long moment. "In that

case, I would think long and hard about whether or not it was what either of us wanted or could handle."

JoJo smiled when she walked into Larry's and saw Pam had already been seated. As always, Pam looked radiant. JoJo could see how Dillon had fallen in love with his wife so quickly.

"I hope you haven't been waiting long," JoJo said as she gave Pam a hug before sliding into the chair across the table.

"Not at all. I took the liberty of indulging in a glass of wine. It's been one of those days."

"Tell me about it," JoJo said, grinning. "I was under the hood of eleven cars too many today."

"But you enjoy your work," Pam said.

"Immensely."

Pam smiled. "And from your phone call I understand there's a man you're trying to impress?"

"Yes." JoJo paused when the waiter came to take her drink order. When he left she said, "I have a good idea where he will be this Saturday night and I want to go there, looking totally different than I do when he sees me at the shop. In other words, I want a grand entrance that will knock off his socks. Can your guy do that?"

When JoJo had talked to Pam yesterday, Pam had said the guy she used as a hairstylist could also do wonders with makeup. He wasn't heavy-handed and applied just enough to reveal a woman's inner beauty.

"Absolutely. Ritz is fabulous and I would love for you to meet him."

Excitement poured through JoJo veins. "I'd like that."

"So you want me to make the appointment?"

"Yes. Please."

Pam beamed. "Consider it done. And you'll probably need a manicure and pedicure. Even a wax."

JoJo tried not to frown as she wondered if Walter Carmichael was worth all the changes she was about to make.

"And what about an outfit?" Pam interrupted her thoughts to ask.

The waiter sat JoJo's glass of wine in front of her. She took a sip. "Stern thinks I should wear a dress."

Pam lifted a brow. "Does he?"

JoJo nodded. "He said I have a great pair of legs and that I don't show them enough."

"Interesting," Pam said, looking at JoJo over her glass of wine.

"In fact, the entire makeover thing was his idea."

"Was it really?" Pam asked.

"Yes."

Pam didn't say anything for a few moments, as if she was giving JoJo's words serious thought. "Well, I'm free on Friday and I'd love to go dress shopping with you. I know just the boutique that might have selections that would interest you. And, if you don't mind, I'd like to ask Chloe to join us. She's sort of a fashion expert."

JoJo knew that to be true. Chloe was married to Ramsey Westmoreland, the oldest of Stern's cousins. Chloe also was editor-in-chief of a national best-selling woman's magazine. "I think that will be wonderful!"

"Then I'll check to see if she is available. How early can we get started Friday morning?"

JoJo lifted a brow. "Friday morning? I thought it would be something we could squeeze in after I get off work."

Pam shook her head. "I wouldn't advise limiting yourself to those hours. Usually when you're shopping for just the right outfit it can take the entire day."

The entire day? JoJo couldn't imagine such a thing.

"Well, okay. I'll divvy up my work orders with the other guys on Friday so I'm free the whole day."

"That's wonderful!"

JoJo took another sip of her wine. She was starting to wonder if getting a new outfit and a makeover was really wonderful or not.

Five

It was close to nine o'clock when Stern drove out of the parking garage connected to Blue Ridge Land Management. He felt good about the work he'd completed. He had cleared a number of files off his desk and the few cases remaining would be finalized before the week ended.

As he steered his car toward the interstate that would take him to Westmoreland Country, his thoughts shifted to JoJo. Although they didn't indulge in long telephone conversations every day, the norm was for him to call her at least once to see how she was doing. He had deliberately not called her today because the last thing he wanted was for her to bring up their kiss last night—or his offer to help her improve on it.

Stern knew JoJo better than he knew anyone, and he of all people understood the depth of her innocence when it came to men. In all the years he'd known her, she'd only had one crush on someone—Frazier Lewis in the eleventh grade. Frazier had been well-known around school, a popular athlete and ladies' man—and, as far as Stern was concerned, a real jerk.

Frazier had pretended to return JoJo's affections long enough for JoJo to install running boards and state-of-the-art speakers into his truck. But once he'd gotten what he wanted, she hadn't been good enough to be asked to the prom. Frazier had asked Mallory Shivers instead. And if that hadn't been bad enough, Frazier had bragged about how he had used JoJo to help with his truck. Otherwise, he'd said, he would never have given her the time of day. She wasn't his type. She wasn't pretty enough and he'd even called her a grease monkey.

Frazier had ended up regretting his words when Stern whipped his behind after school. To this day, Stern doubted JoJo knew about the butt-whipping he'd given Frazier. Now, he hoped history wasn't about to repeat itself.

She still refused to tell him anything about the guy she was interested in, which made him uncomfortable. The last thing he wanted to deal with was JoJo crying in his arms the way she'd done after Frazier had dumped her.

As far as Stern was concerned, nobody would mistreat JoJo and live to tell about it without feeling some kind of pain. Which was why he was determined to find out this Walter guy's full name and where JoJo planned to hook up with the man this weekend.

Stern shook his head as he merged into traffic on the interstate. Only JoJo would assume that teaching her the fundamentals of kissing would be no different than teaching her how to play checkers. She trusted him and knew he wouldn't take advantage of her. But she didn't fully understand the inner workings of a man's body. Even with the best of intentions, a man could not just *stop* desiring a woman…even when that woman was his best friend.

Stern would admit that he'd been pretty angry when he'd left Zane's house last night, mainly because his cousin had tried pushing unacceptable thoughts into his head. It was only after he'd gotten home, showered and crawled into bed that Stern saw what had really taken place. His cousin hadn't pushed anything into his head. Zane had only tried to get him to admit the thoughts that were already there. Thoughts that had been planted a while ago but hadn't been watered and hadn't sprouted. But somehow they'd now started to grow.

And that was the main reason he couldn't teach JoJo how to kiss. He had *felt* things, and, for a moment, he'd gotten so absorbed in the kiss that he forgot he was kissing JoJo. She'd made him lose his head, which wasn't good.

But even though he didn't want to lose his head with her again, another part of him couldn't forget Zane's warning: if Stern didn't do the teaching, then someone else would. The idea of JoJo locking lips with any other man grated on Stern's insides and sent a shiver of anger up his spine.

He was convinced that sudden spike of emotion was what made him push the button on his steering wheel to connect to his car's operator. "Yes, Mr. Westmoreland?"

"Connect me with Jovonnie Jones."

"Business or residence?"

"Residence."

"Just a moment for the connection."

"Thank you."

It took less than a minute for JoJo's voice to come on the line. Immediately, an unexpected shiver of desire rushed up Stern's spine. He tightened his gut. What the hell was that about?

"Hi, Stern."

"Hi. You're doing okay?"

"Yes. I worked on eleven cars today, came home,

showered then met with Pam for drinks at Larry's. We talked about my makeover."

Yes, he'd heard about that meeting from Dillon. "How did it go?"

"Okay. I have an appointment with Ritz, her hairstylist and makeup artist, on Saturday morning, and she, Chloe and I are going shopping for an outfit the day before, so I won't be in the shop. Can you believe it might take the entire day just to find one outfit?"

Yes, he believed it. He'd hung around the females in his family enough to know about their shopping sprees.

"So what are you doing now?" he asked her.

"Reading a chapter of this book you gave me before going to bed. Why?"

He swallowed deeply. "I worked late tonight and just left the office a few minutes ago," he said, already getting off the exit to go back toward town. "I figured tonight would be a good time to stop by and get you started with Kissing 101. Are you game?"

He heard the catch in her voice when she answered, "Yes, I'm game."

Less than twenty minutes later JoJo heard the sound of Stern's car pulling into her driveway and she drew in a deep breath. A tiny shiver stirred her belly. He'd made this unexpected visit just so she could indulge in Kissing 101.

Ever since she'd hung up the phone she'd tried to convince herself that his visit was no big deal. She needed to improve her kissing and he was willing to show her how it was done. It wouldn't be the first time he had helped her improve a skill. When she'd wanted to be a better water-skier, he had taken her to Gemma Lake. When she had wanted to improve her violin playing, he had assisted her with that.

Upon hearing the sound of Stern's car door closing, she moved toward the front door and opened it just as he walked up the steps to the porch. He smiled and tilted the brim of his Stetson. "You look nice tonight, Jovonnie."

Jovonnie? Look nice? She was still wearing the brown slacks and beige top she'd put on for her meeting with Pam earlier. JoJo figured he must have decided to throw some playacting into her kissing lessons to set the mood. Without saying anything, she stepped back as he entered the house. Something about the look in his eyes gave her pause.

"Stern," she said, trying to fight the lust consuming her. "Thanks. You look nice, too." She moved toward the center of her living room.

He closed the door behind him and walked toward her with movements that were so full of virility she felt weak in the knees. And when he came to a stop with only one inch keeping their bodies from touching, she realized she was attracted to him more than ever before. He was tall and handsome, with a beautifully proportioned body that would make any woman take notice.

The outline of his body strained against the fabric of his dark jacket and emphasized the width of his shoulders. The denim jeans covered his long muscular legs and rounded off what she considered a powerfully sexy male physique.

He cupped her face in his hands and whispered in a deep, husky voice, "Have I told you lately just how utterly beautiful you are?"

Utterly beautiful? She dismissed his words, trying to remember they were playacting. Even so, as she looked into the darkness of his eyes, she heard herself saying, "No, not lately."

He smiled and the way his lips curved made a deep yearning spread all through her stomach. "Definitely an error on my part," he said huskily. "One that I need to correct immediately." Then he lowered his mouth to hers.

He didn't take her mouth right away like he had the last time. Instead, he hovered over her mouth as if to allow her to absorb his heated breath into her own. Then he leaned in closer and slowly slid his tongue between her parted lips.

On instinct, her own tongue was there to meet his and they began a dance that had fire rushing through her body. She closed her eyes as the sensations became almost unbearable.

The kiss intensified. He locked their lips in a way that made hers a willing captive to his. He greedily feasted on her mouth, causing her to moan deep within her throat. This kiss was deeper, more thorough and more arousing than the other one had been, though she wasn't sure how that could be possible. How could a kiss meant for teaching be so convincingly arousing?

All too soon he released her chin and dropped his hands. She slowly opened her eyes and looked at him. As he tried catching his breath, she tried doing the same. Even as he drew in deep gulps of air he gazed at her with a seductive look. She couldn't help wondering how he'd been able to play his role so well.

"So," she said, finally finding her voice. "How do you think I did just now?"

The look of obvious approval in his eyes pleased her. "Very well," he said softly as his eyes raked boldly over her.

It was then that she had to remind herself that the look

in his eyes was only a part of his role-playing. The person who'd just kissed her was her best friend—Stern—and the kiss hadn't been a real kiss at all but a lesson. But it had been some lesson!

He reached out and took her hand in his. "Come on, let's sit down on the sofa and talk about it."

She lifted a brow. "Talk about it?"

He nodded. "We need to cover every aspect of that kiss in full detail."

She swallowed tightly, thinking, *Oh, boy.*

Stern sat down on the sofa and gathered JoJo to his side, not ready to let her get too far away just yet. The kiss that had been meant as a learning lesson for her had overwhelmed him, making him fully aware of just what power JoJo packed and how easy it might be for a man to take advantage of her vulnerability.

His reaction to the kiss had been quick and magnetic— and that really wasn't supposed to happen. He was supposed to remain aloof, detached and indifferent. Definitely disengaged.

But he'd gotten engaged, connected and way too involved.

"Well?"

He saw her watching him expectantly. Turning to her, he continued to hold her hand. If she found it odd, she said nothing about it. It seemed her focus was on what he had to say.

"First of all," he started off, "my approach tonight was one of setting the mood. You should have picked up on what my intentions were the moment I arrived."

She nodded. "I did. I saw that look in your eyes and noted your body language and knew you had gone into playacting mode."

He wondered what she would think if she knew he hadn't been acting. When she'd opened the door and he'd seen her standing there, his reaction to her had been purely sensual and definitely real.

"To start things off," he said. "I gave you a compliment about how nice you looked. That was intended to soften you up, make you mellow. That should have been another hint at my intentions. However, there shouldn't have been any doubt in your mind what I intended to do when I cupped your face."

She nodded. "There wasn't."

"Good. That kiss was one I classify as an *I like you* kiss. A French kiss between two people wanting to know each other better. Not too light and not too heavy."

"Do you think that's the type Walter will use?"

Stern flinched at the thought of the man kissing her using any method. "More than likely, if he's a smooth sort of guy," he said, forcing the words from his mouth. "If he tries rushing things, then he'll use one of those *I want you* kisses. Those can be dangerous."

"In what way?"

"Those are intended to make a woman lose her head because the man has only one thing on his mind—getting you into the nearest bed."

"Oh," she said.

He watched her nibble at her bottom lip and knew she was thinking about what he'd said.

"So what should I do if he gives me that kind of kiss and I'm not ready for it?"

"End it immediately," he said with more force than necessary. "A woman can end a kiss at any time, especially if she thinks it's aggressive or if it's more than what she's ready for."

"Okay," she said nodding. "Let's try one."

He raised a brow. "Excuse me?"

"I said, let's try one of those. I need to make sure I can tell the difference between an *I like you* kiss and an *I want you* kiss."

Grinning, he said. "Trust me, you'll be able to tell the difference, JoJo."

"I want to be sure."

He stared at her, certain she had no idea what she was asking of him. "I don't think it's a good idea."

"Why? It's me, Stern. JoJo. I'm the last person you would want to take to bed, but for this kiss I need you to pretend so I can know the difference. I want Walter to like me, but I'm not ready to sleep with him."

Stern sighed deeply, glad to hear that.

"But I don't want him to catch me with my guard down. What if I return the kiss not knowing what kind it is? That wouldn't be fair to him and he might think I'm a tease."

Stern didn't give a royal damn what this Walter guy thought. And he had to bite his tongue not to tell JoJo that very thing. She was trying to impress a man who might not deserve all the trouble she was going through.

"Stern?"

He looked at her and saw the pleading in her eyes. She actually didn't know the power of such a kiss, much less where it could lead. Maybe he should make sure she did. "Okay, JoJo, but only because you asked."

He stood, removed his jacket and placed it across the back of the sofa before sitting back down. "Remember, with *any* kiss you can pull back at any time."

"What if I pull back and the guy doesn't stop and keeps kissing me anyway?"

"Then you slap the hell out of him."

She smiled. "Okay."

He returned her smile, knowing she wouldn't hesitate to do so. "All right, let's get started. Be prepared because there's an intense degree of French kissing in this sort of kiss. Just thought I'd warn you."

"All right."

He leaned toward her. She smelled good, and whether she knew it or not, she exuded a heavy dose of femininity just the way she was. She had her hair in a ponytail, didn't have on any makeup and was wearing slacks and a blouse. Although he'd been the one to suggest a makeover, he wasn't sure whether one would suit her. She was JoJo, and as far as he was concerned, she had an inner beauty that was an innate part of her no matter what she was wearing on the outside.

"Stern?"

It was only then that he realized he'd been sitting there staring at her. "Yes?"

"Is something wrong?"

He could come clean now and tell her that yes, something was wrong—he just didn't know what. He could also tell her he didn't want this Walter guy to come within five feet of her, but if she asked why, he wouldn't know what to tell her other than *just because.*

"No, nothing's wrong. I'm just trying to figure out why someone as beautiful as you are doesn't have men constantly knocking at your door." He pulled the band off her hair and then wound his hands into the dark strands.

She rolled her eyes. "Role-playing again?"

"Yes…" *If that's what she wants to believe...*

"Then I guess I need to get into the act, too," she said, placing the pad of a finger into the dimple in his chin. She'd done that before but her doing it now had his flesh zinging.

"I like this dimple right here," she said, smiling.

"Apparently," he said, trying to control the way her touch was making him feel. "Just like I have a thing for your hair."

"Do you?"

"You know I do. I'm not very fond of your cap."

She chuckled. "But you know why I wear it. Can't have hair falling in my face while changing a battery." She thought for a minute. "I think my profession turns off most men."

"And I can see how it can turn some men on."

She lifted a brow. "Really? How?"

"A woman who can change spark plugs and a tire in record time and doesn't need a man to install brake pads has to be dynamite in every other facet of her life."

"I like that theory of yours."

"And I like you." Stern felt a web of desire building between them and knew it wasn't pretense. It was the real thing. Suddenly, he reached out and swept her from her spot on the sofa and into his lap, ignoring her surprised gasp. Before she could skim out of his grasp, he placed his arms around her.

"Now," he said huskily, "this is where I want you for the time being. Do you have a problem with it?"

She stared down at him for a long moment before saying, "No, I don't have a problem with it."

A part of JoJo wondered whether or not she should have problems with this scenario. Stern had no idea of her feelings for him, of how she constantly fought them. He had no clue that it was his face that invaded her dreams at night, that it was his lips she fantasized about kissing. He had no idea how much she *wanted* his kisses. This role-playing was kind of fun. She could let herself go, let herself enjoy the attraction she felt for him without him knowing the truth.

"JoJo?"

Was she mistaken or had his eyes gotten darker? She must be mistaken. "Yes?"

"We can decide not to do this and call it a night."

Was that reluctance she heard in his voice? "No, I'm good. I want to do this, Stern. I need to do this."

More than you could ever know.

He stared down at her, and then he asked, "Does this Walter mean that much to you?"

She thought about his question. It was on the tip of her tongue to say that no, Walter didn't mean that much to her, Stern did. She wanted to say that she was only using Walter to make her forget about Stern. Instead, she said, "I don't know the answer to that. All I know is that I want him to notice me. To take me seriously. I want him to see me as someone other than the mechanic who keeps his car in check."

"Well, I'm going to be plenty angry if I find out he doesn't appreciate you and the beautiful person that you are. And I'm not saying that as your best friend—I'm saying that as a man who has dated a lot of women and can recognize a gem when he sees it."

His words filled her. No reply could come out. She felt tears trying to gather at the back of her eyes. Why did he have to go and say such sweet things to her? Words that would give any woman pause and make her long for a man like him?

"Thank you," she finally said when she was capable of speaking.

"Don't ever thank me for any compliments I give you, JoJo, because I mean them."

JoJo bit her lower lip to keep it from trembling as her

heart pounded in her chest. She wished he wouldn't play his role so well. It only made her wish even more that they could move beyond being best friends. Unfortunately, that would never happen. They were best friends and that was all they could ever be to each other.

But, for a short while, as he educated her in the fine art of kissing, she could pretend—and boy would she pretend. "Kiss me, Stern."

He fanned her face with his heated breath as he eased his mouth closer to hers. "Asking a man to kiss you in a voice like that can be dangerous. He'll think he's already won half the battle."

At that moment, she didn't care and to prove she didn't, she placed her arms around his neck. In one smooth, forward motion she leaned up and tilted her mouth to his, blatantly inviting him to do just what she'd asked.

He took her lips in slowly and leisurely, as if he had all the time in the world and intended to make sure she felt every demand he was making on her mouth. He tightened his arms around her and took her mouth with a greed that had her head spinning. This kiss was definitely different from the other two. Its intensity made a moan escape her lips. As he continued to enjoy tasting her, she settled back against his chest, sinking deeply into his warm embrace.

If the purpose of this kind of kiss was to make a woman willing and ready for the bedroom, then she could see it happening…but not with Walter. She doubted she could get into a kiss like this with him. In fact, a kiss like this from him just might turn her off because she would be pretending he was someone else. She would imagine Stern as the man holding her in his arms, as he was doing this very minute. Stern was the man using his lips and tongue to send warm shivers through her.

She wasn't certain who shifted first, but her back was

suddenly pressed against the sofa cushions and she was no longer in Stern's lap. She was laying on the sofa with him over her.

He hadn't let up with his attention to her mouth and he hadn't let go of her. The hunger in his kiss was building a passion in her she'd never experienced before. The kiss had started off slow and drugging. Now it was fiery and hot, sending ecstasy spiraling within her, nearly robbing her of all conscious thought.

But she knew the exact moment when he began unbuttoning her blouse, and she moaned when air touched her chest. Then his hands were there, rubbing against the material of her bra and—

Her cell phone rang and Stern jerked away from her as if he'd been burned. He almost tumbled over in his quickness to get off the sofa. She eased up into a sitting position and, after buttoning her blouse, she picked up the phone off the coffee table. It was a cousin calling her from Detroit and she let it go to voice mail.

"Why didn't you stop me?" Stern asked, seeming to barely get the words out. He had a fierce expression on his face.

She shrugged before saying, "Because I liked it," she told him honestly.

He stared at her for a second before grabbing his jacket off the back of the chair. Angry eyes pinned her when he said, "Not sure these kissing lessons were a good idea. I'll call you sometime tomorrow."

By the time she was on her feet, he was already out the door and had slammed it shut behind him.

Six

The next day Stern paced his office in a bad mood. He was glad Dillon hadn't called any meetings today and that he mostly had the office to himself. Riley was out for the rest of the week because he and Alpha had flown to Daytona to visit her parents. Canyon had taken off at lunch to meet with Keisha and go shopping for a swing set for their son, Beau.

Stern stopped in the middle of the floor and rubbed his hand down his face. He hadn't called JoJo like he'd told her he would, and he didn't plan to do so until he pulled himself together. That kiss last night still had him reeling in a way no kiss ever had before.

He let out a deep sigh. It wasn't as if they were lovers. Far from it. They were best friends who'd agreed to study Kissing 101. The prior kisses with her had left him believing he'd probably imagined their impact. But after last night he knew his imagination wasn't responsible. That kiss, the one that was supposed to be the *I want you* kiss had done just that—it had left him wanting her with a vengeance. That's why he was so angry and annoyed with himself. She trusted him in a way she trusted no other man and last night he had violated that trust. He had been two seconds away from stripping her naked.

He drew in a deep breath when his cell phone went off and he recognized JoJo's ring tone. He wasn't ready to talk to her yet. He needed time to come to terms with last night. To her, it might have been a kissing lesson, but to him it had been more.

Now, what he was going to do about it?

When she woke up Friday morning JoJo was convinced Stern was avoiding her. She'd called him yesterday to make sure things were okay after he'd stormed out of her place Wednesday night. But he hadn't returned her call. Usually, even if he was in a meeting when she called, he would call her back at the first opportunity. But he hadn't this time.

Sliding out of bed, she headed for the bathroom to shower and dress. She was to meet Pam and Chloe at the Cherry Creek Mall when the doors opened at ten. That would give her time to stop by the coffee shop to grab coffee and a bagel. Hopefully by the time she met Pam and Chloe she would have her head together. At the moment it was still all messed up.

Shaking off the glum knowledge that she was losing her best friend, she stripped and stepped into the shower. Over the past thirty-six hours she had replayed what had happened over and over in her mind. Stern had readied her for the kiss by telling her what kind it would be. She had been prepared. Sort of. She doubted any woman would have been fully prepared for a Stern Westmoreland kiss. It had knocked her off her rocker, but that hadn't been what surprised her.

What she couldn't figure out was Stern's attitude. Had

she gotten more involved in the kiss than he had wanted? Enjoyed it too much? Had she not followed some unwritten script? Had she not ended the kiss when he felt she should have? Was she wrong in suggesting that he help her improve her kissing in the first place?

There was a lot about men that JoJo didn't know, but things had been going great in her life until she'd developed these crazy feelings for Stern that had escalated into love. Now she was trying like heck to rectify the problem by finding someone else to love. Under no circumstances could Stern ever find out how she felt about him. And if that meant no more Kissing 101, well…she'd deal with that decision when she came to it.

A few hours later she placed a smile on her face and joined the two ladies standing in front of the entrance to the mall. Even at ten in the morning both of them looked radiant, beautiful and classy. JoJo would just love looking like that any time of the day. But she had to be realistic. Her job required that she *didn't* look like that. However, she wanted tips on how to present herself in a better light when she went out. She would be celebrating her thirtieth birthday in less than a year. It was time she made some changes.

Giving the two women hugs, JoJo told them how glad she was to see them and how much she appreciated their help. Then, after telling her how much they enjoyed having a chance to help her, Pam and Chloe pulled her toward the first dress shop.

Stern glanced up when he heard the knock on his office door. "Come in."

When the door opened and Zane walked in Stern placed his pen down and leaned back in his chair in surprise. "What brings you out of Westmoreland Country in the middle of the day?"

Zane, his cousin Derringer and Stern's brother Jason were partners in a horse breeding and training company along with various other cousins in Montana and Texas.

"I had to come to town to meet with a potential client. I think we've made another sale," Zane said, sliding his muscular frame into the chair across from Stern's desk. "Since I was out this way I figured I'd check on you."

"Why?" Stern asked, reaching for a couple of paper clips and then tossing them back on his desk.

"Because the last time we talked you seemed rather frustrated."

If truth be told, he was still frustrated, even more so. He would admit to being overwhelmed by the events of the past few days. There was no doubt in his mind that JoJo was wondering why he hadn't returned her call from yesterday. He'd never done that before.

"The situation with JoJo has worsened," he said in an exasperated tone.

Zane straightened in his chair with a concerned expression on his face. "How so?"

"I decided to do the kissing lesson as you suggested. However, I almost lost control, Zane. You were right. When I was kissing her, I didn't see her as my best friend, but as a potential lover."

"And you still have a problem with that? I'm sure there are several situations where best friends become lovers, Stern. People change. Feelings change. Relationships change. Your feelings for her probably have been shifting for a while now without you even realizing they were doing so."

Stern frowned. "But you know how I am when it comes to women, Zane. I date them and don't give them another thought. Some I take out more than once or twice, but that's seldom. And the thought of a lasting relationship with any of them never crosses my mind. I couldn't treat JoJo that way."

"No, you couldn't and you wouldn't. She means too much to you, which brings up another issue."

"What?"

"When are you going to admit to yourself that you're falling in love with her?"

Stern looked stunned. Then he looked indignant. "What are you talking about? I am not falling in love with her."

"Are you sure about that? I almost lost Channing because I refused to acknowledge I had feelings for her. I think if there's any possibility you might be falling for JoJo, you're doing her a disservice not to let her know. And you need to do it before it's too late."

Stern pushed away from his desk, stood and moved over to the window. He thought of everything that had transpired since the week he and JoJo had spent at the lodge, when she'd first brought up the fact that she was interested in a man. He didn't have to think hard to recall his emotions, his anxieties and his fears. Could they have been based on the fact that he had hidden feelings for her? Feelings he'd had for a while, possibly for years, tucked deep inside?

He turned back to Zane. "It's already too late. She's set her sights on someone else, remember? This Walter guy."

"So? Is that supposed to mean something?"

Stern sighed and shook his head. Sometimes he wondered about Zane and all the wisdom he was supposed to have bottled inside that Westmoreland brain of his. "It would mean something to most people, I would think."

Zane shrugged his massive shoulders. "Not to a Westmoreland, not when he wants something bad enough. It's up to you to determine, first, if you're falling for JoJo, and if you are, what you're going to do about it. If you want to lose her to another man, then that's your business. But if it were me, I wouldn't give up my woman without a fight."

Stern rolled his eyes. "First of all, she's not my woman. All JoJo feels for me is friendship, Zane, regardless of whether I'm falling for her or not."

Zane stood. "Then if I were you, I'd give this Walter guy a damn good run for his money. And I would definitely start letting JoJo know how I feel. You might be surprised. You might discover she feels the same way. I've said for years that the two of you had a strange relationship. Best friends or not, you are in each other's pockets."

Stern released a deep breath. As far as he was concerned, nobody had been in each other's pockets more than his cousin Bane and his longtime girlfriend Crystal and look what had happened to them…but that had been years ago and was another story. "I'll give your advice some consideration," he said.

Zane chuckled as he headed for the door. "Yeah, you do that. It's time for you to think like a Westmoreland."

JoJo bit her bottom lip as she looked at all the dresses Pam and Chloe were holding up. She was convinced she had checked out more than a hundred today and it wasn't even two o'clock yet.

"Well, which ones do you like?" Stern's cousin Megan, who was a doctor of anesthesiology, had joined them when they'd taken a break for lunch. It didn't take long for JoJo to discover that Megan enjoyed shopping just as much as Pam and Chloe did.

Which *ones* and not just which *one?* Jeez, she'd already purchased six dresses. In addition to the one she planned to wear tomorrow night, the ladies said she would need additional outfits for all her other dates with Walter. They had more faith in her ability to nab his interest than she did. "I like the yellow one and the multi-colored one," she said.

Megan beamed. "Good choices. Those were my favorites, too." And Pam and Chloe nodded their approval. Frankly, she'd liked all the outfits she'd purchased today and she had looked good in them.

"After we get these paid for, then we need to visit Sandra's Lingerie Boutique. We've taken care of the outerwear, so now it's on to the underwear," Pam said, smiling.

JoJo thought she had plenty of underwear back home in the top drawer of her dresser, but the three women had stressed earlier that she needed something new and sexy. Honestly, she didn't know why. Even if she and Walter hit it off, there was no way she would sleep with him the first night. Nor the second. Or the third. She might be interested in Walter, but that interest had its limits when it came to sex.

"That was Lucia," Chloe said, sliding her mobile phone back into her purse. "She thought it would be fun to let our guys babysit tonight while we have a girls' night out dinner with JoJo after our day of shopping. So she, Bella, Keisha and Kalina will join us for dinner at McKays."

JoJo thought that was a great idea. She had known Megan, Gemma and Bailey all her life, and because she was best friends with Stern she also had gotten to know the women his brothers and cousins had married.

A half hour later she was in Sandra's Lingerie Boutique looking at undies. Never had she seen so many shapes, sizes and colors. She would have to admit she was drawn to the matching sets. There was just something special about wearing a bra that was the same color as your panties.

"Okay, are you a thong, briefs, bikini or hip-hugger kind of girl?" Pam asked as they moved around the display looking for her size.

"Excuse me?"

Pam smiled. "Here, I'll show you." She held up each type for JoJo.

"I'm a briefs girl," JoJo said now that she had a clearer understanding of the question.

"Um, not tomorrow night," Chloe said, holding up a thong. "This is what you're going to need with the dress you selected."

JoJo gazed at the itsy-bitsy scrap of almost nothing and thought...*seriously?*

"You don't want any panty lines to show," Megan explained.

"Oh." She didn't worry about such things when she wore jeans.

"And we plan to be there tomorrow when you get dressed," Chloe announced.

JoJo blinked. "You do?"

"Of course. We want you to knock your guy off his feet."

After having spent almost the entire day going from store to store and trying on dress after dress, she certainly hoped she would knock Walter off his feet. Absently, she pulled the phone out of her purse to see if she'd missed any calls...specifically, any calls from Stern. She fought back a feeling of disappointment when she saw that he hadn't called.

"Any ideas on your hairstyle, JoJo?" Chloe asked, interrupting her thoughts. "I understand Ritz is taking care of your hair and makeup, and he's good."

"That's what I hear," JoJo said, checking out matching bras.

"Are you going to get it cut?"

JoJo glanced over at Pam. "No, Stern likes it long."

"Stern?" Megan asked, frowning. "Who cares what Stern likes? He's not the one you're trying to impress."

As JoJo continued to pick out matching panties and bra sets, she thought Megan had a point. But still…

Think like a Westmoreland…

Zane's words flowed through Stern's mind as he locked up his desk and prepared to leave the office later that day. How should a man who was used to being pursued switch focus and become the pursuer? It would definitely be one hell of a game changer.

He stood just as his cell phone went off. He checked his caller ID and saw it was Dillon. "Yes, Dil?"

"I'm just giving everyone a head's up. There's been a change in tonight's chow down."

It was customary for the Westmorelands to get together on Friday nights for dinner. "What's the change?"

"The men are doing the cooking since our ladies decided to take JoJo out to dinner after her long day of shopping."

"Oh."

"To keep things simple, I'm asking every man to bring their specialty. Since you don't have one, you can drop by the bakery on your way home and pick up something for dessert."

"That will work."

"And Stern?"

"Yes?"

"Those of us with kids are babysitting, which means they eat what we eat, so don't buy a rum cake."

Stern chuckled. Everyone knew rum cake was his favorite. "Gotcha."

After hanging up with Dillon, Stern sat back down in his chair. *Think like a Westmoreland.* A few minutes later he glanced at his watch. Smiling, he pulled his cell phone from his jacket and punched in a few numbers.

"The Golden Wrench Automotive Repair Shop. This is Wanda. How may I help you?"

"Hi, beautiful. This is Stern. And you can help me by giving me some information I have a feeling you know."

Seven

JoJo stepped out of her bedroom, walked into her living room and was met by a chorus of collective gasps.

"JoJo, you look stunning."

"Sensational."

"Hot."

"You don't even look like the same person."

JoJo smiled at the women staring at her. "Thanks. I feel like all those things tonight," she said, glancing down at herself.

She looked back up at the ladies who filled her living room. "I want to thank all of you for your help. Not only for shopping with me yesterday and being there for the hair and makeover today, but just being here for me now. Giving me the confidence to pull this off."

There was no need to tell them that the one other person she wanted here with her, the one person she needed to give her a confidence boost and his blessing, was her best friend. But Stern wasn't here and she hadn't heard from him since Wednesday. His actions had pretty much let her know things were no longer the same between them. His reaction angered her every time she thought about it. It had been his idea for the makeover. And he had kissed her first! Was it wrong for her to want to improve her kissing skills?

"I went online and checked out your Walter," Bailey Westmoreland broke into JoJo's thoughts to say. "He's a cutie, but his profile picture makes him look like a stuffed shirt in that business suit. Are you sure he frequents a place like the Punch Bowl? That used to be Derringer and Riley's hangout. For a long time we thought they had purchased stock in the place."

"It would be just my luck if tonight is the one night he changes his mind and stays home or goes someplace else," JoJo said, hoping that wouldn't be the case.

"Then it will be his loss," Pam said, smiling. "But I have a feeling this is going to be your lucky night."

JoJo drew in a deep breath. She hoped so. Glancing down at her hands she remembered how Ritz had fussed about how awful they looked and how many wonders he'd had to pull off to make them look presentable. Her nails were painted a pretty shade of pink, which looked good with the multiple colors in her dress.

"And I'm glad you didn't cut your hair after all," Chloe said. "The way Ritz has it styled makes it look fuller around your face. I can't say enough just how gorgeous you look."

And if it never happened again in her life, at least for tonight she felt gorgeous. She looked at her watch. "Well, it's time for me to leave. I want to thank all of you again for tonight and yesterday. Because of you, I feel special."

"You are special," Megan said, smiling. "And before you leave I want to take plenty of pictures. I can't wait to show Rico how beautiful you look."

* * *

"Thanks for letting me perform here tonight, Sampson."

The older man, who had prepared Stern's mother for her first piano recital at age eight, looked up from the piano and smiled. "My pleasure, Stern. Once in a while I was able to talk Riley into sitting on this bench and whenever he did, the crowd would go wild. Your mom made sure all her boys had an ear for music."

Stern nodded. His mom had made certain all seven of her sons loved music as much as she did. Dillon and Micah mastered guitar; Riley and Bane, the piano; Canyon the French horn and Stern the violin. After his parents' death, Dillon made sure they continued developing their love for music by calling on Sampson to give them lessons.

"Riley much preferred being in the audience surrounded by the beautiful ladies vying for his attention." Sampson shook his head. "It's hard for me to believe lover boy is getting married at the end of the month."

"You, me and a number of others," Stern said, grinning. "But once you meet Alpha you'll understand."

Sampson glanced at his watch. "The show starts at eight, but if you want you can go out front and enjoy yourself for a while. Just tell Sweety to put any of your drinks on my tab."

"Thanks, but I'll hang back here until showtime." Stern decided not to mention that sitting on the stool backstage by the observation window gave him a good view of the customers without them knowing they were being watched. His cousin Ian had a similar set up at his casino in Lake Tahoe.

"But you can tell me something," Stern added.

Sampson looked over at him. "What?"

"Walter Carmichael. I understand he comes here a lot. Is he here tonight?"

Sampson leaned up and strained his neck over the piano to look out through the glass. "Yes. He's here. You know him?"

Detecting Sampson's disapproving tone, Stern met the older man's gaze. "No, I don't know him but someone mentioned this is his hangout on the weekends."

"It is most of the time, unfortunately. He has lots of money and likes throwing it around to impress the women. Some he can impress, and others he can't. He gets annoyed quickly with those he can't. I think he feels entitled to any woman he wants. And I hear he has a mean streak. A few months ago, he tried roughing up one of the ladies when she refused his advances. It didn't happen here—otherwise Sweety wouldn't let him come back. I understand they met here but then he took her out on a date a few weeks later. Rumor has it that his daddy paid the woman a lot of money to drop the charges."

"His daddy?"

"Yes. Carmichael's from the Midwest and his family is pretty well off, which is why he drives that flashy car and wears expensive clothes. I understand he only works because his father decreased his allowance a couple years ago, although he's been known to boast that his mother sends him money on the side. I also heard he's in Denver because he had to flee from Indiana amid a scandal involving a married woman whose husband threatened to kill him." Sampson lifted a brow. "Anything else you want to know?"

Stern had heard enough. From the rundown Sampson had just given him, there was no way he would let someone of Carmichael's character become involved with

JoJo. "Yes, there is something else. I need you to point him out to me."

If his request seemed odd, Sampson gave no sign of it. He looked through the one-way glass and Stern followed the direction of his gaze. "That's him in the navy blue slacks and tan jacket, looking like he just stepped off the page of one of those fancy magazines."

Stern studied the man's features. He was hanging with a group of guys at the bar, laughing at something one of them had said. Stern decided then and there that he didn't like the guy. Sampson was right; Carmichael had the look of rich-boy entitlement written all over him.

Stern was about to turn around to say as much to Sampson when he noticed Carmichael, his friends and several other men in the Punch Bowl look toward the entrance of the club. Stern's gaze shifted to see what had snagged everyone's attention. His eyes widened and the breath was snatched from his lungs. Wow! Holy…

It was JoJo. And she looked absolutely, positively hot. Damn, what had she done to herself? Her hair was fluffed up on her head in a style that showcased the beauty of her face. Her face was perfectly made up and not overdone. Her lashes appeared longer, her cheeks a little rosy and her lips a luscious ruby-red.

And then there was what had to be the sexiest dress he'd ever seen. The hem was shorter in the front, barely covering her thighs, with the skirt only a little longer in the back, showing off her gorgeous legs in a pair of blue stilettoes. And the plunging neckline supported firm breasts that made him wonder if she was even wearing a bra.

"Nice-looking lady," he heard Sampson say. "I hope she knows what she's doing by coming here looking that hot without a date. The hungry wolves are certainly out tonight. Look."

Stern switched his gaze from JoJo to the crowd. Every man in the place had eyes on her. Some were even licking their lips. Stern felt his blood pressure shoot sky-high.

He saw the moment she noticed Carmichael and smiled at him. But Stern knew JoJo better than anyone and he could tell by the way her bottom lip quivered beneath that smile that she wasn't as confident as she appeared to be.

"This room is soundproof if you need more practice time," he heard Sampson say.

"No, I don't need any more practice time," he replied, not taking his eyes off JoJo. "I'll be ready to do what I need to do when the time comes."

Unknown to Sampson, Stern's response had double meaning. As far as Stern was concerned, tonight he would be squashing any plans JoJo had for her and Carmichael.

JoJo slowly drew in a breath as the hostess led her to a table. When she'd entered, the first set of eyes she'd met had been Walter's, but he didn't seem to recognize her. Granted she looked very different without her uniform, work shoes and cap, but surely something about her would be familiar.

"The show starts in half an hour." The young woman whose name tag read Melissa smiled. "Would you like some wine?"

"Yes, a glass of Moscato."

"Good choice. I'll be back in a minute."

While waiting for the hostess to return with her drink, JoJo forced herself not to glance back over at the men standing at the bar. She'd made eye contact with most of them when she'd first walked in and she didn't want to give them the impression that she was hungry for anyone's company…anyone other than Walter, that is. What if another guy approached her before he did? She would have to turn him down nicely and let him know she wasn't interested. But if that happened and then Walter finally did approach would he feel like the one who'd grabbed the golden ring? Would he feel entitled to whatever he wanted?

"Excuse me. This might sound like a pickup line, but I have a feeling we've met before."

It was Walter. He was smiling down at her in a way that made his lips crinkle at the corners and his eyes sparkle with intense interest. She was relieved he was the first one to approach her. He looked good tonight, but for the life of her, she couldn't recall why she and Wanda had ever thought he favored over Stern. Stern had him beat in the looks department hands down.

She returned his smile, thinking that the night was already going just as she wanted. "We have met, Walter," she said, deciding not to play coy.

She could tell he was surprised and pleased that she knew his name. "Really? It must only have been in passing. There's no way I would have held a conversation with you and not remembered."

He was smooth, but he would have to try a lot harder to truly impress her. She was best friends with the master of lines, and she'd heard Stern use them often enough.

Which reminded her that she hadn't heard from Stern since Wednesday, and he had refused to return her calls. JoJo knew he wasn't sick because none of his cousins had mentioned him being under the weather. That could only mean he was still upset and taking it to a ridiculous level by refusing to talk to her. The only other time they had stopped speaking to each other was in the tenth grade when he'd sworn that she'd deliberately given him chicken pox…like she would deliberately do such a thing. She'd contracted it first and he had caught it within days—right before he was supposed to compete at a band fair.

To keep his siblings and cousins from catching it, which would have meant bad news for Dillon and Ramsey, her father had invited Stern to stay with them while he was recovering. Her father had figured if he had to tolerate one sick and demanding child with the pox he might as well tolerate two. By the end of the second week, Stern had realized she was blameless for his condition and that being sick hadn't been so bad anyway, especially because her father had given him tons of car magazines to read. In fact, if she remembered correctly, he hadn't wanted to leave her house when his time was up. He'd claimed he'd had more fun being sick at her place than being well at his.

Drawing in a deep breath, she forced thoughts of Stern from her mind. The whole point of tonight was to forget about her feelings for him. It wasn't fair to keep comparing Walter to her best friend.

"So where have we met?" Walter asked.

She held his gaze, wanting to read his expression when she told him who she was. "My shop."

He lifted a brow. "Your shop? And just what kind of shop do you have?" He shoved his hands into his pockets and stood in what some women would probably think was a sexy pose.

A smile spread across her lips. "I just saw you this week. I'm surprised you didn't recognize me right away. My name is Jovonnie Jones, from the Golden Wrench. JoJo."

She saw the shocked look in his eyes and it lingered way too long to suit her. What he did next really got to her. He reached out, picked up her hand and checked her nails. What exactly did he expect to find? Grease on her fingertips? Annoyed, she pulled her hand out of his. "Is anything wrong?"

He shook his head as if he was trying to come to terms with what he'd just discovered. "No, I just can't believe you're the same woman who…who…"

It seemed he was having a hard time filling in the blanks, so she said, "The same woman who repairs cars? Always wears a uniform? Puts her hair under a cap?"

"Yes," he said, grinning. "All those things. You clean up rather nicely," he said, his tone dropping as he looked her up and down. "I never would have thought."

Cleaned up rather nicely? Did he assume he was giving her a compliment? The thought made her even more annoyed, but she tried pushing away her aggravation. She had to remember he served a purpose in her life. Little did he know he was making it harder and harder to believe that he could be the one to make her forget about her feelings for Stern.

"Here's your drink," the waitress said, placing the glass of wine in front of her.

"Thanks."

"Are you expecting someone to join you?" Walter asked.

She glanced up at him, tempted to lie outright and say that she was. But she quickly reminded herself that he was the reason she was here tonight. He was the reason she had spent an entire day shopping till she dropped. And today, because of him, she had gotten plucked, waxed and trimmed.

"No, I'm not expecting anyone. I'm here alone."

"I'm here alone, too," he said in a deep, husky tone. "Mind if I join you?"

She forced a smile. "No, I don't mind."

"You okay, son?"

"Yes, I'm okay."

Stern had been so focused on the interactions between JoJo and Carmichael that he'd forgotten Sampson was still in the room. Now Carmichael was sitting at JoJo's table, engaging her in conversation that had her smiling. A player like Stern could easily recognize player instincts in another man, and there was no doubt in his mind that Carmichael was laying it on thick. Now he was pouring more wine into JoJo's glass, and Stern couldn't help wondering if the man's play was to get her drunk. Stern chuckled. If that was Carmichael's plan, he'd better come up with another one because JoJo's body was resistant to alcohol. It was as if the stuff didn't affect her.

"Show's about to start so I'm leaving to open."

Stern glanced over his shoulder. "Okay. And again, thanks for adding my number to tonight's lineup."

"No problem. I figure there's a reason you called last night wanting to perform." Sampson looked past Stern and through the glass to the table where JoJo sat. He then looked at Stern. "Now I know."

Stern swallowed. "Do you?"

"Yes. When a man loves a woman it's hard to keep certain feelings hidden."

Stern frowned. "It's not like that. She and I are just good friends. We're best friends."

"I see."

Was Sampson seeing him in the same way Zane had? That possibility didn't sit well with Stern because he couldn't see what they were seeing. He was glad when the older man opened the door and left. It kept him from having to say anything more.

Stern leaned back on the stool, bracing his back against the wall as he remembered how fast things had moved yesterday. He didn't have to pump Wanda for information; she'd given it willingly. And once he'd gotten it, setting up his own plan had been easy.

This place used to be Riley and Derringer's favorite hangout and Derringer had called it "pickup alley." Basically, women came here alone to meet men, so this was where men had a tendency to hang out to meet those women. It stood to reason this is where Carmichael would be on the weekends. And the live entertainment was probably the best in Denver, with Sampson on the piano and Mavis on bass.

Stern had come up with the idea of performing, playing his violin, and all it had taken was a phone call to Sampson to make it happen, no questions asked. Even tonight when Sampson had observed how intently Stern stared through the glass at JoJo, the man hadn't asked any questions. He'd just made his observations—with precision accuracy. Except for the part where Sampson had insinuated that Stern was a man in love.

When Stern walked out on stage he was going to give JoJo the shock of her life. Stern was the last person she expected to see here tonight. And she definitely wouldn't expect him to break up her and Carmichael's little party.

The house lights dimmed for the show and Stern saw Carmichael move from sitting with his back to the stage to sitting beside JoJo to face the stage. It was an understandable move, but it was too close to JoJo for Stern's liking.

He grabbed his violin. He was ready to play and clear

his mind of negative thoughts. Because, right now, quite
a few were flowing through his head.

"You know you want to leave here with me, so what
are we waiting for?"

JoJo took another sip of her wine and wondered what
the jerk sitting beside her was drinking. It had to be something strong if he really believed she wanted to leave here
with him. Over the past twenty minutes she had realized
just what a mistake she'd made in singling him out as a
man worthy of her affection. This man didn't deserve the
heart of any woman. The only thing he had on his mind
was sex, sex and more sex.

She'd lost count of how many times he'd hinted that
he wanted to leave with her. To take her to bed. His, hers,
even the nearest hotel would do. Granted she looked different from when he'd seen her last, but now she wondered if she'd had a sign plastered to her forehead during
her makeover: Ready to Get Screwed.

Deciding to ignore his last remark, she said, "Oh, good
the show is about to begin."

"Come with me and we can have our own show at
your place. Or mine."

JoJo drew in a deep breath. She'd encountered very
few pushy men in her life, but obnoxious ones she'd come
across often enough. Those came into her shop asking
specifically for Beeker to work on their cars because she
was a female and couldn't possibly know what she was
doing. Their way of thinking annoyed her but she'd long
ago decided not to lose sleep over it. Men thought what
they wanted to think and there was no changing them.
Just like Walter. He thought she was easy, but he was
wrong. And he thought he was God's gift to women, but
he was wrong about that, too. He had spent most of their

conversation bragging. She would never have believed any man could be so into himself.

Walter Carmichael was a real disappointment. After all the work she'd put into transforming herself from a woman no man would look at twice into a woman they looked at…but for all the wrong reasons. Just like Stern had said.

The saddest part was that the person she had hoped Walter would replace in her heart was no longer her best friend. It seemed her obsession with attracting Walter had driven Stern away.

She was glad when the band struck up. Hopefully Walter would shut his mouth and listen for a while. She would stay long enough to enjoy the music, then she would leave and rethink how she could get herself out of the mess she was in with Stern.

After the band had performed a couple of jazzy numbers, an older man, Sampson Kilburn, stepped onstage to a standing ovation. He was the headliner, and she'd heard he was good on the piano. Moments later he proved the rumor true. The man was truly gifted.

"He's good, isn't he?" Walter whispered close to her ear. "As good as I know the two of us will be in bed."

JoJo bit down on her bottom lip, coming close to telling the man to go screw himself. But she didn't bother because at the first intermission she intended to leave.

Stern stood at the glass and stared at JoJo. He wasn't sure what Carmichael had done, but even in the dimly lit room he could tell by her expression that the man had somehow pushed several wrong buttons. That might be good for Stern because he wouldn't have to go through the trouble of breaking up their little party, but it couldn't be good for JoJo.

He knew how much she'd wanted to impress that guy and all the trouble she'd gone through to do so. He hoped she realized the mistakes were not hers; they were all Carmichael's. Now the music he intended to play for her would be more appropriate than ever.

Sweety stuck her head in the door and smiled. "You're up next, Stern. Sampson is bubbling all over himself to have one of his protégés perform with him."

Stern chuckled. "It's really my pleasure. Sampson kept our music lessons real and kept us focused after Mom died. He was even able to handle my baby brother Bane for a while, and that wasn't easy to do."

Moments later, Stern walked with his violin toward where he would stand until he was called out onstage.

Eight

"I'm leaving after this number," JoJo leaned over and whispered to Walter.

"Good. I'll be right behind you."

She frowned. Evidently he had drawn his own conclusions about how this night would end. She figured it was time to let him know, in very clear terms, that when she left she would be leaving alone. However, before she could do so, Sampson Kilburn finished his number and began speaking.

"It gives me great pleasure to bring onstage a former student of mine who I think you're going to enjoy. I want all of you to give a big round of applause for Stern Westmoreland and his violin."

Air left JoJo lungs as she stared at the stage. *Stern? Here?* She watched as he walked out with his violin, smiling for the audience. She couldn't believe it. What was he doing here? Had he found out this was where she would be? No, how could he have? They hadn't spoken in days. More than likely he had no idea she was in the audience.

She watched as he readied his bow amid whistles and

applause. His smile deepened when he said, "I hope all of you enjoy my musical rendition of this song about true beauty. I'm dedicating this to a special lady in the audience, Jovonnie Jones."

For the second time in less than ten minutes, air left JoJo's lungs. Stern's gaze unerringly found hers and he smiled. He *had* known she was here. But how?

"Hey, that guy's talking about you. You know him?" Walter asked, sounding annoyed.

"Yes, I know him," she said, trying not to show any emotion. "He's my best friend."

"Best friend," he snorted. "Yeah, right. When it comes to a man's and a woman's relationship, there's no such thing."

Whatever words Walter said after that were drowned out when Stern lifted the violin to his shoulder. Accompanied by the band and Sampson at the piano, he played, moving the bow across the strings to produce perfect notes. JoJo had heard that particular song many times, but not until now had she truly been pulled into the melody. Stern was putting his heart and soul into the music and she couldn't help but recall how he'd taught her to play that same instrument when they were in high school.

She felt Walter tug at her hand. "Come on, we were about to leave. If that guy's your best friend, as you claim, then you can hear him play anytime."

JoJo ignored Walter's rudeness as she continued to sit at her table, totally mesmerized by the sight of Stern playing his violin. She was in awe of his skill, as was everyone else in the room.

She'd heard him play a number of times, but tonight was different. He was playing for her. Knowing he'd selected that piece for her sent a warm fuzzy feeling through her. Somehow, and she wasn't sure how, he'd known she would be here. And somehow he'd also known that tonight hadn't gone as she'd hoped it would. Somehow her best friend had known. And he was here, making her feel beautiful nonetheless.

He continued to play and hold her gaze. In her heart and in her mind she felt he was affirming that no matter what, their friendship could withstand anything. Even the Walter Carmichaels of the world.

At the end, when Stern lowered his violin, he got a standing ovation. On wobbly legs she stood and clapped until her hands began to hurt. He winked at her, and she couldn't help but laugh and wink back. They had a lot to talk about, but she was just happy that her best friend was back.

"Okay, I'm ready to leave," Walter said again. He had stood and was tugging at her arm with a little more force.

She snatched her arm away. "Then by all means go, but I'm not going with you."

Walter's eyes darkened to a cold stony black. "Moments before your *best friend* took to the stage, you suggested we leave."

JoJo frowned as she sat back down. "I suggested no such thing. I told you I was leaving. At no time did I invite you to leave with me."

He leaned down near her face. "Don't you dare tease me. I don't take kindly to women who play with me. I don't think you know who you're messing with."

"And I don't think you know who you're messing with."

JoJo blinked when Walter's face broke into a smile. "Okay, I get it. You like being the dominant one. This time I'll let you, but when we get to your place we'll reverse roles."

JoJo tilted her head and stared at him. Was he crazy?

She stood up and parted her lips to give him the put-down of his life when Stern approached.

"Is everything all right?" he asked.

She saw the concern in his gaze. "Yes, everything is all right. I've got this."

"Okay."

She knew Stern agreed to stay out of it only because he knew she had it under control. Turning to Walter, she said, "Read my lips, Walter. I am not going anywhere with you and you aren't going anywhere with me. I misjudged your character and evidently you've misjudged mine. Now get out of my face."

The stony look returned to Walter's gaze. "I don't like being made a fool of. I am not wrong about you. You walked into this club dressed like a woman anxious to get laid."

JoJo quickly reached out and touched Stern's hand when he took a step toward Walter. "No, Stern," she said firmly. Her eyes flashed fire as she stared at Walter, fully aware that people were beginning to stare. "I don't like a man assuming things about me and treating me with disrespect."

"Respect? I can treat you anyway I please," he said with a sneer. "Do you know who I am?"

JoJo narrowed her gaze. "Yes, a little boy in a man's suit who needs to grow up."

A few chuckles came from behind them, from the bar where his friends were still standing. Walter Carmichael had the good sense not to say anything else. Instead he gave JoJo another glacier-cold look before walking out of the club.

"You okay, JoJo?"

She slid her gaze from the club's exit door to Stern. "Why wouldn't I be?"

Stern touched one of the curls in her hair before running a slow hand down the side of her face and touching the collar of her dress. "Because you did all of this for him," he whispered. "I'm sorry."

She drew in a deep breath, tempted to say that she'd only done it for Walter as a way to forget about Stern. The last thing she wanted was for Stern to feel sorry for her, especially when she was trying hard not to feel sorry for herself.

"It's okay. I'm fine. Thanks for the musical piece you performed. It was beautiful and touching. I felt special. How did you know I was here?"

Stern looked around and she noticed at the same time he did that they still had an audience. "I don't have another performance tonight," he said. "Come on, I'll follow you home and then we can talk."

She nodded and together they walked out of the club.

"I'm making coffee. You want a cup?"

Kicking off her shoes, JoJo entered her living room and watched Stern head for her kitchen. "Yes," she called out after him. "And you know how I like it."

She placed her purse on the table and eased down onto the sofa, thinking about how badly things had gone tonight. Perhaps she should have done something differently? She hadn't teased Walter as he'd claimed. They had been having a conversation about a recent movie when suddenly, without warning, he shifted the conversation to sex. Rather explicit sex. He told her right out what he liked women to do for him and that he thought a roll between the sheets was a great way for two people to get to know each other. Then he tried to talk her into leaving with him.

"Don't do that," Stern said, coming back into the room and taking the wingback chair across from her.

"What?"

"Gnaw off your bottom lip. He's not worth it."

"I know but…"

"But what?"

"But I can't help wondering what makes some men turn into total jerks."

Stern leaned forward and stared at her for a moment. "What exactly did he do to get you so riled?"

"He insisted that I sleep with him. Tonight. Dammit, Stern, we hadn't even kissed yet. All he wanted, all he was looking for, was a one-night stand. I wanted more. I wanted to develop a relationship with him. I thought he would be someone I truly wanted to get to know better."

"He didn't deserve the things you wanted, JoJo."

"I know." She rested her head against the sofa cushion to stare up at the ceiling. "So you want to tell me how you happened to be there tonight?"

He stood. "Let me pour our coffee and then we'll talk."

JoJo lowered her head and watched him leave the room. It was so unfair that the guy she'd fallen in love with was the one person she could not have. She heard Stern in her kitchen, opening cabinets to get two coffee cups. He knew his way around her house as much as she knew her way around his, and he didn't hesitate making himself at home whenever he visited. It was the same with her whenever she was over at his place. No limitations and no restrictions. As far as she knew, she was the only nonfamily member who had a key to his place.

He came back into the room carrying a tray with two cups and her coffeepot. He proceeded to pour the hot liquid into their cups. "I thought about making you tea instead. Drinking this will probably keep you up tonight."

She had news for him. She would probably be up late tonight anyway, trying to recover from everything that had happened. She took the cup from him. "Thanks." She took a sip knowing she would enjoy it. Stern had a knack for making good coffee.

She watched as he returned to the chair he had been sitting in earlier. Why did they have to be best friends? If they weren't best friends, then...

She drew in a deep breath and stared down into her cup.

If he wasn't your best friend, then he would have no reason to be sitting in your living room, tonight or any night. He probably wouldn't even know you existed. Men who look like Stern don't date girls who do what you do for a living. And when they do, they are only after one thing.

She frowned, refusing to lump Stern into the same category as Walter.

"You're frowning, JoJo. Is the coffee that bad?"

She shook her head and looked over at him. "No, I was just thinking."

"About Walter?"

No, you. Instead she said, "Yes, Walter." That was partly true.

He took a sip of his own coffee. "May I ask you something?"

"Yes?" she replied.

"What did you ever see in him?"

JoJo couldn't help but chuckle. Only a man would ask a question like that. Although Walter had acted like a total jerk tonight, that did not change the fact that he was a nice-looking man. "Um, possibilities."

She figured they should leave it at that for now, especially because she had her own questions. "You knew I would be at the Punch Bowl tonight. How?"

He stretched his long legs out in front of him and leaned back in her chair. "I have my sources. Since you refused to tell me where you were going or the name of the man you were interested in, I decided to do my own investigation."

She nodded. It wouldn't be hard to find out his source because she knew every single person who had the information. She met his gaze. "You didn't return my calls."

She watched as he looked down into his coffee cup, seeming to gather his thoughts. He then looked back at her. "No, I didn't. I needed time to think."

"About that kiss we shared?" There was no reason not to directly address what she knew had bothered him.

"Yes, about that kiss we shared."

"But why? We knew starting out that the kiss meant nothing, Stern. We even talked about it before we did it. I don't understand why you made such a big deal out of it when you were merely helping me improve my skills."

Stern looked down into his cup of coffee again. How could he explain to JoJo that the kiss did mean something? Although he'd wanted to believe that kiss had been about helping her improve her skills, in fact it had not been about that at all, which was why he'd felt the need to back off. Now he wondered if what Zane had said, and what Sampson had alluded to, were true. Was Stern beginning to feel something for JoJo that had nothing to do with friendship but everything to do with a man desiring a woman?

Even now, she was sitting across from him looking sexier than he'd ever seen her look. He could see why all the men at the bar had been so taken with her tonight.

Whoever had performed her makeover had done an out-standing job.

But then, that was part of the problem. The makeover only emphasized the beauty on the outside. Those other men had failed to see the beauty that was on the inside. In his opinion, she hadn't needed a makeover to empha-size that beauty. It was always there with her. Carmichael hadn't wanted to see past her looks.

"Stern?"

He drew in a deep breath and decided to answer her question truthfully…as best he could. "Yes, we talked about the kiss and it was supposed to be nothing more than a way to improve your skills. However, I lost con-trol, JoJo, and I shouldn't have. If your phone hadn't in-terrupted us, I would have tried stripping you naked."

She held his gaze for a moment before waving off his words. "You would have stopped."

"No, I wouldn't have. Hell, JoJo, I had unbuttoned your blouse."

And she had let him, which proved just how much she had trusted him to do the right thing. But, at the time, doing the right thing had been the last thought on his mind.

"So you unbuttoned my blouse—no big deal."

He wondered why she was making light of what he'd done when he had taken his inappropriate behavior seri-ously. He hadn't been able to sleep much that night, but it hadn't been remorse that had kept him awake. It had been the memory of how aroused he'd gotten from touching her skin and kissing her lips. Why, after all these years, was he being drawn to her this way? Why, all of a sudden, was there this full-blown attraction he couldn't fight?

"Although Walter was a big disappointment," JoJo said, interrupting his thoughts, "I don't think this weekend was a complete waste. I got to spend time with your cousins and sisters-in-law. Ritz and his assistant were a hoot and I liked the way they did my hair and makeup. They even told me how to apply the makeup myself if I ever decide to indulge again. So I should thank you for suggesting the makeover. "

He wasn't sure she should thank him. He wasn't all that concerned about things not working out with Carmichael because he had planned to sabotage that anyway. He might as well come clean about that, too.

"I have a confession to make."

She glanced over at him. "What?"

"I didn't want you and Carmichael to hook up tonight. In fact, I was hoping you wouldn't. I had even planned to do something to interrupt you if the two of you left together."

JoJo lifted a brow. "Do what?"

"Become a nuisance. And when Sampson told me what a jerk Carmichael can be with women—to the point that he's rumored to have roughed up a few who dismissed his advances—I knew I didn't want you with him."

She got up from the sofa and moved to where he'd placed the tray with the coffeepot. She poured another cup. His gaze followed her movements in that too-sexy dress. She'd removed those killer stilettos and was in her bare feet, allowing him to appreciate her gorgeous legs.

"Want some more?" she asked, turning around.

He met her eyes. "What?"

"Coffee."

"No, I'm good," he said, taking a sip and wishing he had something stronger. His attraction to her tonight was fiercer than ever. That's the last thing either of them needed. She needed a shoulder to cry on, not a friend with a hard-on. And he felt himself getting harder as he watched her walk back over to the sofa and tuck her legs beneath her, which raised the hem of her dress and gave him a glimpse of luscious thighs. He knew it was time for him to go, but there was no way he could stand up just yet.

She took a slow sip of her coffee before meeting his gaze. "Explain something to me, Stern."

"I will if I can."

"You didn't know Walter. Why wouldn't you want things to have worked out for us?"

"I told you what Sampson said."

She nodded. "So, you only planned to make a nuisance of yourself after finding out about Walter's character?"

"No."

He saw her forehead crease and figured he was confusing her. There had always been total honesty between him and JoJo, which was why their friendship had lasted so long and had remained so strong.

"Let me explain something to you about men in general, JoJo. We're made to desire women and made to want to make love to women."

She frowned. "Please tell me you're not trying to justify Walter's behavior."

Stern shook his head. "No, definitely not. Mainly because a real man also knows how to respect a woman. Not to talk down to her. You were right on point when you said he was acting like a little boy in a suit, although I don't think he liked hearing it."

"I was just being honest."

"Well, there are some who don't prefer honesty."

She shrugged. "Then it's their problem, not mine." She took another sip of her coffee.

Stern watched her. What was it about being here with her, alone, tonight? He'd done exactly this a number of

other times without feeling anything more than friendship. It could be the way she looked tonight, sexy, displaying all those attributes she usually kept well hidden.

She looked good in that dress, with red on her sultry lips and those sexy earrings dangling from her ears.
And damn, what was that fragrance she was wearing? It
was such an alluring scent. Her hair, styled in feathery
layers around her face, brought out the darkness of her
eyes, the fullness of her cheekbones and the lushness of
her mouth. He was tempted to move close to her and run
his fingers through the silken strands of her hair right
before taking her sultry lips with his. Were things just
as Zane claimed? Had Stern's feelings for JoJo shifted
without him realizing it?

"So why did you plan to make a nuisance of yourself,
Stern? Especially when you knew all the trouble I'd gone
through to make a good impression on Walter?"

Something inside of him almost snapped. Why was
she so fixated on Walter Carmichael? He mentally replayed everything that had happened between them since
that day at the lodge when she'd asked him how to make
a man want her. His jealousy for the unknown man had
started then and it had increased each and every time
she'd brought up this mystery man.

"Stern?"

He gave her a sharp look. "Do you really want to
know?"

"Of course I want to know," she said in exasperation.

He'd tried to explain it before but for some reason she
just wasn't getting it. "What if I said I didn't like the idea
of you chasing behind a man?"

She lifted her chin. "I wasn't chasing behind him,
not exactly. I saw him and decided he had potential. He
would do."

He lifted a brow. "Do for what?"

"Doesn't matter."

He thought it did. As far as he knew, JoJo had never been intimate with a guy. Had she selected Carmichael as the man she'd wanted to share her first sexual encounter with? JoJo would not sleep with someone she didn't care about, so Carmichael had blown his chance when he'd tried making her a one-night stand.

Stern stood. "Whatever the reason, it did matter." He placed his cup down on the tray. "Come on and walk me to the door. It's getting late."

He went over to her and reached out his hand. She took it as she stood. He couldn't resist letting his gaze move up and down her body. "You look beautiful tonight, JoJo."

She smiled as she walked him to the door. "I actually felt beautiful tonight. I'll do this again. The hair, the makeup, the dress. It's a good change."

"Yes," he said when they came to a stop in front of the door. "It's a nice change."

Giving in to temptation, he locked a curl of her hair around his finger. "You didn't cut it."

"No, I didn't cut it. Ritz just trimmed the ends."

"Whatever he did, I like it."

"Thanks."

"Don't cover it up with a cap for a while."

She chuckled. "Can't make you that promise. Can you see me changing spark plugs with curls falling in my face?"

He grinned then. "I guess not."

"But Ritz showed me how to work it back into this style whenever I want to."

Stern didn't know what there was about her hair that made him want to go after her lips whenever he put his hands in it. He felt himself staring deeply into her eyes.

Then, as if of its own accord, his mouth slowly inched closer to hers. Why was his body aching so intensely to hold her in his arms?

The moment their lips touched, merged, latched together in a hungry connection, she let out a small gasp. Whether it was one of shock or one of pleasure, he wasn't sure. All he knew was that she tasted of sweet coffee and he wanted to consume every inch of her mouth.

The moment she leaned into him, his hands automatically left her head to wrap around her waist as their tongues dueled in a fiery exchange. There had been no reason to kiss her tonight. But then he quickly decided that yes, there had been. Tonight she was a woman who deserved a man's attention and he had no problem giving it to her.

He finally released her mouth, then leaned in and kissed around her lips several more times, inhaling her scent and feeling her quiver in his arms. And just like with those other kisses, she had again followed his lead. She'd kissed him back just now in a way that made him want to kiss her that much more.

"Stern?"

"Hmm?" he said as he continued to place soft kisses around her mouth.

"Why are you kissing me?"

"Because I want to."

He hadn't said it to be smart. He was being completely honest with her. So he decided to carry that honesty a little further. He pulled back slightly and touched her chin with the tip of his finger, tilting it up to give her another full kiss on the lips. "In case you haven't figured it out yet, JoJo, there's something happening between us that I don't think either of us expected."

"What?"

He smiled as he took a step backward. Instead of answering her question, he said, "I'm leaving town on Monday for a business trip to Florida and won't be back until Thursday. Let's do something when I get back."

"All right. What about going bowling on Friday night?"

"How about the lodge?"

She raised a brow. "The lodge?"

"Yes. Let's spend the weekend at the lodge."

"But we just got back from the lodge."

"And I want to go again," he said. "Something is happening between us. I don't know what it is, JoJo, but I think maybe it's time we find out."

He leaned in and kissed her lips again before opening the door to leave.

Nine

"Hey, JoJo, you need to look like a girl more often," Sony Wyatt said, grinning. He was standing with a group of guys who worked at the shop as they passed around her pictures from Saturday night. She had brought them in for Beeker and Wanda, but it seemed the pictures were now making the rounds.

"Funny, Sony," she said, grabbing a hose to flush out the carburetor of the car she was working on and ignoring the men's whistles as they looked through the pictures.

"You don't look like the same person," Leon Shaw, another worker, added.

She rolled her eyes. "Well, I am the same person, and need I remind the four of you that I am also your boss? So be nice."

"Did Stern see these?" Charlie Dixon wanted to know.

She lifted her head from underneath the hood of the car. All the guys who worked for her knew that she and Stern were best friends. "Why?"

"Just wondering."

She shrugged and placed her head back under the hood

to finish up the work on the Corvette. Charlie would be surprised to know Stern hadn't needed to see the pictures because he had seen the real thing. In fact, she was still trying to wrap her mind around just what had happened Saturday night from the time she'd walked into the Punch Bowl and met Walter's gaze to later that same night when Stern had kissed her good-night in her foyer. Even now, she was tempted to touch her lips to remember what she'd felt at the kiss he had placed there.

And it had been a real kiss. Nothing he'd done as part of any lesson. She had enjoyed it, and she had a feeling he had, too. For a moment, they had forgotten they were nothing but best friends and had kissed like…like two people attracted to each other. Even now she couldn't understand it. Oh, she understood perfectly from her end because she was in love with him. But what had driven him to kiss her like that? That's what confused her more than anything, and she wouldn't be satisfied until she found out the answer.

At least he was aware something was going on. Before he'd left his exact words had been, *"In case you haven't figured it out yet, JoJo, there's something happening between us that I don't think either of us expected."*

She drew in a deep breath, wondering if there was a way she could multiply those feelings so he'd realize the full extent of what was happening. It had already happened to her. How could she make sure it happened to him?

A few hours later, back in her office doing paperwork and still trying to wrap her mind around everything about this past Saturday night, Wanda knocked on the door. Recognizing the knock, JoJo called out for her to come in.

"Apparently you didn't tell me everything about Saturday night," Wanda said, entering the office and taking the chair across from JoJo's desk.

Knowing she wouldn't be getting any work done for the next minute or so, JoJo closed the file she was working on. "And just what do you think I didn't tell you?"

"How you apparently pissed off Walter Carmichael."

JoJo nibbled her bottom lip. She'd told Wanda the same thing she'd told anyone else who'd asked about Saturday night: things between her and Walter hadn't worked out and when they left the club they'd gone their separate ways. That hadn't been a lie...she'd just deliberately left out everything involving Stern. "What makes you think I pissed him off?" she asked, even though she knew she had.

"Because he just called Beeker and wants his auto records transferred to Carl's Automotive across town. He told Beeker he doesn't plan on ever coming back here again."

JoJo stood and crossed the room to pull open a drawer in the file cabinet. "Great! He's the last person I want to see anyway," she said, pulling out Walter's folder and slamming the drawer shut. She then went back to her desk, sat down and handed the folder to Wanda.

Wanda leaned back in her chair. "Hmm, so tell me, JoJo. How can there be trouble in paradise when you hadn't quite reached the island yet?"

JoJo looked across her desk at Wanda. "Do you really want to know?" Before Wanda could respond, she said, "Then I'll tell you." She allowed herself an irritated breath before saying, "Walter Carmichael is a jerk who assumed I had gotten all dolled up on Saturday night just so he could poke me. All he did the entire evening was try to talk me into leaving the club with him so we could find the nearest bed. What ever happened to two people getting to know each other first?"

Wanda smiled. "I think that went out the window when women became just as interested in one-night stands as men. Couples don't want to get to know each other anymore. All they want is to get into each other."

"Well, that's not what I want."

Wanda nodded. "And I assume you told him that and he didn't take it well."

JoJo rolled her eyes. "Like I said, the man's a jerk. How could I ever have thought he and I could get something going?"

"So, your plan to replace Stern in your heart didn't work. What do you plan to do now?" Wanda asked.

JoJo closed the file on her desk again and leaned back in her chair. "Nothing. I'll grow old and die a virgin."

"Doesn't have to be that way, you know."

JoJo bristled at Wanda's words. "It does have to be that way. At least for me it does. I'm not into one-night stands or casual sex, and there hasn't been another guy who has caught my eye."

"Then don't concentrate on another guy. Just concentrate on the guy you really want."

"Oh, please, I wish it was that simple. But as you know Stern is off-limits."

"Why? Because he's your best friend?"

"Yes."

Wanda didn't say anything for a moment. "Haven't you ever heard of friends with benefits?"

"Of course."

"Then get with the program."

JoJo shook her head. Wanda was old enough to be her mother and the woman was promoting sex. "That sort of thing wouldn't work for me and Stern, either. We aren't

just friends—we're *best* friends. Besides, he's still freak-
ing out over those kisses."

Too late she realized what she'd said and quickly
opened the folder again when Wanda sat up straight in
her chair and stared at her. JoJo knew the possibility
that the woman hadn't caught her last sentence was too
much to hope for.

"What kisses? You and Stern *kissed?*" Wanda exclaimed after sucking in a shocked breath. "And don't
you dare shut up on me now, JoJo. You might as well tell
all. Don't let me ask Stern for the—"

"You wouldn't dare," JoJo said, rising from her seat
to lean over her desk toward Wanda.

Wanda's blue eyes shot up as she leaned forward, too.
"Wanna bet?"

No, JoJo didn't want to bet. She had all but admitted to Wanda last week that she had fallen in love with
Stern and she wouldn't put it past Wanda to try her hand
at matchmaking. "Okay, we kissed. More than once."

"And?"

JoJo rolled her eyes. Did the woman need all the details? "I enjoyed it and I believe he did, too. It started
out as a lesson on how to improve my kissing technique
for Walter and—"

"You've got to be kidding," Wanda interrupted in an
incredulous tone.

"No, I'm not kidding."

"And Stern went along with it? Giving you kissing
lessons for Walter?"

"Yes, and then he felt bad because he lost control."

JoJo wondered at the smile that touched Wanda's lips.
"Go ahead, JoJo. I'm still listening."

"Well, anyway, we kissed again Saturday night after
he took me home."

Wanda raised a brow. "Saturday night? After he took you home?"

"Yes." Seeing no way out of it, JoJo leaned back in her chair and decided to tell Wanda the whole story.

"Wow," Wanda said, after JoJo finished telling her what happened. "So you and Stern are going to the lodge this weekend to figure out things."

JoJo shrugged. "He's the one who has to figure things out. I already know why I get into our kisses. But I'm sure it has to be confusing for him since he doesn't feel about me the way I feel about him."

"Are you sure that he doesn't?

"Of course, I'm sure. Why would he?"

Now it was Wanda's turn to shrug. "Um, I don't know. It could be because you're a nice person, the two of you have a special relationship and he knows you better than anyone. It could also be that he sees what others don't see."

"What?"

"The fact that you have inner beauty *and* outer beauty."

JoJo shook her head. "Thanks, but no. With Stern, it's a man's thing. He all but said so Saturday night. That's why he lost control."

"But he knows something is happening between the two of you and he's willing to investigate to find out what, right?"

"Yes."

A huge smile spread across Wanda's face. "Then use this weekend to your advantage. You already love him, so do whatever it takes to make him fall in love with you."

JoJo frowned. "I may not know a lot about men, but what I do know is that a woman can't make a man fall in love with her."

"There is a possibility she can. Especially if he's half-

way there. So take a chance and shock Stern this weekend. Suggest that the two of you become best friends
with benefits and see what happens."

"So, how was the trip?" Riley asked, entering his
brother's office.

"Great," Stern said, smiling as he looked up from a
stack of papers. "That land deal in Florida is a go."

Riley smiled. "Good news to hear. And I also hear
you're headed back to the lodge this weekend."

"Yes, both JoJo and I need a break."

"The two of you just got back less than two weeks
ago," Riley said, sliding into the chair across from Stern's
desk.

"And we're going again. We enjoy it there."

"Apparently. And I saw the pictures that Megan took
of JoJo's makeover. She looked gorgeous. I'd forgotten
how much hair she had under those caps she likes wearing. And those legs. Wow!"

Stern frowned. "Aren't you getting married at the end
of this month?"

Riley threw his head back and laughed. "Yes, but I
can still appreciate a beautiful woman when I see one.
And don't worry. Alpha has my heart, totally and completely. Who has yours?"

Stern lifted a brow. "My what?"

"Your heart."

A sly grin touched Stern's lips. "Okay, I admit it.
Alpha has my heart totally and completely, as well."

"Smart-ass," Riley said, chuckling. "You know what
I'm asking."

"No," Stern said, shaking his head. "Honestly, I don't."

"If you don't, I have a feeling it won't be long now

before you do," Riley said, standing and heading for the door.

"What do you mean by that?" Stern called out.

Riley paused before he opened the door and glanced back at Stern. "Man, you're in love and don't even know it."

A short while later Stern stood in his office, looking out the window. Now yet another person assumed more was going on between him and JoJo than just friendship. In a way, he shouldn't be surprised by Riley's assumption. Zane claimed most of the family believed there was more going on.

Riley was wrong. He *already* knew how he felt about JoJo. He had fought the truth for as long as he could but would now admit that he'd fallen in love with her. He might have loved her all along like Zane and the others suspected, or he might have realized his true feelings just recently. It didn't matter at this point. The most important thing was that he loved her.

But that only compounded his problems.

He wasn't a man who pined after a woman, but he had longed for JoJo this week. He had talked to her every night on the phone while in Florida but it seemed as if she deliberately kept the conversations brief. He wasn't sure if he'd imagined it or not. But, to be fair to her, she'd had busy days this week and had wanted to get to bed early. It wasn't her fault that he had missed her, ached for her, yearned for her.

He had found himself watching the clock and counting the days. Thursday hadn't gotten here soon enough to suit him. He had planned to stop by the shop after he'd landed and left the airport. But when he called, Wanda told him JoJo had left early for a dentist's appointment.

So, instead of going straight home he had come into the office instead.

Now he couldn't wait until tomorrow. Until this weekend.

Because he realized that Zane was right and Stern wanted more than just friendship with JoJo. He wanted forever. But how was he supposed to change the nature of their relationship without scaring her off?

Zane had made another prediction, too, one Stern hadn't bought into. For some reason, Zane suspected JoJo might have feelings for him. Stern would admit he had racked his brain trying to recall a time recently when those feelings had been displayed and he couldn't think of one. For the past few weeks she had been into Walter Carmichael and trying to turn herself into the object of the man's affections. Well, Carmichael had blown it and lost out. As far as Stern was concerned it was his turn to do something the other man hadn't done: win JoJo's heart.

Stern shoved his hands into his pants pockets. Tomorrow evening he and JoJo would leave town for the six-hour drive to his hunting lodge for the weekend. During that time he would make his move. They'd be returning on Sunday, so he would only have Saturday night.

He had one night. One night to prove that they could move their relationship to a whole new level and become much more than best friends.

Ten

Stern tilted his Stetson back and blinked several times when JoJo opened her door. "Your hair."

"What about it?" she asked, handing him her overnight bag.

"It looks like it did Saturday night."

JoJo chuckled as she pulled the door shut and locked it behind her. "Is that a crime?"

"No, but I didn't expect it."

There will be a lot happening this weekend that you won't expect, she thought as they walked to his four-wheel-drive SUV. "I told you that Ritz showed me how to do it myself when I'm not wearing my cap. Of course it doesn't look as good as when he did it, but it will suffice."

"Well, I think you did a great job."

"Thanks. How was your trip?"

"It was okay. I missed you, though," he said, putting her bag next to his in the backseat.

JoJo couldn't ignore the flutters in her stomach as he opened the car door for her. This was not the first time he'd gone away on a trip and come back to tell her he'd missed her. But this time felt different. Of course, it was all in her mind, but still.

"I missed you, too," she said, meaning it. Although they had talked every night, she had deliberately kept the calls short, afraid she would slip and say something stupid—like confessing she loved him.

"Anything interesting happen at work this week?" he asked after getting in the car and snapping on his seat belt. It was then that he turned those dark, sexy eyes on her.

She sucked in a breath. It was as if she'd taken a dose of some kind of sexual stimulant. The air suddenly felt charged. She could place the blame on all those dreams she'd had about him all week. Or that romance novel she'd read this week thanks to Wanda. The love scenes had almost blistered her fingers they'd been so hot.

"Nothing happened. Except Walter called Beeker on Monday and transferred his auto records. I guess I've lost him as a customer."

"You don't sound too sad about it."

She smiled. "I'm not. So how did things go with you in Florida? Did you close the deal?"

"Yes."

Her smile widened. "I'm happy for you."

"Thanks."

She reclined her seat. Stern preferred to do all the driving. All she had to do was sit back and relax or take a nap.

"Tired?" he asked when he came to a traffic light.

"Yes. Busy week. Any weekends when I can get away are nice. Thanks for inviting me to come with you."

"You're always welcome."

She wondered if she would be welcome when she brought up the next topic of conversation. Even though Wanda had been the one to suggest it, the more JoJo thought about it, the more she liked the idea of them becoming best friends with benefits. She just wasn't sure how receptive Stern would be to the idea.

She glanced over at him. "Stern?"

"Hmm?"

"I've been thinking."

"What about?"

"You. Me. Our relationship."

He quickly glanced over at her before returning his eyes to the road. "What about our relationship?"

"We've been best friends forever."

"True."

"And there's no other man I trust more."

"Thanks."

"I'm getting older."

"So am I," he countered.

She nodded and smiled. "Okay, we're both getting older, but there are plenty of things you've done that I haven't tried yet."

"Such as?"

"Sex."

Stern braked to avoid running into the back of the car in front of him. He then checked his rearview mirror before pulling to the side of the road. Killing the engine, he turned to JoJo. "What did you say?"

JoJo didn't realize she'd been holding her breath until now. She began nibbling on her bottom lip while he stared at her. "I said, you've had sex and I haven't."

"Were we supposed to be competing or something?" he asked, frowning.

She could feel heat gathering in her cheeks. Of all the topics they'd talked about over the years, sex had never been one of them. She'd only known that he'd become sexually active when she found condom packs in his be-

longings. Once, a pack had fallen out of his book bag at
school, and she had quickly picked them up and given
them back to him. All that day she'd wondered if what
she'd heard about him and Melanie Hargrove was true.

"Nah, we weren't competing, Stern. I was just making an observation."

"Why?"

"Why?" she repeated.

"Yes, why?"

She nibbled on her bottom lip again. "I'm in a dilemma."

He frowned. "What kind of dilemma?"

"I'll be thirty in a few months."

"And?"

"And I'm still a virgin."

She watched the way his Adam's apple moved in his
throat. "So?"

She shrugged. "So, I know it's my problem, but I was
hoping you could help me out."

"How?"

His curt questions were beginning to annoy her.
"How?" she repeated.

"Yes, how? How can I help you out?" he asked.

"By agreeing to do something."

He raised a brow. "What?"

She drew in a deep breath. "By agreeing that we become best friends with benefits."

Stern could only stare at her. Of all the things he'd
assumed she would ask, *that* was not it. Never in a thousand years would he have expected a request like that to
flow from her lips. But she had asked, and whether she
knew it or not—and he was certain that she probably
didn't—she had made things easy for him. All last night
and earlier today he had racked his brain trying to figure

out how he would seduce her without coming across as a jerk like Walter Carmichael.

At one point, he'd decided that just coming out and confessing that he loved her would be the best thing to do. But then he doubted that she was truly ready to believe him. So he'd decided that his original plan—to use their one night to prove that they could be more than best friends—was the best way to go.

Now, though, she had taken the decision out of his hands and he planned to run with it. All he had to do was go along with her idea and he'd have his chance to prove to her that best friends with benefits could easily transform their relationship into something more meaningful and everlasting.

And there was no doubt in his mind he wanted forever with JoJo.

"Okay," he said.

"Okay?" she asked, staring at him.

"Yes, okay. Best friends with benefits it is."

She lifted her brow. "You're agreeing? Just like that?"

"Yes. Were you expecting me not to?"

She shrugged. "I guess not. But I *had* expected you to think about it."

"What's there to think about? I want you."

She looked surprised. "You do?"

"Yes. I had time to think about us when I was in Florida, and I believe one of the reasons I have a tendency to lose control when we kiss is because deep down I want you. That explains a lot of things."

"It does?"

"Yes. I guess the desire has been there for a while and kissing you brought it to the forefront."

"Oh."

"But then I need to be sure that you want me and that I'm not a replacement for Walter Carmichael."

"You're not."

He thought she sounded pretty sure of it. "Are you certain?"

"I'm positive. I didn't know Walter, but I thought I wanted to get to know him. In the end, I discovered he wasn't anyone I wanted to know after all."

"So you hadn't fallen in love with him?"

"Of course not! In fact, I can't believe he's the one I picked to replace—"

She stopped talking rather abruptly, leading him to believe she'd almost said something she hadn't wanted to say.

"He's the one you picked to replace what?" he inquired.

"Nothing. Not important."

He remembered having bits and pieces of this same conversation before and suspected she was hiding something that *was* important. "Okay, so we're in agreement that our relationship will be changing. Right?"

"Right."

He smiled as he pressed the keyless ignition back on. "You sound tired. Why don't you relax and take a nap. I'll wake you when we get to the lodge."

"All right."

Stern watched as she closed her eyes. She looked beautiful while asleep. When he'd picked her up and she'd opened her front door he had blinked when he saw her hairstyle. And instead of wearing jeans she had on a denim skirt with leggings and boots. Her attire was definitely new and she looked damn cute. But she still looked like JoJo. *His* JoJo.

As he headed the car toward the interstate, the knowledge that she didn't do casual sex weighed heavily on his mind. So if she was willing to experiment with him in the bedroom, that meant something. Hell, he hoped it did.

Could Zane have been right on all accounts? Could JoJo feel something more than friendship for him, too? But if that was the case, why had she gone after Walter Carmichael? Stern wasn't sure, but he was determined to find out.

"It won't take but a minute to start up the fireplace, JoJo."

"Okay."

JoJo looked around. She loved it here and always enjoyed coming to the lodge with Stern. It seemed fitting that any change in their relationship should take place here, where she had first realized she loved him. Shivers raced through her at the thought that they would probably share a bed tonight. She'd dreamed of him for months and months. At some point while she was here all of her dreams would come true.

She jumped when Stern eased up behind her and placed his jacket around her shoulders. She glanced up at him. "What's this for?"

"You were quivering. For you, that means you're cold or nervous. If it's the latter, you have no reason to be nervous with me, JoJo. No matter what might change, I won't. I'll still be your Stern."

Her Stern... Boy, she wished. She knew in the real world, a lot of women would love to make that claim. He'd always been a heartthrob and she had found the number of women who had envied their relationship amusing. She was certain there were some women who still did envy them. She knew there were some who questioned their relationship, too. But never had Stern let any of them diminish their friendship. She'd heard he'd put several women in their place when they had tried.

She watched him walk back over to the fireplace. Usually, he would call ahead to have Mr. Richardson, the older man he paid to look out for the lodge, get the fireplace roaring with heat before they arrived.

"Did you forget to call Mr. Richardson?" she asked.

He was kneeling and she couldn't help but appreciate the way his jeans stretched tight over his muscular thighs. And that blue sweater he was wearing looked good on him. She'd known it would when she'd purchased it for him last year as a Christmas present. He had just the chest for it, hard-muscled and solid.

While she was thinking of all the things she'd done to that chest in her dreams, he glanced over his shoulder at her and said, "No, I didn't forget. He and Mrs. Richardson left a couple of days ago for a two-week cruise to Hawaii. It's their fiftieth wedding anniversary."

She smiled. "That's wonderful. We need to send them a gift when we get back."

He returned her smile. "Yes, we do." He then went back to starting the fire.

She could stand there and ogle him all night but decided she needed to help in some way, to stay busy for a while. It was way past midnight, but because she had slept on the long drive here, she was wide-awake. "I'll go upstairs and check the bedrooms...I mean the *bedroom*... to make sure it's okay." Oops. Already she'd forgotten they would need only one bedroom because they would be sharing a bed.

He straightened to stand. "Come here for a minute, JoJo."

Swallowing deeply, she crossed the room and came to a stop in front of him. "Yes?"

She couldn't help noticing that he was staring at her mouth. And then instead of answering her, he leaned down and captured her lips with his. She heard herself moan on a breathless sigh, which gave him the opening he needed. Immediately, his tongue slid between her lips and lured her into a mating that made her wrap her arms around his neck.

Stern knew how to do more than stoke the fire in the fireplace because his kiss was definitely stoking the fire in her. His tongue left its mark on every area it touched. Instinctively, she leaned into him and moaned again when she felt his erection pressing into her stomach.

A rush of desire consumed her. She tried calming her body down but couldn't do so. It was as if her mouth had finally gotten what it had longed for. She was consumed with love for him and he was doing a good job stoking their passion. It would not have bothered her in the least if he'd stripped her naked and made love to her right here in front of the fireplace.

Too soon to suit her, he ended the kiss and stepped back, taking her hand in his. "We need to talk, JoJo. While you were asleep in the car, I had six hours to really think about this."

Her heart took a dive into her stomach. "And you've changed your mind about everything." She stated this as if it was a fact and not a question.

Stern wrapped his arms around her waist. "No, I haven't changed my mind. But what I want you to do is really think about what you want for us."

"I know what I want."

"Do you?"

"Yes."

"Are you sure?"

"Yes."

He stared at her for a moment before easing her down with him onto the huge throw rug so they could sit facing the fireplace. "This best friends with benefits thing... What exactly is your definition of it?"

She nibbled at her bottom lip and then said, "Just like it says. Basically we have to be best friends, and we get the benefits of that friendship...which I guess is something we've been doing all along." She paused a moment and said, "Except..."

"Except what?"

"We also get to explore a level of intimacy we haven't explored before."

"You haven't ever slept with a man, JoJo."

"Yes, and that's one of the advantages of friends with benefits. The sex."

"And you only want to indulge in sex because of this age thing?"

"No. I want the sex because I want to know the pleasure I can feel. But I don't want to share it with just anyone, Stern. That would make it too casual for me. Meaningless. Sharing it with you makes it personal. Special. I trust you. And if you're worried that I'd assume there will be a commitment between us, don't be. I know that won't be the case. It will be whatever it is."

He didn't say anything for a minute but looked at her in a way that had her heart jumping. He took a step closer. "Now that's where you're wrong, JoJo. If we start this, it won't be reserved just for when we get an itch to make love. I couldn't handle a relationship with you that way. Somehow it cheapens what we share."

"Oh."

"I couldn't sleep with you tonight and then sleep with

someone else next week. That would make me no better than the Walter Carmichaels of the world. If we become best friends with benefits, we'll also become a couple."

"We will?"

"Yes."

"And you'd want that?"

"Why wouldn't I want it?"

She shrugged. "Your lifestyle. You're single and you've stayed that way for a reason."

"Yes, but then so have you, right?"

"Yes, but it's different for me. There's not a flock of men running behind me like the flock of women running behind you. You seem to like the chase and I can't see you giving it up."

"I will give it up. I'll be dating you. Only you."

She frowned. "But will I be enough?"

He smiled. "Oh, yes, you'll be enough."

She was skeptical. "This is going to be harder than I thought."

"Why?"

"I honestly never thought of us dating exclusively," she said.

"But you have thought of us having sex?"

She figured she could be honest with him about that. She didn't want him to think that her desire to be intimate with him was just a hormonal thing. "Yes."

He arched a brow, surprised. "When?"

"Recently. Most of the time."

A slow smile curved his lips. "You don't say?"

Now she wished she hadn't said. She wasn't sure it was cool, letting a man know you wanted him.

"And how did Carmichael fit into this? The last time we were here you insisted I give you some ideas about how to make him want you."

JoJo leaned back on a pillow and stared into the fire that blazed and sent warmth all through her. She then shifted her gaze to Stern, knowing he was waiting for her response. She nibbled on her bottom lip again. "It's complicated, Stern, and I'd rather not go into details. All you need to know is that I thought he was someone I wanted to get to know and I was wrong."

He stared at her for a long moment and she could imagine what he was thinking. He probably assumed she was fickle and shifted her interest from one man to another at the drop of a hat. But to tell him the truth— that she loved him when he didn't love her back—would make her feel pathetic. For him to commit to become her lover was one thing, but for him to find out she loved him might make him run in the other direction.

"Like I told you before, I recently figured out that the reason I enjoyed our kisses so much is because I was becoming attracted to you."

"Wow," JoJo said, smiling. "It still feels nice to hear that. I was becoming attracted to you, too, so this best friends with benefits thing would have happened between us eventually."

Stern wasn't so sure about that. He wanted to believe that eventually their attraction would have prompted them to note the change in their emotions and then to decide to become lovers with a strong commitment, with a future that included marriage.

"So, do we get to sleep together tonight?"

He heard both anxiousness and nervousness in her voice. "No. I want you to think about everything and give me your answer tomorrow. Like I said, I want a commitment. That means becoming a couple in front of everyone. My family and yours. My friends and yours. Everyone. Can you handle that?"

"Yes. They'll think it's strange at first, but I think everyone will be okay with it in the end."

"And if they aren't?"

She lifted her chin. "What we do is our business, right?"

"Right."

He eased to his feet and pulled her up with him. "Let's share a cup of hot chocolate before we go to bed. Think about things tonight and tomorrow you can give me your answer. I don't want you to feel like you're being rushed into anything."

"It was my idea, Stern."

"Doesn't matter. I still want you to be sure."

As he led her into the kitchen, Stern knew it was important to him that JoJo *did* think this through because as far as he was concerned he had their future all mapped out. They would date exclusively for a while and then, when he thought the time was right for both of them, he would pop the question.

He wanted her as his wife. She was an intricate part of his past and he couldn't imagine a future without her.

Eleven

Stern was up early the next morning, busy preparing breakfast. Although Mr. Richardson hadn't been able to get the place warm for them on this trip, he had gone grocery shopping, stocking enough food for their weekend visit.

One of Stern's favorite rooms in the lodge was the kitchen. It was huge and spacious and would be a chef's dream. When he had purchased the place he had replaced all the appliances with stainless steel ones and installed granite countertops. Because the kitchen was so massive, he had an island breakfast bar built, which he used for eating and as an additional countertop.

He had kept the original cherry oak cabinets and he'd let JoJo pick out all the fixtures and the tile for the floor and the backsplash. He had wanted her to feel this place was just as much hers as it was his. At the time, he hadn't thought much about that decision, but now he couldn't help but question it and others he'd made concerning JoJo. No wonder his family had suspected his true feelings for her long before he had.

He had heard JoJo move around upstairs about half an hour ago and was anticipating her joining him for breakfast. Had she given yesterday's request more thought and decided she didn't want the best friends with benefits thing after all? He'd known that encouraging her to think more about it was a risk that might prompt her to change her mind, but he wanted her to be sure she was truly ready for taking such a step.

Last night, before going to bed, they had shared hot chocolate and Danish rolls while he brought her up to date on what was going on with the investigation of his great grandfather, Raphel Stern Westmoreland.

A few years ago, the family had discovered that Raphel, who they'd always assumed was an only child, had actually had a twin brother, Reginald Scott Westmoreland, who had roots in Atlanta. It seemed Raphel had left home at the age of twenty-two, becoming the black sheep of the family when he ran off with the preacher's wife, never to be heard from again and eventually assumed dead. Raphel had passed through several states before finally settling in Colorado.

It also appeared that his great grandfather had a colorful past. He'd taken up with several women along the way. Everyone in the family was curious about those women because he was rumored to have married all four.

Recently they had met Reginald's ancestors and had formed a close relationship with those cousins in Atlanta. Now everyone was anxious to see if there were more Westmoreland cousins out there somewhere, resulting from any of those women Raphel had supposedly married.

Rico, Megan's husband, was the private detective handling the investigation. A few months ago, Rico discovered Raphel had a child he hadn't known about. A child who was ultimately adopted by a woman with the last name of Outlaw. And now Rico was investigating information about the woman who was rumored to be Raphel's fourth wife, Isabelle. Just yesterday morning, the family had assembled at Dillon's for breakfast to get an update from Rico. He had informed everyone he was still trying to collect data on Isabelle's family and that he was getting close to obtaining information on the Outlaws. So far he'd traced them to Little Rock and there the trail had ended.

"Good morning."

Stern glanced up from the chopping block and stared at JoJo. Her hair was again styled around her face and she wore a cute maxi sweaterdress that showed off her great shape. It was mint-green and made her look soft, totally feminine and sexy as hell. The material hugged her hips, cushioned her breasts and emphasized her waistline. He definitely liked the cowl-neck collar that bared a little skin. Instead of her boots she had leather flats on her feet. He thought she looked amazing. Gorgeous. Hot. The dress was one that would be easy to slide into and out of. He definitely wouldn't mind seeing her slide out of it.

"Good morning, JoJo. Did you get a good night's sleep?" he asked, trying to control the desire rushing through his bloodstream.

She'd come to stand in the middle of the kitchen. "Yes. After sleeping on the drive here, I figured I would stay awake most of the night, but I didn't. I think I went to sleep as soon as my head touched the pillow."

Did that mean she hadn't thought any more about her proposal? "Glad to hear it. I'm chopping up everything for the omelets. Have a seat at the breakfast bar. I should be finished in a minute."

"Okay."

He watched her walk off, noticing how the wool clung to her shapely backside. And when she eased onto the breakfast bar stool the hem of her dress inched up and showed off a gorgeous pair of legs. Seeing her wear something other than a T-shirt and jeans would take some getting used to.

"About what we discussed last night, Stern…"

He shifted his gaze from her legs to her face. His gut tightened. "Yes?"

"I did sleep on it, and I haven't changed my mind."

He released a slow, relieved breath. "Okay."

The kitchen quieted for a moment and then she asked, "Need help?"

"Nope." He went back to slicing the green peppers.

That's usually how things went with them. He would end up in the kitchen because he liked cooking more than she did. She would ask if he needed help and he would decline. Nothing had changed. But in reality things *had* changed. Now the air between them was charged, explosive, volatile. Desire thickened inside of him each and every time he glanced over at her. It wouldn't take much to cross the room and…

"So what's for breakfast in addition to the omelet?"

He glanced up from the ingredients. "The usual— French toast, fruit, orange juice and coffee."

"Can you add something else to the menu?"

"Sure. What?"

"You."

Stern held her gaze for the longest moment. Every pore in his body filled with a degree of hunger he'd never felt before. A fire burned inside of him, spreading fast and furious through his veins. For the first time in his life, a woman had him sizzling. He gathered all the sliced vegetables in the palms of his hands and dropped them in a bowl. Taking a couple of steps back, he placed the bowl in the refrigerator.

After wiping his hands on a kitchen towel, he slowly crossed the room toward her. "I had planned a picnic for us later today, and then I figured we would have movie night. I'd even selected several DVDs for us to watch." Coming to a stop in front of her, he lifted her off the bar stool to stand in front of him. "I didn't want to rush you. I wanted to court you first."

"That's not necessary," she said, leaning her body into his. "I know what I want. Before today, I figured having that particular want was an impossibility. However, I woke up this morning knowing I could finally have what I desire."

He thought she had a way with words and for the next few hours he intended to lap any and all of them from her lips. Starting now. He leaned down and painted feather-light kisses around her mouth, then he licked around the edges of her lips with the tip of his tongue before nibbling around her ear.

"I think it's time for us to take this to the bedroom," he said huskily. Then he swept her off her feet and into his arms.

JoJo wondered how Stern managed to carry her up the stairs as if she weighed no more than a child. Wrapped in his arms, with her ear pressed against his chest, she heard the erratic beat of his heart. She felt his desire and it fed her own.

She'd woken up that morning feeling happier than she had in a long time. Although Stern hadn't said he loved her, he did say he wanted her, his best friend, and he wanted her the same way she wanted him. For her, that was a start.

JoJo felt the mattress beneath her when he placed her on the bed. He stepped back and she held tight to the gaze of the one man who knew her better than anyone else. The one man who'd shared her happiness and her sorrows. He had been her protector, her confidant and, when she needed it, her critic. He'd encouraged her to follow her dreams and had been there to tell her when she'd gotten in too far over her head. She had loved him as her best friend—in fact, she still did. But now she also loved him as the one man who could make her feel complete.

He moved toward the bed, placed his knee on the mattress and tenderly stroked her cheek. "Last chance."

She knew what he meant. "Thanks but I'm not taking it," she whispered, still holding his gaze.

"You've thought this through, then?"

"Very much so. I want you," she whispered.

"And I want you."

He pulled her into his arms and took her mouth with a passion that plunged her senses into overload. The way his tongue devoured hers created a torrid storm within her that made her moan deep in her throat.

He pulled away and she felt air touch her skin as he whisked her dress over her head, leaving her wearing only her thong.

"Ah, hell." Stern felt his guts twist into knots as his gaze raked over JoJo. *Heaven help me.* She was perfect. Long graceful neck, firm breasts, beautiful skin and an adorable flat stomach.

This would be her first time with a man, and he wanted to be gentle. He wanted to take it slow, make it last, make it good and keep it mellow. But seeing her nearly naked, wearing just a tiny scrap of a thong, was more than he could handle. The sight made him want to take her hard and fast, but he knew there was no way he could. He would never hurt her.

Fighting for control, he said softly, "Lie back and lift your hips for me. I want to take this last piece off of you."

She followed his request and he slid the thong over her hips and down her legs. His fingers trembled when they came in contact with her soft skin. He caught a whiff of her feminine scent and he hardened even more, pressing against the zipper of his jeans.

When she lay completely naked before him, he knew he'd never seen a body as beautiful as hers. Unable to fight temptation, he leaned toward her, his greedy mouth targeting her nipples.

He sucked, nibbled and licked to his heart's content. And his hands, of their own accord, drifted slowly down her body, touching her waist, running circles around her belly button and moving even lower, toward the essence of her heat.

When he touched her womanly core, she tried to close her legs on his hands in surprise. "Let me, baby," he said softly, lifting his face from her breasts to gaze up at her. Using his hands, he reopened her legs, spreading them wide.

She moaned when he slid two fingers inside her wet center. He held her gaze as he stroked her, needing to see the play of emotions on her face. Pleasuring a woman had never meant so much to him and he loved the way her eyes dilated, the way her lips parted on breathless moans, the way flames of passion spread across her cheeks.

His fingers moved inside her swiftly, thoroughly. When her inner muscles clamped tight, he deepened his strokes until he couldn't take anymore. Her womanly scent aroused him. He had to taste her. He wouldn't be satisfied until his tongue delved into heated bliss.

"Enjoy," he whispered, before shifting his body and lowering his head between her legs. She tensed but his mouth quickly replaced his fingers and he gripped her hips to keep her steady. He swirled his tongue inside of her, loving her taste, loving the sounds of her lusty moans.

"Stern!"

Her body quivered beneath his mouth but he wouldn't let up or let go. He intended this day to be one of never-ending pleasure for her. It would be one he didn't ever want her to forget.

JoJo was convinced she was dying and Stern's mouth was to blame. All sorts of sensations shot through her, but she felt them mostly right beneath his mouth. He kept kissing her there, using his tongue to do all kinds of wicked things to her.

She was loving it.

She closed her eyes and lifted her hips, brazenly wanting more. Never in a million years would she have seen herself behaving this way. It was as if he had brought out something wild and untamed inside of her and all she could do was…*enjoy*…just like he'd told her to do.

Then she felt something building inside of her, a stirring pressure in her belly and even more erotic sensations where he kissed her. Then he did something with his tongue—she wasn't sure what—but she felt it all the way to her womb. Her body bucked and that building sensation exploded. She screamed his name, clenching his head and trying to clutch his shoulders. It seemed as if that overwhelming sensation had broken into fragments that she felt in every bone, every pore, every part of her.

Her body felt like molten liquid. She breathed his name, convinced she had died and accepting that if she

had died then it had been a damn good death. If she had
to go, this was the way to do it.

Even when he had removed his mouth from her, she
laid there. She was too weak to even open her eyes,
lift her hand, close her legs. She had to force herself to
breathe, slowly and deeply.

"JoJo."

In the deep recesses of her mind she heard Stern's
voice. With all the strength she could muster, she opened
her eyes, one at a time. Then she widened her gaze when
she saw he was removing his shirt.

Surely he didn't think she was up for anything else
after that amazing experience. She would need an entire
day to recuperate. Maybe two days. Possibly three. She
was new at this and he had to know there was no way
her body could rejuvenate itself this soon.

"Stern?" she called out when she heard him sliding
down his zipper.

"Yes, baby?"

"I can't move." Hopefully that would tell him something. Evidently it didn't. He kept removing his clothes
and was now easing his jeans down his legs, followed
by his briefs. And then she saw him. Oh, boy did she
see him. She had to widen her eyes to make sure what
she was seeing was real and not an illusion. Was it even
possible?

That's when something unexpected happened. A stirring spread through her. Her nipples hardened, her belly
quivered and the juncture of her legs began to throb. She
was zapped with renewed energy and she couldn't fathom
the source. All she knew was that suddenly she had the
strength to move her body. She eased up on her haunches.

"I thought you couldn't move."

A smooth smile touched the corner of his lips. He'd

known her body would come back to life. Of course he'd known. He was a pro at this. He'd known her body would blaze with desire all over again just by looking at him.

"I wanted to make sure I wasn't seeing things," she said, staring at what she knew was probably every woman's fantasy. But she was trying desperately to figure out how this was going to go down.

He evidently saw the deep concentration on her face. "It will be okay, trust me," he said softly.

She hoped so because her body was already affected by what she saw. Streaks of desire, tugs of sexual urges, patches of warmth began to consume her, seeming to touch every inch of her body, even those places she figured should still be recovering from her orgasm.

"Are you still on the Pill?"

She looked up into his eyes. "Yes."

There was no need to ask him how he knew. He'd picked up her prescription once or twice when she'd been ill. He also knew why the doctor had prescribed them for her. More than once Stern had held her hand when painful cramps had forced her into bed.

"I can still use a condom," he offered.

She tilted her head to study him once more below the waist. He was probably used to doing so, but it couldn't really be easy. "That's not necessary."

"You sure?"

She was certain she wanted to go through with this, but she still wasn't convinced it would work. "Yes, I'm sure."

"In that case." He slowly moved toward the bed, and she watched him, fascinated and nervous at the same time. He had a powerful stride, a magnificent body. He was definitely an alpha male. He watched her watching him and by sheer willpower alone her breath came from her lungs evenly. He had the physique of masculine physiques—tight abs, nice solid chest—but what held her attention was the engorged erection nested in a thick bed of curly hair.

Who would have thought Stern would one day have this kind of effect on her? She'd often wondered how her first time would be and with whom. Who would have thought that he would be the one? But he was, and she couldn't be happier. That's why a smile touched her lips.

When he reached the bed, she eased up on her knees and extended her arms out to him. And when he pulled her against that hard chest, she met his gaze and knew this was right. This was how it should be.

Capturing her mouth with his, he lowered them both to the bed. She should be familiar with his kisses by now, but she wasn't. She was a firm believer in his ability to design a kiss to give maximum pleasure. He kissed her deeply, thoroughly, taking possession and staking a claim.

Her fingers dug into his shoulders. The feel of her breasts pressed against his chest electrified every single cell in her body. Every kiss was better than the last. Her mouth had been made just for his.

He released her mouth only to begin kissing the side of her face and neck. And she knew the exact moment when he added his hands to the mix. His strokes on her thigh felt purely sensual. She closed her eyes as intense pleasure eased up her body. And when his mouth moved from her neck to her breasts, licking, sucking and nibbling, flames rushed through her.

His hands eased between her legs and she moaned out his name. "I want you, JoJo. I want you," he whispered. "You're wet and ready."

He eased up and slid his entire body over hers while

still gazing down at her. His hands entangled with hers by the side of her face. And then she felt it—his engorged erection pressing against her womanhood. His gaze remained locked with hers as he slowly slid inside of her, inch by incredible inch, and, amazingly, her body stretched to accommodate him.

"Just a little more to go," he whispered.

Sensations concentrated right there, where their bodies were connected. She tightened her inner muscles around him. "Ah, hell," he said, thrusting hard inside her, making her suck in a deep gasp of surprise.

"You okay?" he asked, looking down at her.

She felt him. He was in. All the way. Astonishing. "Yes, I'm okay." She was elated.

He then began moving, with slow, powerful thrusts that stimulated her in a way she'd never been stimulated before. His movements fueled her desire, created needs she'd never encountered, encouraged her to take what he was offering.

He lengthened his strokes. He went deeper and her inner muscles clamped down even more. He let go of her hands and gripped her hips, increasing his pace, establishing a rhythm that nearly pushed her over the edge.

JoJo gripped the bedspread as he began thrusting harder, going deeper. She moaned out his name as sensations whisked through her, withdrawing and then going back in again.

"Stern!"

She screamed his name and clutched his shoulders, lifting her hips to meet his. Over and over and over... then he bucked, threw back his head and growled her name. Her body exploded at the same time that his did. She seized his hips to hold him right where she needed him and she felt his release inside of her.

"JoJo!"

"Stern!"

And as their bodies stilled, he kissed her in an exchange that was bittersweet, passionate and intimate all rolled into one.

She knew she could never love him any more than she did at that very moment.

Twelve

To Stern's way of thinking, nothing hit the spot like good food, fine wine and a beautiful woman. And this evening he was enjoying all three. The sun was going down over the mountains and the trees reflected the autumn leaves in aspen gold, brilliant yellow and tinges of orange and red. From the deck, the sight was picturesque. Scenic. Vivid.

He shifted his gaze to JoJo. How would he describe her? Beautiful. Striking. Sexy. Yes, definitely sexy. She sat in the chair, sipping her wine and watching the view. She was wearing another dress, this one in a paisley pattern. He appreciated the low-cut neckline and how the shirred crossover bodice complimented her breasts. She looked as hot as she had earlier that morning in the kitchen.

The lower part of his body throbbed when he remembered the morning. After making love, they'd dozed off, waking up right before lunch to eat the breakfast they should have eaten earlier. Starving, they'd devoured the omelets with French toast, juice and coffee, then ravenous for each other again they'd gone back to bed and stayed there until their stomachs had sent another signal it was time to be fed.

They'd gotten up and showered together. He had grilled a couple of steaks and she had prepared the salad, selected the wine and set the table on the deck. It was a little chilly so he'd fired up the fire pit he'd had built on the deck for days just like this. The heat from the pit warmed them and made being outside enjoyable.

"It's hard to believe it's been a week."

He took a sip of his wine and glanced over at her. "A week?"

"Yes, since my makeover."

Yes, it had been a week and he doubted he would ever forget how she'd looked when she'd walked into the Punch Bowl. "So other than Carmichael calling to say he wanted his auto records transferred, you haven't heard from him?"

"No, and I don't expect to, either. He found out the hard way that he didn't impress me. I still find it hard to believe that he acted the way he did."

Stern didn't find it hard to believe, especially after what Sampson had shared with him. "So tell me. Do I impress you?"

She looked at him and smiled. "Yes, you impress me."

He reached over and touched her arm, liking the feel of her soft skin. "You impress me, too."

At that moment, he considered telling her he loved her, but he knew it was too soon. He needed to give her time. Give them time to become a couple. He thought of how often they'd shared an afternoon on the deck like this. But tonight things were different. They were officially lovers. And one day they would be husband and wife.

"Thanks for being patient with me today."

He chuckled. "You must have me mixed up with some-one else. I don't recall being patient. In fact, I almost ripped your dress off."

She chuckled. "You whipped it over my head before I even realized you were doing it. You have such practiced hands."

Stern thought about all the women he'd hooked up with over the years. His numbers weren't as outlandish as Riley's, Zane's or Derringer's, so he'd never really thought of himself as a ladies' man. He'd always been just a guy out for fun. He'd dated, never lied to a woman about his intentions and kept moving on.

He had enjoyed being single, had preferred not having to answer to anyone. He had actually cringed when the die-hard bachelors in his family got married.

Derringer had been the first a few years ago when he'd married Lucia, and now Derringer had settled down to the role of father and husband rather nicely. Riley was getting married at the end of the month and Zane over the Christmas holidays. Stern had understood Canyon's quick wedding last month because there had been a child involved, but for his other relatives, he just couldn't figure why any man would willingly give up his single status.

Now he did.

Once you'd fallen in love everything else became sec-ondary to the woman you desired above all else. Thanks to her father, JoJo was independent, and Stern had always admired that streak in her. He still did. But he wondered how she would adjust now that he was more than her best friend, now that he wanted to be more than her lover? How would she feel about him as a possible husband?

"So, what movie did you pick out for us?" she asked, breaking into his thoughts.

He glanced up. She had stood and was gathering their

dishes. His body stirred. Why was he reacting to her every time she moved? "What do you suggest? You know the kind that I prefer."

"And you know the kind I like," she countered.

Yes, he knew the kind. Once in a while he appeased her by watching some chick flick and then he normally fell asleep at some point before it was over. "We could play cards," he suggested. "Or chess."

"We played those the last time we were here. Where's that Scrabble game? We haven't played that in a while."

"And I don't want to work my brain to play it now." An idea came into his head. "I know a game I'm sure we haven't played in years. It's usually played with a group, but it should be interesting with just the two of us."

"What game is that?"

"Simon Says."

She gave him an incredulous look. "Simon Says?"

"Yes." She scrunched her forehead, giving his suggestion some thought. "How do we decide who gets to be Simon?"

"We can toss a coin. The rules are as follows. If you get to be Simon and can make me follow a command that's not Simon's, then I will be at your beck and call for the rest of the night. If you can't, then you will be at my beck and call."

"Beck and call?" she asked raising a brow.

"Yes, beck and call."

She gave him a slow smile as if the idea appealed to her. Evidently she saw a lot of possibilities in his suggestion. "And just how many commands are we talking about?"

"No more than twenty."

She nodded slowly before saying, "Okay, that will

work. Let me take these dishes into the kitchen and then we can meet in the living room. Just be ready."

Stern smiled. He would definitely be ready.

Stern won the coin toss and JoJo would have thought it was rigged if she hadn't been the one who'd tossed the coin. On top of letting her toss, he'd been nice enough to let her pick heads or tails. She would be hard-pressed to make the claim that something wasn't aboveboard.

So here she was, standing in the middle of the floor, waiting for Stern to issue the first command. She hadn't played this game in years and wondered what possessed him to think of it, although a part of her had an idea. In fact, with him standing a few feet in front of her with a silly grin on his face, she had more than an idea.

"Oh, yeah," he said as his smile deepened. "As in most Simon Says games, there is no talking. Just follow the command like you're supposed to, but only if Simon says you can."

"Whatever."

"All right, let's get started. Simon says hold up your right hand."

She followed that command.

"Put it down."

She kept her hand up. If he thought he was going to catch her with that one, he had another think coming.

"Simon says put it down."

She put her hand down.

"Put it back up."

She kept it down.

He smiled. She smiled back.

"Simon says stand on one leg."

She followed his command.

"Simon says go around once in a circle."

She frowned at him because it wasn't easy maneuvering that command and she had a feeling he knew it. She went around once in a circle.

"Simon says you can put your leg down."

She did.

"Put it back up."

She didn't. JoJo wasn't sure if he was keeping count but she was. So far he'd issued eight commands and she was still in the game. Twelve more to go and she would be home free. Already her mind was buzzing with the things she could have him do. Painting her toenails sounded pretty good.

"Simon says take off your clothes."

Her head jerked in his direction and she frowned. She had known he was up to no good. Just as she parted her lips to say something, he quickly spoke up. "Remember, if you talk you forfeit the game."

JoJo closed her mouth and frowned some more, thinking that he would pay dearly for this. When she was declared winner and he was at her beck and call, she'd not only make him paint her nails, she would also have him go out in the cold without a shirt and collect more firewood.

"Simon says he doesn't have all day," he said, grinning. "So I repeat, Simon says take off your clothes."

Glaring, she slowly eased down her side zipper before tugging the dress over her head. That left her standing in front of him wearing only her tangerine-colored bra and matching panties. If his intent had been to get her naked, why hadn't he just suggested strip poker?

"Nice," he said, raking his gaze over her. The heated look in his eyes warmed her body. Now she was glad that his girl cousins and sisters-in-law had talked her into getting rid of her white panties and bras and buying colorful matching sets.

"Simon says remove your bra and panties."

After removing her bra, she eased her panties down her legs.

"Slowly lick your bottom lip."

JoJo caught herself in time before doing that command. This was a mind game and she had to stay focused on what Stern was saying and not on how he was looking at her while she stood before him wearing not a stitch of clothes. She'd never felt this exposed, this vulnerable. Even when they'd made love earlier she had stayed under the covers, while he'd walked around the room unashamedly showing himself. Had he detected her uneasiness regarding putting her body on display?

Stern drew in a deep breath as a knot of desire tightened his chest. Heat sizzled through his veins, making his erection throb. Never had he seen such a beautifully made woman and he had known, when they made love that she had a problem showing her body.

Oh, he'd seen the tiny scar on the side of her hip, the one she'd gotten when she'd fallen off her skateboard at the age of fourteen. And then there was the sister scar from the same accident, located above it, near her waist. They weren't noticeable unless attention was drawn to them. Little did she know he thought she was exquisite. Perfect in every aspect. He wanted to show her that he could stand there and stare at her all day…even while his body was getting more aroused by the second.

"Come here."

When she didn't move, a slow smile touched his lips. He then said, "Simon says come here."

She slowly walked toward him. When she came to

a stop within a foot of him, he said, "Simon says undress me."

She stared at him for a minute before pulling his sweater over his head. Then she eased his belt through the loops before removing it completely and tossing it aside. Next was his jeans. She slowly eased down his zipper before crouching down to tug the pants, along with his briefs, down his legs. Lucky for her, he had removed his shoes earlier so all he had to do was step out of his jeans when she had worked them past his knees to his ankles.

Before standing back on her feet she was face-to-face with the swollen length of him. He hadn't planned to give the next command, but when she glanced up at him and he'd seen the clash of desire and curiosity in her gaze, he said in a husky tone, "Simon says taste it."

A smile touched her mouth before she parted her lips and slid him deep inside. He thought he would drop to his knees in pleasure. Instead, he threw his head back and released a guttural growl. His hands grabbed a fistful of her hair while she tasted him in a way no one ever had. Her curiosity made her bold, audacious and confident as she used her tongue to explore every single inch of him.

He was close, too close, and their game would be over before he had a chance to finish all his commands. Tightening his hold on her head, he uttered thickly, "JoJo stop."

When she kept right on with her torture he recalled what he needed to say. "Simon says stop."

She slid her mouth off him and stood to her feet with a satisfied grin. He inwardly chuckled. She knew exactly what she'd been doing, the little vixen. But he had no complaints.

He studied her as she stood in front of him, waiting for Simon's next command. She had no idea just how much he loved her, adored her. He intended to do everything within his power to make her realize just how much he wanted her to be a part of his life forever.

He grabbed one of the chairs from a nearby table and sat down. He glanced up at her. "Simon says straddle me."

She slowly eased her body into his lap, straddling his thighs. The warmth of her skin touched his and he breathed in her scent. He held her gaze as they sat face-to-face. "Simon says to take me inside of you."

She lifted her hips and shifted a little. He moaned when he felt his engorged shaft penetrating her wet flesh and he slid slowly inside of her. He had one more command left and he intended to make it last. It didn't matter that she'd won the game. All that mattered was that in the end they'd both get what they wanted.

He licked the side of her face right beneath her ear and whispered, "Simon says ride me hard."

She obeyed the command at once, rotating her hips, pumping on him. He drew in a sharp breath when she grabbed his shoulders and showed him just what her body could do.

He buried his face between her breasts before tilting his head to the side to take a nipple into his mouth. He grabbed her thighs as she gyrated her hips, her inner muscles clenching him. When he felt her body explode and she screamed his name, he tightened his hold on her, screamed her name and let the essence of his release blast off inside of her.

"JoJo!"

He thrust deep within her, exploding inside her a second time as sensations rushed through him. She trembled in his arms and he knew he was trembling, too. As their breathing slowly returned to normal, he held her in his arms. He needed the feel of her, chest to chest, hearts connected.

Stern whispered, "We need to take this to the bedroom, don't you think?"

She chuckled against the side of his face. "As long as you remember that, for the rest of the night, you're at my beck and call."

He drew in a deep breath. "I have no problem with that, sweetheart. No problem at all."

Thirteen

If anyone had asked, JoJo would have admitted that her life over the past few weeks had been perfect. While at the lodge, she and Stern decided they deserved another day and instead of leaving on Sunday, they'd left Monday evening, arriving back at her place before midnight.

He had spent the night at her place, and then she'd spent a night at his place. They'd been inseparable practically every night since, when he wasn't traveling.

She would also admit that making the transition from best friends to lovers had its perks. With him, she could be herself, the JoJo she'd always been. And she could also discover who else she wanted to be. She'd found she could be brazen, shamelessly so, and, at times, Stern would blatantly egg her on. She totally and thoroughly enjoyed it when he did.

It was hard to believe two weeks had passed since their decision to become best friends with benefits. Tonight, he was taking her to a fund-raising dinner for heart research, and she was happy about going with him. They'd gone out to dinner a few times, attended movies and football games, but this would be the first evening where they would be seen together at a public event as a couple. She was rather nervous about it.

Which was why she'd looked at herself in the mirror a dozen times since she'd finished dressing. She loved her gown and thought she looked striking in it. Stern had picked it out and purchased it for her. She had been surprised and elated when she had received the huge box.

When she'd pulled out the very flattering white gown, she'd been in awe. The dress gave the illusion that the person wearing it was a goddess. Silver beads ran the length of the gown but were only visible when she walked. It definitely made a stunning statement and the feel of the soft georgette on her skin was fabulous. And to think that he'd known her body measurements to a tee!

Really, she should not be surprised. He seemed to love touching her. He would spend time just running his hands all over her body, and she loved when he did it. Her independent side had made her offer to pay him for the gown, but he would not hear of it, telling her to consider it an early birthday present. And because her birthday was next month, she had conceded.

Her heart jumped when she heard her doorbell and she couldn't stop the smile that broke out on her face. After looking in the mirror one last time, she grabbed her purse off the table and moved toward the door.

The man she loved had arrived.

Aiden Westmoreland glanced over at his cousin. "JoJo looks simply breathtaking tonight, Stern."

Stern nodded, refusing to let his gaze leave JoJo as she danced around the ballroom with Derringer. "Thanks. Yes, she does."

He'd been in Los Angeles on business and had spotted it in the window in a boutique in Beverly Hills. As far as he was concerned, JoJo's name had been written all over it so he'd bought it for her.

"So what's going on with you, Aiden?" His cousin was the newest doctor in the family and had decided to do his residency at a hospital in Maine.

"Nothing, just hard at work. I needed this break."

"Did you?" Stern asked, taking a sip of his wine as he studied his cousin. He could remember when Aiden and his identical twin, Adrian, and their sister Bailey and Stern's brother Bane, were the terror of Denver. "So your being home has nothing to do with the fact that Jillian decided to come home this weekend, too?"

Stern inwardly chuckled when Aiden almost choked on his wine. He gave his cousin a couple of whacks on the back. "Wine go down the wrong pipe, Aiden?"

Aiden glared at him. "Did you have to hit me on the back so hard?"

"Yes, I thought it would knock some sense into you. I hope you know what you're doing with Jill. If you're trying to mess her over, then—"

"What do you think you know about me and Jill?"

"Only what I saw the last time you were home. I was out riding Legend Boy that morning you were supposed to take Jill to the airport. From what I'd heard from Pam, Jill was supposed to be there at five in the morning, which is why you had volunteered to take her. So I'm sure you can imagine my surprise when I saw you whip Jillian out of the car and into your arms that morning and carry her into Gemma's house." Gemma's house stood empty because she had married and moved to Australia.

"It's not what you think," Aiden said in his defense.

"I'm not the one you need to be telling that to. All I've got to say is that you'd better hope Pam and Dil don't find out what you're up to."

"I love her."

"Then why the sneaking around?"

Aiden didn't say anything for a moment. "You know Pam's plan for Jill. After she finishes medical school in the spring, Pam hopes she'll—"

"What does Jill want?" Stern interrupted to ask.

Aiden didn't say anything for a moment and then he responded, "She wants us to be together but doesn't want to disappoint Pam."

Stern shrugged. "Either way, the two of you should come clean and let everyone know how you feel."

"Like you've come clean and let everyone know how you feel about JoJo? I don't see you standing on the highest rooftop shouting out anything."

Aiden's words stirred Stern's gut because what his cousin had said was true. He hadn't told anyone how he really felt about JoJo, not even JoJo, but then most who truly knew him were probably well aware that he was a man purely smitten. But still…

"Sorry, I shouldn't have said that, man," Aiden said. "Everyone in the family knows how crazy you are about JoJo. Look over me tonight. I'm in a bad mood about Jill right now because we argued earlier. I want to go to Dil and Pam and tell them the truth, but she's against it. And that bothers me more than anything. I don't like deceiving them, but I'm doing it anyway."

"It sounds like you and Jill need to make some decisions."

And it seemed, Stern thought, that he needed to make some decisions, too.

* * *

JoJo strolled out of the ladies' room and walked right into someone blocking her way.

"Well, well, if it isn't the grease lady. You can take the woman out of the auto repair shop but you can never really get the grease off the lady. I'm sure there's grease somewhere on that body of yours."

Anger sliced through her. His insulting words were deserving of a slap to the face, but she refused to make a scene tonight like she'd done at the Punch Bowl. Besides, Walter Carmichael wasn't worth it. Deciding to ignore him and move on, she tried to walk past him. He reached out and grabbed her arm with force, jerking her to him.

"You embarrassed me that night at the Punch Bowl and you also straight out lied about your relationship with Westmoreland. Best friends, my ass. There's more going on between you two—anyone can see that. And I'm going to make sure you pay for being a tease."

"Get your hands off me before I knock your eyeballs out of their sockets."

He immediately let her go and she quickly walked off without looking back. She tried not to fume, but Walter had her riled. When she reentered the ballroom, she met Stern heading toward her.

"You okay?" he asked her in a voice filled with anger.

She studied his features. "Yes, why wouldn't I be?"

"Lucia said she saw a man grab for you when you came out of the ladies' room. I figured it was Carmichael since I saw him earlier. What did he say? What did he want?"

She thought about mentioning the threat Walter had made but decided against it. The man was all bluster, and the last thing she wanted was to ruin Stern's night like Walter had tried to ruin hers. Besides, she had handled it.

"Nothing and nothing. At least nothing worth mentioning. I shut him down. It's okay."

"It's not okay. If he manhandled you, then—"

"I took care of it," she said. "I don't need you handling my business."

He stared at her for a long minute and then asked softly, "Has it ever occurred to you that your business is my business?"

She shrugged. "No, because I don't recall that being part of the deal when it comes to being best friends with benefits."

"Then maybe we need to discuss just what our relationship entails," he said.

JoJo detected anger in his voice, and she couldn't understand why. Was Stern missing his role of ladies' man? He didn't seem to be, but she couldn't help but wonder, especially when she saw women vying for his attention. He'd always said that he enjoyed the chase.

She would admit she was a little annoyed at the number of women who had tried to make a pass at him tonight. Some so brazen it was ridiculous, going so far as to approach him as if JoJo wasn't there. Maybe some of them assumed she and Stern were still nothing more than best friends, but even when he'd placed his arms around her waist in a more intimate gesture and introduced her as his date, most gave her a haughty look as if to say, "Good luck trying to hold on to him."

"JoJo, are you listening to what I said?"

Honestly, she hadn't been. She did recall he'd said something about them needing to discuss what their relationship entailed. "If you think we need to talk, fine. But when it comes to Walter Carmichael, I can handle myself. I don't need you to fight my battles."

She then walked off.

* * *

Somehow Stern held his anger in check for the rest of the night, but he couldn't help noticing that things between him and JoJo were strained. She barely said anything on the drive home.

As soon as the door closed behind them at her place, he knew they had to talk. "What's bothering you, JoJo?"

She looked at him with fire flashing in her eyes. "Nothing's wrong with me other than the fact that you have some brazen ex-girlfriends. I've never met women so disrespectful."

He was well aware that jealousy had driven a few of those women tonight. They'd wanted to get a rise out of her. "I hope you didn't let their behavior get to you. When I saw what they were doing I did set them straight, didn't I?"

"Yes, you did, but…"

"But what?"

"Nothing."

He crossed his arms over his chest. "You've used that word a lot tonight, don't you think? And I know you. When you say 'nothing,' most of the time there is something. So come on, let's talk."

He tugged her over to the sofa and into his lap. "Now tell me."

She didn't say anything for a moment. "Before, you liked women. Lots of women. And you enjoyed the chase. Now you're stuck with dull little me. You must miss your old lifestyle."

Stern looked at her for a long moment, knowing she didn't have a clue. What she'd just said didn't come close to being factual. So maybe it was time he told her the truth. "I love you, JoJo."

She waved off his words. "Of course you love me and

I love you, which is why we've put up with each other all these years and—"

He placed a hand over her mouth to stop her from talking. "Listen to what I'm saying for a second. I love you. I love you the way a man and a woman love each other."

Stern was certain JoJo would have fallen out of his lap if he hadn't been holding her so tightly. Her eyes widened and her mouth dropped open as she stared at him. She then shook her head. "No, you can't love me that way."

"Why can't I?"

"Because that's the way I love you."

Now it was Stern's turn to be stumped, and he was speechless. He shifted JoJo's position so they were facing each other. He wanted to look into her face while they were talking. "Are you saying that you're in love with me…the same way I'm in love with you?" he asked her.

She shrugged. "I don't know. What way are you in love with me?"

He knew she hadn't asked to be funny but truly wanted to know. "I'm in love with you in the way where I think of you all the time, even when I'm at work. In the way where I think I smell you even when you aren't there. I'm in love with you in the way where you are the first person on my mind when I wake up in the morning and the last person on my mind before going to bed at night. In the way where having sex is now making love. And in the way where whenever I'm inside of you I want to go deeper and deeper because I want to be consumed by you and you by me. No matter what, I will always be here for you, even during those times when I know you can take care of yourself. Loving you makes me want to take care of you anyway."

JoJo had tears in her eyes. "I've never heard a declaration of love stated so beautifully." She swallowed. "When did you know?"

"To be honest with you, I'm not sure. I might have loved you forever. My family suspected I did, but it's only been revealed to me lately. Your fascination with Carmichael made me realize what you meant to me."

She nibbled on her bottom lip and then said, "I was only fascinated with Walter because of you. I thought I needed him."

Stern lifted a brow. "I don't understand. What do you mean? You needed him for what?"

He tensed and she wrapped her arms around his neck. "I noticed I was becoming attracted to you when we were together at the lodge in the spring. It was more than attraction, really. I knew I had fallen in love with you and it scared me because I'd never been attracted to a man before…and especially not to you. You were my best friend, and I couldn't fall in love with my best friend. So I came up with what I thought would be the perfect plan."

"Which was?"

"To find someone else to fall in love with."

A smile touched Stern's lips. "I don't think it works that way, JoJo."

"That's what I found out."

Stern didn't say anything for a moment. "So are you telling me that this whole Carmichael thing was a plan you concocted because you'd fallen in love with me and were trying to fight it by trying to fall in love with another man?"

"Yes. Sounds crazy, huh?"

Stern chuckled. "No crazier than the fact that I've been denying loving you, even when Zane called me out on it."

"He did?"

"Yes, more than once. Riley called me out on it, as

well. You and I did admit at the lodge that we were attracted to each other, but what we should have done was come clean with our true feelings."

"Yes, we should have. So let's do it now. Stern, I love you as my best friend, my lover and the man I will always want in my life."

A smile curved his lips. "And Jovonnie 'JoJo' Jones, I love you as my best friend, my lover and the woman I will always want in my life."

"Oh, Stern, I was afraid if you found out how I felt that I could lose you all together. And with all your brothers and cousins getting married, I was worried about you falling in love and that woman not accepting our close relationship and forcing you to cool things between us."

He nodded. "That crossed my mind, too, when you seemed so obsessed with Carmichael. I was afraid he would come between our friendship, and I couldn't let that happen."

Both of them were quiet for a few moments and then Stern said, "I wish I had leveled with you about my feelings before now, but maybe things happened as they should have for us."

She stared at him. "You mean becoming best friends with benefits?"

"Yes. But now we know the truth. What I need you to understand is that loving someone means caring for that person, comforting that person, being their protector and their strength whenever they need it. I know all of your skills as a marksman, a karate champ and an archer, but that doesn't eliminate my desire to look after you. To want to protect you. And those times that I do want to protect you, just humor me, okay."

She smiled. "Okay."

He then leaned forward and kissed her with a hunger

and need he felt throughout his body. The connection with her was different now because he knew how she felt and she knew how he felt. When she quivered in his arms, he tightened his hands around her waist.

Moments later, he pulled back and forced air into his lungs before taking her mouth again in a kiss that was hungrier than before. Then, suddenly, the need to make love to her was fierce. Intense. Extreme. Powerful.

Stern stood up from the sofa with her in his arms. His destination was the bedroom upstairs, but he only made it to the wall near the staircase and pressed her against it. "I can't go any farther," he moaned, taking her lips again.

He put his hands everywhere, but mostly underneath her gown. When he'd first seen the gown he'd liked it, but now there was too much of it. He finally found the zipper in the back and with practiced hands slid it down. Then he shifted his body away from her just enough to grip the gown at her shoulders and quickly yank it off her.

He heard her suck in a deep breath. "Stern, can you slow down? You're going to ruin my dress."

"No, I can't slow down and I'll buy you another one."

He went still when he saw what she was wearing beneath her gown. A sexy white lace garter belt set with matching thong and back seam stockings. Stern was convinced he'd never seen anything or anyone so sensual in his entire life. "Nice," he said on a tortured moan.

"I'll be sure to let your cousins and sisters-in-law know how much you appreciate it. Just another thing they talked me into buying when we went shopping earlier this month."

"I'll make sure they take you shopping more often. Now, I'm taking it off you."

"I think that was the idea."

In no time at all, Stern had removed every stitch of

her clothing. Not to be undone, JoJo stripped him naked, too. Beginning with his tux jacket, which she shoved off his shoulders, she removed all his clothes. "Now, we're even."

"If that makes you happy," he said, lifting her off her feet and pressing her back against the wall once more. He smiled up at her. "I so enjoy getting into you."

She returned his smile. "And I so enjoy you getting into me."

With that said, he widened her legs with his knee before sliding his engorged shaft inside her, not stopping until he was as deep as he could get. She felt tight. She felt right.

She wrapped her legs around him as he moved, thrusting, filling her, withdrawing and then filling her again. Over and over. Her scent overwhelmed him, stimulating him, and the feel of her soft skin against his swamped his senses. The sounds of her moans only made his body want more.

He tried to slow down and make it last, but then she'd clamp her inner muscles, overpowering him with sensation. He was close, but he refused to climax without her.

He sucked a breast between his lips. She arched her body in a perfect bow while crying out her pleasure. The heels of her feet dug into his back, her fingernails plowed into his shoulder, but all he could feel was the ecstasy of being inside of her.

And then she screamed his name. His mouth left her breast to claim her lips and there it stayed, even when his body jerked from the force of his own orgasm.

He felt more than just love for her. He adored her, cherished her. He would always and forever honor her.

When he slowly disconnected their bodies and eased her legs down, it was only to lift her back into his arms.

"I think we were headed this way before we got side-tracked," he said, moving up the stairs.

"Getting sidetracked can be a good thing," she whispered, placing kisses on his chest.

When they reached her bedroom, they fell on the mattress together, fully intent on making this a night they would both remember for a long time.

Fourteen

JoJo glanced over at the clock when she got up from her desk to pour another cup of coffee. It was close to ten. It had been a long time since she had worked this late at the shop. But it was the end of the month and paperwork had to be completed. Due to federal regulations regarding hazardous wastes, air emissions and wastewater, she had a ton of reports to finalize. It seemed there were more this month than the last. Wanda had stayed as late as seven, but she had a date with her ex and had to leave.

Stretching her body, JoJo took a sip of coffee. It wasn't as good as Stern's but it would do. She couldn't help but smile when she thought of her best friend turned lover. It seemed that after declaring their love for each other last week, everything was falling in place.

They'd decided not to make any definite plans for their future until after Riley and Alpha's wedding. The entire Westmoreland family was excited about the upcoming wedding and expected many of their cousins from out of town to begin arriving this weekend. She had met most of them at one time or another, and she looked forward to seeing them again.

As soon as she sat back down at her desk her cell phone rang and she felt giddy all over when she saw the caller was Stern. He and Canyon had left two days ago for Miami to finalize a deal, and they weren't expected back until sometime tomorrow morning.

She clicked on her phone. "Hello."

"Hello, beautiful."

She smiled. "You wouldn't call me that if you could see me. I'm still at the shop."

"The shop? Why so late?"

"Reports. I have to keep the government happy. I miss you."

"I miss you, too. But guess what."

"What?"

"Canyon and I finalized everything and decided to return home early."

She sat up straight. "How early?"

She could hear his chuckle. "Tonight. Our plane just landed."

"You're back in Denver?" she asked, unable to contain her excitement.

"Yes. Canyon has gone to get the car. I was going to have him drop me off at your place, but you won't be there."

Already she was placing the papers on her desk in a stack. "Wanna bet? I'm leaving now so I'll make it home before you do."

"Um, I don't want to come between you and Uncle Sam."

"I'll finish the reports tomorrow." Just then she heard a crash. "Hold on, Stern. I think I heard something," she said, getting up from her desk.

"Wait! You're there alone?"

"Yes."

"Then stay put and call the police."

JoJo rolled her eyes. "Stern, I can handle—"

"I know you can, but humor me. Canyon just pulled up and we're headed there. We're less than ten minutes away."

JoJo let out an exasperated sigh. Only if they flew. "The alarm is on. It's probably nothing but a stray cat that somehow got locked up inside. It's happened before."

"I know, but I prefer being the one to check it out to make sure. Is your office door locked?"

"No."

"Then lock it and stay put."

Rolling her eyes, she left her seat to go lock the door just as the door crashed open.

"Walter!"

Walter?

Stern went still. He'd clearly heard the name she'd called out but now all he heard was muffled voices. Then her phone went dead. "JoJo? What's going on? You still there?"

When he didn't get a response, he punched in the emergency number. An operator picked up immediately. "I'd like to report a break-in at the Golden Wrench Auto Repair Shop. I was talking to the owner when a man named Walter Carmichael burst into her office. Carmichael has a history of harassing women."

Chills went up Stern's spine when he remembered what sounded like JoJo's door bursting open. "This is Stern Westmoreland," he said when the operator asked that he identify himself.

After hanging up the phone, he glanced over at Canyon, who was driving. Canyon caught his eye and then pressed his foot on the gas and sped down the interstate.

"I heard. We're on our way," Canyon said. "I just hope we get to the shop before JoJo takes the man apart. Evidently, he doesn't know who he's dealing with."

Anger consumed Stern. "Evidently."

"Take your filthy hands off me, Walter."

"Not until I'm good and ready. And you have a lot of nerve calling me filthy, grease lady."

JoJo drew in a deep breath, trying to control her anger. Otherwise, she would break every bone in his body. She still might. She had been so shocked at seeing him that she'd hadn't had time to defend herself. He'd quickly dived at her and grabbed her, knocking her hard against the desk and sending her cell phone flying to the floor. She wondered if Stern was still on the line. Had he heard anything? Was he calling the police?

"Why are you here, Walter? What do you want?"

"I warned you that I would make you pay for being a tease. You owe me a night and I'm getting it. It doesn't matter to me if I have to take it."

She'd like to see him try. Did he really think he would force himself on her and get away with it? "You're willing to risk your reputation, your job, your—"

"My old man will handle you like he did all the others."

JoJo swallowed. "What others?"

"All those women who tried bringing charges against me, as if they didn't enjoy what I did to them. But Dad proved they all had a price, which I'm sure you do, too. My old man will pay up. He always does, to keep things quiet." Walter then made the mistake of shoving her away from him before shouting, "Now take off your clothes!"

Now he'd really made her mad. Thinking about those other women, who had been at his mercy, and his father, who had bought them off, really had her blood boiling. "Take off my clothes? For you? Don't hold your breath," she snarled.

She saw anger flash in his eyes. He seemed furious that she had the nerve to refuse him. Intense anger distorted his face as he moved toward her. "No problem, I'll take them off myself."

She noticed he didn't have any kind of weapon. Apparently he assumed he could handle her with his bare hands. "Stop, Walter!" she said, issuing her warning. "I don't want to hurt you."

He laughed hard. "You can't hurt me, but I intend to hurt you."

He lunged for her.

Canyon, Stern and a patrol car arrived at the Golden Wrench at the same time and everyone was out of their cars in a flash. Stern saw one of the officers was Deputy Pete Higgins, Derringer's best friend. They were racing toward the front of the building when they heard a chilling scream…from a man.

Canyon glanced over at Stern and a wry smile touched his lips. "Sounds like we're too late."

"The bastard got what was coming to him," Stern said angrily.

The lock on the entry door had been jimmied. With guns drawn, the two officers cautiously made their way inside the building. Ignoring the officers' orders to stay back, Canyon and Stern were right behind them.

The door to JoJo's office was wide-open, barely hang-

ing on by the hinges. When they walked inside they
found Walter Carmichael in the middle of the floor, holding his crotch and sobbing like a baby. A cool, calm and
collected JoJo sat behind her desk working on her reports.

She glanced up at them and smiled sweetly. "I stayed
put just like Stern told me to do."

More patrolmen arrived on the scene, reports were
taken and Walter would be taken to the emergency room.
While he lay on the stretcher, still sobbing, Stern walked
over to him.

"Didn't you know that besides being a black-belt
champ JoJo's also a marksman? You're lucky she didn't
shoot you. She's also a skilled archer. Can you imagine
how it would feel if she'd used a bow and arrow?"

Stern paused to let his words sink in before saying,
"You're going to jail for what you tried to do. Just in case
your old man's money gets you off, I suggest you not
come back this way. JoJo holds grudges."

When Stern saw stark fear in the man's eyes, he
couldn't help but chuckle before walking off to where
JoJo was giving a final report to Pete.

"Can I take her home now?" Stern asked.

"In a minute," Pete said, frowning. "I'm trying to figure out how Carmichael got past your alarm system."

"My new guy," JoJo said. "Walter bragged about paying my new guy, Maceo Armstrong, money to report
whenever I'm here working late. And he paid extra to
have Maceo cut a wire in the alarm system."

Pete nodded. "You got Armstrong's address?"

"Yes. It's on file in my office."

"Good. We're going to pick him up."

An hour later, Stern and JoJo were at her place. She

was in the shower and Stern was in the kitchen pouring glasses of wine. He entered the bedroom just as she walked out of the bathroom wearing a velour bathrobe.

"Here, you need this," he said, handing her a glass of wine. "You deserve it."

She took a sip and smiled at him. "Mmm, delicious." She then sat down on the edge of the bed. "Walter got just what he deserved, you know."

Stern chuckled. "You'll never be able to convince him of that. It was pathetic to hear a grown man cry."

She shrugged. "Like I said, he deserved it. The nerve of him, thinking he could rape me without me doing anything about it."

"He might not be able to walk again," Stern said, smiling, liking the idea. "Or have sex," he added, liking that idea even better. He paused and took a sip of his wine. "I hope I never make you mad."

"You can handle me."

Stern thought about what she'd said. Yes, he could handle her, but after a night like tonight, he was glad she could also handle herself. "I propose a toast," he said, lifting up his wine glass.

"To what?"

"To whom. Your daddy, who had the insight to raise a daughter who could take care of herself."

JoJo thought about what he'd said and got kind of misty-eyed. She held up her glass and clinked it against his.

"And to you, Stern. For being a man who knows me, inside and out, and who loves me anyway. And for being a man who lets me know it's okay to be myself and ask for what I want. That means a lot."

After taking a sip of wine, she placed her glass on the

table beside the bed, stood and pushed her robe off her shoulders. "I think you know what I want now."

Yes, he knew.

Stern pulled her into his arms and kissed her hard and deep.

Epilogue

Tucking her hand into Stern's, JoJo sat beside him in the packed church as everyone watched Riley and Alpha join their lives together as man and wife. It was a beautiful ceremony and, not surprisingly, the bride, who was an event planner, had arranged the entire thing with help from the Westmoreland women. It had truly been a storybook wedding. The groom was devastatingly handsome and the bride was outrageously beautiful.

When JoJo had woken up that morning to an empty bed, she'd later found Stern standing outside on her patio staring up at the sky and drinking coffee. She'd tightened her robe around her before opening the French doors to step outside and join him.

He'd turned when he saw her and smiled.

"You okay?" she asked him.

This was the last weekend in September and the weather was turning colder. The wind blowing off the mountains was brisk.

"Yes. I was thinking about just how blessed the Westmorelands are, especially the men. They have been lucky to find women who complement them, women worthy of loving forever. I see my brothers and how happy they are with their wives and families, but I never entertained the thought of finding a woman to share that same happiness with me. Now I know why."

She glanced up at him. "Why?"

"Because I had that woman by my side all along. You were my best friend and the woman destined to be a part of my life forever, as my soul mate, my wife…the mother of my children."

Tears stung JoJo's eyes. "What are you saying, Stern?"

He turned to her and smoothed her hair back from her face. "That I love you and want to marry you. I want you to share my name and be with me always. Will you marry me, JoJo?"

She smiled through her tears. "Yes! Yes! I'll marry you."

Loud clapping intruded into JoJo's thoughts and brought her back to the present. The minister had just presented Riley and Alpha as man and wife and everyone was on their feet, clapping and cheering. Riley swept his bride into his arms and walked out of the church. It had been a beautiful wedding and now it was time to leave for the reception.

Still holding her hand, Stern led her outside where they joined Canyon and his wife, Keisha, and their son, Beau, along with Zane and his fiancé, Channing. Zane and Channing would be tying the knot around the holidays, so another Westmoreland wedding would be taking place in a few months.

JoJo and Stern hadn't yet announced their engagement to anyone, preferring to let Riley and Alpha enjoy their day without any new family news.

Stern leaned down and kissed her on the cheek. "What was that for?" she asked.

"Being you."

"Oh." She leaned up on tiptoe and returned the favor.

"And what was that for?" he asked her.

She gave him a bright smile. "For not just seeing me on the outside but appreciating the inside, too."

He leaned down and whispered sexily, "And I do enjoy the inside."

She was sure her cheeks darkened.

"Come on," he said, tightening her hand in his. "Let's go talk to my cousins from Atlanta who are chatting with Dillon and Ramsey. I think I'll ask Thorn to build us a couple of bikes."

JoJo liked the idea. "Okay. Who is that young woman with Thorn and his wife, Tara?"

"That's Tara sister. She might be relocating to the area from Florida, and Thorn and Tara wanted her to meet all of us."

JoJo nodded. "She's very pretty."

"Come on, let me introduce you," Stern said.

"All right."

As they walked toward the group, for some reason, the thought of Walter Carmichael crossed her mind. He was still in jail awaiting trial. Unfortunately, the Carmichael family had suffered a major setback when the judge had denied bail. Even Walter's father's money hadn't helped him. JoJo believed Walter had a mental illness and she hoped he would get the help he needed.

Maceo Armstrong had gotten into trouble for assisting Walter. And then the young man had gone on to confess that he had been the reason for all her missing inventory. He had been stealing auto parts from her and selling them. She had liked him and had been very disappointed in his duplicity.

Before they reached the group of cousins, Stern stopped walking, pulled her into his arms and spun her around. "You're beautiful and I love you," he said, placing her back on her feet.

She laughed, catching her breath. "And I love you, too."

He leaned down and said, "I have plans for you later."

She smiled up at him, the man who held her heart. "And I definitely have plans for you."

* * * * *

Don't miss Aiden's and Adrian's stories,
coming soon!
Only from Brenda Jackson and Harlequin Desire!

BACHELOR UNTAMED

To the love of my life, Gerald Jackson, Sr.

To all the members of the
Brenda Jackson Book Club. This one is for you.

Apply your heart to instruction,
and your ears to words of knowledge.
—*Proverbs* 23:12

Prologue

"Go ahead and do it, El. You've been dying to kiss him forever. Do it. I dare you."

Ellie Weston rolled her eyes at her best friend Darcelle Owens's statement. She was used to Darcy getting them in trouble with her dares. But, this was one dare that she was more than tempted to carry through.

The two of them stood hiding in the thicket of trees and bushes while spying on the guy Ellie had had a crush on forever. It didn't matter that Uriel Lassiter was twenty-one to her sixteen and a senior in college. All that mattered was how her heart started beating fast in her chest whenever she saw him.

"Come on, El. He's leaving tomorrow to go back home, and you're going to hate yourself for a missed opportunity. This will probably be the last time you'll see him until who knows when. He graduates next spring and will probably never come back here for the summer."

Ellie felt a thump in the pit of her stomach and pondered Darcy's words. With Uriel graduating from college next year, he probably wouldn't be coming back to the lake, at least not as often. Uriel's parents owned a summerhouse right next door to her aunt's home on Cavanaugh Lake, a few miles outside of Gatlinburg. For an entire month during the summer she would visit her aunt, and it was only then when she would see Uriel. The thought that she might not ever see him again was too painful to think about.

She could recall only one summer that he hadn't come, and that had been last year. She'd heard that he and his five godbrothers had taken a trip abroad that summer. It had been the most boring summer of her life.

Ellie glanced over at Darcy and whispered, "If I take you up on your dare, what do I get?"

Now it was Darcy's turn to roll her eyes. "I would think to lock lips with your dreamboat would be enough. But since you want to be greedy, if you take me up on my dare you can have my autographed picture of Maxwell."

Ellie's eyes widened. She had been scheduled to go to that Maxwell concert with Darcy, but had come down with the mumps and missed it. "You'll risk the chance of losing that?" she asked, since she knew what a big Maxwell fan Darcy was. She probably sang "Fortunate" in her sleep.

"Yes, but only if the kiss lasts for more than a minute. I don't want to see just a peck on the lips, El. You're going to have to make him kiss you for a long time."

Ellie was aghast. How was she supposed to do something like that, when she'd never kissed a boy before? "Any bright ideas how to pull that off?"

Of course Miss-Know-It-All Darcy would have all the answers. "You're going to have to use your tongue. I heard Jonas tell one of his friends that he liked kissing girls who used their tongue."

Ellie lifted a brow. Jonas was Darcy's oldest brother,

who was a senior in high school, so he would know. All the girls back home in Minneapolis just loved Jonas and he loved all the girls. "And he said guys actually liked it?" Ellie asked, to be sure.

Darcy nodded her head. "Yes, I heard him say it. He and Leroy Green didn't know I was hiding under the bed."

Ellie knew better than to ask Darcy what she was doing hiding under her brother's bed. "Well, okay. But if he doesn't want to keep his mouth on mine I can't make him. But I'll try."

Darcy's eyes brightened. "You're going to do it?"

Ellie released a deep breath. "Yes, but you can't make a sound."

"Okay, but remember the kiss has to last for at least a whole minute."

Ellie frowned. "You don't have to remind me."

Uriel glanced to the side when he heard the sound of footsteps crunching on fallen leaves.

Ellie Weston.

Good grief! She was only sixteen, but last week when he had arrived to join his parents at the lake, he hadn't been able to believe how much she changed since two summers ago. She was no longer a tall, lanky girl, but now she had curves in places that he couldn't help notice.

She had been wearing a pair of shorts and a blouse and she looked quite stunning. The fitted top she wore outlined breasts that were full and perfectly formed. She had the tiniest waist he'd ever seen, and her hips flared out rather nicely, to join a pair of gorgeous long legs.

He swallowed, trying not to notice how she was dressed now. She was wearing another pair of shorts and they were way too skimpy for his comfort. And the way her blouse fit exposed a sliver of her bare stomach.

He frowned, trying to deny the attraction. He was five years older than her, and shouldn't be thinking about her this way. Damn, but he could remember when she was a kid in braces climbing trees. Now he could imagine them hooking up as a couple. He shook his head slightly to clear his thoughts.

"Hey, Uri. What are you doing?" she asked, coming closer.

He shifted his gaze from her legs to glance out over the lake. "Fishing. Where's your friend?" He nearly let his fishing rod fall in the water when she came and sat on the pier beside him.

"Oh, Darcy's taking a nap. We were both up late last night."

He forced his gaze to stay straight ahead. "Why aren't you taking a nap, too?"

"Umm, not sleepy. I was taking a walk, and then I saw you and thought I'd come keep you company."

He was about to tell her not to do him any favors, but decided against it. She had no way of knowing he was seeing her in a whole new light. Her aunt, Ms. Mable, would probably kill him if she knew what kind of light that was.

"So, how is college?" she asked him.

He shrugged. "It's okay. What about you? Are you looking forward to the end of the summer to head back to school?"

She giggled. It wasn't a kid's giggle, either. It had a sensuous twang to it. At least he thought so. "Heck, no. I don't like school. I can't wait to get out," she said.

He heard her words and recalled feeling that way when he'd been her age. "Don't you have plans to go to college?" he couldn't help but ask.

"No. I want to get married."

Now that got his attention and he couldn't help but

glance over at her. Then he wished he hadn't. She had brought her face close to his. Too close. He could actually see the dark irises staring back at him. That cute little mole on the side of her nose was even more visible. And the shape of her lips... When had they gotten so full? So well defined?

He swallowed, tried forcing his gaze back to the lake, but his eyes refused to budge. "Why do you want to get married?"

She smiled and his gut pulled so tight he could barely breathe. "I want to get married because..."

Her voice had lowered and he could barely hear her words. And was he imagining things, but had she just inched her face a little closer to his? Or was he the one leaning in closer?

"Because of what?" He somehow found his voice to ask her, and couldn't stop his gaze from dropping from her eyes to her lips.

"Because I want to know how it is to sleep with the man I love. To feel his body beside me in bed. To become acquainted with his lips on mine."

He felt himself leaning in closer to her. "Aren't you too young to be thinking of such things?" he managed to ask in a voice so deep he barely recognized it as his own.

"No." And then in a move that was totally unexpected, she leaned over and plastered her lips to his.

The first thought that came to his mind was to push her away, but her lips felt so soft and sweet that he found himself entranced. His body shuddered as he sank his hand into her hair, deepening the kiss.

"That's it, El. Hang on in there! You've made the one-minute mark, so now you can go for the gusto!"

Uriel jerked up, and in the process nearly tumbled them both into the water. He had to catch his breath before he could say anything, and then he looked from Ellie Weston and her thoroughly kissed lips, to her friend, the one that should have been napping.

He narrowed his gaze, first at the other girl and then at Ellie. "What's going on, El?" he asked in a rough voice.

Before Ellie could reply, Darcy spoke up, grinning proudly, "You kissed her for one minute and twelve seconds, so she won the dare."

Those words hit him hard in the chest. That kiss had been part of a dare. He had been the butt of these girls' joke? That very idea made his blood boil and intense anger rushed through him. He glanced over at Ellie. "Is that true, El?"

Her face had tinted in embarrassment, and she looked everywhere but at him, mostly glaring over at her friend. "I asked you a question, El," he said, when she didn't say anything.

She drew in a deep breath and then glanced back over at him and said. "I can explain, Uri."

He shook his head. "No explanations. Just answer the question. Was that kiss about a dare between you and your friend here?"

"Yes, but—"

Not giving her a chance to say anything else, he snatched up his fishing rod and angrily began walking off the pier. He got halfway, turned back around and said directly to Ellie, "The next time I come to Cavanaugh Lake, I'm going to make sure that you aren't here."

And then he turned around and kept walking, while wishing that he could forget the sweet taste of her lips.

One

Ten years later

"To Flame, with all my love. D."

Ellie Weston studied the elegant sprawling handwriting across the bottom of a framed picture on the wall in her aunt's bedroom.

She lifted a brow. Aunt Mable had probably purchased the painting at one of those garage sales she'd enjoyed getting up on Saturday mornings to drive forty miles into Knoxville to attend. In fact, Ellie had noticed several new paintings in all of the bedrooms as well as the living room. However, this particular one caught Ellie's eye because it wasn't one she would have expected her unmarried seventy-year-old aunt to be attracted to.

Ellie studied the painting some more. It was a colorful piece of art that showed a faceless but very naked couple in a risqué embrace. So much in fact, that upon closer study it appeared they were having sex.

She felt a heated blush stain her face as she stepped back and glanced around. It seemed that rather recently

her aunt had gotten a new bedroom suite—a king-size
Queen Anne four-poster bed in beautiful cherry mahog-
any. The bedroom suite had a romantic flair that Ellie
liked. And there was a matching desk in one section of
the room with, of all things, a computer. When had her
aunt entered the computer age? Ellie hadn't been aware
she'd owned one. If she'd known, they could have been
staying in contact by email.

To Ellie, her aunt's two-story house had always seemed
too large for one person. It had a spacious layout that
included a huge living room, a bathroom, dining room
and eat-in kitchen downstairs, and four bedrooms and
three bathrooms upstairs. The wood paneling had been
removed and the walls had been painted an oyster-white.
The bright color actually made the entire interior appear
larger, roomier.

Had it been five years since she had last visited her
aunt here? Although she had stopped coming to the lake
house when she'd turned twenty-one, she and her aunt
still got together every year when she could convince
Aunt Mable to come visit her in Boston, where she had
moved after college. It had worked well for the both of
them. It gave her aunt a chance to leave the lake and visit
someplace else, and it gave Ellie a chance to not dwell
on the most embarrassing memory of all her visits here.

She had stopped speaking to her best friend Darcy for
an entire month after that kissing incident with Uriel Lassiter, regardless of the number of times Darcy had told
her how sorry she was for getting carried away with her
excitement. In the end, Ellie had accepted full responsi-
bility for ever accepting Darcy's dare in the first place.

And it was her fault that Uriel had kept his word and
had made sure their paths never crossed at Cavanaugh
Lake again.

She had not seen him in ten years. He had been out of the country, unable to attend her aunt's funeral last month, but her parents had mentioned getting a nice floral arrangement from him.

Ellie shook her head, remembering that Uriel's parents had gotten a divorce two years ago. Who would have thought the Lassiters would ever split? And according to her parents, Carolyn Lassiter was now involved with a much younger man, one only a few years older than her own son.

The last Ellie had heard, according to Aunt Mable before she'd died, was that Anthony and Carolyn Lassiter were in court, battling over who would get ownership of the lake house. As a result of the bitter embroilment, the courts had ruled that the house should be put up for sale and the proceeds split. Aunt Mable had no idea who'd bought the lake house next door and hadn't met her new neighbor before she'd died.

Deciding she needed something to eat before she began unpacking, Ellie left her aunt's bedroom and began walking down the stairs, remembering how her aunt, who hadn't been sick a day in her life, had died peacefully in her sleep. Although Ellie knew she would miss her, she felt it was befitting for her to go that way—without any type of sickness to destroy her mind and body. And from what she could tell, although Aunt Mable had probably been lonely at times living out here at the lake, her aunt was happy. At least she had appeared happy and content the last time Ellie had seen her. And she had left everything she owned to her one and only grandniece. Ellie was overwhelmed by such a grand gesture of love.

She walked into the kitchen and immediately noticed the new cabinets. It seemed her aunt had given the house a face-lift, one that had been beautifully done. There were new marble countertops, stainless steel appliances and polished tile floors.

The drive from Boston had been a long one, and Ellie had stopped by one of those fast-food places to grab a hamburger, fries and a shake before getting off Interstate 95. Then, once she had reached Gatlinburg, she stopped at a market to pick up a few things for dinner, deciding that later in the week she would take an inventory of what she would need for her month-long stay at the lake. It was a beautiful day, the first week in August, and the first thing Ellie intended to do tomorrow was open up the windows to air out the place. The living-room window was huge, wall-to-wall, floor-to-ceiling and provided a lot of sunlight and a beautiful view of Cavanaugh Lake, no matter where you stood or sat.

Crossing the kitchen floor, she opened the pantry and wasn't surprised to find it well stocked. Her aunt was known to prepare for the winter months well in advance. Settling on a can of soup for dinner, she proceeded to warm it on the stove.

Standing at the kitchen sink, she glanced through the trees to look at the house that used to be owned by the Lassiters. She could easily recall how often she would stand in this very spot, hoping for a glimpse of Uriel when he would come outside. But she had discovered long ago that the best view from her aunt's bedroom window was that of the backyard and pier.

A half hour later, Ellie had finished her soup and was placing her bowl in the sink when she glanced out the window and saw that a car was parked in front of the house next door. She lifted a brow, wondering if perhaps the new owners had decided to spend some time at their lake place.

Ellie had parked her car in the garage, so they would not know someone was in residence at her place. Her place. That seemed so strange, when this home had be-longed to Aunt Mable for so long.

She was about to turn around and go upstairs to start unpacking when something caught her eye. She drew in a tight breath as she leaned closer toward the window to make sure her eyesight wasn't playing tricks on her.

The man who had come to stand outside on the front porch, while talking on a cell phone, was older-looking now, but was just as handsome as she remembered. She was twenty-six now, which meant he was thirty-one.

She might be mistaken, but it appeared he had gotten taller. She figured his height to be at least six foot three. The T-shirt he was wearing covered broad shoulders and his jeans were molded to firm thighs. Her gaze slid to his face. The color of dark chocolate, his features were and always had been striking, a pleasure to look at.

Ellie scanned his face, from the thick brows that can-opied a pair of beautiful dark eyes, to the long, angular nose that sat perfectly in the center of his face and more than highlighted the sensuous shape of his lips, to the perfect lines of his jaw. Strong. Tight. Every feature was totally flawless. Him standing there in his bare feet made her think of a chocolate marshmallow all ready to eat.

The thought of that made her stomach stir, generated a tingling sensation even lower, and it made the nipples of her breasts that were pressing against her blouse feel achy. She quickly moved away from the window, crossed the room and sat down at the table.

Uriel Lassiter had returned to the lake house, and the one thing she knew for certain was that he hadn't made sure she wasn't there.

Uriel threw his head back and laughed. He was still in shock. One of his closest friends from college, who was also one of his investment partners, had called to let him know he was getting married. He just couldn't believe it. Who in their right mind would have thought that there was a woman somewhere capable of winning the heart of Donovan Steele. *The* Donovan Steele. The man who always claimed he wanted to be buried wearing a condom, because even then he knew he would be hard.

Uriel had the pleasure of meeting Donovan's woman a few weeks ago. With a PhD and a professorship at Princeton, Natalie Ford had just as much brains as she had beauty. And she *was* a beauty. That was one of the first things Uriel had noticed that night when she had come storming into the Racetrack Café, ready to give Donovan hell about something. Evidently, their disagreement had gotten resolved, since Donovan was now talking about a wedding.

"Hey, Don, we're going to have to get together when I return to Charlotte," he said. "And we'll make it one hell of a celebration. Have the two of you set a date yet?"

"We're having a June wedding," Donovan replied easily. "After we marry, she'll take a sabbatical to write another book and work on several projects with NASA. You can't imagine how happy my family is."

Uriel could just imagine. Donovan, the youngest of the Steele brothers, headed the Product Administration Division of the Steele Corporation, and Uriel was Vice President of Lassiter Industries, the telecommunications company his father, Anthony Lassiter—CEO and president—had founded over thirty-eight years ago.

Although both he and Donovan had major roles at their family owned businesses, years ago, right out of college, they had partnered in a co-op. They had started out by flipping real estate, and later moved on to small businesses. The co-op had proven to be highly successful, and they had moved on to even larger investments, like the publishing company they had recently purchased.

Two years ago, Uriel's father had taken a leave of absence due to stress and depression brought on when the wife he'd been happily married to for over thirty-five years asked for a divorce. That had forced Uriel to take over the day-to-day operations of Lassiter Industries.

Uriel was glad his dad had finally snapped out of his depression, decided life was too short to drown in self-pity over a woman whom you still loved but didn't want you, and had returned to Lassiter Industries sharper than ever. Uriel had quickly turned things back over to him and decided to take some much needed R and R. The lake house was his first choice. His parents had been forced to sell it, so he decided to be the buyer.

"While you were in Princeton yesterday, I signed my part of the paperwork, so that the consulting firm could proceed with our most recent acquisition," he said of the publishing company they'd just purchased. "Now, you need to make sure you swing by their office on Friday to put your John Hancock on the papers, so they can officially begin going through the books to see what areas we want to keep and those we want to trim.

"I know Bronson has a race next weekend in Michigan, and I promise you'll be out of Manning's office in no time just in case you're planning to go," he added, mentioning their friend, Bronson Scott, who raced for NASCAR.

"Yes, I'm going and will be taking Natalie with me. I can't wait to introduce her to the world of auto racing. What about you? Will you be there?" Donovan asked.

"Umm, not this time. With Dad back at the helm at Lassiter Industries, I'm staying here at the lake for an entire month, and plan on getting in a lot of fishing. And I did bring some papers with me on the publishing company, to do my own evaluation. I'll let you know what I come up with, and I'll compare it with the recommendations of those consultants."

Less than five minutes later, Uriel was ending the call with Donovan. He slipped his cell phone in the back pocket of his jeans and decided to sit down on the porch swing his father had built for his mom years ago.

His mom.

Uriel could only shake his head with sadness whenever he thought of her and the pain she had caused his father. The pain she had caused him. When his parents had first told him they were getting a divorce, they'd shocked the hell out of him. All it took was to see the hurt and sadness in his father's eyes to know that a divorce hadn't been Anthony Lassiter's idea.

Neither of his parents had wanted to talk about the reason for the divorce, and had asked that he simply accept their decision. It hadn't taken long for him to find the reason. His mother had been going through a midlife crisis, which had been evident when she'd hooked up with a boy toy within months of leaving his father. His mother, for God's sake, was openly living with a man only six years older than him.

Carolyn Lassiter, he had to admit, was a beautiful woman at fifty. The first time Uriel had seen her lover with her at a restaurant, Uriel had wanted to smash the dude's face in. No man wanted to think of his mother in the arms of any man other than his father.

Her actions had not only nearly destroyed his father, but had left a bad taste in Uriel's mouth where marriage was concerned. That was the reason he had joined the Guarded Heart Club, a private fraternity he and his five godbrothers had established. Each had his own reasons for wanting to remain a bachelor for life.

He was about to get up from the pier and go inside, when he glanced through the trees at the house next door. He'd been sorry to hear about Ms. Mable's passing and missed her already. Whenever his parents would arrive for their three-month summer stay, the older lady would be there ready to greet them with a cold pitcher of the best lemonade he'd ever drunk and a platter of her mouthwatering peanut butter cookies.

He pulled in a deep breath thinking how much he loved it here. Gatlinburg was less than ten miles away, and there were only two houses on Cavanaugh Lake. The only other homes were about five miles down the road on Lake Union. Both lakes were nestled in a wooded area within a stone's throw of the Smoky Mountains.

The fresh August air filled his lungs. Nothing relaxed him more than sitting on the pier with a fishing rod in his hand and a cooler of beer not far away. As he'd mentioned to Donovan, he brought along some reading material, but he would work it in. At the moment, well-deserved R and R was at the top of his agenda.

He stretched his body thinking after taking a nap he would go skinny-dipping. It was something he could truthfully say he'd always wanted to do. Now he had the chance. With the house next door vacant, he didn't have to worry about shocking the socks off anyone.

He lay back and looked forward to his naked swim, all alone in the lake.

Two

Ellie finished putting the last piece of her clothing away, after deciding to sleep in her aunt's bedroom instead of the guest room she'd used whenever she would come to visit. Tomorrow she would start going through her aunt's things. She would donate the clothes to the Salvation Army, and any items of her aunt's that Ellie considered as keepsakes would be put away in the attic, to one day be passed on to her offspring.

She could only shake her head, wondering how she could think of a family when she didn't even have a boyfriend. Her last serious relationship had been a few years ago, right out of college.

His name was Charles Wilcox, and the affair had lasted far longer than it should have. Never had she met a more boring man, one whose sole purpose in life other than his job as a computer programmer was his fixation with pro wrestling. He practically lived for the *WWE Smackdown*.

She had landed her first job after college as a financial advisor with a major bank, and she thought her career was set for a while—only to get laid off in the first year.

Instead of trying to compete in a job market that hadn't seemed to be going anywhere, she decided to go back to college to obtain her master's degree. She had graduated last week, but intended to chill a few months before going back into the job market.

She glanced out the bedroom window. The sun had gone down and pretty soon night would come, and she would need to turn on the lights. Once she did, there was no way Uriel wouldn't know someone was occupying her aunt's home. Would he immediately assume it was her? And if he did, would he hightail it back to Charlotte?

But then, there was a possibility he didn't even remember what had happened that summer day on the pier. After all, ten years had passed. However, she could not forget the ice-cold look he had leveled at her when he'd pretty much told her he never wanted to see her again.

She was about to leave the room to go downstairs when the ringing of her cell phone stopped her. Her parents were presently out of the country, taking a well-earned vacation in the Bahamas. It was probably them checking to see how she was doing. Being the only child, she'd always had a special relationship with her parents.

A quick check of the caller ID screen indicated the phone call was from Darcy and not her parents. "Hello."

"What's up, El? You didn't call to let me know you'd arrived safely."

Ellie smiled. Darcy was acting the mother hen as usual. "Sorry, but I got busy as soon as I got here," she said, dropping into the chair next to the window.

"Have you started going through your aunt's things yet?"

"No, not yet. I've decided to put it off until tomorrow. Right now the only thing I want to do is rest. I don't care if I ever read another book again," she said.

Darcy laughed. "Hey, you just haven't read the right book. Now that you have time, you need to read one by Desiree Matthews."

Ellie rolled her eyes. Darcy, who was a corporate executive with the city of Minneapolis, had gotten married right out of college and had gotten a divorce within the first year, when her husband, Harold, began showing abusive tendencies. The first time it happened, by the time the police arrived, Harold had been on the losing end, discovering how well his wife could defend herself. Evidently, Darcy had never told him she had taken karate while growing up.

"Thanks, but no thanks. I don't need to read a book that gets me all hot and bothered," Ellie said, pushing the curtain aside when she thought she saw movement through the trees.

"Trust me, reading about it is better than doing something stupid like making booty calls. Besides, sex isn't all Desiree Matthews's books are about. They're love stories, and there's plenty of romance between the two people. You root for the hero and heroine to work out their problems and get together."

"Yippee," Ellie said, rolling her eyes and twirling her finger in the air. "Romance or sex is the last thing I need right now. You have a tendency not to miss what you never got a lot of anyway."

"Yeah, I guess so. And speaking of romance and sex, did that guy you went out with two weeks ago call you back?"

Ellie shook her head. "Nope. Just as well. He was ready for us to make out on the first date, and that wasn't going to happen."

She was about to pull the curtains together when something again caught her gaze. She strained her eyes to look through the trees and blinked, not believing what she was seeing. A naked Uriel Lassiter. "Damn."

"El? What's wrong? Why did you curse just now?"

"Trust me. You don't want to know," she said, easing back from the window so she couldn't be seen, but keeping her gaze glued to the man walking toward the pier.

"I do want to know. What is it? Tell me. Tell me now."

Ellie wanted to roll her eyes at Darcy's persistence, but didn't. If she rolled her eyes she might miss something, and she intended to keep her gaze focused on Uriel.

"Ellie Mable Weston, tell me!"

Seeing that Darcy wasn't about to let up, she said, "It's Uriel."

There was a pause. And then, "Uriel Lassiter?"

"Yes."

"He's there at the lake house? Oh, El, that's wonderful."

"What's so wonderful about it?" Ellie asked as she continued to stare at Uriel. The only wonderful thing she could think of at the moment was seeing such a nice looking hunk of dark chocolate. The man was built, superbly so. She wasn't close enough to see his front, but his profile and back were simply magnificent.

Ellie couldn't believe that he was walking around stark naked, regardless of the fact he assumed no one was living at her aunt's place.

"I think it's wonderful that he's ten years older and so are you. Chances are, he's forgotten all about that stunt we pulled that summer."

"Don't count on it. Some men have long memories."

"Well, what did he say to you when he saw you? Did he act like he is still angry?" Darcy asked.

"He doesn't know I'm here yet. I'm upstairs in my aunt's bedroom and watching him through the window."

"Oh. What is he doing? What is he wearing?" Darcy asked excitedly. As usual, she wanted every single detail. "Has he changed much over the years? Is he still good-looking?"

"Nothing."

"Nothing? What do you mean, nothing?"

"Darcy, please keep up. You asked what Uriel was doing and what he was wearing, and the answer to both questions is nothing."

There was a pause. "Nothing? Are you saying the man is naked?"

"Yep, that's what I'm saying. I think he's about to go skinny-dipping in the lake."

"What parts of him can you see?" Darcy was not ashamed to ask.

"Mostly the back—and before you ask, the answer is yes. He is as fine as fine can be. Extremely well built. It's quite obvious that he works out regularly." Ellie nervously bit her lip when Uriel eased into the water. It was only then that she rested her eyes. "I shouldn't be spying on him like this. It's not right."

"Hell, yes it is," Darcy almost screamed in her ear. "If I was there I would be pulling out a pair of binoculars and getting an eyeful. Men are known to girl-watch, so what's wrong with us boy-watching?"

Ellie smiled at the logic in that. "Nothing. But then I shouldn't be discussing it with you."

"Why not? We tell each other everything. Don't try holding out on me now."

Ellie couldn't help but laugh at that. She glanced back at Uriel. He was just getting out of the water, and when he pulled himself up onto the pier, he was facing her and she nearly caught her breath. The man was an Adonis. Perfect in every way.

As if in a trance, she rose from her seat to lean closer to the window, literally pressing her face against the glass to see more clearly, to check out every inch of him. Her gaze took in his wet, muscular thighs, strong-looking legs, tight abs—and she blinked at what she saw at the apex of his legs. His thick shaft seemed to glisten proudly in the sunlight as it lay nested in a thick, curly bed of hair.

At that particular moment he had to be the most beautifully built man she'd ever seen out of clothes. And her eyes took their fill. She stood there entranced. Mesmerized. Captivated. Every bone in his body seemed possessed of strong density: muscular, solid.

She mentally dismissed the familiar landscape that encompassed him and the body of water surrounding him. The only thing occupying her mind was his body in all its glorious and masculine splendor. Without a stitch of clothing, he appeared rough, unmanageable.

Untamed.

She felt a tug in the pit of her stomach and wondered how it would be to tame such a male. She doubted such a thing could be done. At least not by her.

"Ellie? Are you still there? What's going on? Why aren't you saying anything? What do you see?"

Ellie swallowed tightly. There was no way she could tell Darcy what she was staring at. Barely breathing through constricted lungs, she merely said, "I'll call you back later." Refusing to listen to any argument from her best friend, she clicked off the phone.

As if the clicking sound had the ability to travel through the frame of the house, through the trees and toward the lake, Uriel glanced up toward her house, and before she could move out of the way, his gaze found hers as she stood staring at him through the window like a deer caught in headlights. He returned her stare.

She felt the flush of embarrassment flicker from the top of her head to the bottom of her feet. Uriel Lassiter had caught her watching him in his very impressive birthday suit.

Three

Uriel's lips formed in a tight line when he recognized the woman who was standing at the window spying on him.

Ellie Weston.

Oddly, he felt not even an ounce of shame at having been caught naked. How was he to have known she was over at Ms. Mable's house?

He grabbed his towel, deciding he had given her enough of a peep show. Since she was still standing there, he wondered if she had a fetish for naked men. Too bad the show was over.

Wrapping the towel around his waist, he broke eye contact with her and began walking back toward his house like he had all the time in the world, fighting the temptation to glance back at her. She was the last person he wanted to see, and in the past he would have asked his parents about her comings and goings at the lake to make sure their paths never crossed. But he hadn't done so this time. Big mistake.

Uriel kept walking, and when he made it to the back door and went inside, he leaned against the kitchen counter and pulled in a deep breath. At a distance, from what he could see through the window, Ellie Weston had grown from a pretty-looking sixteen-year-old to an attractive twenty-six-year-old woman.

He frowned, thinking, so what? It had been expected. Her mother was a nice-looking lady, so Ellie had probably inherited some pretty good genes.

Moving away from the counter he opened the refrigerator and pulled out a beer. He popped the top and took a huge swig, not caring that he was standing, dripping-wet, in the middle of his kitchen. His mind was filled with too many thoughts of the woman he hadn't seen in ten years.

Woman.

It was safe to think of her as a woman now, and not a kid any longer; although, at sixteen, she hadn't really looked like your average kid, not at the rate her body had been developing. Even now he could recall how she had looked that day she and her friend had pulled one over on him.

He wondered how long had she been standing by the window watching him? How much of him had she seen? He would be the last person to admit to being an exhibitionist, and would never have considered a skinny-dip if he'd known someone was next door—especially if that someone was her.

When he finished off the beer, he sat the empty bottle on the counter, wondering if he was being unreasonable for still holding a grudge after all this time. She had been sixteen, and teenagers had a tendency to act silly and do stupid things. Hell, at that age he could remember all the trouble he and his five godbrothers used to get into. They would spend at least a week together every year while growing up, and would get into and do all sorts of crazy stuff.

He then thought about Ms. Mable and all the kindness she had bestowed upon him as a kid, and even through his adulthood. Although he hadn't made it to the funeral, he had sent a floral arrangement. But he hadn't spoken to anyone in the family.

The decent thing to do would be to go over there and offer his condolences in person. That was the least he could do. Nothing less. Nothing more. In addition to that, the gentlemanly thing to do would be to apologize for going swimming in the nude.

And with that decision made, he moved up the stairs to get dressed.

Ellie paced her bedroom, feeling the heat of embarrassment enflame her body with every step she took. Why did she have to share her most humiliating moments with Uriel Lassiter? First it had been the kiss, and now this. He had actually caught her spying on him while skinny-dipping. She didn't want to think what he probably thought of her for doing such a thing. This was a great way to renew their acquaintance after ten years.

Realizing that wearing out the floor wasn't getting her anywhere, she decided to sit in a chair—the same one she had sat in earlier, before getting into so much trouble. At least now she had pulled the drapes, so if he decided to go streaking across his back porch he would be doing so without having her as a captive audience.

She wished she could place the blame squarely at his feet without feeling guilty. After all, no one told him to parade around without any clothes on. She was a woman. Of course she was going to look. Come on now, get real.

The only thing real about it was how good he had looked. Even from a distance she had appreciated every inch of him that she saw; every body part, individually and collectively. She sighed deeply. When had she developed an interest in male body parts? Probably after seeing such outstanding workmanship on him earlier today.

Her cell phone rang and she didn't have to wonder who it was. No doubt Darcy was calling to see what was going on after she'd all but hung up on her earlier. But given the choice between checking out a naked man and talking on the phone to Darcy, the naked man would win hands down.

She reached for her cell phone. "Yes?"

"Girl, you were wrong for doing what you did. The only reason I'll forgive you is if you say you hung up because you decided to get naked and go join Uriel for a swim."

Ellie rolled her eyes. "You've been reading way too many of those romance novels, Darcy."

"I haven't been reading enough. That's how it goes when you don't have a love life. It's me, a good book and Bruce when I need him. It's safer that way."

Ellie couldn't help but smile. Bruce was the name Darcy had given her little toy. Her friend was simply scandalous. "You have no reason not to get out and start dating again."

"I do, too. I'm not ready. And until I am, Bruce will have to do. Now, enough about me, what about you and Uriel?"

Ellie frowned. "You're saying it like we're a couple."

"You could be. You've always had a crush on him, you know. Some things you were able to outgrow, but I don't think Uriel Lassiter was one of them."

"I did outgrow him."

"I don't think you did, but I won't argue with you about it. Just tell me how he looks now, and I'll settle for above the waist, since you're determined not to tell me about anything down south."

Settling comfortably in the chair, Ellie closed her eyes and envisioned the much older Uriel. "Oh, Darcy," she said, not realizing how much in awe she sounded. "He was always handsome. But now that I'm older, I see more things than just his eyes that used to make me drool. He has a cute nose and a nice set of lips." Lips she once kissed. "I never realized until today how perfectly they're shaped."

"And you saw all of that from your aunt's bedroom window?"

"Pretty much—especially when he looked up and saw me."

"What! Are you saying he caught you watching him?"

Ellie opened her eyes, feeling her cheeks heat up all over again. "Yes, he caught me, so I can only imagine what he's thinking about now. I acted no better today than I did that day ten years ago."

"He was probably flattered that you were watching. Men like women who show an interest in their bodies. Besides, like I said earlier, he probably doesn't even remember what happened then. Men typically don't hold grudges."

Ellie wasn't all that convinced. "I hurt his pride. I could see it that day in his eyes. Men don't typically forget something like that. I should have apologized about it. I never did."

"What you should do is let it go and hope he has, too."

Darcy's last words were still ringing in Ellie's ears a full hour later, after she had left the comfort of her bedroom to come downstairs. She planned to go to bed early, to get a good night's sleep so she could be well rested in the morning.

Her mom had offered to postpone her vacation to come and help her pack up Aunt Mable's things, but it was something she wanted to do by herself, no matter how long it took. There were a lot of fond memories in this house, and there was no rush. She had an entire month, and if she needed more time she would take it. Her aunt's attorney, Daniel Altman, would be dropping by on Thursday evening to give her a listing of all the bank accounts her aunt had transferred to her name. When she had spoken with him on the phone last week, he'd given her the impression there were several of them.

She found that odd, since her aunt's only source of income that she knew about was the monthly pension check from working forty years as an English professor at the Smoky Mountains Community College.

It had just started to turn dark, and Ellie went through the house, turning on the lights. With the approach of night, she suddenly realized that she had never been here in this house alone. All the times she'd visited, her aunt had been present. She hadn't realized just how quiet things were at night.

Ellie had checked all the doors and was about to go upstairs and settle in for the night, when she heard a knock at the front door. The hard rap against the wood startled her, and automatically her hand flew across her chest at the same time she took a deep breath. The only person she could imagine at her door was Uriel.

The thought of coming face-to-face with him again after all this time gave her pause. Was he coming to have words with her for staring at him through the window? A part of her doubted it, reasoning that if that was the case, he would have done so sooner.

She moved toward the door, inhaling and exhaling deeply. She hadn't expected company, but she figured she looked decent. She had changed her outfit earlier, putting on another shorts set, and a pair of flats were on her feet.

She took a look through the peephole to make certain it was him, but even after verifying that fact, she asked anyway. "Who is it?"

"Uriel Lassiter."

Glancing down again, reassuring herself that she looked okay, and trying to keep her fingers from trembling, she slipped the chain off the door and slowly opened it. Uriel stood there, and at that moment she had to literally catch her breath.

On her porch, while leaning against a post with his ankles crossed and hands in his pockets, standing beneath the beam of light from a fixture in the ceiling, he looked like he ought to be on the cover of one of those hot and steamy romance novels Darcy enjoyed reading. He had the right height and the perfect build, she thought, trying to keep her gaze from roaming all over him. She had done that enough earlier, and definitely knew how the body beneath the pair of jeans and white shirt looked. And speaking of shirt, she tried not to notice how his was open at the collar, with the first two buttons undone, giving her a glimpse of the spray of hairs there. Something about them nearly had her mesmerized.

She forced her gaze to his face and met his eyes. "Uri, this is a surprise."

Surprise in what way? To see him in clothes instead of naked?

She suddenly realized just how lame her words had sounded, especially after having spent the past few moments checking him out.

"I hope I'm not bothering you this late," he said, in

what she thought was a deep and throaty voice. "But once I realized you were here, I felt I should come over and apologize. Had I known, I would have dressed more appropriately for swimming."

Thinking it was probably rude to have him standing on the porch while they engaged in any kind of conversation, she took a step back and automatically he entered inside. "No apology necessary."

And to move on past that, she said, "And how have you been? It's been a while."

A smile touched both corners of his lips and she almost melted into a puddle on the floor. He'd always had a knock-your-socks-off smile. It was still devastating, when he flashed pearly white teeth against chocolate skin.

"Yes, it has been, and I've been fine. What about you? I regret hearing about Ms. Mable. I'm sure her passing was hard on everyone, especially for you. I know how close the two of you were."

"Thanks, and yes, it was, but at least she hadn't been sick or anything. She passed away in her sleep."

He nodded. "That's what I heard."

She recalled that she had more manners than she was presently displaying, and asked, "Would you like to sit down for a minute?"

Belatedly, she realized how that sounded. It was as if she was putting a time limit on how long he could stay. But if he had picked up on it, he didn't show it. He merely crossed the room and sat down on the sofa.

"Would you like anything to drink?" she asked, and then couldn't help noticing how his jeans stretched tight across his thighs when he sat down.

"Yes, thanks. Water will be fine, unless you have something stronger."

She couldn't help but smile, since she'd brought a bottle of wine at a market in Gatlinburg. "Umm, I think I might be able to find something a little stronger. What about a glass of wine?"

"That will definitely work."

"Okay," she said, backing up slowly. "I'll be right back." She then turned, to head straight for the kitchen.

"Take your time."

She glanced over her shoulder and met Uriel's gaze. It was the same gaze that had looked at her earlier, when she'd been standing at the window. She drew in a deep breath, turned back and kept walking.

Her heart was racing a million beats a minute, and she was suddenly beginning to feel a tingle in her inner muscles. Ten years had passed and their parting hadn't been great. Now they were alone. And other than giving him a glass of wine, she had no idea what to do with him.

Uriel pulled in a deep breath the moment Ellie left the room. *"Damn,"* he muttered, and the word nearly got caught in his throat. When he'd seen her standing at the window he knew she had turned out to be a beauty; however, he hadn't figured on that beauty being so spellbinding that it had the ability to strip a man of his senses.

And one of the first things he noticed right off the bat was that she still had the ability to wear a pair of shorts. She still had the flat tummy, curvy thighs and long, gorgeous legs for them. The T-shirt she was wearing was a bit too large for her medium-built frame, but it looked sexy on her instead of baggy.

He tried getting his thoughts together by studying the room. The last time he had been here was about two years ago, right after he'd been told about his parents' divorce. He had needed to get away, and his father had suggested that he come here for the weekend. Ms. Mable had invited him to dinner. It seemed that she had spruced up the place since then. New furniture, new paintings on the wall and a different throw rug on the floor.

"Here you are."

He glanced around and his gaze met Ellie. Another thing he noticed was that her brown hair was shorter. He really liked the stylish cut and thought it was perfect for her oval face. Her almond-shaped eyes were framed by perfectly arched brows, and her high cheekbones blended in well with the sexiest pair of lips he'd ever seen. They had eased into a smile when he mentioned he'd like something stronger than water. That smile had emphasized the smoothness of her mocha-colored skin.

He crossed the room to take the glass from her hand, and suddenly wished he hadn't. The moment their hands touched he felt it: a spark of sensation that went straight to his toes. A quick glance at her face and the surprise she was trying to hide indicated she had felt it, as well. "Thanks." He said the words as calmly as he could.

"You're welcome" was her quick response.

He moved to sit back down on the sofa, took a sip of his wine, and after a moment of trying to get his pulse under control, he said, "Your aunt Mable was a special woman. Everybody liked her." He figured discussing her aunt was a safe topic.

"Yes, and I miss her already," she said.

He saw the sad look in her eyes and quickly thought discussing her aunt wasn't a safe topic after all. He took another sip of his wine.

"I understand you've moved back to Charlotte," Ellie said.

He glanced over at her, wondering how she'd known that, and figured her aunt must have mentioned it to her at some point. "Yes, I had moved to Detroit after graduating from college, to open a new branch office of Lassiter Industries, but two years ago I moved back home."

There was no need to tell her that his father had needed him back in Charlotte. The blow of a divorce had ended up being more than Anthony Lassiter could handle.

Evidently his parents' marriage had had issues that even he hadn't known about, hadn't even realized, until they'd announced they were going their separate ways. Even at his age it had been hard on him. It had been even harder to remain neutral and not take sides. He loved them both.

Uriel suddenly picked up on Ellie's nervousness and knew there was something she wanted to ask, even if only out of politeness. So, to make things easier for her, he said, "If you're wondering how my parents are doing since the divorce, they're fine. Dad still goes through life day-to-day, trying to cope, and Mom is out there having the time of her life. She has turned into a real party animal."

He stared down into this wine glass, truly regretting that he might have sounded bitter, but the truth of the matter was that he was. That was something he knew he had to work on.

"And how are your godbrothers?"

He glanced up, as her question made him smile. She had deliberately changed the subject and he appreciated that. She had met all five of his godbrothers during their visits to the lake on several occasions. So she had gotten to know them pretty well.

"They're all doing fine. All successful in their own right."

"That's good to hear. I liked them. They were nice guys."

Uriel chuckled as he took another sip of his wine. She was right, they were nice guys. Most people were only blessed with one good friend, but he had five, which hadn't happened by accident.

Almost forty years ago, his father and five close friends who were in their senior year at Morehouse had made a pledge that not only would they stay in touch after graduation from college, but that they would become godfathers to each other's children, and that the name of each of their first sons would begin with the letters U to Z. The men had kept their promise, and all six sons, Uriel, Virgil, Winston, Xavier, York and Zion, became godbrothers to each other.

"Do you see them often?" she asked.

He met her gaze, deciding it wouldn't be wise to tell her about the club they had formed, the Guarded Hearts Club, and that they met at least once or twice a year, usually on the ski slopes or abroad in Rome, where Zion, who'd become a world-renowned jewelry designer, had lived for the past three years.

"Yes, we get together on occasion, several times a year. They are still single and prefer remaining that way. Don't be surprised if they show up while I'm here."

He then tilted his head, met her gaze and decided it was time they got something out in the open, discuss it if she felt the need, but definitely put it to rest. "And what about that girlfriend you used to hang around? Darcy what's-her-name? Do the two of you still keep in contact?" he asked.

He watched as she shifted nervously in her seat while taking several sips of her wine. Saying Darcy's name had brought up the past, specifically that day ten years ago, and they both knew it. After taking yet another sip of her wine she met his gaze and said, "Yes, Darcy and I are still close friends. In fact, I talked to her earlier today on the phone. She's divorced and still living in Minneapolis, and she works for the city government there."

She breathed in deeply and then said, "Uriel, about that day when we…"

"Kissed?" He went ahead and supplied the word when he saw she was having trouble doing so.

"Yes. My first kiss, actually. I wanted to see how it was done and decided I wanted you to be the one to show me. Darcy knew it as well and dared me to take matters into my own hands."

After pausing briefly, she then said, "I owe you an apology. What I did was stupid. But then, during those days I did a lot of stupid stuff."

"I understand," he said, finally accepting that he did. She was right. When you're young you sometimes do foolish things.

"Do you really, Uri?"

He saw the intense look in her eyes. Her need for him to know that she had regretted her actions that day was there for him to see. Evidently, the rift between them had bothered her over the years. Some young women would not have given a damn. But she did.

"Yes, I do," he finally said. "I'd admit at the time I had gotten pretty pissed off about it, but it didn't take me long to get over it."

Now that was a lie if ever he'd heard one. He hadn't been able to get over it as quick as he'd made it sound, mainly because it had taken him a long time to eradicate her taste from his mouth no matter how many women he'd kissed after that day.

"I'm glad. I'd hoped that you had, but hadn't been sure when I never saw you at the lake again. I knew you came whenever I wasn't here, because my aunt would mention it, and I always assumed it was deliberate."

"Just a coincidence," he said, lying again. No need to send her on a guilt trip. Ten years was ten years. Now they were older, wiser and from the sexual chemistry he felt flowing in the room, just as attracted to each other. But then, that was the crux of his problem. He never really knew if she'd been attracted to him back then as much as he'd been to her, or if it had been nothing more than playacting as part of her dare with Darcy.

That was a mystery he needed to solve, a curiosity that he needed to explore. "So, how long are you staying out here on the lake?" he heard himself asking her.

"A month."

He nodded. So was he. That meant he had a month to satisfy his curiosity about a few things.

He gave the room one final glance, thinking for some reason that, with all the changes, it now suited Ellie more than Ms. Mable. Everything seemed much too modern for an older woman's taste. It was as if Ms. Mable had somehow known her niece would take up residency here one day.

Uriel returned his gaze to Ellie before placing his wineglass on the table and standing. "I just wanted to come over and apologize about my state of undress earlier today as well as to convey my condolences regarding Ms. Mable."

"Thanks."

"It's good seeing you again, Ellie. I'll be here for a month as well so if you need anything I'll be next door. You can call on me anytime," he offered.

She smiled. "Thanks, Uri, I'll remember that," she said, walking him to the door.

"Do you have a lot of plans for this week?" he asked as they crossed the room.

She shrugged. "Not really. I'll be busy going through Aunt Mable's things. I plan on starting that tomorrow."

"Okay." He paused for a moment and then said, "I'll be going into Gatlinburg on Tuesday to get a bunch of supplies. If you make a list of the things you need I can pick them up, as well."

He could tell by the smile on her face that she appreciated his generous offer. "Thanks."

"You're welcome. Good night." And deciding he had stayed longer than he should have, a lot longer than he'd planned, Uriel opened the door and left.

Four

The next morning, Ellie's eyes opened and she blinked a few times before remembering where she was. Then she closed her eyes, deciding to just lie there for a moment in the big bed until her mind and body became functional. Too much wine last night was definitely to blame for her feeling hungover this morning, a state she didn't need to be in, considering all she had to do today. But she couldn't get herself to move just yet. She wanted to lay there awhile, get herself together while remembering the unexpected visit she'd gotten last night from Uriel Lassiter.

She hugged the pillow to her chest as she remembered how sexy he'd looked sitting on the sofa. It had been nice of him to pay her a visit, to clear the air between them, so to speak. And now, with what happened ten years ago behind them, they could move on and be friends. From what he'd said last night, he would be staying at his lake house for as long as she intended to stay here, which meant they would probably be seeing each other on occasion. She could deal with that. He'd mentioned that his godbrothers would probably be visiting him while he was here. What about a girlfriend?

If she had a man who looked anything like Uriel, she wouldn't let him go anywhere without her for thirty days. Although she'd never heard of him ever bringing a woman to the lake with him before—at least Aunt Mable never mentioned it—Ellie refused to believe Uriel didn't have a special woman in his life. For some reason, she just couldn't imagine him being unattached.

One thing was for certain—although they had both downplayed it last night—sexual chemistry had stirred in the air between them, especially after their hands touched. She had felt a sense of relief when he hadn't acted on it. Some men would have, and she doubted she was ready for the likes of Uriel Lassiter if he were to come on to her. The man was sexual magnetism on legs.

After he left, she had tried doing a few things—had even made an attempt to rearrange her aunt's pantry, which was a wasted effort, since her aunt was known to be meticulously neat. For some reason, she hadn't been able to sleep. After tossing and turning for what seemed like hours, she ended up getting out of bed around three in the morning and indulging in another glass of wine. She didn't remember much after that.

Ellie slowly reopened her eyes and glanced at the clock. The day had already started without her, and she needed to get out of bed and begin getting some work done.

She had just thrown the quilt off her body, ready to ease out of bed, when a noise outside caught her attention. Deciding she didn't want to be caught staring out the window just in case Uriel had decided to go skinny-dipping again, she slid off the bed and slowly pulled back the curtain and looked out.

She had a clear view of Uriel's backyard, and he was out there jumping rope. And it looked like he was going at it one hundred times a minute. He was shirtless, and the only thing that covered his bottom was a pair of dark-colored gym shorts. No wonder the man was in good shape, with solid muscles. Her gaze scanned his body and she saw he had worked up a sweat. At that moment, her imagination went wild with thoughts of that hot, sweaty body rubbing against hers.

She swallowed deeply as she tried convincing herself there was no need for her to feel guilty about the tingling sensation she was feeling between her legs. After all, she was a woman who hadn't been involved with a man in a while—almost four years now. She had been too wrapped up in schoolwork to care. But with school behind her, her hormones were letting her know she had more time on her hands; and after seeing a naked Uriel yesterday, her body was forcing her to realize that those needs she had placed on the back burner were now clamoring for attention of the primitive kind.

When Uriel stopped jumping rope and leaned over to pick up a set of barbells, she quickly dropped the curtain in place. It wouldn't do well to be caught spying on him again. Besides, she needed to take a shower, get dressed and get some work done.

She made her way to the bathroom, thinking the best thing to do today was to stay busy. Then she wouldn't have a reason to think about her neighbor next door.

Uriel opened his refrigerator and pulled out a bottle of cold water. He chugged it, not caring that a few drops missed his mouth and oozed down his chin to join the sweat on his chest.

He emptied the bottle and wiped his mouth with the

back of his hand. He'd needed that. He had doubled the amount of exercises he normally did each morning, just to work off a hard-on that wouldn't go away.

He had awakened around three in the morning, unable to sleep, and had gone outside on the porch to sit a spell. He had known the exact moment the light had gone on in the upstairs bedroom next door, and his gaze had sought out the same window that Ellie had been staring at him from yesterday.

While he sat there in the swing, he had seen her pass by the window a few times before she finally came and stood there with a glass of wine in her hand and a skimpy nightie covering her body. She stared out the window at the lake and sipped her wine. The angle at which the lamp had shone on her had given him a pretty good view of her body through the thin material of her short, bright yellow gown. He had gotten a very private viewing, one he doubted very seriously she knew she was giving. She probably figured that, since his house looked totally dark, he was in bed, asleep. But he hadn't been. His focus had stayed intently on her. He hadn't moved, had barely breathed the entire time.

He was no longer ashamed of the thoughts that had flowed through his mind, or the fact that his senses as well as his libido, had gotten aroused. She had captivated him enough to sit there in the dark, fighting off occasional mosquito bites, while keeping his gaze glued to her.

From his porch, he hadn't seen all of her, but he had seen enough, and his body had been aching ever since. The thin material of her nightgown had barely covered a curvaceous body and a pair of firm breasts. Because of the way the window was made, he hadn't been able to see anything below her waist, so he could only imagine. And that imagination had gotten the best of him. It still was.

He drew in a deep breath and decided it was time for a cold shower. Since coming of age he'd had his share of women, but he'd never been in what he would consider a serious relationship with any of them, and he'd always made absolutely sure the two of them were on the same page. He hadn't wanted any woman to assume anything, and felt it was up to him to make sure they didn't. One or two had tried and were dropped like a hot potato as a result.

Uriel wanted to think of himself as an unselfish lover, and he would be quick to admit to being in control of all his relationships. There hadn't been any woman who'd made him regret walking away. There might be some things beyond his control, but managing a woman wasn't one of them.

As he headed up the stairs for his shower, he decided that he would stay inside most of the day and get some reading done—and try like hell to forget about his next door neighbor. He figured she would be staying inside most of the day, as well.

She'd indicated last night that she would be going through her aunt's things. He wondered if she was up, or if she was still sleeping off the effects of the wine she had downed. He had watched her consume a whole glass at the window, not to mention the glass she'd had while he had been there.

He recalled how he had felt sitting across from her in that living room last night. Once they had cleared the air about what had happened that day ten years ago, he had relaxed and opened up his mind and thoughts to numerous possibilities. Some had been too shocking to dwell on in her presence, so he had left before he was tempted to get into trouble.

He might have retreated last night, and would lay low

most of the week, but when he felt the time was right, he would do something that was beginning to vex him. He had kissed the sixteen-year-old Ellie ten years ago, and now he had a strong urge to see how the grown-up Ellie tasted.

Ellie glanced around her aunt's desk. The drawers were locked, and she figured there had to be a key somewhere. A serious expression appeared on her face as she tried to consider just how her aunt's mind worked. Where would Aunt Mable hide the key?

She smiled and then reached out and picked up the framed photo of her and her aunt taken last year when Aunt Mable had visited her in Boston. On this particular night they had gone to a musical featuring a renowned pianist. It had been around Easter and the weather in Boston had been freezing. They were all bundled up in hooded coats while smiling for the camera.

That had been less than six months ago. Ellie fought the tears that threatened to fall at the memory. No, she wouldn't cry. Her aunt had lived a good life, a full life, and she had been happy. Ellie wished she could live as full a life as her aunt had.

Instinctively, she carefully pulled the back off the frame and her smile widened when the key dropped out. Feeling quite smug at her accomplishment, she picked up the key and began opening the drawers. Most of the items, all neatly arranged, were office supplies—computer paper, ink cartridges for the printer, pencils and pens.

She opened another drawer and pulled out a stack of papers that were rubber-banded together. She lifted a curious brow when the first sheet said, in a bold font, *Make Me Yours,* by Flame Elbam.

Flame.

Ellie quickly recalled where she'd seen the name "Flame" before and glanced across the room at the risqué painting on the wall. Raising her brow, she settled back in the chair, flipped through the pages and swiftly came to the conclusion that these pages were part of a manuscript. Who did it belong to?

She stopped flipping the pages when a word—one that denoted a male body part—jumped out at her, quickly grabbing her attention. She blinked a few times and then, for clarity's sake, decided she needed to read the entire sentence, but she ended up reading the complete paragraph. Afterward, she swallowed deeply, felt the heat that infused her body and wondered where the heck an ice-cold glass of water was when you needed it. Whew! What on earth was her aunt doing with something like this?

Although that one raw word still stuck out in her mind, Ellie decided she needed to start reading at the beginning and not jump to any conclusions. After all, just because this was found in Aunt Mable's desk really didn't mean anything. Her aunt was a retired English professor, so she was probably editing the book for a former student as a favor.

Ellie figured that had to be it, and she was certain her aunt hadn't started reading the manuscript yet—and could imagine her aunt's gray hair turning a quick shade of white if she had read that passage she'd just read.

Taking the banded papers in her hand, Ellie went to sit at her favorite chair by the window. After she'd settled in comfortably, she began reading.

Uriel reached over to pick up his cell phone. "Yes."

"How are things going, son?"

Uriel smiled, glad to hear his father's voice. "Things are going great, Dad. I've been getting some reading done about that publishing company Donovan and I recently acquired. What about you? How are you doing?" Although his father had returned to work, Uriel was still somewhat concerned about him overdoing things. Long workdays were becoming a norm for Anthony Lassiter.

"I'm doing fine. In fact, I just wanted you to know that I'll be flying out later today for Rome. I have a meeting with one of our distributors there and plan to stay for a few days."

Uriel raised a brow. "Anything serious?"

"No. In fact, it's something one of the managers can handle, but I decided to go myself. Besides, it will give me a chance to see Zion. It's been a while since I've spent some time with godson number five."

All that was well and good, but unfortunately, Uriel was reading between the lines. His father's eagerness to leave town could only mean one thing. His parents had been invited to the same social function, and instead of making an appearance while his ex-wife paraded her boy toy around, he had opted to be somewhere else instead— somewhere like another country.

Uriel pulled in a deep breath. "I understand, Dad," he said, and in all honesty he really did. "Have a safe trip."

"I will. And by the way, I ran into Chester Weston the other day, right before he and Nancy left for a vacation in the islands. He mentioned that Ellie would be packing up Mable's belongings at the lake house. Have you seen her yet?"

His father's question triggered memories of Ellie standing at the window last night. "Yes, I've seen her," he said, deciding not to mention to what degree he'd seen her.

And because he didn't want his dad to ask any more questions, he said, "Okay, Dad, I better get back to reading those documents. But if you need me to return to Charlotte to handle things while you're away, then—"

"No, no. The company will be in capable hands while I'm gone. I just wanted to let you know. Take care, Uri."

"You do the same, Dad."

When Uriel hung up the phone a part of him could actually feel his father's pain. He knew that more than ever he needed to have a long talk with his mother. What could she be thinking? He already knew the answer. Only of herself.

Stretching his body, he decided to walk out to the pier for a while. He had been holed up inside reading for a couple of hours now. Walking through the kitchen, he opened the door and stepped out on the porch. Instinctively, his gaze moved to the window across the way.

Uriel squinted his eyes against the sun, and he could see Ellie sitting in a chair by the window, where it seemed as if she was doing the same thing he'd been doing before receiving his father's call. Reading.

He hoped that whatever papers she was reading were a hell of a lot more interesting than the ones he'd just gone over.

Five

Ellie pulled in a deep breath at the next chapter break, inwardly acknowledging that she evidently had lived a sheltered life. How on earth had the author come up with this stuff? And did people actually do those kinds of things in the bedroom?

Well, to be honest, about eighty percent of the time they weren't in the bedroom, but were in places she would not have thought of making love, not even in her wildest dreams. It was plain to see that the imagination of the person who had written this story was a lot more vivid than hers.

The story wasn't just a bunch of pages filled with nothing but hot and heavy sex. The couple was in love with each other; however, neither was ready to face up to that fact. The reader knew their true feelings, though. So, all the time the hero claimed that he could never love any woman— that it was nothing more than sex—the reader knew differently. Ellie already knew that the heroine was chipping away at the hard casing that surrounded the hero's heart.

The intimacy they shared in the bedroom was what

sexual fantasies were about, and only someone who not only understood the lovemaking act, but who was familiar with it as well could do these scenes justice. They were gripping, so earth-shakingly passionate. Ellie was dying to find out which of her aunt's acquaintances had that much bedroom experience and passion to pen such a romantic masterpiece.

Ellie thought about the many times Darcy had tried getting her to read a romance novel, and how she had rebuffed the very thought of doing so. Now she knew what she'd been missing.

The only downside to reading about such passion was that it made you realize how much you lacked in your own life. To have a man kiss you to the point that you actually felt like swooning, or to think that something like multiple orgasms could actually occur during a lovemaking session, was too much to consider. But there had been something about the intensity of the love the couple shared that easily took your breath away.

At that moment, her stomach growled and she glanced over at the clock, unable to believe she had read through lunch. She was eager to finish the book, but she knew she had to eat and do a little of what she'd intended to do today. But a part of her couldn't wait to see what the next scene would bring.

Placing the pages on the bed, she stood and stretched. Glancing out the window, she saw Uriel sitting down on the pier, fishing. It reminded her of the day she had pulled that prank on him. Not wanting to remember, she moved away from the window and headed downstairs to the kitchen.

Uriel grimaced. He had been sitting here for a couple of hours and had yet to catch a single fish. For some reason, they weren't biting today, which for him was a huge disappointment as well as an aggravation.

He had stopped reading, to give his eyes a rest. From all accounts, Vandellas Publishing Company, whose home office was in Houston, with a little more than a hundred employees, was financially sound, which was the reason he and Donovan had purchased it. They would hold on to it a few years before reselling it for a profit. That meant they needed to do anything they could to keep it financially sound until then.

He glanced at his watch. One thing for certain was that he wouldn't be enjoying fried fish for supper. He was glad he'd taken a hamburger patty out of the freezer.

Because he couldn't resist the temptation any longer, he glanced over his shoulder to Ellie's bedroom window and noticed she was no longer sitting there reading. He wondered what had captivated her to the point that she'd sat in that chair by the window for at least four solid hours. He wondered, too, what happened to her plans to go through her aunt's things today.

Reaching the conclusion that it wasn't really any of his business, he turned his attention back to the lake and to another question he was wondering about. Did Ellie have a boyfriend? Was that the reason she'd been standing at the window last night? Had she been hot and restless for a lover who hadn't been able to make the trip with her? Did that mean she would be expecting company any day now?

And why in the hell did the thought of that nag him?

He stared intently at the lake, refusing to dwell on the thought. Hell, if truth be told, he was probably the hot and restless one. He treated sex as the sport it was, and knew, without thinking too hard about it, just when was the last time he'd played. Valentine's Day. The woman was someone he'd met at the Racetrack Café. They had dated a few times before she'd begun getting possessive. She'd found out rather quickly that he didn't do *possessive* very well. On occasion she would call. He had yet to call her back. One day she would learn that most men appreciated women who knew how to curtsy out of the picture gracefully.

He decided he'd spent enough time out here on the pier. He always enjoyed fishing, whether he'd had a good day or not. There was something about sitting on the water, especially Cavanaugh Lake with a fishing rod and a six-pack. It was peaceful and relaxing. That was the main reason he'd bought the lake house from his parents.

He eased into a stand and gathered his tackle box and fishing gear and began walking back toward his house. He glanced up at Ellie's window. She was back, and he immediately felt a tug in his gut. From the looks of things, she was back to reading again.

Something, he wasn't sure what, made her look up at that moment, as their gazes connected. He felt it. More than a mere tug in his gut or a stirring in his blood. It was a rush of desire that he knew had everything to do with how he'd seen her last night while standing at that window. Sexy couldn't get any better.

Figuring they didn't need to pass the time away just staring at each other, he threw up his hand to acknowledge her presence. Smiling amiably, she waved back.

That was that. At least he quickly told himself so. Shifting his gaze away, he kept on walking.

Ellie watched until Uriel was no longer in sight, and thought that he was just as handsome as Grant Hatteras, the hero in the manuscript she was reading. Grant, the man who had captured Tamara Carrington's heart.

In her mind, Uriel had all of Grant's physical attributes.

He was handsome as sin and had a body that could make a woman drool. And he could kiss you in a way that made your toes curl. She'd been only sixteen when she'd kissed Uriel, but that single kiss had made a gigantic impact on her and had been the basis of comparison for all the other kisses she'd shared since. No one had come close.

When she'd confided in Darcy about it, her best friend had rolled her eyes and said that every girl remembered her first kiss and thought it was special. But Ellie truly believed that, for some reason, it was more than that for her. And she wanted to believe that Uriel had gotten caught up in the kiss as much as she had, before Darcy had made a mess of things. She couldn't help but wonder how far things would have gone if Darcy hadn't shown up. What if the two of them had been completely alone, with no one spying on them? Would he have been her first in more ways than one?

She drew in a deep breath, thinking that reading about Grant and Tamara was putting her into a romantic mood. She could actually feel the chemistry flowing between them, the surge of energy that would flow from Grant whenever he knew that Tamara was near. Even when they would stand across the room from each other and their gazes would meet, there was something there, a desire that went so deep that merely reading the passages left Ellie breathless.

She glanced around her bedroom, specifically at the clothes hanging in the closet. Aunt Mable's clothes. She was supposed to start packing them up today, but since she had started reading this manuscript, she'd been so entranced she couldn't think of doing anything other than finishing it. So she would. For however long it took. She hadn't taken the time to read for pleasure in years, and if she wanted to take a few lazy days, then she deserved to do so.

With that decision made, she curled up in the chair and continued reading.

Six

The next morning, Uriel stepped out on the back porch with a cup of coffee in his hand, and glanced around. It would be another beautiful day, and he couldn't help wondering if the fishing would be better today than it had been yesterday. In a few hours, he would grab his fishing rod and a cooler for his six-pack and find out.

He pulled his cell phone out of his pocket when it rang, and grimaced when he saw the caller was his mother. Apparently she did remember she had a son every once in a while. He was well aware she had her own life now, but was finding it annoying that she only called when she wanted him to do something.

He still couldn't grasp how well he *didn't* know her. His mother was a totally different person than the one he'd known growing up. The one who would carpool him and his friends to school and attend all those activities he had been involved in. The one who would lovingly tuck him into bed at night. The one he thought was not only a fantastic mother but a wonderful wife to his father. She had always seemed so happy. But both he and his father had discovered she had actually been very sad.

"Yes, Mom?"

"Uri, how are you, sweetheart?"

He leaned back against a rail. "I'm fine, Mom, and how are you?"

"Busy. I need a favor from you."

Like there would be any other reason for your call. "What do you need?"

"I know this is short notice, but I need for you to escort Allison Hampton's daughter, Charity, to that dinner and dance Saturday night to raise money for diabetes."

Uriel figured that that must be the same function his father was avoiding this weekend. "Sorry to disappoint you, Mom, but I'm not in Charlotte. I'm out at the lake." Not that he'd have taken snooty Charity Hampton anyway.

"Oh."

He couldn't help wondering if her mind was reliving any memories of how things used to be when she, his father and he would spend time at Cavanaugh Lake.

"Well, have fun at the lake," she said, interrupting his thoughts. "I'll talk with you again soon."

Yes, when you need another favor, he thought before saying, "Goodbye, Mom."

She clicked off the line before returning his goodbye.

He put his phone back in his pocket, thinking he would make sure he and his mother had a serious conversation, once he returned to Charlotte.

He took a sip of coffee and glanced over at the house next door—specifically at the upstairs bedroom window. Ellie was back, sitting at the window, reading. What in the world was she reading that was still holding her interest? Late yesterday evening after dinner, when he'd come outside to relax, she had been sitting in that chair by the window. And around two in the morning, when he hadn't been able to sleep yet again, he had come outside. From the brightness of the light in the bedroom, he could make out her silhouette behind the drawn curtains, as she sat in that same chair. If she had come outside the house at all yesterday, he hadn't been aware of it.

He checked his watch. He needed to go into Gatlinburg to grab a few supplies, and had volunteered to pick up whatever she needed for her month-long stay, as well.

After drinking his coffee, he would head over next door for her list.

Ellie rubbed her hand over her face in frustration, not wanting to believe it. An unfinished manuscript!

Whoever had sent her aunt these pages to edit could possibly be somewhere working on it at this moment. But that wasn't helping Ellie, who had gotten caught up in the couple's passion as well as the love they were both trying to deny.

She wondered if she should call Smoky Mountain Community College and speak to Aphelia Singleton, a librarian who'd worked with her aunt for years. Maybe she would know of someone named Flame Elbam.

The more Ellie thought about it, she had a strong suspicion that Flame Elbam wasn't really the person's true name but a pseudonym. A pseudonym for a woman well-versed in lovemaking. Flame Elbam certainly had a vivid imagination, and Ellie was convinced the person had to be a sexual goddess.

Ellie had gotten pulled into Grant's and Tamara's sexual adventures, to the point where she had put the pages down last night only when she hadn't been able to keep her eyes open any longer. And even after that, she had dreamed about all those sumptuous lovemaking scenes she had read. Her body had gotten unbearably hot, and she had awakened that morning infused with a need that had her wishing, of all things, that she'd had her own Grant.

To make matters worse, Uriel had been back outside, exercising again this morning. As inconspicuously as she could, she had watched him from the window and found herself emerged in all kind of fantasies. It didn't take much to imagine her legs snugly wrapped around the width of his shoulders and her bare breasts coming into contact with the solid wall of his chest.

Unable to deal with further torment, she had forced her gaze away from his flat abs, deciding to let him finish his workout without being spied on. But that didn't stop her from imagining how his sweaty body would feel on top of hers. At sixteen, she used to have visions of Uriel kissing her, and now she was envisioning a whole lot more than mere kisses.

She was halfway down the stairs, headed toward the kitchen, when she heard a knock at the door. She stopped and breathed in deeply. It was as if her thoughts had conjured up Uriel Lassiter.

As she made her way to the door, she couldn't help wondering what he wanted.

After taking a deep breath and pasting a light smile to her lips, she opened the door. "Hello, Uri, what brings you over?"

Uriel figured it couldn't be helped, when his gaze automatically moved from Ellie's face and went straight to her outfit. One thing that hadn't changed over the years was her propensity for wearing those short shorts. They weren't Daisy Dukes, but they were a close cousin. And she looked good in them. Hell, she looked better than good. Seeing her up close was a lot better than seeing her from a distance at the window. Although that nightgown was his favorite outfit on her so far, these shorts were a close second.

"Uri?"

His gaze moved back up to her face and he pulled in a steadying breath. "Yes?" He then watched as she took the tip of her tongue and traced it over her upper lip.

"Is there something you wanted?"

Slowly, he drew in a deep breath, thinking that was a loaded question if ever there was one. Here she stood at the door, looking like someone he would love to crawl back in bed with this morning, and she had the nerve to ask him a question like that?

Inwardly telling himself to get his libido under control, he said, "Today is Tuesday."

When a dumbfounded look appeared on her face he said, "Remember, I told you I was going into town today. Do you have your list ready?"

"Oh, my gosh, I forgot," she said, slapping the palm of her hand against her forehead. "I've been so busy—"

"Reading."

Ellie inwardly gasped. "How do you know that?"

He shrugged. "I noticed. You've been sitting by the window a lot, and it looked like you were reading."

She nodded, surprised that he had noticed her. Her aunt's home was not in his usual line of vision, which meant he had deliberately looked up at the window.

"Yes, I've been reading," she said. But she had no intention of telling him just what she'd been reading and how he had fit into her fantasies. "I decided to put off going through my aunt's things for a while and enjoy a few lazy days."

He smiled. "There's nothing wrong with that." And then, after a brief pause, he said, "So, is there anything I can get you from town?"

"Yes, but I don't want to hold you up, and—"

"I'm in no hurry. In fact, why not come with me? That way you can get everything you need, and you'll probably see a few things you don't know you need."

She blinked. "You want me to ride into Gatlinburg with you?" she asked in an incredulous tone.

He lifted a brow. "Yes, I believe that was the offer I just made. You have a problem with it?"

Considering the slight frown appearing on his face, she figured he didn't get it, so she said, "No, I don't have a problem with it, but I'd hate for your girlfriend to hear about it and get the wrong idea."

His frown was replaced with a sexy smile. "That's nothing you should concern yourself with, because I don't have a girlfriend."

He studied her features for a moment before asking, "What about you? Is there some serious guy for you that I need to be worried about?"

The only serious guy in her present was Grant Hatteras. The man had been playing with both her and Tamara's emotions for the past eighteen hours. "No, I'm not involved with anyone. I've been too busy with school."

"In that case, there's no reason you and I can't share the same vehicle to go into town and get supplies. Besides, even if we were seriously involved with other people, you and I go way back. We're nothing but friends, right?"

Ellie quickly forced last night's dreams from her mind. Friends didn't do all the things they had done. "Yes, of course. If you don't mind waiting while I grab my purse, it won't take me but a second."

"No problem. I'll wait right here. I don't need to come inside."

She nodded, and then she rushed off to get her purse, leaving him leaning in her doorway.

Seven

"I can't believe you actually eat that stuff."

Ellie couldn't help but smile at how Uriel had scrunched up his face at the asparagus she had placed in the plastic bag. Upon entering the grocery store, they had gotten their own individual carts, but by silent, mutual consent decided to shop together.

"It's good, Uriel. You need to try it."

"I'll pass."

She laughed. "No, honestly, it's all in the way it's prepared. The next time I cook some I'll be sure to share. I think you'll be surprised."

Ellie then glanced at the items accumulating in his basket. She didn't want to sound like a busybody, but she couldn't help but say, "You do know there's a lot of sodium in those microwave dinners, don't you?"

A smile touched the corners of his lips. "Yes, just like I'm sure you know how many grams of fat are in that half gallon of chocolate chip cookie dough ice cream."

Ellie couldn't help but laugh. "Point taken. From now on I'll just worry about what's going into *my* cart."

"Thanks, I'd appreciate that."

Ellie couldn't help but inwardly smile. There was something rather intimate about going grocery shopping with a man. She was getting an idea of the foods he liked and those he didn't like. And she was discovering other detailed personal information, like the brand of soap he used, what shaving cream and that he liked peppermint candy.

"Are you planning on checking out a movie?"

His question reclaimed her thoughts. She looked over at him with a confused expression. "You've got a lot of stuff in your grocery cart that's symbolic of movie night," he explained.

She couldn't help but smile when she saw she did indeed. In addition to the microwave popcorn, she had gotten a bag of gummy bears, a big bag of nachos and a canister of the melted cheese. Then there were the sodas as well as the wine coolers.

"No, I hadn't thought about it actually. These are things I figured I'd treat myself to at least some time during the month I'm here. I couldn't tell you the last time I watched a movie or went to one. Schoolwork came first."

A look of disbelief appeared on his face. "You mean you haven't seen anything?"

He then went through a list of recent movies.

"Afraid not."

"Then I'm going to have to fix that. You decide on the night, and then you do the popcorn and wine coolers and I'll bring the movie. I have a collection of DVDs I've brought to the lake with me. We'll make it a movie night."

Ellie reached for a bottle of Tabasco sauce, refusing to look over at Uriel. She wondered if he realized what he'd just suggested sounded like a date. Probably not, she figured as they kept walking, sharing space in the aisle.

After all, he had defined their relationship as being nothing more than friends.

A half hour later, with their carts fully loaded, they had left the store but not before several people who'd recognized her as Mable Weston's niece approached her to convey their condolences.

Uriel was very organized when he arranged everything in his SUV, making sure her items were in the back so they could be removed first. "Are there any other stops you'd like to make before we head back home?" he asked.

She wondered if he'd noticed that he'd asked the question as if they were a married couple who'd just done grocery stopping together and was returning to the same house. "No, I'm fine."

"Do you mind if I stop by Logan's hardware store? I need to get some more hooks."

"No, I don't mind."

After making the stop at the hardware store, Uriel suggested they grab something to eat at one of the diners in town, since it was so close to lunchtime.

"What about your frozen dinners?" she decided to ask. "And the ice cream?"

"Thanks for reminding me. We'll get our orders to go," he said as he pulled into Buddy's Diner.

As she resettled in the truck, she couldn't help but appreciate how easily they seemed to get along. They teased each other mercilessly about their purchases, but it had all been in fun.

"Next time we decide to ride into town together to pick up a few things, we'll grab lunch before hitting the grocery store," he said, glancing over at her and smiling.

She didn't say anything, just let the words flow between them while fighting the flutter in the bottom of her stomach. That was the third time today he'd said something that made them seem like a couple. Were they words spoken between friends with no hidden meaning? Or was he throwing around some type of hints of possibly something more?

When Ellie snapped her seat belt in place she decided not to put more stock into something that really wasn't there. The little innuendos Grant would occasionally say to Tamara were getting to her, making her dissect Uriel's every word for some hidden meaning. She had to pull her mind out of fantasy land and back into reality. They were not the hero and heroine in a hot and steamy romance novel. The man sitting beside her was Uriel and she was Ellie. And the conversation they had been exchanging was merely words spoken between friends. Nothing more.

As he tightened his grip on the steering wheel, Uriel muttered a curse that was too low for Ellie to hear. What was with all these slip-ups he was making?

Damn. He was getting too comfy with Ellie. Letting down the guard he usually kept up with most women. It could possibly be the result of his dream last night and the visions that keep popping up in his head. In his dream, she had been sitting cross-legged in the middle of his bed. Naked. And waiting for him to tear off his clothes and join her there. The dream had been as erotic as any dream could get, and before he could join her on the bed, something had awakened him.

Unable to resurrect the dream, and with no sleep in sight, he got up at 2:00 a.m. for the second straight night and had gone outside to sit on the porch. He had fervently hoped he would be lucky and she'd be standing at the window, half-naked again, with her glass of wine. To his disappointment, she hadn't been.

He gripped the steering wheel even tighter, and kept

his focus on the road while trying to come up with one good reason he shouldn't pursue a relationship with Ellie. She was no longer a minor, but a full-grown woman who could make her own decisions. He was attracted to her big-time. She didn't have a significant other and neither did he.

Something else he needed to consider was that their families knew each other, which in a way wasn't a bad thing, but it wasn't necessarily a good thing, either. She already knew more about him than he would have shared with a woman, especially the situation with his parents. He was sure she had heard the story about his mother and her boy toy. Hadn't practically everybody?

He loosened his hold on the steering wheel when the thought of an affair with Ellie began to take shape in his mind. A month was long enough to indulge in an affair. Hell, that was longer than most of his affairs.

"Are you still into photography?"

Her question made him glance quickly over at her, before returning his gaze to the road. He was surprised she remembered that. "Not as much as I used to be," he responded. "That was something I outgrew, especially when I found out that I would be responsible for buying my own film. Too much out of my allowance. So I got another interest that didn't cost as much."

When he came to a stop sign he glanced over at her. "What about you? Did you ever write your book?"

Ellie blinked, and then she couldn't help but chuckle when she remembered. Gosh, how long ago had that been? She was probably no more than twelve that one summer when she'd decided after reading a Nancy Drew Mystery that she would pen one of her own. She had interviewed everyone for her book, including him, and she hadn't gotten past the first chapter when she decided writing was too much work.

"No, but when I got to college I did enough writing, with all those term papers."

He nodded. "So, are you through with school, or will you go ahead and get your PhD, like your parents?" Both of her parents were college professors.

"I've had enough of school. I'm hoping my entrance into the workforce this time is better than the last. I only had the job a year before I got laid off. That's why I went to grad school."

"What is your field of study?"

"Finance."

As he rounded the lake, he said. "Hopefully, with the economy improving, you won't have a problem finding a job and keeping it."

"I hope not."

The SUV came to a stop in front of her house. "I'll help you get your stuff inside. Just unlock the door for me."

"Thanks."

While he unloaded her purchases, she quickly walked ahead, unlocked the door and pushed it open. When he strolled by her she got a whiff of his aftershave, the same one that had played havoc on her senses during the ride home. The same one that reminded her of what a strong male he was—not that she could forget.

She followed him into the kitchen where he sat her bags on the table. "I'll go get the rest of the stuff," he said, before walking out. She began going through the bags, immediately taking out the ice cream to place in the freezer. She was putting away items in the pantry when he returned after a couple of trips.

"Okay, that's everything that's yours."

Ellie moved away from the pantry to where he'd placed

the other bags on the table. She hadn't realized she bought so much. "Thanks, Uri, for everything."

"No problem. I'll check you out later."

Uriel turned to leave, almost got to her kitchen door when something stopped him. It could have been a number of things. It could have been the dream he'd had last night, or the memory of the kiss they'd shared all those years ago that had been playing on his mind a lot lately. It could be something as simple as the fact that he was a man and she was a woman, and the chemistry between them had been more potent today than ever. It could have been any one of those things or all of them.

She noticed she hadn't heard the back door close behind him, so she glanced over—at *him*. Met his gaze.

He stood there with his focus directly on her, while trying to figure out what there was about her that made him want to strip her naked, right here in this kitchen, but not before he got to taste her again, to see if the flavor of her mouth had changed, and to see if she could still work her tongue like she had before.

His eyes slowly shifted lower to her breasts. He pulled in a choppy breath when he saw her nipples start to harden right before his eyes. Hell, if just a look could do that to her, he wondered what would happen if he were to touch her, taste her kiss.

He could feel his own eyes darkening with heat, and he knew the moment she saw it, as well. She continued to hold his gaze, then asked, "Is there something else?"

He couldn't help the smile that touched his lips. She could ask the damnedest questions. This time he would give her an answer, and he hoped she was ready for his response. "Yes, there is something else," he said, walking back toward her.

He came to a stop in front of her, and because of their

difference in heights, she tilted her head back to look up
at him. He figured, at some point she must have figured
what this was about. He had to kiss her. For no other purpose than to appease the curiosity between them, harness
this sensuous pull, take control of the sexual attraction.
And that was precisely what he intended to do. Now.

He lowered his head toward hers, and when their
mouths were mere inches apart, when he could feel the
heat off her lips radiating toward his, he paused. He was
giving her a chance to pull back, resist what he was about
to do. But when she darted her tongue out of her mouth
to moisten her top lip, he decided it was too damn late.

Before she could put her tongue back, he sank his
mouth down on hers, taking it all. He immediately
grabbed hold of her tongue with his and began sucking
on it, as he had in his dream. And when she moaned deep
in her throat and wrapped her arms around his neck, every
nerve in his body began to flicker, his erection began to
throb. To let her know just how aroused he was, he pulled
her closer into his arms, and pressed the lower part of his
body to hers.

It didn't take long for Uriel to see that this kind of kiss
could turn dangerous, especially if he listened to what
his aroused body was begging him to do. It wouldn't
take much for him to push everything off the table and
take her there. Hell, taking her against the refrigerator
sounded even better. The bottom line was that he wanted
to take her. Somewhere. Now. Standing up in this very
spot would even work. All he had to do was pull her
shorts and panties down, undo his zipper and get to work.

But he realized that the first time he entered her body
he wouldn't want it to be a quickie. He would want to
savor the moment, enjoy the buildup. So, until that time
came, he would enjoy this, the meshing of their tongues,

while he got aroused by her taste. It was nothing like he remembered. The flavor was more intense, her tongue more controlled.

The kiss was everything he'd known it would be, everything he'd imagined as well as dreamt about. Every lick sent sensations rushing all the way to his toes, had blood rushing through his veins and made something in the pit of his stomach stir to the point where he couldn't help but deepen the kiss, pull her closer to his body and begin backing her up toward the refrigerator after all.

The moment Ellie felt the refrigerator against her back she pulled her mouth free from Uriel's and whispered, "Wow."

Her mind began reeling, her pulse was racing and tingling sensations were having a serious confrontation between her legs. She gazed into Uriel's eyes that were so close to hers. He hadn't backed up any. It was as if he just wanted her to get her breath, since he wasn't quite through with her yet.

The intensity in the gaze holding hers said as much. She could only stare back, transfixed. Pressed against the fridge, she should have felt trapped. Instead, she felt provoked into seeing just how far he would take this.

Ellie pulled in a deep breath. She needed to think, and then quickly decided that, no, she didn't. What she seriously needed to do was play this out, see where it would go and put a stop to it if it became too much. This was Uriel. He wouldn't force her to do anything she didn't want to do. Although he had initiated the kiss, she hadn't fought it, because she had needed it. Seeing him naked, and then seeing him every morning working out, had been too much for a woman who hadn't had sex in quite a while to handle.

Staring into his face, she knew he was waiting for her

to make the next move, since she'd been the one to end the kiss. She detected patience in him and knew he would wait, give her time to make up her mind. But she also understood, and very clearly, that if the decision didn't go the way he wanted, his untamed side, the one she detected he possessed, had no qualms about using seduction to sway her to what he wanted. The very thought of being seduced by him had her drawing in another breath, just seconds before she leaned closer and touched her mouth to his again.

And he took things from there—immediately deepening the kiss, to make up for lost time. In a way, she wasn't the least bit surprised or shocked by the intensity of the kiss. He was kissing her with the confidence of a man who knew exactly what he was doing. A man who knew what he wanted, with no qualms about getting it, but making sure he enjoyed it in the process. A man who knew how to combine an ample measure of warmth with his hunger, an enormous amount of sensuality with his greed, and who had the ability to ignite passion around with a force that made her weak in the knees.

When she felt his hands move to the waistband of her shorts, felt his fingers inch lower, tracing a path past her panties, seeking hot bounty, she pulled her mouth away. "We have to stop."

His brow lifted with an arrogance that she found totally captivating. "Do we?"

The man was too much. "I think we'd better," she whispered.

He held her gaze. "You think so?"

"Don't you?" she countered.

His response was quick. "No."

She couldn't do anything but drop her head to his chest and mumble against his shirt. "You're not helping matters."

"Am I supposed to?"

She lifted her head, gazed into his eyes and tried smiling reassuringly. "That would really help."

"All right."

He then pulled his hands from within her shorts, but he didn't move away, just backed up. A little. A quiver slid down her spine at the intensity of the gaze holding hers. And she knew he was in a waiting mode, to see what she would do or say next.

"How did we go from just friends to this?" she heard herself asking, while still trying to force air through her lungs. She had never been kissed that way. Had never participated in anything so intense that it nearly snapped her senses.

He shrugged and then said, "I've wanted you pretty bad ever since I saw you that night at the window."

She lifted a brow. "You saw me at the window one night?" At his nod, she asked, "When?"

"A few nights ago. Evidently, you couldn't sleep and neither could I—which has been happening a lot lately—so I thought I'd sit on the back porch awhile. The lights came on in your bedroom and sometime later you came to the window to look out at the lake. You were wearing a very short and ultrasexy nightie. I couldn't see everything, but I saw enough."

Ellie swallowed deeply. Yes, she could tell by the look in his eyes that he had seen enough. She remembered that night. She hadn't been able to sleep and had drunk more wine than she really should have. "I didn't know you were watching."

"I know. It was dark, and not once did you glance over at the porch. You just stood there staring at the lake. I could understand why. It was a beautiful night and a full moon was in the sky. You were satisfied with just staring at the lake and I was satisfied with just staring at you. I've been back every night since then, feeling restless, edgy, but you haven't been back."

"And?" she asked, wondering why he was telling her this.

"And there's nothing else to tell. Like I said, you hadn't been back and I've been fine at fighting the temptation."

Until today, evidently, she figured. He had been fine until today, when they had gone into Gatlinburg together. "And what made you kiss me?" she asked him, hoping he would answer, since he seemed not to mind talking about it.

"That day at the lake, when you took your friend up on that dare, I had enjoyed kissing you. I was curious to see if I would enjoy kissing you now. And today I just couldn't leave until I found out."

"And?" she asked as she relaxed back against the refrigerator.

His brows rose. "I enjoyed it. Couldn't you tell?"

Yes, she had been able to tell, but then it definitely had been a mutual exchange. "I need to finish putting things away," she said, deciding it was time for her to rein in her senses and for him to do the same with his.

An affair would be a waste of their time, because it would be an affair that went nowhere. He wasn't into long-term, and she'd figured whenever she did get back into the dating scene, that she would be. She never intended to spend the rest of her life alone, without a special man in it, as her aunt had done. She wanted to marry, have children. She wanted the white picket fence and the house that it surrounded. She had a feeling he didn't.

"All right, I'll let you call time out for now," he said, taking another step back, giving her a lot of space.

"Excuse me?" She must not have heard him correctly.

"I know what's probably going through your mind right now. You're probably wondering if an affair—a short-term affair—with me is worth it. We'll be here for a little less than thirty days, so the way I see it, we could either be bored to death or we can really enjoy each other's company."

She lifted her chin. "What makes you think I'd be bored?"

"Just a guess."

Unfortunately, Ellie thought, he had probably guessed right. If she had the rest of that manuscript to read, then she would have had something to look forward to doing for the next couple of days. And packing her aunt's things would keep her busy, but only for a while. But no matter how you looked at it, indulging in an affair with Uriel Lassiter was too much to think about. She wasn't sure she could handle him. The man had more sexual energy than any man she knew. His kiss had confirmed that.

"I propose we have a summer fling, Ellie. At the end of the summer, when we leave here, you will go your way and I'll go mine. No attachments. No follow-up visits or phone calls. No cards in the mail during the holidays, nor any getting together for an Easter feast. And when we do see each other again we'll be friends. Former lovers who'll always be nothing more than friends."

He paused and she knew he was letting his words sink in. "I'll give you a few days to think about it," he said, backing up.

The lines around his lips eased into a smile. "You know where I'll be once you've made a decision."

She didn't say anything, just stood there and stared at him and then stared at the door when he left.

Eight

Uriel pulled the dinner out of the microwave and placed it on the table before moving to the refrigerator to pull out a can of soda. It was a nice day, and he had thought about eating outside on the porch but changed his mind. There was no way he could sit on his porch and not look over to where he knew Ellie was.

It had been two days since he had kissed her. He'd told her that he'd give her a few days to consider an affair between them, but hadn't really expected for her to take all this time. What was there to think about? They were attracted to each other. There was strong sexual chemistry. They had enjoyed kissing each other, which meant sleeping together would be enjoyable, as well.

That night, when he'd gone to bed and thought about it, he had figured out why she was holding back. Her parents' marriage was a good role model for her to go by, and she wanted the same thing they had. So she was holding out for marriage and was not into casual affairs.

Sitting down at the table, he bowed his head and said grace before digging into his meal. He couldn't help but grin when he recalled how she'd warned him about the amount of sodium in his microwave dinner. He would have to admit that he had enjoyed going grocery shopping with her that day, the first time with any woman. For some reason it had seemed natural to be with her in that store.

He wondered how long she would stay locked up in that house. Was she deliberately avoiding him or was she actually busy packing up Ms. Mable's belongings? He had seen the Salvation Army truck over there yesterday. Still, the last two days had been nice ones, so she should have been outside enjoying them.

He was tempted to go over there once or twice, but had changed his mind. But that hadn't stopped him waking up around two every morning, easing onto the porch and sitting in the dark, hoping that he would catch a glimpse of her standing by the window again. He hadn't. In fact, the light in her bedroom never came on, which meant she was getting a good night's sleep, even if he wasn't.

For the past two days, he'd been lucky with his fishing rod and had caught enough for a fish fry this weekend. He wondered if Ellie would be interested in joining him. No matter what her ultimate decision would be about an affair, they would remain friends, although it was hard to be friends with a woman you wanted to take to bed.

At that moment he heard a car door slam, and wondered if someone was paying him a visit. Four of his god-brothers were here in the States and knew where they could find him, but he doubted they would come looking for him.

He stood and walked through the kitchen to the living room, to glance out the window. The car he'd heard was actually next door. Someone was paying Ellie a visit, and it was a man. He frowned. She'd said she was not involved with anyone, so who would come to the lake to see her?

Uriel squinted his eyes against the sun and saw it was
Daniel Altman, the man who had been Ms. Mable's attorney for years. Evidently, the older man needed to finalize a few things with Ellie regarding her aunt's estate.

Satisfied this was nothing but a business call, he
headed back to the kitchen to finish his dinner, refusing
to admit that for a moment, his deep, dark thoughts had
been those of a jealous man.

"I wasn't aware my aunt's estate encompassed all of
this," Ellie said, after Daniel Altman had gone over everything with her.

The older gentleman smiled. "Yes, your aunt invested
wisely, and that's a good thing, considering how the stock
market has taken a beating. Other than the money she's
set aside for that scholarship at Smoky Mountain Community College, everything of hers is now yours."

The man then shifted uneasily in his chair. "Your aunt
was a very private person, and there was one business
deal she was involved with where she preferred that any
correspondence relating to it come directly to me. I would
deliver the mail to her."

Ellie lifted a brow. "Why?"

"I believe this letter will explain everything. It's ad-
dressed to you, and she would update it every so often
to try and keep it current," he said, handing Ellie the
sealed envelope.

He glanced at his watch and said, "I need to leave now,
but if you have questions about any of this, just give me
a call tomorrow."

He paused a moment and then said, "I'll be retiring
from practicing law in a few months and will be moving to Florida. I bought a small place in Ocala. I'm getting too old to handle the harsh winters here any longer."

She smiled. "I am happy for you, Mr. Altman," she said, getting up off the sofa to walk him to the door. "I'm going to miss seeing you around."

Her aunt had left her enough money to open her own financial consulting company, and she was considering doing just that, and to work from here at Cavanaugh Lake.

Mr. Altman turned to her and said softly, "I considered your aunt a close friend as well as a good client, and there was nothing I wouldn't do for her."

Ellie's smile brightened. "Thanks, Mr. Altman. And I believe I speak for my parents as well as myself when I say that we have appreciated your friendship and loyalty to my aunt over the years. She always spoke highly of you and indicated you always provided outstanding service."

She thought she actually saw the man blush when he said, "I did my best." He then quickly opened the door and left.

Ellie stood at the door and watched him hurry to his car, and couldn't help wondering what that was all about. For some reason, she thought Mr. Altman had begun acting rather strange. For someone who was about to retire, he didn't seem all that happy about it. In fact, if she didn't know better, she'd think he was sad. Shrugging her shoulders, she went back into the living room to read the letter her aunt had left for her. It had been dated a month before she died.

To my beautiful niece,
If you're reading this letter, it means I am no longer with you. There's a lot I shared with you and some things I didn't share. There are some things I could never bring myself to talk to you about. I admit I took the coward's way out, but after reading this letter I hope you will understand.

A few years ago I did something that I thought I would never do, and that was to fall in love.

Ellie nearly dropped the letter. Aunt Mable? In love? She blinked and reread that passage of the letter again, to make sure she had read it correctly, and when she saw she had, she quickly read on.

He was a widower and we talked about getting married, but I had been alone for so long, all I really needed was companionship, and he provided that for me; and with this being such a small town, and not wanting our relationship to be dictated by traditional ideals, we preferred being discreet and keeping our business to ourselves. Anyway, I've always wanted to write, and he encouraged me to do so. I wanted to write a love story, and after much encouragement I sat down and started on it.

Ellie was feeling the hairs on the back of her neck stand up, and she had a strong suspicion what her aunt was about to tell her.

I'm hoping by the time you read this I've gotten published. That is my dream. That is my goal. A publisher out of Texas has purchased my first story. They loved it! They gave me an advance, and understanding that I was a new writer, they were gracious enough to give me a year to complete it. I am attaching my agent's card to this letter. Her name is Lauren Poole. She's been a jewel to work with and the book has been a jewel to write. The manuscript is my baby. I'm entrusting it into your care if something were to happen to me. I'm writing under the name of Flame Elbam. Note that Elbam is Mable spelled backward. That's kind of cute, don't you think? I'm hoping by the time you read this letter, I would have finished plenty of novels.

Always know that I love you and I hope that one day you will share the kind of love that I have shared in the past few years. Don't wait as long as I did to find love. There is nothing more precious for a woman than sharing the love of a man that she can call hers.
Many kisses and much love,
Aunt Mable

Ellie couldn't fight back the tears that fell from her eyes. It was hard to believe. Her aunt, who had never married, had become Flame Elbam and had penned a beautiful romance filled with more passion than Ellie could ever imagine.

It was a story she hadn't finished, and now, with her passing, it would be a story that would never get finished.

Ellie shook her head at the cruelty of it all. She removed the agent's business card denoting a New York address. Ellie would call her tomorrow, to see if there was something that could be done. Maybe a ghost writer could finish the final chapters. Surely, the publisher could find someone to do that.

And if that option wouldn't be acceptable to the publisher, Ellie would make sure the company got back every dime of its advance.

She then wondered about the man who had been her aunt's lover, and when she recalled the artwork hanging on her aunt's bedroom wall, it all made sense.

To Flame, with all my love. D.
Her aunt never said who her lover was, but Ellie had

a strong suspicion that the man who'd given her aunt the
risqué painting and the man who had delivered the papers
to Ellie this afternoon were one and the same, although
she would not have thought so in a hundred years. But
that just proved you couldn't discount what people did
in their bedrooms. In order for her aunt to write about
such passion, she'd had to experience it at the hands of
Daniel Altman.

Ellie stood. She would call Lauren Poole, and whatever it took, she would make sure the manuscript her aunt
considered "her baby" got published.

"No, Xavier, I really mean it. The fish have really been
biting the past few days," Uriel said to one of his godbrothers, the only one who also lived in Charlotte.

"If I didn't have plans for this weekend, I'd be tempted
to head your way," Xavier was saying.

Uriel nodded. He didn't have to figure what kind of
plans Xavier had. Like him, all of his godbrothers were
Bachelors in Demand, who had no desire to marry anytime soon—or ever.

He and Xavier talked for another fifteen minutes or
so, and then they ended the call. Uriel had been enjoying
a movie every night this week, and had been getting in
bed before ten. That would be just fine if he slept through
the night, but he did not.

Tomorrow, after his early morning workout, he would
start cleaning all the fish he'd caught, and then, if Ellie
still hadn't made contact with him by Saturday, he
planned to go over there and have a talk with her. She'd
made it pretty clear she did not want to indulge in an affair, and that was fine, although he wished otherwise.

He noticed Daniel Altman hadn't stayed long, and now
the house was completely dark. The lights in the upstairs

bedroom were off, which meant she'd gone to bed and was probably getting a good night's sleep.

He decided to take a shower and then check out the sports station to see what was happening there. He didn't want to admit it, but he missed seeing Ellie over the past couple of days and hoped he got a chance to see her tomorrow.

Ellie tossed around in the small bed, trying to get comfortable. Instead of sleeping in her aunt's room for the past two nights, she had slept in the guest room, which was located on the opposite side of the house. That way, Uriel wouldn't know when she turned on a bedroom light.

She hadn't wanted him to know, especially that first night, that the kiss they'd shared had definitely made an impact on her. She knew he was still waiting on a decision regarding an affair, but she didn't have one to give him. She didn't want a short-term affair and he didn't want a long-term one. A relationship would not work out between them, because they wanted different things in life. She had tried avoiding him, but eventually she would have to go outside.

And when she did she would see him. She remembered the kiss that nearly scorched her toes. The kiss that still could render her breathless, just thinking about it.

To keep Uriel off her mind, she had been able to pack up a lot of her aunt's belongings over the past two days and had everything ready for the Salvation Army truck when it arrived. More than once, she had been tempted to call Uriel over to handle a big box for her, but had quickly changed her mind, not wanting to give him any ideas. He had pretty much told her what he was looking for in a relationship, and it wasn't the same thing she wanted. He wanted a summer fling that would last while the two of them were here on the lake. But she couldn't risk that because when it was over, her heart would break.

She'd had this crush on Uriel for years—one that had lasted through her adolescent years and all through her teens. Even after that incident that day on the pier, when he had walked off from her with anger in his eyes at what she'd done, she had still loved him and had come to the lake each year after that for five straight years, hoping the anger within him would have subsided. She had even tried calling him a few months later at college to apologize, after getting his cell number from his father, only to get cold feet and hang up when she'd heard his voice. When it became apparent to her that he would keep his word and not come to the lake while she was there, she had stopped coming.

And now, after ten years, they were both back at the lake; they were adults who were attracted to each other, though for her it went a little further than that. A part of her still loved Uriel and would always love him. For some women, teen crushes faded over time; but not for her, which was why she could not consider a fling with him. She would need something more lasting than that.

Nine

"Okay, El, start at the beginning."

Ellie rolled her eyes as she slumped down in her favorite chair. She glanced out the window. Uriel was in the middle of his workout. It was close to nine, which meant he'd gotten a late start this morning for some reason. She'd had a sleepless night, and she couldn't help wondering what his excuse was.

She tried turning her attention away from Uriel and back to her conversation with Darcy. She had meant to call her aunt's agent first thing this morning, but before she could do so she had gotten a call from Darcy, who in a very excited voice had told her about a job offer she'd gotten with the City of New York.

Ellie was happy for her friend and knew it had been Darcy's lifelong dream to live in the Big Apple. Darcy worked hard and was good at what she did as a city planner. Minneapolis's loss was now Manhattan's gain. After going through all the congratulations and deciding when the two of them could get together to celebrate, Ellie, needing someone to talk to, had unloaded on Darcy, telling her all the things that had happened over the past two days, namely Uriel wanting a summer fling and her aunt being, of all things, a romance author of erotica fiction.

"Just what part didn't you get, Darcy?" she finally asked.

"Both."

Ellie pulled in a deep breath as she went through everything again. From her time spent in Gatlinburg with Uriel to their heated kiss, and then his proposal that they have a summer fling, all the way to the letter her aunt had left with her attorney. Surprisingly, Darcy just listened and let her talk without any interruptions.

When she was finished Darcy had her turn. "Okay, let's take one issue at a time. I understand about you and Uriel. You've been hooked on the guy forever, and you're not bad-looking, so quite naturally he would come on to you. Personally, I expected it. And if you recall, that day the two of you kissed on the pier, he was enjoying it. He only got pissed off because I interrupted things. You were too busy kissing him back to notice that he was attacking your mouth just as much as you were attacking his."

Darcy paused briefly, then continued. "Now fast-forward to present day. Most men his age aren't ready for commitment. In a way, I wish Harold hadn't assumed that he was. It would have saved me a lot of misery. I applaud a guy who won't marry until he feels that he's ready. And in the meantime, do you really expect him to twiddle his thumb and lay off women until then? Come on, El, that's not how it works. I read plenty of romance novels, but this here is the real world. Men prefer affairs, and believe it or not, some women do, too. Things are less complicated that way."

"Are you saying that maybe I *should* consider having a summer fling with Uriel?"

"It's your decision, Ellie, and I can't help but admire Uriel for giving you the time to make it. Most men, especially ones our age, would use this time to seduce you into one. From what you've said, Uriel has kept his distance, giving you a chance to think straight, without him being around. In other words, he hasn't sought you out."

Ellie gnawed on her bottom lip, deciding it wasn't necessary to tell Darcy that it had been the other way around. She had sought him out, without him knowing she'd done so. Uriel had no idea that she watched him work out every morning or that she would often watch him fish from the pier.

"Now, with this issue involving your aunt. I can't believe she actually penned a romance novel. And one with love scenes. How hot were they?"

Darcy's words pulled Ellie's thoughts back in. "They were hot. Actually a bit erotic. But the love scenes fit the story."

"So you enjoyed it, hmm?"

Ellie knew what Darcy was getting at. "Okay, I did enjoy it. It was different from what I've been reading, so I was quickly pulled in. After the first chapter, I knew it was more than that. It was truly a well-written story. I hate that the manuscript didn't get finished."

"So, what are you going to do about that?" Darcy asked.

"There's nothing I can do but contact her agent to let her know Aunt Mable passed on, and to find out how much of an advance she received so that I can return it to her."

Darcy didn't say anything for a moment, and then said, "You know there is another option, don't you?"

Ellie raised her brow. "And what option is that?"

"You can finish it."

"What!" Ellie exclaimed, jumping out the chair. "Are you nuts, Darcy? There's no way I can finish that book. First of all, I know nothing about writing a novel, and then, did you miss the part when I said that it's a *romance* book, with plenty of sensuality and passion—two things I know nothing about?"

"Calm down, Ellie, and listen to me for a second, because I think you're wrong. You *can* finish it. I think you owe it to your aunt to do so. You read what she wrote in that letter. It was her dream to get that book published. And you said there're only a few chapters left. The only thing you need is to get romantically and sexually inspired, and we both know the person who can serve as some real-life inspiration."

Ellie frowned. "Don't even think it."

"Sorry, too late. I'm already thinking it. I think it's perfect. If the book is that good, then you owe it to Ms. Mable to finish it, even if it means that summer fling with Uriel to get inspired, to feel how sensuality and passion work hand-in-hand."

Ellie rolled her eyes while shaking her head. "That doesn't mean I would be able to finish that book, Darcy. I'm not a writer."

"But you are your aunt's niece. Her favorite niece. Her only niece. You even got her name, Ellie *Mable* Weston. So, in essence, a Mable Weston *would* have written the book."

"Jeesh" was the only comment Ellie could make, not believing Darcy's logic.

"And I believe, once you start writing, that Ms. Mable will also inspire you with the right words to write," Darcy tacked on.

Ellie didn't say anything for a moment. Would her aunt do that? She didn't necessarily believe in the paranormal, but if it was possible, her aunt would find a way to reach her. "But what about Uriel? He would never go along with being used that way," she said.

"You're talking nonsense now, Ellie. The man asked you to indulge in a summer fling. It's all about sex, girl, so get real. If you agree to it, do you think he'd care one iota that he's inspiring you or that you're doing research for a book? In fact, why even bother telling him? The fewer details men know about certain things, the better. Uriel thinks your aunt was a sweet old lady. Do you really want him to know she was a hot tamale?"

"Darcy!"

"Sorry, but you know what I mean. Think about my suggestion. Your aunt was given until the end of the year to finish that book. If I were you, I would finish it and turn it in as soon as possible. If the agent thinks it doesn't work she will let you know it. If it flows and turns out to be a good book, like I know it will be, at least there will be one book on the shelf written by Flame Elbam, and no one will know the truth but me and you. And if the agent wants another book, we can tell her then that your aunt passed away. We don't have to tell her when."

Ellie eased back in the chair and closed her eyes. Sometimes she actually thought that Darcy was in the wrong profession. She could plot deception too easily. "I need to think about this."

"Then think about it, and if you decide to let Uriel be your inspiration, all you have to do is let him know you'll agree to that summer fling. You don't have to give him a reason. And then, who knows? In the midst of it all, Uriel just might figure out that you're the best thing to ever happen to him, and you'll cure him of his commitment phobia."

* * *

Ellie used the rest of that day to pack up some more
of Aunt Mable's things. Around noon, she had stopped
for lunch, and later that day she took a break for dinner.
It was only later, when the sun had finally gone down
that she decided to call it a day, take a shower and relax.

She sat downstairs on the sofa with a glass of wine
and her aunt's letter and unfinished manuscript, to pon-
der her options. She hadn't called Lauren Poole today,
deciding to give Darcy's suggestions some thought first.
Was finishing this manuscript something she could actually pull off?

She took a sip of wine and then reread her aunt's letter.
Afterward, she placed it aside and picked up the manuscript and began reading it again.

The room was quiet, and reading her aunt's words a
second time was just as exhilarating as the first. After
she finished the first chapter, she took another sip of wine
and smiled to herself. Darcy really had a lot of confidence
in her abilities, if she thought she could just come in and
finish this story without a reader recognizing it hadn't
been written by the same person. But then, as she continued reading, she had thoughts and ideas on just how she
would want the book to continue and then to conclude.
But would those have been her aunt's thoughts and plans
for her hero and heroine?

Ellie lifted her eyes from the manuscript and sighed
deeply. And what about those hot and steamy lovemaking scenes, where sparks were flying off the pages? It had
been years since she'd actually shared a bed with a man,
and even then things had been kind of rushed each time.
Could she actually write the love scenes after obtaining
some real-life inspiration?

In a way, Darcy was right. Uriel had asked her to indulge in a summer fling. If she decided to go along with it, did he have to know her motives for doing so? Darcy was probably right in thinking that he wouldn't care. Especially since he'd made it known he was not interested in anything long-term. They would be former lovers who were nothing more than friends. Those had been his words, and not hers.

She took a sip of her wine and continued reading. A short while later she lifted her gaze from the page to draw in a deep breath. With each lovemaking scene she could actually feel when Grant stroked Tamara's skin. When he whispered words into Tamara's ear he might as well be whispering them into hers, as well.

Ellie loosened the two top buttons of her blouse, then shifted positions when the cotton material of her shorts suddenly seemed sensitive against her skin. She was beginning to feel hot. Aroused. Sexually deprived. Her lips curved. Maybe she was enjoying too much wine tonight. Too much wine and not enough man.

At least, not a *certain* man.

She could actually admit, in all honesty, that she'd only really been kissed twice in her life. And both times by Uriel. Kisses she'd receive from other men didn't even come close. For one, long heartbeat of a moment, she stared into space as she remembered the kiss that had taken place a few days ago in her kitchen. She recalled how her back had felt pressed against the refrigerator while a very hungry mouth had devoured hers.

There was no doubt in her mind that Uriel was all the real-life inspiration she would need, and that he was not only capable of stimulating her body to where she would probably not only put sexy words on paper, but talk all kinds of stuff in her sleep. Especially if the size of the erection she'd felt that day, pressing hard against her, was anything to go by. No doubt he would teach her a lot, inspire her plenty and leave her wanting more, only to deliver time and time again.

The thought was tempting, so much so, in fact, that she could feel her inner muscles quivering, the area between her legs tingling and the heat invading her body and taking over her common sense.

Was this the opportunity that she had been waiting for all her life, at least since the time she'd decided she would love Uriel forever, marry him one day and have his babies? Even then, those had been the dreams of a teenager who didn't know, hadn't a clue just what she'd been hoping for. Now she knew.

She sighed deeply and placed the rubber band back around the unfinished pages, placed the letter on top to put the items away. Her decision had been made. She would be the one to finish her aunt's manuscript. Darcy was right. Aunt Mable would want it that way. She would pay Uriel a visit tomorrow and tell him that she would indulge in an affair with him.

Picking up her items, she carefully balanced everything in her hands as she climbed the stairs. She turned on the light in her aunt's room and went to the desk, placed the manuscript and letter in a drawer and locked it. She then glanced over at the clock. It was close to 2:00 a.m. Had she been reading that long?

She turned off the light to leave the room, when her gaze traveled to the window. She then recalled what Uriel had said about not being able to sleep sometimes at night, and that one of those nights he had been outside, sitting on the porch, and had seen her at the window, wearing a nightie.

Was he outside now, sitting on the porch? Restless, edgy, possibly even a bit horny? What would he do if she appeared at the window, pretended she didn't know he was there and started removing her clothes, piece by piece? Feeling naughty, wild, with a burst of erratic hormones she hadn't realized she had until now, she turned the light back on and moved toward the window.

She might wait and give Uriel her decision tomorrow, but she intended to send him a very intimate message tonight.

Uriel stood at the kitchen sink and wet his hands to wipe across his face. He felt hot, filled with a fiery sensation, a primal urge, that even sleeping in the nude hadn't eased. So he had slipped into a pair of shorts to come downstairs. He glanced at the clock on the stove. It was two in the morning. He should have guessed. This restlessness, edginess, was becoming a nightly thing around this time.

As usual, he'd had his dreams, and as usual, he had awakened just seconds before joining his body with Ellie's. Would there ever be a dream when he would complete the act and relieve himself of his misery? When would he feel what it would be like to be inside her body, have her inner muscles clench him tightly, milk him dry? He would have to settle for a dream, since it seemed she had decided an affair with him was not what she wanted. This had been day three, and he had pretty much gotten her message loud and clear. There would be no summer fling between them.

In the morning he would go over there, give her some of the fish he'd caught and offer to fry them for her. He would then tell her that he'd accepted her decision and, as nothing more than friends, they could at least enjoy each other's company for the rest of the summer.

But during the wee hours of the night, while alone in his bed, he would continue to dream about her and to do to her in his fantasies what she refused to let him do in reality.

He crossed the darkened kitchen and headed for the back door, opened it and stepped outside. It was hot, but the cool breeze from the lake was swirling around, spraying a light mist on his naked chest. The moment he sat down in the swing he glanced next door, and his pulse rate accelerated when he saw the light was on in Ms. Mable's bedroom. The first time in three days.

He sat there with his gaze transfixed to the window. He had told her he'd sometimes sit out here at night and look over at the window. For that reason alone, Ellie would probably not come close to the window, knowing there was a possibility that he would be watching.

But still, that didn't stop him from sitting and staring. He figured, sitting out here, being hopeful, was a hell of a lot better than going back to bed and dreaming and being disappointed,

The light went out and he mentally swore, followed by the muttering of a few choice words under his breath. This was pathetic. He had a cell phone filled with the names of a number of willing women, women he could call even now, at this hour, to initiate a long-distance booty call. Over the phone, they could engage in some pretty dirty sex talk, and he knew any one of them would follow it up with a visit to the lake by morning. Probably before the sun even came up, there would be a knock at his door. So why was he sitting here with a hard-on as big as the state of Texas?

While he was pondering that question, the light came back on in the bedroom next door. Evidently, Ellie had decided she wasn't ready to go to bed after all. He watched, and then his breathing almost thickened when he saw a slight movement of the curtain, a flutter. Was his imagination getting the best of him?

He slowly stood, deciding he wouldn't torture himself any longer, when the curtain moved again. Actually moved. And then she was there.

At the sight of her he sucked in a deep breath and his already hard body got harder.

She was wearing a pair of shorts and a blouse. He couldn't see all of her shorts but he could see most of her blouse. And it was open. Unbuttoned all the way to her navel. And she wasn't wearing a bra.

He blinked. For a second he couldn't breathe. He refused to do so. He could only watch, stare, all but gape, while making out the fullness of her breasts that he could see from a distance. His lips firmed. Did she have any idea what she was doing?

He dropped back down in the swing with his gaze glued to the window. It was dark over at his place, so Ellie didn't know he was sitting on the porch watching her. Or did she?

He leaned back in his seat. If she was deliberately putting on a show, he fully intended to watch. With a barely functional mind, he took in all he was seeing, and when she slowly eased the blouse from her shoulders, letting it drop nonchalantly to the floor, leaving her bare, he couldn't fight the rampant sensations, the hard-hitting desire that seeing her naked breasts evoked.

Intense heat seared through him, making his already hot body even more enflamed. And as he continued to watch, she leaned over and he could tell she was removing her shorts. After taking them off she held them in her hand, up to her chest, before tossing them aside. And then he could tell she was easing something else off her body and figured it was her panties. Moments later, she held them up on her finger and, as if they were a trophy, she twirled them around in the air on her finger a few times, before tossing them away, as well.

The sudden flick of his tongue across his sensitized lips made his breathing almost come out in a growl. He couldn't see much of her below the navel, but just knowing she was completely naked made his pulse increase to heart-attack range. She caressed her stomach the way a lover would, before placing both hands on her naked hips and traveling them lower.... Then she drew the curtains.

He eased out of the swing and putting one foot in front of the other. He moved down the steps, not caring that his bedroom slippers were not meant to be worn outdoors. Nothing mattered except for the woman who'd had the nerve, the audacity and the boldness to tempt him. Excite him to no end. Coax the untamed beast in him to come out.

He stalked through the trees toward her front door. Ellie evidently assumed the show was over. But he was about to let her know, in no uncertain terms, that as far as he was concerned it was just beginning.

Ten

Smiling, Ellie slipped into her nightie. Never in her life had she done anything so brassy and bold. Outlandish. Brazen. And she felt good about it.

There was a chance Uriel hadn't been sitting out on his back porch tonight, and had missed her little show, but that was okay. She had taken the chance, not knowing one way or the other. And she had liked pretending that he was out there, sitting and watching. Getting aroused.

That possibility had made her shamelessly daring. She hadn't intended to do that piece with her panties, but at the last minute she thought she might as well go for the gusto.

She could imagine him staring up at her with that intense look on his face, no smile, just a look of complete concentration, deep, unyielding attentiveness and hot-blooded awareness.

She breathed in deeply. The only problem now was that she was left in a bad way. Being an exhibitionist had made her realize more than ever just how sexually deprived she was. That was why her skin suddenly felt hot to the touch. The juncture of her legs was tingling something awful, and the nipples of her breasts felt tender. She needed to take a cold shower to get rid of all these sensations before she became crazed with lust of the most potent kind.

Deciding a cold shower wasn't such a bad idea, she was about to turn toward the bathroom when she heard a pounding downstairs on her front door. She sucked in a quick breath the same time her pulse began racing. There could only be one person at her door. The same person she had performed her little act for at the window. Evidently, he'd been awake. He had watched. He had interpreted her message.

And he wasn't waiting until tomorrow to let her know that he'd received it.

She stood glued to the spot, not sure what she should do. Maybe if she didn't do anything he would assume she was asleep and go away. Fat chance. She had a feeling she had unleashed the uncontrolled beast in her neighbor, that same wildness she had detected the other day. A controlled Uriel she could handle. An uncontrolled one she wasn't so sure about.

The pounding stopped and she wondered if he'd gone away. Or…had he decided to come into the house anyway? Because her aunt had been getting up in age, both Uriel and his parents knew Aunt Mable kept a spare key taped underneath the cushion of her wicker chair. Would Uriel be so bold as to enter her home uninvited?

Deciding not to wait and find out, she quickly put on her robe and moved toward the stairs. As soon as her feet touched the living room floor the pounding at the door started again.

Nervously, she walked over to the door, having a good idea of the voraciousness of the lust she might have released, not only within herself but within Uriel, as well. When she got to the door she leaned on it, could actually feel the fierce pounding of her heart against the heavy wood panel. "Who is it?"

"Uriel."

Hearing his name spoken from such a deep, throaty voice effectively made her heart beat even faster. On tiptoes she looked out the peephole, and although it was dark, she could make out his muscular form in the shadows. At that moment her entire body intensified with a need she hadn't known until tonight that she was capable of feeling.

Her racing pulse didn't abate as she flipped the lock and slowly opened the door. She pulled in a tight breath when they stood facing each other. It was as if he'd walked straight out of his bedroom, wearing nothing more than a dark pair of scandalously sexy shorts and slippers. She held his gaze as intently as he was holding hers, saw that his breathing was just as rapid. Noticed the center of his throat and saw how his pulse rate was beating just as fast as hers.

She was tempted to lick her lips with her tongue, and then thought better of it upon remembering what the action had sparked within him the last time. Instead she swallowed deeply and said as calmly as she could, "Uri, is there something that you wanted?"

"Yes." He advanced forward, which prompted her to back up when he crossed over the threshold and closed the door behind him. He didn't stop walking until he stood directly in front of her. "There's something I want. And you're it."

Uriel studied the look on Ellie's face. He sharpened his gaze. She knew why he was here, although he could tell she was surprised by his appearance. Did she actually think her little performance at the window wouldn't prompt him to rush right on over and take her up on what she'd been offering?

"I saw you at the window," he said, and when she didn't respond he raised his brow and added, "I assume that was to let me know you've decided on the summer fling. Am I right or wrong?"

She held his gaze and for a second he thought she would claim that he was wrong, and that she had no earthly idea what he was talking about, and that he must have imagined the whole thing. But she didn't. He watched as she gave a little bit of relief to those lips she had pressed so tight and said softly, "No, you're not wrong."

She drew in a deep breath and then added, "But I didn't expect you to come tonight."

He took another step toward her, coming so close the nipples of her breasts pressed against his bare chest through the material of her robe. "You actually thought I would wait?"

"Yes."

His scowl eased into a smile. "Baby, if you thought that, then you don't know men very well. And you most certainly don't know me. But I plan to change that. By the time our fling ends you'll know me better than any other man you've ever been intimate with."

Ellie tightened her lips before she made the mistake of uttering that she hadn't been intimate with many men, and could basically narrow it down to one—which had truly been a waste of her time. But she had a feeling that any time spent with Uriel would not be wasted.

Holding his gaze, she thought about getting to know him intimately. That meant they would be spending a lot of time together between the sheets. But then, wasn't that what she needed to get inspired?

She then thought about how Tamara would handle it

if she was in the same dilemma and immediately knew the answer. Tamara was confident with her sexuality and would face up to Grant at every turn. So likewise, Ellie fixed Uriel with a challenging stare and said, "And you'll know me better than any other woman you've ever been intimate with."

She watched as he slowly raised a pair of arrogant brows. Instead of backing down, she slowly raised hers. And then a smile touched the corners of his lips when he said, "We will see, won't we?"

Before she could respond, before she could draw her next breath, he reached for her, pulled her into his arms and sank his mouth down hard on hers.

Resisting never entered her mind, which was just as well, since she was suddenly caged by his masculine strength—a strength that was more comforting than threatening. And when she felt his hard, engorged erection cradle intimately at the juncture of her thighs, she released a satisfied moan and shifted her full concentration into the kiss.

But then, he was making it impossible not to do so, with the way his tongue was taking hold on hers, savoring it like it was something he had missed and was entitled to making up for lost time. Every flick, every lick and every single thrust of his tongue, as it tangled with hers made her moan even deeper. It elicited intense sensations that were uncontrolled and unrestricted. This kiss was even more hot, demanding and overwhelming than the last, and she hung on, determined to keep up, hold her own and stand her ground.

Unexpectedly, he pulled his mouth back and she used that time to suck in a quick breath. When she met his gaze and he smiled, she knew at that moment he hadn't finished with her yet. She saw the heat in his eyes.

"Do you prefer the bed or right here?"

She blinked. He had spoken, and she nearly blushed upon realizing what question he'd asked. The bed would be her logical choice but the other option definitely intrigued her. "Which do you prefer?" she decided to ask him, curious as to what he would say.

His smile widened into a sexy grin and he replied in a low throaty voice, "Doesn't matter. Either way, I plan on making you incapable of speech for a while."

She lifted a brow. His arrogance was showing again. "And what makes you think I won't be able to talk?"

"Because you'll be too busy moaning. That is, when you aren't screaming."

She didn't know what to say to that, figured there was nothing she could say. And when he leaned down and captured her mouth again, she figured some things were better left unsaid. This kiss would have wiped any words right from her mouth, anyway.

He deepened the kiss seconds before sweeping her off her feet and into his arms. He then headed up the stairs, and she knew once they reached the bedroom that she would be getting more than inspired. She would be indulging in passion of the wildest and most exciting kind.

Eleven

The trip up the stairs took a little longer than expected, when Uriel stopped midway up, after deciding he just had to taste her mouth again. He wasn't sure why he couldn't wait, all he knew was that he just couldn't.

So, leaning against the rail, he balanced her securely in his arms while taking her mouth with slow deliberation, letting his tongue wrap around hers, mate with it, play with it and entice her to respond. She did. And when she entwined her arms around him and returned the kiss with the same intensity, he deepened the kiss even more.

By the time they reached her bedroom, his entire body was quivering with a need so keen and potent that he had to do everything within his power to hold on to what little control he had. Never had a woman brought him to this. Never had he felt so connected to a woman in so many ways. Never had he wanted a woman so badly.

The moment he placed her on the bed, he decided wasting time wouldn't get either one of them anywhere, so he reached out and quickly removed her robe and swiftly dispensed with her excuse for a nightgown. It was one of those short nighties with satin spaghetti straps that didn't cover much, not that he was complaining. The cool mint-green highlighted her complexion, and the nightie was similar in design to the yellow one she'd been wearing that first night he'd seen her at the window.

When she was stretched out on the bed, reclining on her side facing him, his gaze swept all over her naked body, scanning her from head to toe, absorbing every inch of her. He was fascinated by the perfect details of her body, each and every curve, the flatness of her stomach, the graceful smoothness of her thighs, the allure of her long legs. But what part enticed him the most, what captured his gaze time and time again, was the beauty of her feminine mound. He had seen many in his day, but none that seemed more perfect, more alluring than hers. For him, hers held an unexplainable fascination. She had seen him naked before, but this was his first time he'd seen her without clothes, and he couldn't get enough of looking at her. The more he looked, the harder he got. The more his erection throbbed. And the more it ached to get inside of her.

He could tell that his intense stare was making her nervous, so he backed away from the bed to remove his own clothes, which consisted of nothing more than the pair of nylon gym shorts.

Uriel heard her sharp intake of breath the moment he eased the shorts down his legs. He had come ready. He had come hard. What had she expected, after that number she'd pulled at the window? He had been a goner the moment she'd taken her panties off and twirled them around on her finger.

He slowly moved back to the bed, wanting to touch her all over, taste her everywhere, consume her in a manner that would leave no doubt in her mind that he had left his mark. Easing onto the bed to join her there, she shifted her body to make room and he took his place beside her. They faced each other, gazed into each other's eyes, and he could feel the beat of her heart. He thought she had such an arousing scent, one that was reaching out to him on a primitive level, triggering everything male within him to respond, act and proceed.

He reached out and traced his hand up the side of her body, liking the feel of her soft skin beneath his fingers. He traveled a path and touched her hip, paid special homage to a small birthmark on her upper thigh.

His hand then traveled in slow motion upward, toward her breasts, and when he made an unhurried path around her nipples he heard her groan deep in her throat. Easing her down on her back, he lowered his head and captured a breast in his mouth and began feasting on her. And when she grabbed hold of his head to hold him to her breasts, he responded by sucking harder. He had discovered a long time ago that there was something special about Ellie's taste. It was delectable and was a scrumptious flavor to his tongue. And tonight it was his.

He intended to do whatever it took to make her aware of that fact. He didn't want to encounter any regrets when the sun came up tomorrow. One night would not be enough for him. The next twentysomething days might not be enough for him, either. But they would have to do. He would definitely miss their time together, but then all good things eventually came to an end. His parents had shown him that.

"Uri."

He heard her moan and felt her shudder almost uncontrollably beneath his mouth, and knew he had made her come, just from having his mouth on her breasts. He only looked up briefly to see the glow on her face before his mouth began tracing a path down from her breasts toward her belly, and when he took his tongue and drew a wet ring around her navel, her stomach muscles tightened. He liked the feeling beneath his tongue. He liked the sounds she was making. He damn sure liked her.

At that moment, a turbulent sensation washed over him and he knew he had to taste her completely. This wasn't a token hunger that needed to be appeased, this was greed of gigantic proportions, as ravenous as it could get. Her taste, mingled with her just-climaxed scent, was driving him to a state of craziness.

Possession.

And he knew before the night was over he would possess her. That sort of determination seemed odd, out of place for a mere fling, but it was what it was. He would try to make sense of it later. All he knew was that, at this very moment, he had to have Ellie.

With that thought in mind, he pulled away from her stomach and began easing lower, his attention latched on that part of her that aroused him the most, that small nub at her center that he knew provided its own taste of honey. He was there before she'd realized where he'd gone, and, by the time it registered, he lowered his head and took total and complete custody.

She screamed the moment his tongue entered her, and her scream only fueled his fire, intensified his need to taste her this way. And from her initial reaction, it was quite obvious no man had ever gone down on her before. He found it odd but gratifying—that he would be the first one giving her this experience. A first they would share together.

He immediately tossed the thought from his mind, that when it came to Ellie, they shared a lot of firsts. Like right now. No woman had ever mattered so much, no booty call was worth so much that he'd left his house in the middle of the night like a madman, needing her so desperately. Until Ellie. He had rushed over here to her, barely dressed, and was now lapping up her honeyed nub like his life depended on it. He hadn't been prepared for this.

Uriel quickly pulled his mouth away when he realized just how unprepared he was. He was about to make love to a woman and didn't have a condom. Damn! Another first.

If this was any other woman, he would haul ass in a heartbeat and go back over to his place, take an ice-cold shower, drown in a few beers and go back to bed. But this wasn't any woman. It was a woman he needed now, as he needed air to breathe.

Licking his lips, savoring her honeyed taste, he slowly eased his body upward and met her gaze. "I rushed over here so fast I didn't bring any condoms with me," he said in a low voice, hating to admit to such a thing that was so unlike him. "Would you happen to have one here?" he asked. And if she did, he hoped like hell it was more than one.

He knew what her answer would be before she opened her mouth to speak, and his entire body became infused with intense disappointment. "No. I haven't been intimately involved with anyone for over four years," she said. "But…"

He blinked. There was a *but*. A semblance of hope sprang to life within him, his erection throbbed even more and he waited for her to continue. When she paused and wouldn't say anything else, he prodded. "But what?"

"I'm on the Pill. I've been on them since high school." She blushed when she added, "To keep me regulated each month."

He could tell she'd gotten embarrassed, sharing such personal information with him. Typically, he preferred his own brand of protection, regardless if the woman claimed she was on the Pill. Unless a man was with a woman 24/7 to watch her take the damn thing, there was no way he could be absolutely sure, and Uriel had better sense than to take any woman's word when it came to birth control. He knew of several guys who had "Pill babies" walking around, that they were paying child support for.

But this wasn't just any woman he was dying to make love to. It was Ellie—and if she said she was on the Pill, he felt confident that she was. So, in essence, she'd just thrown him a lifeline, one he intended to take. It would be for this one time, he assured himself. He would be well prepared from here on out.

He met her eyes. "I'm a stickler for safe sex, Ellie, and assure you I'm in good physical shape and I get regular checkups, so I know I'm healthy and free of anything." Now that the issue of birth control had been resolved, he felt the need to address another concern.

She nodded. "And I'm healthy, as well," she followed his lead by saying. "I get a checkup annually."

Satisfied they had talked about what needed discussing, he leaned up and lowered his mouth to hers, to return her to the state she was in before the interruption. It seemed every bone in his body was on fire at the thought of making love to her in a way he had never done with another woman.

He couldn't help but revel in the sensations that kissing her this way evoked, and she clung to his mouth, accepting all he was doing to hers: feeding greedily, without any restraint. And the thought of making love to her the same way made his erection throb that much more. It was begging for attention, demanding it.

He pulled away from her mouth to raise his body slightly, then to straddle her, to pin her to the huge bed.

He reached down to the juncture of her legs and touched her wetness. He had tasted it earlier and knew she was ready. So was he.

He met her gaze when he settled his body in place, so that his erection was right at her entrance. He wanted to be looking into her face, staring into her eyes when he entered her. He wanted to see her expression the moment she felt his unsheathed shaft. Knowing he couldn't hold back any longer, he leaned to her ear, whispered what he intended to do once he got inside her, and when he watched the blush that colored her cheeks, he met her gaze as he slowly entered her.

He kept his eyes locked with hers as he inched slowly, taking his time, savoring each second. She was tight—in a way, too tight to have done this before, and he decided the man before him hadn't known what the hell he was doing. Only when he finally felt her body opening for him, taking him in, letting him forge his way to the hilt, did he release her gaze to lean forward and take her mouth with his.

The kiss—along with the fact that he was buried deep inside of her, and could feel her muscles tighten around him—made him shudder in a way he'd never before done while making love to a woman. He began moving, then withdrawing and thrusting back inside, over and over again. As he did, he threw his head back, thinking this much pleasure was not possible, but every deep stroke into her body only proved that it *was*.

He pulled his mouth from hers and threw his head back to let out one hell of a fierce growl, and his body trembled with a need that had him panting for breath. She screamed then and it echoed off the walls and ricocheted into him, causing him to thrust harder into her, lifting her hips under him, until the force of his release threatened to consume them both.

He greedily took her mouth as the orgasm tore into him, shredding his body into a million pieces and letting him feel each slice cut straight to the core of him, a part he'd always kept well protected. But not now. At this moment, it was open, raw, totally exposed, and he was powerless to fight it.

When the sensations finally ran their course, he felt weakened, totally spent. He slumped down upon her, his muscles unable to move. He'd had orgasms before, but none had left him feeling so sated, so drained. Struggling to ease his weight off her, he pulled her into his arms, and wrestled with what he was feeling, trying to fully understand why making love with Ellie had been so intense, so different and so mind-blowingly perfect.

No, he would think about that later. Much later. For now, all he wanted to do was hold her in his arms while the magnificent sensations rushed through him, leaving him blissfully sated, splendidly drained and gloriously weak.

Ellie sat cross-legged in the bed and stared at Uriel while he slept. He was sleeping so peacefully that, if it hadn't been for the slow movement of his chest denoting he was breathing, she would have wondered if he was still alive.

Over the years, she'd often heard her mother remark about her father's snoring. It was just the opposite with Uriel. If it hadn't been for the warm, hard body that had been next to her, and the solid arms that had held her close all through the night—she would not have known he was in the bed. He had been just that soundless and motionless.

She had never spent the entire night with a man before, and when she awakened during the night it had felt odd. But knowing the man was Uriel had comforted her, and she had closed her eyes and returned to peaceful slumber.

Now she was wide-awake and she couldn't help but sit there and watch him sleep, while remembering all the sensations he had stirred within her. When she had reached the peak of sexual fulfillment, not once but twice during the same lovemaking session, her orgasms had been nothing like she'd ever experienced before. And Uriel had made it happen.

She angled her head as she continued to stare at him. She had never known a more assured man, confident in his abilities. He didn't just talk the talk, he delivered. He had made good on his promise to make her incapable of speaking for a while. She doubted she could speak now. She had very little to say, since she was still in awe of it all. In awe of it and in awe of him, but then it was hard to separate the two.

She glanced over at the clock. It was close to six in the morning, and the sun was peeking up over the mountains. Typically, on most mornings, he would be up, dressed in his gym shorts and in the backyard working out. But today, after a night spent with her, he was still asleep, with no signs of waking up.

Ellie smiled. She would love to think she had worn him out after their night of lovemaking. She would be the first to admit it had been intense.

A small piece of lint off the bedspread had settled in his hair and she wondered if she could remove it without waking him. She leaned over and reached out, and when he suddenly opened his eyes, her hand froze in midair. His dark, intense eyes met hers, and she wondered if he was trying to figure out where he was and why they were in the same bed. She pulled her hand back. "There's a piece of lint in your hair and I was going to get it out," she explained.

He held fast to her gaze and asked in a voice that was raspy from sleep, "Is there?"

"Yes."

His gaze slowly moved from her eyes and shifted upward to her hair. "What do you know? There's a piece of lint in yours, as well."

And then he reached out and his hand first went to her hair, before he cupped his hand behind her neck and drew her face down to his, capturing her mouth.

Ellie was so absorbed in the kiss that it took her a while to notice he had shifted positions again and she was now underneath him. After an intense mating session with their tongues, he pulled back and let his gaze run over her. "You put your gown back on," he said in a throaty murmur.

She smiled up at him. "Yes. Aren't you going to go work out this morning?"

He lifted a brow. "And how do you know I work out every morning?"

She shrugged innocently. "It was a lucky guess."

Tilting his head, he studied her for a moment and then said, "I don't think so. Have you been spying on me again?"

She pretended to be taken aback by his accusation and had to keep the laughter out of her voice when she said, "I can't believe you would accuse me of such a thing, Uri."

When he didn't say anything but continued to study her face, she finally asked, "Well, aren't you going to say something?"

He smiled. "Yes. Do you want to work out with me?"

She couldn't help rolling her eyes. She recalled what

he did while working out, and it looked too strenuous for her. Besides, he was too good at it, and there was no way she could keep up. "No, thank you."

"You sure? I can tone things down a bit."

"Don't bother. Besides, I never liked jumping rope anyway."

"And how do you know I jump rope?"

Too late. She'd been caught. She wondered how she was going to get out of this one, then decided to use the same reason she'd used earlier. "I guessed."

"Once again, I don't think so. That means you will be working out with me this morning, and we'll start with my version of push-ups. But first I need to get rid of this." Rising on his knees, and with a quick flick of his wrist, he removed her nightgown.

Then he kissed the surprised gasp from her lips, and by the time he took his mouth away, she felt her bones seem to soften like jelly. "Now," he whispered close to her mouth as he straddled her body, "this is how it's done."

And he proceeded to show her.

Twelve

Through exhausted eyes, Uriel watched the delicious sway of Ellie's naked hips as she left the bed to go to the bathroom.

He forced his body to roll over, trying to recall just how many push-ups he'd actually done, so many he'd lost count. The only thing he remembered was that her body had been the mat, and each time he'd lowered down to it, his shaft had been dead center to enter her. The tempo had been quick and rapid, the strokes sure and precise, and when an orgasm tore into her, it tore into him, as well; and the final time he came down on her, he locked in to her tightly, as his release exploded inside of her.

He closed his eyes, remembering his vow that last night would be the one and only time he made love to her without a condom. But a condom had been the last thing on his mind every time he'd lowered his body to hers, felt the connection, went inside of her, felt how her inner muscles had tried to clench him before he'd quickly pull out, only to push back in. That had been one hell of a workout, one he doubted he would ever forget.

He opened his eyes when he heard the shower going and had every intention of joining her there. But first he needed to get a second wind. When had any woman made him do that? He glanced over at the clock. It was past ten already. When was the last time he'd stayed in bed this long? Hell, he could barely remember what day it was. All he remembered was how it felt being inside of Ellie, making love to her, releasing a part of himself inside of her.

Uriel closed his eyes again, reliving the moment. He snagged her pillow and buried his face in it, needing to breathe in her scent. He felt at peace, relaxed, sleepy— and although he wanted to join her in the shower, he gave in to sleep.

Ellie stood on her back porch with a cup of coffee in her hand, while gazing out at the lake. It would be another beautiful day because the most beautiful man was upstairs sleeping in her bed. She had expected him to join her in the shower and had been surprised when he hadn't. When she had dried off, and slipped into a pretty pink shorts set, and returned to the bedroom, he was sleeping like a baby.

Going downstairs, she had taken her laptop and— remembering where her aunt's manuscript ended—she picked up from there, to pen her own words, and had been surprised to see just how easily her thoughts had flowed. It had been a scene where Grant and Tamara had met for lunch, and later Grant had invited her to his house. There had been no doubt in either of their minds what would happen when they got there.

Ellie had been surprised just how easily the dialogue had come to her, and she could actually feel the chemistry between them as she typed each word. It was as if she had gotten into their heads. She'd known each time

Grant had wanted to reach out and touch Tamara but had fought the urge to do so, still thinking he didn't need or want a woman in his life.

Ellie had not written the lovemaking scene, deciding she wanted her full concentration when she did so, and didn't want to have to worry about Uriel walking in on her and possibly asking questions about what she was doing.

After what they'd shared the night before, she felt inspired, in awe and quietly resigned to the fact that Uriel could stir up passion within her as if it was his right. And those push-ups…

Where on earth did he come up with this kind of stuff? He had placed his body in perfect formation over her, his chest flat, arms shoulder level, feet apart and parallel. Even after the first contact with her body, he had kept his body straight, although he had cheated a few times by bringing down his hips for deeper penetration. He thrust inside of her each time he lowered his body, inhaling as he did so, only to exhale when he would raise his body from inside her. He had done two sets of fifty, and she hadn't been able to handle any more, and had tumbled over into an orgasm so strong it nearly drowned them. It seemed her orgasm triggered his, and they both had gotten washed away. She had discovered firsthand just what strong muscles he had.

"Why didn't you wake me?"

She swung around. Uriel was standing in the doorway with a cup of coffee in his hand, and the only stitch of clothing he had on was the gym shorts from last night. Now in the daylight, she could see just how scandalous those shorts looked on him, exposing his muscled thighs and strong legs. She knew how those legs felt cradling hers.

She moved her gaze from the lower part of his body

back to his face, and noted the sleepy look in his eyes. Sleepy and sensually hazed over. "I figured you needed your rest," she said, her gaze slipping back to his shorts, specifically the middle, and what was so obvious. Could he be aroused this morning already? But then she'd heard that some men woke up with erections that had nothing to do with sexual desire. However, with the way Uriel was looking at her, she wasn't so sure.

"Have you eaten breakfast already?" he asked, taking a sip of coffee.

She smiled. "No. Are you hungry? I can throw something together in—"

"The reason I asked is because I wanted to treat you to breakfast this morning. I had a good week fishing, and I know how much you like fried fish. At least, you used to like it."

Her smile widened. "I still do."

"Then give me a chance to shower and get things set up outside. I'm going to use that big fryer Dad stored in one of the closets," he said.

"Wonderful! Is there's something I can do? Anything you need me to bring?"

He didn't say anything as his gaze moved over her, and she could tell by the way he looked at her that he liked her outfit. Figuring she'd be alone at the lake, she'd purchased several shorts sets that were comfortable, feminine and so easy to wear. She'd also figured it'd be hot, although not this kind of hot. The way Uriel stared at her had her blood nearly boiling.

"Uriel?" She tried to get his attention away from her bare legs.

His gaze roamed back up to her face. "Yes?"

"I asked if there was something I could do and if you needed me to bring anything."

He moved away from the doorway and walked toward her. When he came to a stop in front of her, he reached out and brushed a strand of hair from her face. He then lowered his mouth to hers and kissed her in a slow, drugging fashion. The taste of coffee on her tongue mingled with the taste of him. But it wasn't just his taste that she found intoxicating, it was the way he used his tongue. He was a master at making each and every kiss memorable.

He pulled back, met her gaze and said in a husky voice, "I'll let you know what you can do when you get there. And as far as bringing anything, just bring yourself. You will be more than plenty."

He moved away to walk down the steps, and then looked back at her, smiled and said, "I promise to return your coffee cup, but this is the best coffee I've drunk in a long time, Ellie Weston. You're good at everything you do."

She watched him walk away, thinking that if his compliment was meant to butter her up for some reason, it was working.

Ellie decided to prepare something to bring anyway. It was the least she could do, since he was frying the fish. And though it was close to noon, and breakfast had turned into brunch, she would bet any amount of money he would be cooking a pot of grits.

It hadn't taken her long to throw together a container of coleslaw, and while she was at it, she decided a nice dessert was in order, so she had baked a batch of peanut-butter cookies, using her aunt's recipe. She even made a pitcher of lemonade, Mable Weston's own blend.

While the cookies were baking, she sat at the kitchen table with her laptop. Although she couldn't see him from where she sat, Ellie could hear the commotion Uriel was making as he set up the deep fryer outside. The last time she recalled it had been used was for Uriel's eighteenth birthday party.

His birthday was in September, but his parents had decided to celebrate a month early, since he would be leaving home and going off to college at the end of August—and it would have been the ideal time for his five godbrothers to attend. That had been the last time she had seen all six of them together. As she made her way over to Uriel's, she thought it was wonderful that the men had stayed in contact all these years.

"I was wondering when you would get here," Uriel said, smiling at her when she appeared through the trees. He hurried over to take some of the items from her hands. He was wearing a pair of denim cutoffs and a T-shirt.

"What's all this?" he asked. "I thought I told you that you didn't have to bring anything."

She returned his smile. "I know, but I couldn't resist. There's nothing like coleslaw to go along with fish and grits. And I couldn't resist baking some of those peanut-butter cookies you love so much."

His eyes lit up. "You have your aunt's recipe?"

She laughed. "Of course. Aunt Mable left me everything." She refrained from saying: including her unfinished manuscript. "I've even made a pitcher of lemonade that I need to go back to get."

She glanced around and saw he'd already placed several pieces of fish in the fryer. She knew they had been coated with his father's fried fish batter recipe, and the aroma of mouthwatering fried fish was circulating through the air. "It seems like you have everything under control," she said, smiling over at him.

He grinned. "Did you doubt for one moment that I would?"

"No, not really. If it's okay, I'll go inside and put the slaw in the refrigerator."

"No problem, go ahead."

"Thanks."

"And while you're in there, how about grabbing me that hush puppy batter I have in the fridge."

"Okay."

The moment Ellie opened the back door and went inside Uriel's home, memories assailed her and she glanced around the kitchen. Everything basically looked the same, and she was surprised he hadn't made any changes. Maybe that had been deliberate, and he wanted to remember earlier times when his parents had been happy together, or so he'd assumed. She wondered if he knew the reason behind his parents' failed marriage of thirty-plus years, and if it had a bearing on how he viewed relationships. She hoped not. But then, she would be the first to admit that she believed in a strong marriage for herself, because her parents had one. If she found out different, would she think otherwise? She didn't think so, but one could never be absolutely sure how they would react in certain situations.

After placing the slaw in his refrigerator she remembered he had asked her to bring back the hush puppy batter, so she grabbed the foil-wrapped container. Moments later she was headed back outdoors, but stopped when she got to the screen door, and glanced out. She couldn't stop the grin that touched her lips. Standing in front of the fryer with tongs in his hand, Uriel looked relaxed, as if he was actually enjoying what he was doing.

Just as he'd enjoyed what he'd been doing last night, as well. At least he had given her the impression that he had enjoyed himself. She knew that *she* had. He was an experienced man in the bedroom, and there was so much he could teach her, so many ways to inspire her. But a part of her knew finishing the manuscript was only a small part of her wanting to be with Uriel. She would be fooling herself if she convinced herself otherwise. She truly wanted to be with him—to spend whatever time she could with him was a dream come true for her, and she intended to be satisfied with that.

He must have felt her gaze on him, because at that moment he looked over her way and smiled. "Are you standing there drooling over me or the fish?" he asked, taking a few pieces out of the fryer. She all but licked her lips when she saw they were a golden-brown.

"The fish," she said smiling as she opened the screen door and walked out on the porch. "Why on earth would I be drooling over you? And here's the hush puppy batter."

"Thanks, just set it on that table. The first batch is out, hot and ready to eat, just as soon as I get a few hush puppies going. I hope you're hungry."

"Starving. I'm going to get the lemonade. Is there something I can do or get for you before I leave?"

"Yes, there is something. Come here for a second."

She actually thought he was going to ask her to watch the fish while he took a bathroom break, and when she reached out for the frying tongs, he reached out for her. Before she had a chance to react, he bent his head and took her mouth.

Desire as hot as the fryer oil raced through her body with his kiss. When he pulled back, her senses felt totally wrecked. She could only stand there in a daze and look at him.

He smiled. "You can go get the lemonade now."

His words made her blink, and she felt a little embarrassed that she'd been standing there, staring at him like a ninny. "Yes, of course."

As she made her way along the path toward her house, she could only fight the fires that were beginning to rage out of control inside her.

And she knew at that moment that a summer fling with Uriel might be more than she could handle, if day one was anything to go by.

Thirteen

Uriel kept his gaze glued to Ellie until she was no longer in sight. He actually felt the area behind his zipper throb. Okay, so maybe he should have a little more control; but seeing a small waist, flat tummy, curvy hips and a nice tight backside in a pair of denim shorts could do it to him. Nothing could ignite a man's testosterone quicker than a sexy female body, and memories of how it felt being inside that particular body was enough to raise anything. Especially an erection.

He had gotten the last of the fish out of the fryer and had tossed in the hush puppies when his cell phone went off. After wiping his hand on a paper towel, he pulled the phone from his back pocket. "Yes?"

"Start the fish frying, we're on our way."

Uriel frowned upon recognizing Xavier's voice. "I thought you had other plans, X, and who are we?" Now that he and Ellie had decided on a summer fling, the last thing he wanted was company. He had a specific agenda already laid out in his head, and from the look and feel of things last night, they were off to a very good start. He'd known his godbrothers would visit him sooner or later, but a part of him wished it was later.

"My plans for the weekend got canceled, and we are me, Virgil, Winston and York. They showed up this morning to visit your dad, only to discover he's out of the country."

Anthony Lassiter and his friends had forged a tight bond in college and had passed that bond onto their first sons. The elder men had made themselves a part of their godsons' lives. They were men who had set good examples and were deeply admired and respected. Men who in some way, some form or fashion, had always been there for their godsons. Therefore, it wasn't unusual for the younger men to show up, individually or collectively, to check on one of their godfathers. Especially if their health and well-being was an issue. And although Uriel could thankfully say his father's state of mind had improved a lot, his well-being continued to be a concern. A broken heart was worse than a hard kick in the ass. It was a torment that didn't seem to go away. It was the kind of misery that loved company, and it was something Uriel definitely didn't want for himself.

"Dad flew to Rome on business, and he plans to check on Zion while he's there," Uriel said, wondering how long his godbrothers would be staying, once they got to the lake. Uriel had all intentions of sharing Ellie's bed again tonight, and their arrival would throw a monkey wrench into his plans.

"Where are you guys now?" he decided to ask.

"Less than thirty minutes away. We'll be there before you know it. Do you need us to stop and get anything? Need more beer?" Xavier was asking.

"No, I got plenty," Uriel responded. "You might want

to pick up some wine coolers, though. You know how much Winston likes them."

"Okay, we can do that. We'll see you soon."

He heard the sound of Ellie returning when he placed his cell phone back in his pocket. He turned toward her when she stepped into the clearing from among the trees, carrying a pitcher of ice-cold lemonade. He thought it would be best to let her know his godbrothers were coming.

"We're going to need additional food, so I'm going to cook more fish," he said, taking the hush puppies out of the fryer.

"Why?" she asked with a bemused expression on her face.

"Xavier just called. He, Winston, York and Virgil are headed this way. They'll be here in a half hour or so."

He watched as a smile touched Ellie's face. "It will be nice to see them again." Without hesitating, she added, "I'll put this pitcher of lemonade in your refrigerator, and then I'll go back home to make some more slaw. I baked enough cookies the first time around," she said.

"Okay."

He watched as she walked up the steps to his porch and then went inside, thinking how good she looked in those cutoff shorts that showed a lot of shapely thigh, and he knew, if he noticed it, his godbrothers would notice, as well. They were all hot-blooded bachelors.

When Ellie came out of the house, he said, "I prefer being the only man to see you in those sexy-looking shorts while we're involved, Ellie."

He could tell from her expression that his statement surprised her, had caught her off guard. She lifted her chin, probably to put him in his place about thinking he could dictate what she wore, but after their gazes held for a while, she lowered it. He could actually feel heat, desire and longing stroke across his skin, and after their gazes locked for several moments, he could tell that her entire body began to relax. They were in an intimate relationship, and he felt territorial. He could tell that at some point during the past few moments she had decided that she would accept what he'd said as his due for now. "That's fine," she finally said in a yielding tone, before turning to head back over to her place.

No, it wasn't fine, he thought, placing more fish into the batter. He'd never been concerned with the outfit worn by any woman he was involved with, or who might be seeing her in it, no matter how sexy the outfit might have looked. He'd never had a jealous bone in his body. So why was he growing one now?

Uriel turned and looked out at the lake. He needed to think over a few things. Namely, why, for the first time in his life, he was acting like a jealous man.

Ellie looked at her outfit in the mirror. She had changed out of her shorts and top set, and was wearing a pale yellow, crinkled chiffon blouse and a printed flowing skirt with bright yellow daisies. This was another new outfit she had purchased.

She thought about Uriel's request that she change outfits. She would have done so anyway, just because she'd known her shorts would be considered a little too much… or in this case, a little too little, to go parading around wearing, especially among a group of men. To hear Uriel make the suggestion, though, like she hadn't had the sense to know that, at first had gotten her ire up. But, when she had met his gaze, she had seen the possessiveness in the dark depths of his eyes. They had made love. Twice. Had spent the night in each other's arms. Uriel was a man, and once in a while they got foolish thoughts about certain things. As far as she was concerned, this was one of those times. She figured sooner or later he would figure that out on his own, without any prodding from her. But for now, although what they were sharing was nothing more than a summer fling, if he wanted to be territorial and protective, she'd let him have his way.

When she made it back down to the kitchen, she heard the sound of several car doors slamming. She glanced out the living-room window in time to see four men walking up the steps to Uriel's front door.

She studied the men's faces, and although she hadn't seen them since the summer of their last year of high school, she still recognized them. Like Uriel, they were in their early thirties. All were very good-looking—*handsome* would be an even better word to describe them—and, according to Uriel, like him, they were still single.

Going into the kitchen and grabbing the coleslaw out of the refrigerator, she headed out the door.

Uriel couldn't help but smile as he gazed at the four men. Although they might be screwing up his plans with Ellie, he was still glad to see them. They were close—always had been and always would be. Of the six of them, he and Xavier were the only two who didn't have other siblings. But the one thing they all had in common was that they were the firstborn sons of their fathers.

"Okay, U, where's the food?" Winston Coltrane asked, looking around and sniffing the air. Everyone knew how much Winston loved to eat, especially when it came to fried fish from Cavanaugh Lake.

"In the kitchen. And there's plenty, W, so don't plan on eating any off Y's plate," Uriel said, laughing. Since being kids, they'd shorten each other's names with just the first letter.

At that moment there was a knock at the door. York, a former officer for the NYPD, who now owned his own security firm, glanced over to Uriel. "You're expecting someone, U?"

Uriel nodded. York was always on the alert for any type of action. "Yes, I'm expecting someone," he said, crossing the room to the front door. He understood why Ellie would come to the front door instead of the back door. She wasn't sure how he wanted to define their relationship to his godbrothers, and would follow his lead. He appreciated that, because he wasn't sure how he intended to define it—which was odd, because he'd never had this problem before with other women.

He opened the door and his mouth nearly fell open. She had changed clothes, but if she thought what she was wearing would garner less attention, she was sadly mistaken. This was the first time he recalled ever seeing her in anything other than shorts, and the transformation was astounding. The color yellow made her glow in a sensuous sort of way. And the smile she wore jolted his insides.

"I'm back with the coleslaw," she said in a quiet tone, and the texture of her words seemed to flow over his skin. Instead of answering or taking the huge bowl out of her hands, he just stood there staring at her. She'd done something different to her hair. It was all fluffed up around her face, as though she'd put a curling iron to it. And he could also tell she'd put on some makeup. Not a whole lot, but just enough to enhance her full cheeks and eyes. Then there was the lip gloss she'd smoothed on her lips, which made them even more sultry-looking. He felt tempted to lean closer and taste them.

"Hey, who's at the door, U?"

Uriel rolled his eyes. It was Y asking again. Instead of answering, he took the bowl out of Ellie's hands and whispered for her ears only, "Yellow is my favorite color on you."

When her smile brightened even more, he said, "Come on in." He took a step back and hoped he would be able to deal with his godbrothers when they saw her again.

When Uriel stepped out of the way, Ellie walked over the threshold and four pairs of eyes stared straight at her. From the curious expressions on their faces, she knew immediately they didn't remember her, which was understandable, since she'd only been twelve years old when she'd last seen them.

Smiling, she said, "Hi, guys. It's good seeing you again."

Their gazes sharpened, it seemed all at the same time. One man's eyes narrowed more than the others, and she recalled who he was: York Ellis. And he was the one who finally lifted a brow of disbelief when he said, "L?"

The others followed with that same astonished disbelief in their voices. She could only chuckle, and said, "Yes, it's me."

"Damn."

That had come from Virgil Bougard, and it made her laugh. He still could curse.

Over the summers, when they had visited with Uriel at the lake, they had called each other by the first letter of their names, and had told her if she wanted to hang around them and fish—which she did—she had to do likewise. However, they'd said the name "E" didn't do her justice, so she became "L".

"It's been a while," Xavier Kane said, smiling. "The

last time we saw you, you were only a kid. How old are you now?"

"She's twenty-six," Uriel said, coming to stand beside her.

"Twenty-six...." Winston Coltrane said as if rolling the age around on his tongue, while his gaze moved all over her from head to toe.

"Yes, she's twenty-six, but don't even think it," Uriel said in a steely voice.

Winston met his gaze and Ellie glanced over at Uriel as well, thinking he was sounding territorial again. She quickly decided to downplay his actions by diverting Winston. "And how have you been doing, Winston? Do you still have problems with allergies?"

Winston returned his gaze to her and smiled. "No. I must have outgrown them, since I don't have those problems anymore."

But he did have a problem with being a womanizer, Ellie thought, although she doubted he saw it as a problem. It was something she had picked up on from the way he'd been looking at her, which had all but caused Uriel to growl.

"Well, I brought over some coleslaw and also baked some cookies. I'll help Uriel get things set up in the kitchen. It's good seeing all of you again."

"Same here," they said, almost simultaneously.

She was halfway out of the living room when she overheard Winston whisper to Uriel, "Is that the way it is, U?"

And Uriel's response was firm. "Yes, that is the way it is."

Uriel glanced around at his godbrothers, satisfied they had a clear understanding that Ellie was off-limits, which was a good thing. Now he could relax, since it seemed they were all treating her like the kid sister, as they always had. Everyone was enjoying her company, and she was enjoying theirs, as well.

And although he and Ellie had only hours ago agreed to engage in a summer fling—it was easy to see they were a couple. When she found a place to sit at the table to eat, it seemed natural for him to sit down beside her. And, more than once, he had found himself just staring at her, listening to her and his godbrothers converse. That was good because he liked looking at her.

There was something about her blouse, how soft it looked next to her skin, that made him want to reach out and touch it, touch her, rub his hand across her flesh, caress it, taste it. He remembered the taste of her and longed to have her again.

"What's Donovan up to these days?" York asked, pulling Uriel's attention momentarily from Ellie.

"Donovan is doing fine. He's at the races this weekend," Uriel responded. "He called a few days ago to let me know he's engaged."

Shock, total and complete, covered the faces of all the men at the table. "Are you saying that Donovan Steele met some woman who he wants to marry?" York asked as if he refused to believe such a thing was possible.

"Yes, and it shocked the hell out of me, too. But I met her. She's nice, and a looker," Uriel said. He then glanced over at Xavier. "You've met her, too, right, X?"

Xavier stopped eating long enough to nod. A smile touched his face. "Yes, I met her. She is nice. But I have to admit, the night I met her I was more interested in getting to know her friend."

"Who's Donovan?" Ellie interrupted the conversation to ask.

Uriel glanced over at her and said, "Donovan Steele is a

good friend of mine from college, and he and I are in several business ventures together. His company, the Steele Corporation, sponsors a car racing team at NASCAR."

She nodded. "Oh. And why is it so strange for him to become engaged?"

Uriel smiled. "Because he was a devout bachelor. The last person anyone would have thought to consider marrying."

Uriel decided not to add that there was no reason for Donovan to ever consider marrying, because he'd had his pick of affairs. In fact, he had lived for them. Why would a sane man give that up? And Donovan was a sane man. The thought of any woman messing with a man's mind to the point where he'd give up his bachelorhood was simply not good.

He glanced over and saw that Ellie had resumed eating her food. Uriel was about to go back to eating his as well, when he happened to glance across the table and saw his godbrothers all staring at him.

He stared back and read the message in their eyes. Like him, they were all bachelors on demand, which meant that they knew whatever was going on between him and Ellie was short-term. He could tell they weren't particularly overjoyed at the thought of that. Although they understood and supported his desire to remain single, and that it meant he would sow wild oats from time to time, he knew they weren't crazy that the recipient of those oats was Ellie.

Hell, he refused to let them try to make him feel guilty about anything. As he'd told them, Ellie was no longer the twelve-year-old they remembered. She was twenty-six, and old enough to make her own decisions about what she wanted to do.

"How long do you all plan to stay?" he decided to ask them.

It was York who responded. "Probably until tomorrow. Why?"

He smiled, but the smile didn't quite reach his eyes, or his lips for that matter, when he said, "No particular reason. Just asking."

They knew there *was* a particular reason, just like he did. At the silence, Ellie, who'd been concentrating on picking bones out of her fish, glanced up. She looked first at Uriel and smiled, before glancing over at Virgil, Winston, Xavier and York. She smiled at them, too, and they smiled back. When she resumed what she was doing, they dropped the smiles off their faces and glared back at Uriel.

He shrugged and continued eating, refusing to let their attitudes bother him. Moments later, Ellie interrupted the quietness that had once again descended around the table to ask, "Where's Zion?"

It was Xavier who spoke. "Z has been living in Rome for a couple of years now. You do know that he's that well-known jeweler, Zion, right?"

Ellie nodded. "Yes, I know," she said, smiling proudly. "I've seen a few of his pieces, and they're simply beautiful. When the president presented the first lady with a Zion bracelet for her birthday, I knew it was just a matter of time before everyone discovered what gorgeous jewelry he designs," she said.

Uriel took a sip of his lemonade. For some reason, he could picture her wearing her own Zion bracelet, one specifically designed just for her. He could also envision a Zion ring on her finger. He blinked, and then frowned, when he realized just where his thoughts were about to go, and he outright refused to let them go there.

He gave himself a quick mental shake, and for the rest

of the meal he ate in silence, deciding it would be safer to just listen to the conversation and not add anything to it…and to keep all those foolish thoughts out of his head.

"It was so nice seeing your godbrothers again, and spending time with them, Uriel. They're as nice as I remembered," Ellie said as Uriel walked her home later that evening. He didn't have to bother, but he'd insisted because it had gotten dark.

After they'd eaten dinner and dessert, everyone had sat around talking about basically everything. The guys had brought her up-to-date on what had been going on with them and about the different businesses they owned. When she'd teased them about them getting married one day, all four of Uriel's friends rebuffed the very thought of doing anything like that.

She wondered what they had against settling down with the right person, and was tempted to ask Uriel, but figured it was none of her business. Still, she couldn't stop wondering if Uriel felt the same way they did. Was he as dead-set against the idea of marriage as they were? Was that the reason he had stipulated they would share nothing more than a short-term affair?

"I won't be coming over tonight, Ellie."

She glanced up at him, saw the tenseness in his jaw, the firmness of his lips, and knew he didn't like the idea of not spending the night with her. In a way, she felt good that he was regretting it. "That's okay, I understand. It wouldn't look right for you to leave your company."

He stopped walking and she did, too. "Do you understand that I enjoyed being with you this morning, making love to you, cherishing your body? I also enjoyed the time we spent together today, even if we weren't alone."

She couldn't help but smile. "Thanks, Uriel. I enjoyed

being with you, too." And although she wanted to convince herself it was just for inspiration to finish her aunt's book, she knew that wasn't the reason.

When they reached her porch, instead of walking her up the steps to where they would be standing underneath a bright light—giving his houseguests something to see, he touched her arm and walked her over to the huge oak tree, whose branches not only provided shade but also privacy.

When Ellie stood facing him, Uriel studied her features for a second and said, "You look very pretty today, Ellie."

And she had. He had stared at her a lot today, on the pretense of watching out for her. But he knew that wasn't the case. Not one of his godbrothers, even Winston, would have crossed the line once he had established it. And he *had* established it with Winston's question. Now they pretty much knew something was going on between him and Ellie, but they probably weren't sure just to what extent.

As far as Uriel was concerned, they didn't have to know. They'd never kept up with any of his conquests before. Something cut deep within Uriel with the word *conquest.* For some reason, he didn't like thinking of Ellie that way.

"Uriel."

He blinked. Her saying his name reined in his attention. He had been staring at her, but his mind had been flooded with other thoughts. Thoughts of her, but also of his godbrothers. Now he wanted his full concentration on Ellie.

Reaching out, he took her chin in his hand, finally allowing himself to taste the lips he'd been looking at all day, and yearned to kiss. He slowly ran his finger across her lips, liking how soft they felt to his touch, all the while his gaze held hers. "I'm going to miss you tonight," he said in a low voice, one that had deepened to a pitch he hadn't known existed for him.

Although her eyes had begun to darken with the same desire he felt, she managed a small smile and said, "I can always stand at the window and give you something to think about—to remember."

A smile touched his lips, followed by a deep frown. "Don't even think about it. I might not be the only one watching," he said, knowing a couple of his godbrothers had a tendency to get up through the night. "That sort of performance is strictly for me."

While we are together in this summer fling, he thought, but didn't say. When things ended between them, would she be sending out intimate messages to other men? He fought back the knot that began forming in his stomach at the mere thought of that happening. He breathed in deeply, deciding what she did after the summer was her business. He would return to Charlotte and resume his life as it had always been. He would bury himself in work and escalate his sex life up a notch.

But now he just wanted to concentrate on Ellie. His fingers moved from her lips, and he then used his hands to frame her face, capture it gently and tilt it up slightly, at the same time that he lowered his head. The last thought on his mind, before their lips touched, was that he needed this just as he needed to breathe. When she uttered a delicious sigh, it gave his tongue the opening it needed to enter her mouth and taste her delectable warmth. The moment he did so, he heard a groan emit from deep within his throat.

He'd figured he would go easy on her mouth, savor it. A hunger, a need, an absolute greed, made it impossible to do that. Instead, his tongue swept all over her mouth, intensifying the heat, stoking the fire and making him want to stand there and kiss her forever.

Forever? He was suddenly stunned at the thought of that word with regard to any woman. Why would he want to kiss the same woman forever, when there were others out there whose mouths probably tasted just as good? But as he deepened the kiss, a part of him knew it would be hard finding one. At the moment, he was satisfied with this mouth. Ellie's mouth. So utterly satisfied that he could feel blood rushing through his veins, and his erection starting to throb. And he knew at that moment, more than just heat was flowing between them. Desire, as compact as it could get, was invading their senses, and it wouldn't take much to pull her down on a bed of grass and make love to her here. Right now. Forever.

The fear of that one word, of even thinking it again, had him pulling back, stepping away. "I need to go," he said, pulling in a deep breath. "Go on inside, Ellie."

She looked at him, seemed to study his features a moment, before turning and walking up the steps. It was only after she was inside and the door was closed that he leaned back against the oak tree to release the breath he'd been holding. Spending time at his own place, instead of over here, was probably the best thing. He was beginning to act stupidly and think foolishly, and he couldn't allow that to happen. He was a Bachelor in Demand, the last of what seemed to be a dying breed, and he intended to remain that way for life. And no woman, not even someone like Ellie, would make him forget it.

Unable to sleep, Ellie sat in her darkened bedroom and gazed out the window at the house next door. It seemed every room in Uriel's house was lit, which meant everyone was still up and moving around. She knew it had to be close to three in the morning.

When she'd returned home, after taking a shower and changing into a nightgown, she had pulled out her laptop and had typed several scenes, amazing herself at how easily her thoughts had flowed. She had even glanced over her shoulder a few times to make sure her aunt wasn't there somewhere, guiding her fingers across the keyboard, generating the thoughts going through her mind that she was transferring into her laptop. It seemed so easy to continue to read Grant's mind, to see the hard stone around his heart slowly being chipped away. She would admit that he was a complicated man, but he was a man worth loving, and she was glad Tamara knew that.

As before, Ellie wasn't ready to write any lovemaking scenes just yet, although she'd already been inspired by Uriel. Her aunt had done more than connect two bodies in bed, she had created a masterpiece with words enticing the reader to feel, to discover, from the very first kiss. She couldn't attempt to even try to follow in her aunt's footsteps until she felt the time was right.

Sighing deeply, Ellie moved away from the window and crawled back into bed. Funny how after one night, her bed seemed so lonely without Uriel in it. But his masculine scent was embedded in the sheets and the pillow where he had placed his head. She pulled it to her, breathed in deeply and for the moment she was content.

Fourteen

"And what if we told you we've decided to stay with you another week, U?" Xavier asked, grinning as Uriel walked them out to their car.

Uriel frowned. "Then I would tell the four of you to check into a hotel," he said bluntly.

Winston glanced through the trees at the house next door. He then rubbed his chin thoughtfully. "Hmm, if you won't put us up for a while, maybe L will," he said, smiling.

Uriel didn't crack a smile. Instead, he crossed his arms over his chest and said, "Go ahead, W, and try me. I haven't kicked your ass in a long time."

"Sounds like somebody won't be a bachelor in demand pretty soon," York said, chuckling.

Uriel's frown deepened. "If so, I don't know who that will be, because I'm staying put. There's nothing different with what's going on with me and Ellie than with any other woman I've dated. This is no big deal, so why are you making it one?"

Virgil shook his head. "No, U, you're making it one,

and what's so sad is that you haven't realized it yet. You didn't pick any woman to mess around with, you picked L. Even if we thought it was okay, and really not any of our business—which I have to admit it's not—you still have Ms. Mable to deal with."

Uriel lifted a brow. "Ms. Mable?"

Virgil nodded.

Uriel rolled his eyes. "The woman died, or have you forgotten?"

"No, I haven't forgotten. And the way I figure, she's probably rolling over in her grave, thinking about how you plan to treat her niece. Her favorite niece. Her only niece. Her—"

"If you're trying to make me feel guilty, V, it won't work," Uriel broke into Virgil's spiel to say.

Virgil shook his head. "In that case, we're out of here. We'll see you in Aspen in a few months, right?"

"I'll be there."

"And let L know we'll be seeing her again soon," York added. At the dark, threatening look that suddenly flashed in Uriel's eyes, York couldn't help but laugh. "Damn, man, you got it bad."

The four men then got inside their car and drove away.

Moments later, Uriel was still standing in the same spot. The car was no longer in sight. Even when the last of the dust generated from the car on the dirt road was settling back down to earth, he remained in place.

He still hadn't cracked a smile, because basically, his godbrothers were wrong. They were assuming things they shouldn't. Things about his and Ellie's relationship that weren't there. He and his godbrothers were close, but they couldn't read his mind. But still, they knew his situation better than anyone. They knew that, although he'd pretended nonchalance, his parents' divorce had not only thrown him for a loop but had made him look at things differently.

Ellie was a nice girl, and he hoped she would meet someone who would give her all the things in life she deserved. That man was not him, and would never be. All there was between them was a casual relationship. Ellie knew the score. He wanted her, and yes, it was all about sex and nothing more, but she was a grown woman, not a kid. She could handle it. It had taken almost three days for her to make up her mind, which meant she had thought long and hard about it. That night she had appeared at the window undressed, and had waved her panties in the air, it had been an acceptance by her of that decision. Her acknowledgment of what was and what wasn't. No love, just sex.

He glanced at his watch. He had been standing at the kitchen window this morning when he'd seen Ellie back her car out of the garage. She had gotten out of the car to go back inside the house to get something, and he'd seen she was dressed for church, evidently to attend early morning service. She'd been the epitome of a classy lady, from the dressy, wide-brimmed red hat she'd worn, to her red patent leather high-heel shoes. Her dress was black, with a huge, front-draped red sash around her small waist.

He had been tempted to go out on the porch and at least say good morning, and to tell her how nice she looked. Hell, *nice* wasn't a strong enough word. She had looked absolutely gorgeous. But he hadn't gone to the porch, for fear he would have eventually crossed his yard to hers and end up kissing her like a man with no control. Just as he was feeling now.

That was the main reason he knew he should get inside the house, trade his jeans for a pair of shorts, get a beer out of the fridge and chill awhile. Sit on his back porch and appreciate what a beautiful day it was, and be grateful, in spite of what was going on with his parents, that life was good. His business interests appeared to be productive and worthy of every cent he'd invested.

Going back inside and getting that beer sounded like a good plan. Then why was he still standing in the same spot, looking over his right shoulder at the house next door? Why was there an intense longing beginning to build in the pit of his stomach? And why was he turning, placing one foot in front of the other and moving in the direction of where he knew Ellie to be?

And now that he'd passed through the trees and was in the clearing, why was he making his heart rate increase even more by jogging the rest of the way? And why, the closer he got, could he detect her scent, like it was in the very air he was breathing, fueling his heat and intensifying his hunger?

The next thing he knew, he was standing at her back door, leaning against the frame, nearly out of breath—which was unheard of for a man who had a constant workout regime. What he was feeling was anxiousness, not exhaustion. Pulling in a deep breath, he knocked on the door.

She must have been in the kitchen already, because he immediately heard the sound of her voice when she called out, "Just a minute."

While pulling in another deep breath, he heard her footsteps moving across the tile floor. And when she slowly slid the door open and he saw her, looked into her face before moving his gaze to scan over her, to take in yet another sexy short set, he actually couldn't say anything. He just stood there and feasted his eyes on her, feeling a need that for her just couldn't be normal.

His gaze returned to her face and met her eyes. He

didn't say anything, but neither did she. However, he figured she'd seen the appreciative male look in his eyes when he'd checked out her outfit. And he was also certain she could see the hunger that was there now. Hunger for something he'd gotten a chance to sample yesterday and was eager to do so again. He'd never considered himself a horny bastard until now.

He could blame his state on a lot of things: he could blame it on the air that for some reason seemed thick with her scent; or the fact that last night he'd hung around four guys who had nothing better to do than share exaggerated tales of their bedroom escapades while drinking beer and eating pretzels. At least three of them had. Come to think of it, Xavier hadn't said a word, which suddenly made Uriel wonder why.

"Uriel?"

He blinked at the sound of Ellie saying his name, but didn't respond. He couldn't. He just continued to look at her and then, finally, he said, "They're gone."

She nodded. "I know. I was standing at the sink washing dishes, and saw them leave."

That meant she probably saw him standing awhile after they'd left, trying to make up his mind what he should do. She probably even saw him jog over to her house like a madman, which was probably why she hadn't asked who was at the door when he'd knocked. She had known.

Suddenly, something passed through his nostrils and he picked up another scent other than hers. Spaghetti sauce. He lifted a brow. "You cooked?"

A smile touched her lips. "A girl's got to eat. I have plenty left, if you want some."

Heat suffused his body. He was hungry, but it wasn't the thought of consuming spaghetti that had certain parts of him throbbing. He wanted her. He wanted to get inside of her. The spaghetti could wait. "May I come in?" he tried asking softly, but the words came out sounding rather husky, even to his own ears.

Instead of answering, she took a step back and he followed, hoping by the time he stepped over the threshold the flames that were raging wildly through his veins would have suddenly cooled. That wasn't the case. The moment he closed the door behind him and, with a flick of his wrist, put the lock in place, he reached out and grabbed her by the waist to bring her closer to him. He wanted her to feel his hardness and to know what wanting her was doing to him. As much as he liked seeing a pair of sexy-looking shorts on her, he suddenly wanted them off her. But first he wanted to kiss her. He *had* to kiss her.

He lowered his head and took her mouth with a kiss that was meant to temporarily satisfy the flames that refused to cool, intended to slow down the fast beating of his pulse. Instead, it ignited a bigger blaze, one that amounted to a bonfire by the time he took hold of her tongue, mingled it with his and started sucking on it. And his pulse, the one he wanted to slow down, actually picked up speed, which then triggered a blood rush through his veins, making his nerve endings feel as if they would explode.

He wasn't sure at what point something within him snapped, pushed him over the edge, made him crazy with lust, desperate for her. But it happened and he couldn't stop it. His rational mind became irrational. His senses lost all commonality. The need to strip out of his clothes and to get her out of hers was as urgent as anything he'd ever endured.

He groaned deep within the pit of his stomach when he forced his mouth from hers. His hands went immediately to his shirt, nearly tore it from his body, sent buttons fly-

ing everywhere. He glanced over at her when his hands
went to the snap on his jeans. She was leaning against the
counter, drawing in deep breaths as she tried to breathe.

She was staring at him through glazed eyes, watching
as he kicked off his sandals. Then, in one smooth sweep,
he pulled down his jeans and kicked them aside. Before
she could react to seeing him standing stark naked in the
middle of her kitchen, he had reached out for her and was
pulling her top over her head.

Before removing her bra, he leaned down and kissed
her again, and while his mouth was busy on hers, his
hands were inching downward, inside her shorts, just
enough to slip past her panties and go straight for the
center, finding her hot, wet and pulsating to his touch.

He actually let out a low growl as he lifted his head,
ending the kiss, and bringing his hands upward to take
off her bra. Within seconds, his mouth was there on her
breasts, feasting greedily on her nipples like a starved
maniac.

"Uriel."

The sound of her moaning his name in a shuddered
breath alerted him she was close, too close. She was about
to come, but he intended to be inside her when she did.
Backing her up against the refrigerator, he quickly pulled
down her shorts and panties and then kicked them aside,
lifted her up and wrapped her legs around his waist. He
pinned her between him and the fridge, and entered her
with one powerful thrust.

He felt her inner muscles around him begin to throb,
start clenching him, and he drew back out and pushed
back in, over and over again. They were skin-to-skin,
flesh-to-flesh. Her legs were wrapped tightly around his
back, and when she screamed out his name, the sound
triggered an explosion within him that ripped everything

out of him, blasted him off to another hemisphere, made him call her name at the top of his voice, and made him give her all that he had, and then some.

Moments later, he slumped against her, his body still intimately connected to hers. He pulled back, but did not pull out, and looked at her. Her eyes were closed, her face damp with perspiration, her hair falling in her face, and her lips swollen, begging to be kissed.

He leaned and kissed them, still needing to draw this out for as long as he could take it, needing to be connected to her in every way, as long as he desired. And he desired it with every ounce of the strength he'd lost making love to her.

And then, when he couldn't play it out any longer, he swept her into his arms, not caring at the moment that their clothes were thrown carelessly all over her kitchen. He moved through her living room and walked up the stairs, and when they got to her bedroom they tumbled onto her bed and Uriel pulled her into his arms. He spooned her naked body to his, their legs entwined and his hands protectively placed on her stomach. "Rest," he whispered in her ear.

It was only after he heard her slow, easy breathing, indicating that she had fallen asleep, that he closed his eyes to sleep, as well.

Ellie shifted in bed a few times before opening her eyes to a darkened room. She pulled herself up in bed and glanced over at the clock. It was nearly seven at night. Had she slept that long?

And where was Uriel? Had he gone back to his place? Was he downstairs eating spaghetti? She then remembered she had left her laptop still on and sitting on the coffee table. Would he, out of curiosity, see what she was working on? What if he used it to check his email, and noticed the document she was working on?

Not sure of any of those things, she eased out of bed and slid into her robe. She was halfway down the stairs when she heard his voice, loud and angry. She frowned, wondering who he was talking to. She reached the bottom stair and could see him, fully dressed and standing in her kitchen, talking on his cell phone. He'd said he wasn't involved with anyone, but that didn't mean women wouldn't call him. Was he having an argument with an old girlfriend?

Deciding it was really none of her business, and that he deserved to have his conversation in private, she turned to go back up the stairs, when his next words stopped her in her tracks.

"For God's sake, Mom, for once will you think of someone other than yourself? Don't you know every time you hurt Dad, you're hurting me, too?"

Ellie lifted a brow. He was talking to his mother? Mrs. Lassiter? She heard the pain in his voice and also the frustration. Immediately her heart went out to him.

"Look, Mom, this conversation isn't going anywhere. You just refuse to understand what I'm saying. I'll talk to you later. Goodbye."

A part of Ellie wanted to go to Uriel, hold him and tell him everything would be all right, but he might not want that. That would be getting into his business, and until he invited her into it, she had to remain on the outside.

Ellie turned to head back up the stairs, and when she got to the top she eased down to sit on the step. She heard the back door open and close, indicating he had either left or gone outside to get some fresh air. Again she fought the urge to go to him, get him to talk about it.

She was about to get up and go back into her bedroom,

when she heard the back door open and close again and then, moments later, Uriel rounded the corner from the kitchen and glanced up and saw her sitting on the top stair.

He didn't say anything. He just stood there and stared up at her, and even then she felt his anger, but knew it wasn't directed at her. Ellie's natural instinct, the one that loved him, had always loved him, told her to go to him, risk having him tell her she was overstepping the bounds of what was permissible in their affair.

She decided to take the risk anyway, and slowly began walking down the stairs to him. When she reached the bottom step and stood directly in front of him, she wrapped her arms around him and leaned up on tiptoes and joined her mouth to his.

He reciprocated her kiss, reached out and placed his arms around her waist as he eased her closer to him. His hands stroked her back and her backside, while his mouth mated totally and thoroughly with hers.

She gasped when he swept her off her feet and into his arms and headed toward the sofa, sat down and cradled her in his arms. He said nothing for a long time, just sat there holding her, with his chin resting atop her head.

She decided to break his silence by looking up at him and asking, "Are you okay?"

He didn't say anything for a moment, just continued to look down at her, and then he pulled her back into his arms, rested his chin atop her head again and said, "I want to believe that my mother at some point did love my father, but at times, I'm really not sure."

She gave his words a chance to float around them, and then she asked another question, one whose purpose was to make him think. "Why would you even believe that she didn't?" she asked quietly.

He shifted her in his lap so he could meet her gaze,

and then, in a quiet tone, said, "Because she is hurting him so much now. And I can't imagine that a woman who professed to loving a man at one point, could deliberately hurt him the way she is doing. My father left the country this weekend because they were invited to the same party at the country club, and he knew she would be bringing her boy toy. She parades him around like he's the best thing to happen to her since gingerbread. My father still loves her. Nearly had a nervous breakdown when she asked for a divorce."

Ellie didn't know what to say. She had heard bits and pieces of the story from her aunt and her parents, but she hadn't known how deeply the divorce had affected Mr. Lassiter. And she could clearly see the divorce had affected Uriel, as well. She had a question to ask him, mainly because she needed to know.

"Is that the reason you won't consider ever marrying, Uriel? Because of what's happened to your parents' marriage?"

He didn't say anything for a long moment, and she wondered if he would reply. Finally he said, "Yes. I saw my father hurt. I felt his pain. I saw a strong and confident man nearly reduced to a whimpering, poor soul because of his love for a woman, and I made up my mind never to let it happen to me. No woman would ever touch my life that deeply or make me love her that strongly for that to happen. I refuse to let it."

Ellie couldn't say anything. He had pretty much told her in no uncertain terms, that no matter how enjoyable he found her in bed, no matter how much he might take pleasure in her company, when it was time for him to leave Cavanaugh Lake, he would do so without looking back, and possibly, as time passed he wouldn't bother looking her up. If their paths crossed, she would have been just another woman from his past.

"How can I still love her for what she's putting him through, Ellie?"

His question, since he'd asked, was one she felt she could answer. She shifted so she could reach up and place her arms around his neck. "You love her because she is your mom," she said simply. "Our parents don't always do what we want them to do, just like, as their children, we don't always do what they want us to do. We love them anyway, and they love us anyway. Sounds like she's going through a midlife crisis, and it's sad they aren't going through it together."

Her parents certainly had, she thought, remembering how her parents, who didn't even own bicycles, had gone out and purchased his and hers Harleys. And if that wasn't bad enough, they'd joined a motorcycle club and traveled with a group on their motorcycles to Bike Week in Daytona every year. Once she'd gotten over the shock and saw how much fun they were having, she left them alone to do their thing.

"I asked her that, but she said Dad was too busy, never paid any attention to her, because he was working so much. Too bad she couldn't appreciate that he was working so hard to continue to give her the things she'd always wanted. My mother never worked a day in her life. She has a college degree she never used. I never knew how selfish she could be until now."

Ellie said nothing, she just relaxed in his arms and let him vent. It seemed there was a lot he needed to get off his chest. Moments later, when he was finished, he sat there and held her, and she sat there glad to be held. She looked up at him. "Did you get something to eat?"

He nodded. "Yes. Thanks. The spaghetti was good, by the way."

She smiled. "Thank you."

"You're welcome."

She glanced over at the window and saw it had gotten dark outside. She wondered if he would be staying for the night or if he would return to his home. As if he read her thoughts, he leaned closer to her ear and asked in a whisper, "May I spend the night?"

She twisted around in his arms again, and gently pushed him back against the sofa cushion, to sprawl her body over his. She smiled up at him and said, "Yes, you may," before leaning up and placing her mouth on his.

In sleep, Ellie shifted her body to snuggle closer to him, and instinctively, Uriel tightened his arms around her. At least one of them was getting some rest, he thought, as he glanced around the room. They had left a small lamp on near the bedside. He had wanted to see her face while they'd made love. He had wanted to watch how pleasure infused her features when she came. Seeing it would make him explode inside of her, permeate her insides with the essence of him, and she would use her muscles to clamp tight on him, refusing to let him go until she was sure she'd gotten the very last drop.

The thought of a woman wanting that much of him, the thought of wanting to give a woman that much of himself clamored his senses; but then there was nothing about their relationship that was even close to what he was accustomed to with a woman. He had talked about his parents to her. Granted, she knew them, but still, he had told her things he would never have shared with another woman.

And she had listened. He had a feeling that, deep

down, she truly cared. Ellie had offered words of encouragement regarding his father. The main thing he should do now was just hope that his father continued to get involved in things. His dad had agreed to go with them to the next NASCAR race in Indianapolis, and that was good. Another good thing was that he would be spending time with Zion this week.

At thirty, Zion was the youngest of the godsons and the one everyone thought needed the most attention, mainly because Zion was considered the loner, the one who would go for months without staying in touch.

The five godbrothers understood and respected Zion's need for privacy when he was working on his jewelry pieces. Unfortunately the godfathers most often did not. When one would show up unexpectedly, interrupting Zion's work flow, he would be quick to put them to work. Uriel could only smile at the thought that his father was sitting somewhere soldering jewelry pieces at this very minute. At least it would keep his old man's mind occupied for a while.

Another thing Donovan had suggested was that his father start dating. If his mother was all wrapped up in someone, then maybe his father should find someone, too. But preferably, unlike his mother, who'd basically gone and robbed the cradle, he'd choose someone closer to his age. Donovan's cousin Vanessa had hinted at introducing his father to her widowed mother. He'd seen Vanessa's mother, and he would be the first to admit that the lady was very attractive. And Anthony Lassiter, at fifty-five, was a good-looking man who kept himself in excellent physical shape.

Ellie shifted again and whispered his name, but he quashed the urge to wake her up and make love to her again. He'd certainly made up for not having slept with her last night. They had ended up making love on the sofa downstairs, and then had come back upstairs to make love again. And he had enjoyed each and every moment of it.

But he didn't want to dominate all her time during the coming days, and wasn't into her dominating his, especially since he still had a lot of reading about his publishing company to do. Evidently, she had completed whatever it was she'd been reading. He would spend the night, and tomorrow he would return to his place for a while and do a few things over there. Five men could get pretty damn sloppy, even in one day, and he needed to clean up the place.

"Uri?"

He glanced down and saw her sleepy eyes staring up at him. "Did my moving around wake you up?" he asked in a low tone.

"No. I woke up on my own." A smile touched her lips. "And now, since I am awake," she said, pushing him back among the pillows and straddling her body over his, "I might as well take advantage of it."

And she did.

Fifteen

Uriel paused in taking the fish off the hook and glanced over at Ellie. "What do you mean you don't know how to clean fish?" The two of them had gone fishing, and he couldn't believe, he refused to believe what she'd just said.

She shrugged. "I mean what I said. No one has ever taught me. When my dad and I used to fish he would clean them. The times I went fishing with you and your godbrothers, you all would do all the cleaning. There was no need for me to learn."

Uriel squinted his eyes against the brightness of the sun. "Well, I hate to be the bearer of bad news, but there is a need now. We both clean the fish we catch. I believe in equal opportunity."

He couldn't help but laugh at the face she made at him before turning and prancing off the pier and walking toward her house, giving him a delectable view of her backside in a pair of shorts.

"And just where do you think you're going, hot pants?" he called out to her.

She turned around with her chin lifted in the air and

said, "Home. I don't want to play with you anymore. I'm going to take a shower and relax. Later, after you've cleaned *all* the fish, come join me."

He lifted a brow. "Umm, and what do I get?"

"What you've been getting all week," she replied bluntly, before turning around and continuing her walk home.

Uriel couldn't help the huge smile that touched his lips. Damn, had it been a full week already? Actually, it had been more than a week. Ten days, to be exact, and the woman had proven to be temptation and enticement all rolled into one.

Nothing was going as he'd planned. He'd thought he could leave her during the day and just show up at night for sex, but things weren't quite working out that way. He'd tried it the first day, but now he was looking in her face 24/7. And he liked being inside her body, as well. He hadn't missed a day making love to her since his godbrothers' departure, alternating between his bed and hers.

They had taken out the time to go fishing, and she had helped him when he'd decided his living room needed a new coat of paint. They had done a movie night over at his place. He'd even been helping her pack up her aunt's belongings in between bouts of lovemaking. Hell, they made love all the time and he was enjoying the hell out of it. But then they would sit down and talk, as well. She told him about how she was thinking about going into business for herself, but wasn't sure if that would be the right move. She even mentioned just hanging out at the lake house a few more months before getting back into the workforce. And because he had been in the corporate world a lot longer than she had, he'd given her advice on what companies to avoid. One thing he liked was that she listened and asked questions. Bottom line was that he enjoyed her company both in and out of bed.

Picking up both of their fishing rods as well as the bucket filled with the fish they'd caught, he made it back over to his place. He placed the fish in the sink and grabbed a beer out of the fridge, deciding he would cool down before cleaning the fish. Then he would take a shower and go find Ellie, and when he found her he would—

The ringing of his cell phone interrupted his thoughts, but that was okay, since he knew exactly what he would do to her. He pulled his cell phone out of the back pocket of his shorts. "Yes?"

"Hey, Uri, this is Donovan. I'm a new uncle again. Morgan and his wife, Lena, just had a son. He came out looking like a slugger. I bet he weighed every bit of ten pounds."

For the next few minutes, he and Donovan talked about the new baby and how the parents were handling things. And then Donovan asked, "How's the fishing? They still biting pretty good?"

"Yes. You ought to grab your fishing rod and come down a few days." Since Donovan had never met Ellie, he wouldn't feel inclined to protect her honor like his godbrothers had. But Uriel had made up his mind about a few things this week. No matter who else showed up at the lake—except for her parents or his, as a matter of respect—he didn't intend on spending a single night out of her bed.

For him to be involved in an affair was commonplace to Donovan, and he wouldn't think anything unusual. With Ellie living next door, Donovan would only think of it as convenient. Before Natalie had come into Donovan's life, he'd been Charlotte's number-one player. In a way, Uriel still couldn't believe Donovan had given all of it up. Just for one woman.

"Donovan, I need to ask you something," he said, when both confusion and curiosity got the best of him.

"Sure. What?"

Uriel knew that although he and Donovan were thick as thieves, were more brothers than friends, he still wanted to word his question carefully. He didn't want to offend anyone or give the impression Donovan had made one hell of a mistake. But his engagement was still too mind-boggling to think about, and Uriel needed his friend to explain why.

"This thing with you and Natalie. The two of you just met last month. She's a gorgeous woman and a nice person to boot. I liked her off the bat, but you've dated a lot of women—lookers, stunners, women so attractive I could weep with envy. Just think of all the booty calls you're giving up. My question to you is, is it—"

"Worth it?" Donovan finished for him.

Uriel released a long and deep breath. "Yes, is it worth it?"

Donovan didn't say anything for a moment, and then he said, "I wish I could explain it, Uriel, but I doubt if I can. And to answer your question, yes, it's worth it. *She* is worth it. I didn't think I would say that about any woman. You know my philosophy. There were too many out there to settle on just one. Being inside the body of one was no different than being inside the body of another. But I found out that isn't true. There is a difference when something comes into the mix you don't expect. Love. Damn, man, it was the weirdest thing. I think I fell in love with Natalie the moment I met her, and one of these days real soon I'm going to have to tell you all about it. You won't believe how we actually met. And although I thought it was all about sex, and once I took her to bed that would be that, I found out it wasn't. There is a difference, and if you ever meet a woman—the woman who is wearing your name somewhere on her heart—you will know. Maybe not right away, but eventually you will."

Uriel thought about what Donovan was saying. If he didn't know his friend as the man he was, as the player he had been, Uriel would think he was nothing more than a lovesick puppy. But he knew that wasn't the case. Donovan hadn't been out there looking for love. He had been doing what he usually did when it came to women, which was looking for sex. But now he was making plans to spend the rest of his life with the same woman, and he actually seemed happy about it. Uriel could not detect one ounce of regret in his voice.

"Like I said, Uriel, you'll know her."

Uriel frowned, deciding not to waste time telling his friend it wouldn't happen to him. That even if he met this woman, whose name he was supposedly wearing on his heart, he would wonder if she would eventually do to him the same thing his mother had done to his father. The thought of losing his mind over a woman was something he refused to consider.

"I know you met Natalie that one time at the Race-track Café, but I'd love to bring her down to the lake to spend time with you. How about a fish fry next weekend?" Donovan was saying.

Uriel smiled. He had no problem getting out the fryer again. "Sounds like a great idea, and you and Natalie can have the whole house to yourself for the weekend."

"And where will you be?" Donovan asked.

"Next door. The woman next door and I are…friends," he said, knowing Donovan would get his drift.

"Oh, okay. If you're sure it's okay, I'll make certain Natalie will be available for next weekend. I'll call you later today and let you know."

"All right."

After hanging up the phone and placing it back in his pocket, Uriel still felt a bit confused as well as somewhat curious. Maybe seeing Donovan and Natalie interact would help him understand the gist of it all. The one and only time he'd seen them together they'd been at odds with each other, and the only thing Uriel had felt flowing between them were tension and anger, at least from Natalie. Donovan had simply come across as frustrated.

Oh, well, he thought, as he went to work cleaning the fish, love and marriage might be for some people, but it definitely wasn't for him.

A just-showered, fully relaxed Ellie slumped down in her favorite chair by the window, with her laptop in her hand, ready to write a couple of scenes today. And from where she was sitting, she'd be able to see Uriel when he left his house to come to hers.

She began typing, and as if she were in another world, one filled with love and passion, she brought life once again to Grant and Tamara. Her hands seemed to flow over the keys, knowing what they were about to say before they said it.

Moments later, when Ellie finally got to a love scene, she began typing, truly inspired. She and Uriel had been sharing a bed for more than a week and she had never known a more passionate man. Her cheeks couldn't help but color with a blush just thinking about their nights as well as their mornings. And it just wasn't in the things he did, but also the things he said. The man took pillow talk to a whole other level.

She wasn't aware just how long she'd sat there typing, when she heard the sound of a door slamming shut. She glanced up and saw Uriel step off his porch and head over to her place. He glanced up and saw her sitting by the window and smiled before waving at her. She smiled back, noting he had showered and changed clothes.

Ellie shut down her laptop, but not before noting just how much she'd typed. She smiled, pleased with her accomplishment for the day. And she was pleased with how things were going between her and Uriel. It was pretty nice waking up in a man's arms every morning, after falling asleep once she'd been thoroughly made love to at night.

Then there were the other things they did together, like cook breakfast and dinner. He helped her pack up the last of her aunt's belongings to give away and had helped store in the attic those things she wanted to keep. He had driven her into town to a nursery to purchase a couple of fruit trees she wanted for the backyard, and had even chopped wood for the winter months; if she decided to come back later in the year, there would be enough ready for the fireplace. And he had made watching movies with him special.

Sensations suddenly overwhelmed her at the thought that in two weeks he would be leaving Cavanaugh Lake to return to Charlotte. Their affair would be ending. She would remain here and finish the book, which shouldn't take too long. Then she would return to Boston. She had decided to wait until the first of the year to decide if she wanted to go back into corporate America, or start her own business. Uriel had given her good advice regarding the pros and cons of both.

She didn't have to look up to know he had entered the bedroom. She felt his presence. She was intercepting his heat. She knew, at that moment when they went their separate ways, her pain would be almost too much to bear, but she would. She had no choice.

Tilting her head back, she stared at him. He was leaning in the doorway, shirtless and wearing a pair of shorts that, in her opinion, looked just as scandalous as any she'd ever worn. They displayed just what a good physique he had: flat stomach; muscular thighs; strong legs. And a thick arousal pressing hard against his crotch. It wouldn't be so bad if she didn't know what was behind the shorts. She knew every solid inch of him there, had seen it erect and nonerect. Her fingers had touched it, gently squeezed it, had given it her own personal massage. And one night, in a surprise move and with a bold degree of naughtiness, her mouth had tasted it, almost greedily, and several satisfied groans had escaped his lips. She now knew all the things that brought him pleasure, all the ways they could be done, what it took to push him over the edge, make him call out her name in a throaty growl. Remembering made an intense shudder ripple down her spine.

She had opened the bedroom window earlier, and a gentle breeze was coming in, stirring the heat he was emitting as well as his scent. The air between them seemed to spark, and she had a feeling if she didn't say something, didn't start conversation, they were liable to go up in flames just from staring across the room at each other. So to break the silence, she asked, "Did you get all the fish cleaned?"

"Yes, with no help from you."

She couldn't help but chuckle. "You poor baby. Do you want some cheese to go with that whine?"

"Do you really want to know what I want, Ellie?"

"No," she said, managing a faint smile, letting her gaze travel back down to his crotch, then back to his face. "I have an idea."

A smile curved his lips. "And you're probably right.

But I can wait till after dinner for you to be my dessert," he said, coming into the room. "Besides, we need to talk."

She raised a brow. "About what?"

"More company coming. My business partner, Donovan Steele. I think I mentioned he'd gotten engaged."

She nodded. "Yes, you did."

"Well, I invited him and his fiancée to come to Cavanaugh Lake for the weekend for a fish fry."

"This weekend?"

He chuckled. "No, next weekend. I haven't forgotten my promise to take you rafting in the Smokies this weekend."

"Good."

"And I hope you don't mind, but I gave them full use of my place for the weekend, which means I'll be crashing over here," he said.

"No, I don't mind," she responded. He'd been crashing at her place anyway. Since their affair had begun, the only night he hadn't stayed was the one night his godbrothers had come to visit.

"How would you like to take a walk before we get into the kitchen to fix dinner?"

"A walk?" She'd said it like she hadn't heard him right.

He grinned. "Yes, a walk. When was the last time you actually walked around Cavanaugh Lake, all the way to the east bank?"

"Too long ago to remember. Why the interest in doing so now?" She was curious enough to ask.

He leaned back against the dresser and said, "I'm thinking of buying a boat, nothing too big, but it's something I've always wanted. I want to walk to the other side of the lake to make sure that old dock is still there. If it's not, I'm going to have to build one."

She nodded. "If it's there, you might need to get it repaired," she pointed out.

"No problem. So put on a pair of good shoes and let's go," he said, moving toward the door.

She laughed and gave him a hearty salute. "Yes, boss."

He turned around and gave her a charming smile. "I'm not your boss."

"Oh, then what are you?" she asked sweetly.

His gaze seemed clouded in an arousing heat when he said, "Your lover."

He was her *lover*.

Uriel made a mental acknowledgment of the words he had spoken to Ellie earlier that day. That acknowledgment was followed by an image that popped into his mind. It was a scene that had taken place less than an hour ago, right in his bed, before Ellie had drifted off to sleep. It was one that affirmed his claim. Proven without a shadow of a doubt. He was her lover.

Even now, they were lying facing each other, her head resting snugly on his chest, their legs entwined, and their bodies still intimately connected. He felt himself getting hard again, just thinking about how things had started out with her being his dessert in the kitchen, and his late-night snack in the bedroom. And he had basically been hers.

He slid his arms around her, opening his hands on her bottom, to pull her snugly against him for an even better connection when he felt himself starting to get hard again. His shaft was happy, very contented, because it was where it wanted to be. It would probably protest if he were to pull out of her. A satisfied groan flowed from his lips. *He* was happy and very content, as well.

He glanced over at the nightstand at the several packets of condoms. Although he placed them there every night, he had yet to use one. With Ellie, he enjoyed the feel of skin-to-skin, flesh-to-flesh. He enjoyed the feel of exploding inside of her, jetting his hot release into her—something he had never considered doing to another woman. She was on the Pill, but then, every once in a while, when the possibility did cross his mind, he would envision a prissy little girl with skin the color of Ellie's and eyes identical to his. And just like all the other times when such foolish images formed in his mind, he was quick to dismiss them. He felt his shaft grow even harder inside of her and tried like hell to ignore it. No luck. A shudder ran down his body, rippling along his spine, electrifying the hard muscles in his erection.

She must have felt it. She must have felt *him.* Not surprisingly, since he was stretching her again to accommodate his growing manhood. She slowly opened her eyes and met his. She smiled and gave him a sleepy but knowing look.

"Sorry," he apologized. "I didn't mean to wake you, but I guess my friend wants attention." And as he felt himself grow larger still, he added, "No regrets."

She smiled as he held tight to her body, remaining inside of her as he turned and placed her on top of him. She gazed down at him and said, "And that's why your friend and I like each other so much, and why we get along so well—because I have no regrets, either. We don't have time to waste, since it will be the end of the month before you know it."

Her words reminded him of just how true that was. It would be the end of the month soon, and he didn't want to waste time. He wanted to savor every moment that he could with her, because when it ended, it ended. But for now, he was wrapping his arms around her as she began riding him as if her very life depended on it, moving up and down, permeating the air with her scent, his scent, the aroma of their lovemaking. He had this.

His jaw tightened each time he lifted himself to meet her downward movement. This was the best of the best, the cream of the crop, off the charts. This is what made a man appreciate being a man…and what made a man appreciate having a good woman.

He tossed that very claim out of his mind. This woman was his *temporarily.* By rights, she should be doing all the things she'd done to him, and with him, for the past ten days to a man who would be a permanent part of her future. A man who would flood her body with his seed to make babies, a man she could commit her life to, as he would commit his to her. A man who would not place a limit on the time they spent together.

He was not that man; but for now, tonight, until the end of the month, they could both pretend.

Sixteen

"And Donovan, this is Ellie."

Uriel watched Donovan's expression when he turned his attention to the woman by his side. Surprise, confusion and keen interest were showing in Donovan Steele's gaze, but only someone as close to Donovan as Uriel would be able to detect it. Uriel could just imagine what his friend was thinking. Ellie was beautiful, and for him to even consider eventually walking away would be stone crazy. But then, Uriel knew those were the thoughts of the new, engaged and about-to-be-married Donovan.

The old Donovan would have understood and not questioned his motives or decision. He would have patted him on the back for making such a lucrative score—a worthwhile conquest—and would have given him a wink of envy. But not the Donovan who was deeply in love with the gorgeous woman standing by his side, so much so that he couldn't keep his eyes off of her. *Jeesh.* Uriel figured it was going to take some getting used to this Donovan Steele.

After all the introductions were made, Uriel saw how

quickly Ellie and Natalie took to each other like old friends. When the conversation between them shifted to a subject he was certain neither he nor Donovan gave a royal damn about—namely the right shampoo and conditioner to keep the frizz out of your hair in this August heat—he caught Donovan's attention and rolled his eyes, before saying, "I'll help you get the luggage out of the car."

The two women went inside his house while he and Donovan went to the back of the car to open the trunk. Uriel raised a brow when he saw several pieces of luggage. "Hey, Don, you and Natalie are here just for the weekend, not for the rest of the year, right?"

Donovan chuckled. "Natalie wasn't sure what to pack, so she tucked in a little of everything."

Uriel gave him a wry look, knowing how Donovan detested excessiveness in anyone…or at least, he used to. "And you're still going to marry her with this one major flaw?" he asked teasingly.

Donovan threw his head back and laughed. "In a heartbeat. Tomorrow, if she'd agree to it. Hell, I tried, at a weak moment, getting her to fly to Vegas with me, but she refused."

Uriel shook his head. "I guess you're going to have to work harder on her."

"Just like Ellie is going to have to work harder on you?"

Uriel raised a brow, and tried to keep his body from stiffening at Donovan's words. "Meaning?"

"She likes you."

Uriel relaxed somewhat. "And I like her. But nothing is going to keep me from ending our relationship in eight days."

"Then I hope you know what you're doing."

Uriel gave his friend another wry look, wondering if

Donovan realized what he was suggesting. A serious relationship, one that could end in marriage, babies and a little house with a picket fence was nowhere in his future, and Donovan, of all people, knew that.

Deciding it was time to change the subject, Uriel asked, "How are things going with the Steele Corporation? I understand you had a serious internal issue."

"Everything is fine. Fortunately, we identified the person trying to give company secrets to our competitor. A man in Morgan's department who'd worked with us for years. I'm glad we made the discovery before he could do any damage."

Donovan then asked, "So, how does our publishing company look?"

Uriel knew that the reason Donovan was asking had nothing to do with the possibility that they'd made a wrong investment. That wasn't the case, since they had checked out Vandellas Publishing thoroughly before making the purchase. It had been financially sound. Their main concern was making sure it remained a viable acquisition over the next three years, until they were ready to sell.

"I haven't finished going through all the documents as I'd planned."

"I can understand why," Donovan said with a smirk on his face.

Uriel ignored him and said, "But I plan to do so this week. I'm anxious to go over their inventory lists to see how many books they published this year, and how many they plan to publish next year. I'm also curious to see who they gave high advances to and what promotional and marketing strategies they intend to use to make sure those books sell."

They carried the luggage to the door and when they entered they could hear Ellie and Natalie chatting away. He glanced over at Donovan. "They're still talking about hair products?"

Donovan grinned. "Sounds like it."

"Then we need to pull them apart and give them something else to talk about, don't you think?" Uriel said, winking at his friend.

Three days later, Ellie eased out of bed, thinking that this past weekend had been fun spending time with Donovan and Natalie, and in a way, she'd regretted seeing them leave. While Donovan had helped Uriel fry the fish, Natalie had helped her make coleslaw. And for dessert, Natalie had offered to make her aunt's mouthwatering peach cobbler. That meant going to the grocers and getting all the ingredients they needed. During the drive, Natalie told Ellie her and Donovan's love story and filled her in on their June wedding plans.

It only took being around the couple for a brief period of time to see how much in love they were. Ellie couldn't help but wonder how it would feel to be loved that much by any man, to know that you, of all women, had been the one he chose to be with for the rest of his life, to be cherished by him, deeply loved to the point where he would want you to be the mother of his babies, the woman he wanted to make love to for the rest of his days.

Ellie glanced back over her shoulder at Uriel, who was sprawled out naked on top of the mattress, heart-stoppingly breathtaking. From the way his erection was growing before her eyes, he was getting aroused all over again. "Make it go down," she ordered, and couldn't help but giggle as she slipped into the shorts he had removed last night.

Uriel's hand, the one that had been thrown over his eyes to ward off the morning sun coming through the window, slid down just enough to look over at her. "You come back to bed and *make* it go down, because I sure as hell can't. When it wants you, even a cold shower won't work."

Ellie figured there was no use reminding Uriel that *it* had had her several times during the night. But what she *would* remind him was that he'd promised to take her to dinner at that Italian restaurant in Gatlinburg. They were winding down the time they would be spending together, because in four days he would leave to return to Charlotte.

She glanced over at the bed and saw that Uriel had drifted back to sleep. Would he ever give his heart a chance to share a love such as Natalie and Donovan's? Or would he let what happened with his parents' marriage be the reason he would never want that kind of love, that kind of relationship, for himself? And for that very reason, she would never let him know just how much she loved him, just how much her heart would break in a few days when he would be leaving, going back to a world without her in it.

She slowly walked over to the bed, leaned down and placed a kiss on his lips. She then glanced around his bedroom, saw a pen and a piece of paper lying on the dresser, and scribbled a note, letting him know she was going back to her place to shower, and to then start packing the last of her aunt's things.

A short while later, back at her place, and after taking a shower and putting on her favorite shorts set, Ellie headed downstairs, wondering if Uriel was still in his bed asleep. He had mentioned last night that he would be spending the first part of the morning finishing up reading about some company he and Donovan had purchased a month or so ago.

She had just taken the milk out of the refrigerator for her cereal when the house phone rang. She lifted a brow, wondering who would be calling this early on a Monday morning. Most people she knew called her on her cell phone, which meant the caller was probably one of those telemarketers. She decided not to pick it up, but changed her mind, thinking it could possibly be her parents.

"Hello?"

"Is Mable Weston there?"

Ellie frowned. Most people who knew her aunt were aware she'd passed away. "May I ask who's calling?"

"Yes, this is Lauren Poole."

It didn't take long for Ellie to recall the name, and she leaned back against the refrigerator in surprise, quickly remembering that the last time her back had been against the refrigerator Uriel had pinned her there.

"Hello. Are you there?"

The woman's voice pulled her thoughts back to the conversation and the realization of just who Lauren Poole was. "Yes, I'm here."

"May I speak with Mable please?"

Ellie gnawed nervously on her bottom lip before saying, "Sorry, she's resting." She breathed in deeply, while thinking that it wasn't really a complete lie. "This is her niece, Ellie Weston. Is there something I can help you with?"

"Oh, yes, her niece. Mable speaks of you often. She simply adores you."

"Thanks. And I adore her, as well. Is there a message you'd like to leave? I'll be happy to make sure she gets it." Now *that,* Ellie thought, *was* a lie.

"I just wanted to let her know that the Vandellas Publishing Company was sold to another company, but the buyout changes nothing, as it relates to her contract. She still has until the end of the year to turn in the manuscript, and the release date for the book is still July of next year."

Ellie nodded her head, thinking that was good to hear. "I appreciate you calling and will make sure she gets your message."

"Thank you. I'm looking forward to receiving the finished manuscript, and so is her editor at Vandellas. We all thought it was a beautiful romance, and we're eager to get more stories by Flame Elbam."

Ellie drew in a deep breath. Now was the perfect time to tell Lauren Poole that her aunt had died, and that there was no way Aunt Mable, aka Flame Elbam, would supply them with more manuscripts. "Ms. Poole."

"Yes?"

Ellie opened her mouth to tell the woman the truth, but closed it when she recalled the words her aunt had written in the letter Mr. Altman had given to her. Although the publishing company and Ms. Poole probably wouldn't think so, Ellie believed she was doing the right thing by completing her aunt's novel.

"Yes, Miss Weston?"

"Nothing. I'll give Aunt Mable the message."

"Thank you."

After the phone conversation ended, Ellie drew in a deep breath and then slowly released it. She was doing what her aunt would have wanted. And she knew that, in addition to Uriel's inspiration, her aunt was inspiring her, as well. There was no way she could have gotten into the characters so deeply over the past three weeks without her aunt's divine intervention. So she truly believed she was finishing the manuscript with her aunt's blessing.

But what about Uriel's?

Ellie went over to the table and sat down. He had only inspired her because she loved him. To him, this summer fling may have been about nothing but sex, but to her it had been so much more. Every time he had touched her, she fell deeper and deeper in love with him, and she knew that the day he left to return to Charlotte would be the hardest day of her life.

But she wanted him to leave knowing the truth. Although the past three weeks were nothing but an affair for him, she wanted him to know that for her it had meant something more.

Seventeen

Uriel lay in bed and stared up at the ceiling. In four days he would be leaving this place to return to Charlotte. When he pulled out of the driveway on Sunday evening, he would look straight ahead, wonder how well his assistant had managed things in his absence, and look forward to getting back into the swing of things at Lassiter Industries.

He would not dwell on what he'd been doing for the past three weeks, the summer fling he thoroughly enjoyed. Why would he? It had been nothing more than an affair, and affairs were insignificant. After one ended, you rested up, gave yourself breathing room and prepared for the next one. Life moved on.

Then why did he suddenly feel like his was standing still?

Why did the thought of leaving here, not seeing Ellie, not spending time with her, not making love to her, leave an emptiness in his stomach, a vacant spot in his chest surrounding his heart?

An unfamiliar feeling stirred in his gut, and he tried

shoving it away. Instead, it moved to his shoulder blades
and then to the lower part of his back. Agonized, he closed
his eyes, and the only image that could form behind his
closed eyelids was Ellie. He saw her as she'd looked that
night she had stood at her window, stripping for him, giving him her decision to have an affair with him in a style
that even now left him breathless.

And then Ellie as she had looked later when he had
entered her, felt her tightness squeeze him, and her wetness surround him, flesh-to-flesh, skin-to-skin.

He saw, too, the Ellie who had spent the past three
weeks with him, making him enjoy a woman's company
in a way he'd never done before. Sharing breakfast with
her, going fishing with her, going skinny-dipping with
her, watching movies till dawn with her, making im-
promptu love to her, anytime and anyplace—tasting her
with a hunger and need that he hadn't experienced with
any woman. And having unprotected sex with her and
enjoying shooting his seed into her, while actually imagining the baby they could be making together.

He thought of Ellie, and those times she held him
within her body, clenched him with a need that could
make him come. How she would stroke him, take him
into her mouth and love him that way, and how he would
doze off to sleep, wanting her near him, with his hands
between her legs to keep her there. Before now he refused to believe there was a difference in passion. Now
he knew there was lovemaking passion and sex passion.
The passion that flowed through his body whenever he
was inside of Ellie was lovemaking passion.

He opened his eyes and stared at the ceiling again, as
his heart began to pound deep in his chest and every bone
in his body began to quiver. There could be only one rea-

son for him feeling as he did. One reason he needed to finally face up to.

He then recalled Donovan's words of just a few days ago: *"If you ever meet the woman who is wearing your name somewhere on her heart—you will know."*

He knew. He knew at that very moment that it was Ellie's name scrawled on his heart. *Damn.* He eased out of bed, thinking he needed a beer, then deciding a shot of whiskey—preferably Jack Daniel's—would do better. How had he allowed himself to fall in love, after what his mother had done to his father? Was he a glutton for the same type of experience?

He knew that the only thing he was a glutton for was Ellie. She was not like his mother. He would be able to put all his love and trust in her and not be betrayed.

He rubbed his hand over his face. His shower could wait. He needed to see Ellie, and he needed to see her now.

Ellie released a long sigh and wondered why she had called Darcy, when she knew what her best friend would say. "I hear what you're saying, Darcy, but a part of me feels I should come clean and tell Uriel the truth. And if you think it won't matter, then fine. I just don't want him to think these past three weeks meant nothing to me."

"Okay, El, if you think that's what you should do, then fine, do it. But if he's like most men, all that matters with an affair is the outcome, and the outcome was three weeks in his bed. I doubt he would have given that up for anything."

"Maybe not, Darcy, but the bottom line is that I got a call from my aunt's literary agent, to tell me that Vandellas Publishing was sold to another company. I'm glad Uriel was around so I could get plenty of lovemaking inspiration to finish the book for her as Flame Elbam. But the bottom line is that, when he finds out he is going to know that he was being used."

Suddenly, she thought she heard a noise outside, and glanced out the window but didn't see anything. She then pulled in a deep breath and said, "That's why I have to tell him the truth. I have to let him know that he wasn't used. That I love him, and the time I spent with him was special."

She took a deep breath, and was grateful that, for once, Darcy didn't say anything.

"Look, Darcy, I have to go. I have a lot to do before Uriel comes over. And then I will tell him the truth. Everything. He deserves that."

Somehow, Uriel made it back to his house and dropped down in his kitchen chair, while the words he had heard Ellie speak rang so clear in his mind.

He had been about to knock on her back door, when two names she'd spoken grabbed him. Darcy and Vandellas Publishing. Darcy was her best friend, the one who'd talked her into that dare ten years ago, and Vandellas Publishing was the company that he and Donovan now owned. What was Ellie talking about when she said she would finish a book for her aunt for his publishing company? And better yet, how had his lovemaking inspired her to finish the book?

A part of him knew he probably should have just hung around and asked her, demanded a few answers. But the part of him that had just admitted to being in love with her less than an hour ago felt raw and betrayed.

He breathed in deeply as he replayed her words that were still so clear in his mind.

He stood, and slowly walked up the stairs to his bedroom, where he pulled open his briefcase. It didn't take him long to find the papers he was looking for. The first was a detailed listing of all the outstanding manuscripts. He quickly scanned the page and found the name "Flame Elbam," and in parenthesis it showed "Mable Weston."

Uriel blinked. Ms. Mable had been writing one of those romance novels? He pulled in a breath deeply. The woman was in her seventies, for crying out loud, so it had to be one of those sweet and innocent types where the man and woman did nothing more than hold hands, or kiss each other on the cheek.

He nearly swallowed his tongue when, moments later, he saw the category Ms. Mable's book had been purchased for: erotica. The paper he was holding almost slipped out of his hand, and he couldn't do anything but gape his mouth before dropping down on the side of his bed in shock. Sweet little old Ms. Mable had been writing erotica romances? He read further and saw she'd been given an advance of over fifty thousand dollars.

Damn. First his mother and her boy toy, and now Ms. Mable and her erotica romances…the female population never ceased to amaze him. His thoughts then shifted to Ellie. There was nothing on the paper he was holding in his hand to indicate that Mable Weston, aka Flame Elbam, would not be turning her manuscript in, which revealed Ellie's devious plan to outwit the publisher and finish the book herself.

Using him for her research.

Anger consumed him at the thought that, once again, ten years later, she and her friend Darcy had played him for a fool. The years hadn't matured them at all. Instead of getting wiser, they had gotten more conniving and deceitful. It would do Darcy justice to one day meet someone like York, who would see through her with the first blink, and then show her no mercy.

But for him, his bone of contention was with Ellie, the woman he had been foolish enough to fall in love with, the woman who had broken his heart before it had gotten a chance to accept that it could beat for one woman.

Deciding he no longer wanted to be within even fifty feet of Ellie, he went to the closet and threw his luggage out on the bed and moved around the room throwing things into it. There was nothing she could say. Nothing he wanted to hear.

She had made a fool of him for the last time.

Ellie climbed the steps to Uriel's front door, surprised to find it cracked open. It was not like him to forget to lock the door behind him. She had expected him to come over to her place at least by noon, and wondered if he was still asleep. She was prepared to tell him everything.

She entered the house, and when she heard him moving around upstairs, she called out to him as she headed toward the stairs, "Uriel, I'm coming up."

"Don't bother."

She looked up at him and saw that he was standing at the top of the stairs staring back. The look on his face sent chills through her body. And he had his luggage in his hand. She swallowed and wondered what was wrong. Had something happened to his father? His mother?

"Uriel, what is it? What happened?"

The laugh that emitted from his throat was just as cold and chilling as the look he was giving her. "You want to know what happened, Ellie? I'll tell you what happened. Stupid me. Foolish me. Wanting to believe, after ten years, you had grown up and had matured, not just in body but also in mind—only to discover that, once again, you and your friend, Darcy, decided to play me. This time, using me in the bedroom, since you've outgrown a mere kiss on the pier. You needed to finish your aunt's book, and I was the perfect man to research those bedroom scenes you needed to write."

At the surprised look in her eyes, Uriel laughed again and said, "Yes, I was coming over to see you and just happened to overhear your conversation with your friend, Darcy. I heard everything you said. Go play games with someone else, and get out of my house. You aren't welcome here."

"Uriel, please listen. You didn't hear everything, and I wasn't playing a game with you. I had planned to tell you everything about Aunt Mable's book and—"

"When? When had you planned to tell me, Ellie? Once the book was published, and my name appeared in the acknowledgments as the man who inspired you to write all those lovemaking scenes? The man who introduced you to all those various positions? The man you used once again, ten years later."

"Uriel, I—"

"Please leave. And you can have Cavanaugh Lake all to yourself, because I am going back to Charlotte."

He came down the stairs and stood in front of her. The anger on his face was reflected in his eyes as well, when he said, "Now, please leave so I can lock up the place."

Ellie met his gaze and knew that no matter what she said to him, he would not listen. So she turned and headed for the door. But not before looking back one final time, hoping, just hoping, she would once again see his eyes and a smile curve his lips. She saw neither. Instead, she saw the hard, cold expression of a very angry man. A man who had all but told her he did not, would not, allow her back into his life again.

She turned and walked away, opening the door and then walking out of it. She kept walking, refusing to stop until she was safely inside her own home. And then she made it to the sofa, slumped down and covered her face in her hands. It was only moments later, when she heard the sound of his car pulling away, that she let the tears fall, unheeded, down her face.

Kicking off her sandals, she decided to lie down, doubting her legs would be able to carry her anywhere right now. And she closed her eyes and cried some more.

Ellie opened her eyes and looked around, and when she glanced out the window she saw that dusk was covering the earth. She pulled herself up, not believing she had actually slept for over five hours.

But she had slept, and while doing so she had dreamed. It had been a pleasant dream, one of her and her aunt. They had laughed and they had talked, and then her aunt had held her while she cried. It had seemed so real, but she knew it had been merely a dream.

Still, she had come away with something very important. Her aunt wanted her to finish the book, and in doing so, she would be stronger when she confronted Uriel again. If he thought he had seen the last of her, he was sadly mistaken. She would give him time to cool his anger, and then she was going to Charlotte to see him. No matter what it took, she would make him realize her aunt's book was a blessing to them and not a curse.

It might have been the reason she'd agreed to an affair with him, but it hadn't been the reason she had fallen in love with him.

Eighteen

"Have a nice weekend, Mr. Lassiter."

Uriel paused and glanced over his shoulder at his administrative assistant. "Thank you, Karen, and I hope you do the same."

"Are you headed out to your lake place for the Labor Day weekend?" Karen asked, and smiled as he grabbed his briefcase off his desk.

"No. I plan to have a quiet weekend at home."

He quickly left the office, not wanting to engage in any further conversation with Karen, or anyone else for that matter. He'd already seen his father before he'd left for the day. His father had made plans to fly to New York and visit with York and his parents.

Due to the holiday traffic on the road, it took Uriel longer than usual to get home. Normally, he would drop by the Racetrack Café and have a couple of beers with Donovan, Xavier and Bronson. But Bronson was racing this weekend at the Atlanta Motor Speedway, and the guys had gone to Atlanta to give him their support. Uriel thought about going, but had changed his mind. He much preferred being by himself this weekend. Now he knew how his father must have felt. It had been two weeks, and the pain hadn't eased any.

Donovan had accused him of being stubborn and had tried encouraging him to call Ellie, and listen to her—to let her explain her side of things. Donovan had shared with him the mistake he'd made in jumping to conclusions with Natalie. But Uriel's heart had hardened more at the thought of even talking to Ellie.

He let himself inside his home, and again noticed how lonely it seemed. He went into his bedroom, tossed his suit jacket on the bed and decided to slip into a pair of jeans and a T-shirt before ordering take-out. Then he intended to spend the rest of the evening, probably the entire weekend, with ESPN.

He was stretched out on the sofa, watching the NFL preseason highlights, when he heard the sound of his doorbell. Thinking it was the pizza delivery man, he grabbed the twenty-dollar bill off the table and walked to the door in his bare feet and opened it.

Instead of the pizza man, Ellie stood there. He had to blink to make sure he wasn't seeing things, and then, with the anger he hadn't manage to cap, said in a cold tone, "What the hell are you doing here?"

Ellie dragged in a deep breath as she gazed into Uriel's eyes. Two weeks hadn't softened them any. They were just as cold as that day he had left Cavanaugh Lake. But she couldn't let that stop her from doing what she needed to do. What she had to do. It would be the same thing Tamara had had to force Grant to do: to listen to her reasons for doing what she'd done, and make him believe, no matter what or how long it took, that every time he had touched her, had made love to her, she had loved him.

And before she left, she would make Uriel face up to the fact that he loved her, too. She truly believed it, and it had taken finishing her aunt's manuscript to realize it. She was not dealing with make-believe, but hard, cold reality. And no man would have handled her the way he had unless he had loved her. She believed that. Once they got their love out in the open, they would be able to handle the rest. The man standing in front of her was her destiny. Now she had to convince him of that.

"I asked what you are doing here, Ellie."

"We need to talk." Before he realized what she was about to do, she slipped past him and walked into his house. She didn't turn around until she was in the middle of his living room, and when she did, the shocked look on his face almost endeared him to her.

"You weren't invited inside my house," he said, slamming the door shut.

"Then put me out," she challenged, knowing he wouldn't. He wouldn't come close to her. He wouldn't touch her. He was so much like Grant Hatteras that her heart ached. That's why the last two chapters had come easily to her, and she had been able to finish them in ten days.

And since she had decided to come clean, before she sent the manuscript to Lauren Poole yesterday, she had called the woman, confessed to what she'd done. Lauren had been more than understanding, and had agreed to read the entire manuscript as soon as she got it. If Lauren felt everything flowed smoothly, and Ellie had been able to capture her aunt's writing voice, then she would notify Vandellas Publishers, and request that they go ahead and print the book as the first and final work of Flame Elbam.

"You have three minutes."

She glanced over at Uriel. "I'm taking five," she said,

sitting down on the sofa and crossing her legs. "Ten, if I need them."

She'd seen him glance at her legs when she crossed them. She had him figured out, which was why she had worn this particular skirt with the split in the side. And she wondered if he had picked up on the fact that she didn't have a bra on underneath her blouse. He would find out soon enough.

He stared at her. She stared at him. There were some things a man couldn't hide, no matter how quick he might be to do so, and when he came and quickly sat down in the chair across from her she knew. He might be mad at her, but his body still wanted her.

"I'm waiting."

She pulled in a deep breath and then said, "I don't want you waiting, Uriel, I want you listening. Will you listen to what I have to say?"

"Maybe."

Okay, if he wanted to be difficult, then she would show him what being difficult was about in a minute, if he kept it up. "I will start at the beginning. I found my aunt's unfinished manuscript...."

Uriel stared at her. Was he listening? Most of the time. The rest of it was spent watching her lips move, watching that tongue work inside her mouth, watching how she nervously twitched her crossed legs, watching her hand gestures. Just plain watching her. And remembering.

Remembering the lips he kissed. The tongue that had mingled with his, the pair of legs he had been between and the hands that had stroked him. He felt his crotch harden. Felt the way his pulse rate increased. Felt the heat that was beginning to run up his spine.

"Uriel?"

He blinked. "What?"

"I asked you a question."

He frowned. Had she? He shifted in the chair. "Could you repeat the question?"

"Sure. I asked whose idea it was for us to have that summer fling?"

His frown deepened, wondering what point she was trying to make. "It was my idea."

"Why?"

"Why?" he repeated.

"Yes, why?" she almost snapped.

A moment of silence was all it took before he said, "Because I wanted you."

A faint smile took shape on her lips, and then she asked, "For what reason?"

For what reason? A lump formed in his throat. Why was she asking all these questions?

"For what reason, Uriel?" she repeated.

He hesitated before replying, then thought, what the hell. He would tell her just what she wanted to know. "Sex," he said, and just in case she didn't hear it, he said it again, louder this time, *"Sex."*

She was out of her seat in a flash, and he had to draw back when she got in his face. "You're mad at me for wanting you for sex, but you just admitted to wanting me for the same thing. Please explain that!"

Annoyance rushed through him. "There's nothing to explain. It was what it was, and you knew it from the beginning. But *you* had ulterior motives in what you did."

She stared at him, her brows arched and chin tilted. She backed up and returned to stand by the sofa. "I needed to be inspired to finish my aunt's novel. I finished it and I told her agent the truth, and she will tell the publishing company the truth. If the work is acceptable, they will publish it as Flame Elbam."

She didn't say anything for a moment, and then said, "Finishing that manuscript meant a lot to me, Uriel, and I appreciate your giving me what I needed to do it. No man had ever really and truly made love to me before, and I knew you could and would do it right. What was wrong with that?"

He got on his feet, quickly covered the distance separating them, to stand in front of her. He tightened his hands into fists at his sides, or else he'd be tempted to strangle her. He suddenly felt out of control. Untamed. "What was wrong with it was that you should have told me!"

Refusing to retreat, she dragged in a deep breath and then let it out before asking, "And if I had, Uriel? Would you have done anything differently? Would you have?"

He frowned. "That is not the point."

She threw up her hands in frustration. "And what is the point? You got what you wanted and so did I. In fact, I got more than I ever dreamed of getting, Uriel, because for three weeks I made love to the man I have loved since I knew what love was about, or thought I knew what it was about. Even that day ten years ago, I had this huge crush on you. And I always dreamed you would be the first boy I kissed. I got to share so many firsts with you as well as seconds, and I don't regret any of it."

She paused, held his gaze and said, "Yes, I wanted you to inspire me. Yes, you did. And yes, maybe I should have told you about it. But you wanted to have an affair with me. You asked and I consented, whatever the reason. You got from me what you wanted. Now I plan to get from you what I want, then I will leave you in peace."

Uriel's mind was too wrapped up in her admission

of her love for him to pay attention to what else she was saying. He saw her kick off her shoes, but didn't realize what she was about to do until her hand went to the zipper of her skirt.

"What do you think you're doing, Ellie?"

"What does it look like?"

And with that smart-ass response, her skirt dropped to the floor, leaving her clad in a pair of black lace bikini panties. He frowned at her. "Lady, you've got a lot of nerve."

She threw her head back and laughed. "Glad you think so." She reached out and grabbed his jeans by the waist. Before he could resist, she had pushed him back, and they both went tumbling onto the sofa, with her landing on top of him.

He glared up at her. "Is there anything in particular that you're trying to prove?" he asked, not believing how she was carrying on.

"Yes," she said, holding his gaze. "Let me know when it's starting to work."

And then she lowered her head and kissed him, seducing his mouth with the sweetest pair of lips he had ever known, and then tangling with his tongue. He didn't resist—didn't even try—when their mouths began mating with a hunger that would not be denied.

When she finally pulled her mouth back, she whispered against his lips, "I love you, Uriel. It's always been about love for me. Even when I knew you were going to leave me at the end of the month, I still wanted to be with you because I loved you. You could only inspire me because I loved you."

He stared up at her and then he knew. Her name was still written on his heart. It hadn't gotten erased. It could never get erased. He pushed a wayward strand of hair back from her face, and he studied her features and knew that one day he would have a daughter who would look just like her.

"And I love you, too, Ellie," he said huskily, admitting what he should have figured out long before he actually had. "I realized it before leaving the lake, and I had been headed over to tell you that day when I heard you talking on the phone to Darcy."

She nodded. "Had you hung around and listened to all of the conversation, you would have heard me tell Darcy of my decision to tell you everything because I loved you."

Cupping her behind the neck, he brought her mouth down to meet his, and their tongues mingled in a kiss that was beginning to burn him inside out. He could feel the thudding of her heart against his, and then he realized something, her nipples pressing hard against his chest.

He pulled back. "You're not wearing a bra," he said in disbelief.

Ellie couldn't help but laugh. "No, I'm not. I started not to wear any panties either, but with the split in my skirt, I thought that might be too much. Either way, I'd planned on making you incapable of speech for a while."

Uriel smiled. "What have I created?"

Her features took a serious turn when she said, "A woman who will love you forever."

He reached out and brushed his knuckles against the softness of her cheeks and said, "And I am a man who will love you forever, as well." He kissed her. "There's something I think you ought to know. If I didn't know any better, I'd think your Aunt Mable had a hand in all of this."

She lifted a brow. "In all of what?"

"That publishing company. Vandellas Publishing. Donovan and I own it. I didn't know it was the one that was publishing your aunt's work until I heard you talking with Darcy. Just so you know, I plan to remain impartial. It will be the editor's decision as to whether you did your aunt's manuscript justice. If you did, then it will be published."

Her eyes lit up and she smiled. "And if I did a good job and they want another book from Flame Elbam, would you let me write it?"

He shrugged. "I don't see why not."

"And will you inspire me again?" she asked, leaning in closer and using the tip of her tongue to trace around his lips.

"Baby," he said in a quivering breath, "all you have to do is ask."

"I'm asking."

He stood up and pulled her into his arms. As he quickly moved toward the bedroom, he glanced down at her and smiled. "That's one request that you don't have to make twice."

Epilogue

"How did you manage to get married before I did?" a disgruntled Donovan Steele asked Uriel as the two stood with Uriel's five godbrothers for another wedding picture.

Uriel rolled his eyes and remembered something Ellie had once asked him. "Would you like some cheese to go along with your whine?"

Donovan frowned. "Funny."

Uriel shook his head. "Hey, at least the product trade show was a huge success for the Steele Corporation, so I guess you can't have everything. Now, smile for the camera, Don."

After the photo was taken, Donovan strolled to where his fiancée was standing with his relatives. There was no doubt in Uriel's mind that Donovan would try to work on Natalie again, to move up their wedding date. Uriel and Ellie had decided not to wait, and figured a Thanksgiving wedding would suit them just fine. They had a lot to be thankful for.

Ellie had accepted a position at Lassiter Industries, and they made Charlotte their primary home, but kept

Cavanaugh Lake as their weekend getaway, deciding to keep Uriel's lake house as a guest cottage for any visitors.

The editor at Vandellas Publishing had loved the story and could not believe it had been written by two different people, and had asked Ellie to continue writing as Flame Elbam. Ellie had agreed to do one more book, and she would see how that worked out before doing another.

Uriel smiled as he glanced around the room, looking for his wife, but he didn't see her anywhere. He then scoped all the people who had come to see him and Ellie pledge their love and life to each other. It had been a beautiful affair.

He breathed in deeply when he saw his mother with her boy toy, but didn't feel so bad when he noted his father was too occupied talking to Donovan's aunt to notice. Or maybe Anthony Lassiter no longer cared, which was even better.

"How much longer for the pics, U?" Xavier leaned over and asked.

"Why are you in such a hurry?" Winston jokingly asked. "It's too early in the day to be making booty calls, X, so chill."

Uriel knew Winston had only been joking, but he had a feeling W's words had hit a nerve with X, and he couldn't help but wonder why. He then glanced over at Zion. "Thanks for the ring, Z," he said to his godbrother, who had flown in from Rome a couple of days ago.

Zion smiled. "Only for you. I hope she liked it."

Uriel chuckled. "Are you kidding? A wedding set designed by Zion. Come on, man. She loved it."

"I hope you know you're no longer a member of Bachelors in Demand," York decided it was time to point out.

"Whatever," Uriel said, rolling his eyes. He then saw his wife reenter the ballroom with her best friend, Darcy.

He hadn't forgotten Darcy's role in Ellie's two escapades involving him. He left his godbrothers and moved toward his wife to give her a huge kiss.

When the wedding planner came to grab Ellie for a second, he was left standing with Darcy. "I hear you've moved to New York," he decided to say, while sipping his punch.

She eyed him warily. "Yes, what about it?"

Uriel smiled. "No reason." He knew that, although they were both part of the wedding party, Darcy hadn't officially met York; but Uriel planned for them to meet before he and Ellie left on their honeymoon to Paris. He hid his smile, thinking that an introduction ought to be interesting.

Ellie returned to his side. "The photographer is ready for us to cut the cake."

"All right, but I need to talk to you about something for a minute." He glanced over at Darcy. "Please excuse us for a second."

The moment they stepped out of the ballroom and rounded the corner, he pulled her into his arms and lowered his mouth to hers. She surrendered, and he pulled her closer into his arms and kissed her with a hunger that made her moan.

When he finally withdrew his lips from hers, she pulled in a deep breath. "What was that about?" she asked.

A smile curved his lips and he said, "Inspiration."

* * * * *

YOU HAVE JUST READ A

HARLEQUIN®

Desire

BOOK

If you were taken by the strong,
powerful hero and are looking for the
ultimate destination for **provocative
and passionate romance,** be sure
to look for all six Harlequin® Desire
books every month.

HARLEQUIN®
entertain, enrich, inspire™

HALOHDINC13

REQUEST YOUR FREE BOOKS!
2 FREE NOVELS PLUS 2 FREE GIFTS!

HARLEQUIN® *Desire*

ALWAYS POWERFUL, PASSIONATE AND PROVOCATIVE

YES! Please send me 2 FREE Harlequin Desire® novels and my 2 FREE gifts (gifts are worth about $10). After receiving them, if I don't wish to receive any more books, I can return the shipping statement marked "cancel." If I don't cancel, I will receive 6 brand-new novels every month and be billed just $4.55 per book in the U.S. or $4.99 per book in Canada. That's a savings of at least 13% off the cover price! It's quite a bargain! Shipping and handling is just 50¢ per book in the U.S. and 75¢ per book in Canada.* I understand that accepting the 2 free books and gifts places me under no obligation to buy anything. I can always return a shipment and cancel at any time. Even if I never buy another book, the two free books and gifts are mine to keep forever.

225/326 HDN F4ZC

Name _____ (PLEASE PRINT)

Address _____ Apt. #

City _____ State/Prov. _____ Zip/Postal Code

Signature (if under 18, a parent or guardian must sign)

Mail to the Harlequin® Reader Service:
IN U.S.A.: P.O. Box 1867, Buffalo, NY 14240-1867
IN CANADA: P.O. Box 609, Fort Erie, Ontario L2A 5X3

Want to try two free books from another line?
Call 1-800-873-8635 or visit www.ReaderService.com.

* Terms and prices subject to change without notice. Prices do not include applicable taxes. Sales tax applicable in N.Y. Canadian residents will be charged applicable taxes. Offer not valid in Quebec. This offer is limited to one order per household. Not valid for current subscribers to Harlequin Desire books. All orders subject to credit approval. Credit or debit balances in a customer's account(s) may be offset by any other outstanding balance owed by or to the customer. Please allow 4 to 6 weeks for delivery. Offer available while quantities last.

Your Privacy—The Harlequin® Reader Service is committed to protecting your privacy. Our Privacy Policy is available online at www.ReaderService.com or upon request from the Harlequin Reader Service.

We make a portion of our mailing list available to reputable third parties that offer products we believe may interest you. If you prefer that we not exchange your name with third parties, or if you wish to clarify or modify your communication preferences, please visit us at www.ReaderService.com/consumerschoice or write to us at Harlequin Reader Service Preference Service, P.O. Box 9062, Buffalo, NY 14269. Include your complete name and address.

HD13R

SPECIAL EXCERPT FROM

 HARLEQUIN

Desire

What will happen when this beauty tries to tame the beast?

*Here's a sneak peek at the next book in
Andrea Laurence's SECRETS OF EDEN miniseries,
A BEAUTY UNCOVERED, coming
October 2013 from Harlequin® Desire.*

Brody turned on his heel, ready to return to his office and lick his wounds, when she called out to him again.

"Mr. Eden?"

"Yes?" He stopped and faced her.

Sam rounded her desk and approached him. His body tensed involuntarily as she came closer. She reached up to the scarred side of his face, causing his lungs to seize in his chest. What was she doing?

"Your shirt…" Her voice drifted off.

He felt her fingertips gently brush the puckered skin along his neck before straightening his shirt collar. The innocent touch sent a jolt of heat through his body. It was so simple, so unplanned, and yet it was the first time a woman had touched his scars.

His foster mother had often kissed and patted his cheek, and nurses had applied medicine and bandages after various reconstructive procedures, but this was different. As a shiver ran down his spine, it *felt* different, as well.

Without thinking, he brought his hand up to grasp hers. Sam gasped softly at his sudden movement, but she didn't pull away when his scarred fingers wrapped around her own. He was glad. He wasn't ready to let go. His every nerve lit up with awareness, and he was pretty certain she felt it, too. Her dark brown eyes were wide as she looked at him, her moist lips parted seductively and begging for his kiss.

He slowly drew her hand down, his eyes locked on hers. Sam swallowed hard and let her arm fall to her side when he finally let her go. "Much better," she said, gesturing to his collar with a nervous smile. She held up the flash drive in her other hand. "I'll get this printed for you, sir."

"Call me Brody," he said, finding his voice when the air finally moved in his lungs again. He might still be her boss, but suddenly he didn't want any formalities between them. He wanted her to say his name. He wanted to reach out and touch her again. But he wouldn't.

Don't miss
A BEAUTY UNCOVERED by Andrea Laurence,
part of the Secrets of Eden miniseries, available
October 2013 from Harlequin® Desire.

Copyright © 2013 by Andrea Laurence

Kick back and relax with a

book

Passion, wealth and drama make these books a must-have for those so-so days. The perfect combination when paired with a comfy chair and your favorite drink or on the subway with your morning coffee. Plunge into a world of **hot cowboys, sexy alpha-heroes,** secret pregnancies, family sagas and **passionate love stories.** Each book is sure to fulfill your fantasies and leave you wanting more.

HDINCAD1